Acclaim for Julian Stockwin's Naval Adventures

"Stockwin bravely goes where Patrick O'Brian has gone before . . . period dialect and seagoing argot aplenty add credibility to the adventure, and the unworldly Kydd is an apt lens for the reader's journey."

—*Publishers Weekly*

"Comparisons to Patrick O'Brian's saga are inevitable, but Stockwin's debut focuses on the common seamen rather than on the officers. . . . Kydd's first storm at sea is rendered with great drama [and] at times breath-stopping detail. . . . An engaging sea yarn."

—*Kirkus Reviews*

"A brilliantly imagined account of a man overcoming fear."

—*The Boston Globe*

"Salt spray and the aroma of tarred rigging and powder fly off the pages."

—Tall Ships Books

"Adventure and historical fans will delight in this well-crafted yarn."

—*Booklist*

SEAFLOWER

A KYDD NOVEL

JULIAN STOCKWIN

SCRIBNER

NEW YORK LONDON TORONTO SYDNEY

SCRIBNER
1230 Avenue of the Americas
New York, NY 10020

First Scribner trade paperback edition 2004
Originally published in Great Britain in 2003 by Hodder and Stoughton, a division of
Hodder Headline

SCRIBNER and design are trademarks of
Macmillan Library Reference USA, Inc., used under license
by Simon & Schuster, the publisher of this work.

For information about special discounts for bulk purchases,
please contact Simon & Schuster Special Sales:
1-800-456-6798 or business@simonandschuster.com

Designed by Colin Joh
Text set in Galliard

Manufactured in the United States of America

1   3   5   7   9   10   8   6   4   2

The Library of Congress has cataloged the Scribner edition as follows:

Stockwin, Julian.
Seaflower: a Kydd novel / Julian Stockwin.—1st Scribner ed.
p. cm.
1. Kydd, Thomas (Fictitious character)—Fiction. 2. Great Britain—History, Naval—
Fiction. 3. British—Caribbean Area—Fiction. 4. Caribbean Area—Fiction. I. Title.
Pr 619.T66S4 2003
823'.92-dc21
2002042827

ISBN 0-7432-1462-5
0-7432-1463-3 (Pbk)

*To the wind that blows
a ship that goes
and the lass that loves a sailor
—Sea toast*

SEAFLOWER

CHAPTER 1

—⁂—

The low thud of a court-martial gun echoed over Portsmouth in the calm early-summer morning, the grim sound telling the world of the naval drama about to take place. Its ominous portent also stilled the conversation on the fore lower-deck of the old receiving ship lying farther into the harbor. There, Thomas Kydd's pigtail was being reclubbed by his closest friend and shipmate, Nicholas Renzi.

"I wish in m' bowels it were you," Kydd said, in a low voice. He was dressed in odd-fitting but clean seaman's gear. Like Renzi, he was a shipwrecked mariner and his clothes were borrowed. A court-martial would try the sole surviving officer, and Kydd, who had been on watch at the helm at the time, was a principal witness.

There was a muffled hail at the fore hatchway. Kydd made a hasty farewell, and clattered up the broad ladder to muster at the ship's side. The larboard cutter bobbed alongside to embark the apprehensive witnesses. In the curious way of the Navy, Kydd joined diffidently with the petty officers, even though with the death of his ship his acting rate had been removed and therefore he was borne on the books of the receiving ship as an able seaman.

His testimony, however, would be given as a petty officer, his rate at the time.

The pleasant boat trip to the dockyard was not appreciated by Kydd, who gulped at the thought of crusty, gold-laced admirals and captains glaring at him as he gave his evidence, which might well be challenged by other hostile officers.

In fact recently it had not in any way been a pleasant time for Kydd and Renzi. Their return as shipwrecked sailors to the land of their birth had been met with virtual imprisonment in a receiving ship; at a time of increasingly solemn news from the war it was a grave problem for the authorities how to announce the loss of the famous frigate *Artemis*. Their response had been to keep the survivors from the public until a course of action had been decided after the court-martial, with the result that both Kydd and Renzi had not been able to return home after their long voyage. As far as could be known, their loved ones had had no news of them since the previous year, and that from Macao, their last touching at civilization.

The cutter headed for the smart new stone buildings of the dockyard. The last half of the century had seen a massive expansion of capability in the foremost royal dockyard of the country, and it was a spectacle in its own right, the greatest industrial endeavor in the land. As they neared the shore, Kydd nervously took in the single Union Flag hanging from the signal tower. This was the evidence for all eyes of the reality of a court-martial to be held here, ashore, by the Port Admiral. The court would normally meet in the Great Cabin of the flagship, but the anchorage at Spithead was virtually empty, Admiral Howe's fleet somewhere out in the Atlantic looking for the French.

The marine sentries at the landing place stood at ease—there were no officers in the boat needing a salute, only an odd-looking lot of seamen in ill-fitting sailor rig. There were few words among the men, who obediently followed a lieutenant into an anteroom to await their call. Pointedly, a pair of marines took up position at the entrance.

It seemed an interminable time to Kydd, as he sat on the wooden chair, his hat awkwardly in his hand. The voyage across the vast expanse of the Pacific and the early responsibility of promotion thrust on him had considerably matured him, and anyone who glanced at his tanned, open face, thick dark hair and powerful build could never have mistaken him for anything other than what he was, a prime seaman. His past as a perruquier in Guildford town was now unimaginably distant.

"Abraham Smith," called a black-coated clerk at the door. The carpenter's mate stood and limped off, his face set. Kydd remembered his work on the foredeck of *Artemis* in the stormy darkness. Men here owed their lives to the raft he had fashioned from wreckage and launched in the cold dawn light.

The clerk returned. "Tobias Stirk." The big gunner got to his feet, then he paused deliberately and looked back at Kydd. His grave expression did not vary, but his slow wink caused Kydd to smile. Then he thought of the trial, and his heart thudded.

"Thomas Kydd."

Kydd followed the clerk, emerging into a busy room where he was handed over to another. Expecting at any moment to appear before the great court, Kydd was confused to be led upstairs to a much smaller room, bare but for a large table. At a chair on the opposite side was a senior official wearing a grave expression, who motioned him to sit down. A junior clerk entered and took up position at a smaller table.

"Thomas Paine Kydd?"

Kydd nodded, too nervous to speak.

"My name is Gardiner. We are here to determine the facts pertaining to the loss of His Majesty's Frigate *Artemis*," the lawyer announced, with practiced ease. "Your deposition of evidence will be taken here, and examined to see if it has relevance to the case soon before the court."

Perhaps he would not have to appear in court at all. He might be released and allowed home—but then reason told him that his

contribution was a vital piece of evidence. He and Renzi had discussed their respective positions. Renzi was a self-exile with a well-
born past, serving "sentence" for a family crime, and had a more
worldly view. Kydd had a stubborn belief in the rightness of truth,
and would not shift his position by an inch. The result of his stand
would be inevitable.

"Were you, Kydd, on watch on the night of the thirteenth of
April, 1794?" Gardiner began mildly, shuffling papers, as the clerk
scratched away with his quill off to the side.

"Aye, sir, quartermaster o' the starb'd watch, at the helm." The
man would probably think it impertinent of him were he to volunteer that, as quartermaster, he would never have deigned to
touch the wheel—that was the job of the helmsman. He had been
in overall charge of the helm as a watch-station under the officer-
of-the-watch, and as such was probably the single most valuable
witness to what had really happened that night.

A pause and a significant look between Gardiner and the clerk
showed that the point had in fact been caught.

"As quartermaster?" The voice was now sharply alert.

"Acting quartermaster, sir."

"Very well." Gardiner stared at him for a while, the gray eyes
somewhat cruel. His musty wig reeked of law, judgment and
penalty. "Would it be true or untrue to state that you were in a
position to understand the totality of events on the quarterdeck
that night?"

Kydd paused as he unraveled the words. The junior clerk's quill
hung motionless in the dusty air. Kydd knew that any common
seaman who found himself afoul of the system would be lost in its
coils, hopelessly enmeshed in unfathomable complication. Renzi,
with his logic, would have known how to answer, but he had been
asleep below at the time and had not been called as a witness.

Looking up, Kydd said carefully, "Sir, the duty of a quartermaster is th' helm, an' he is bound to obey th' officer-o'-the-watch

in this, an' stand by him f'r orders. That was L'tenant Rowley, sir."

Lines deepened between Gardiner's eyes. "My meaning seems to have escaped you, Kydd. I will make it plainer. I asked whether or not you would claim to be in a position to know all that happened."

It was an unfair question, and Kydd suspected he was being offered the option to withdraw gracefully from the hazard of being a key witness open to hostile questioning from all quarters. He had no idea why.

"I was never absent fr'm my place o' duty, sir," he said quietly.

"Then you are saying that you can of a surety be relied upon to state just why your ship was lost?" The disbelief bordered on sarcasm.

"Sir, there was a blow on that night, but I could hear L'tenant Rowley's words—every one!" he said, with rising anger.

Gardiner frowned and threw a quick glance at the clerk, who had not resumed scratching. "I wonder if you appreciate the full implications of what you are saying," he said, with a steely edge to his voice.

Kydd remained mute, and stared back doggedly. He would speak the truth—nothing more or less.

"Are you saying that simply because you could hear Lieutenant Rowley you can tell why your ship was lost?" The tone was acid, but hardening.

"Sir." Kydd finally spoke, his voice strengthening. "We sighted breakers fine to wind'd," he said, and recalled the wild stab of fear that the sudden frantic hail there in the open Atlantic had prompted. "L'tenant Rowley ordered helm hard a'weather, and—"

Gardiner interjected. "By that I assume he immediately and correctly acted to turn the ship away from the hazard?"

Kydd did not take the bait. "The ship bore away quickly off th' wind, but L'tenant Parry came on deck and gave orders f'r the helm to go hard down—"

Gardiner struck like a snake. "But Parry was not officer-of-the-watch, he did not have the ship!" His head thrust forward aggressively.

"Sir, L'tenant Parry was senior t' L'tenant Rowley, an' he could—"

"But he was not officer-of-the-watch!" Gardiner drew in his breath.

Kydd felt threatened by his strange hostility. The lawyer was there to find the facts, not make it hard for witnesses, especially one who could explain it all.

"But he *was* right, sir!"

Gardiner tensed, but did not speak.

The truth would set matters right, Kydd thought, and he had had an odd regard for the plebeian Parry, whom he had seen suffer so much from the dandy Rowley. He was dead now, but Kydd would make sure his memory was not betrayed. "Ye should put the helm *down* when y' sees a hazard, that way th' ship is taken aback." He saw a guarded incomprehension on Gardiner's face, and explained further so there would be no mistake on this vital point. "That way, the ship stops in th' water, stops fr'm getting into more trouble till you've worked out what t' do."

"And you allege that Lieutenant Rowley's act—to go away from the hazard—was the wrong one?" Gardiner snapped.

"Aye, sir!" Kydd's certainty seemed to unsettle Gardiner, who muttered something indistinct, but waited.

"We sighted breakers next to loo'ard, an' because L'tenant Rowley had come off the wind, they were fast coming in under our lee an' no time to stay about!"

There was a breathy silence. Gardiner's face hardened. "You are alleging that the loss of *Artemis* was directly attributable to this officer's actions?"

There was now no avoiding the issue. He must stand by his words, which he must repeat at length in court, or abjectly deny them. "Yes, sir!" he said firmly.

Gardiner leaned back slowly, fixing Kydd with his hard eyes. Unexpectedly, he sighed. "Very well, we will take your deposition."

There was a meaningful cough from the clerk. Gardiner turned slightly and something passed between them that Kydd was unable to catch. Resuming his gaze Gardiner added, "And in your own words, if you please."

Concentrating with all his might, Kydd told the simple story of the destruction of the crack frigate, from the first chilling sight of breakers in mid-Atlantic to her inevitable wrecking on an outer ledge of rock on one of the islands of the Azores.

But he said nothing of the personal heartbreak he felt at the death of the first ship he had really loved, the ship that had borne him around the world to so many adventures, that had turned him from tentative sailor to first-class seaman and petty officer. He also omitted the story of the nightmare of the break-up of the wreck during the night and his desperate swim for his life among the relentless breakers, the joy at finally finding himself alive. Those details would not interest these legal gentlemen.

"Thank you," said Gardiner, and glanced at the clerk, whose hand flew across the paper as he transcribed Kydd's words. "It seems complete enough." His detachment was a mystery after the savage inquisition of before.

The clerk finished, sanded the sheet and shuffled it in together with the rest. "Ye'll need to put y'r mark on each page," he said offhandedly.

Kydd bristled. He had debated Diderot and Rousseau in the Great South Sea with Renzi, and never felt himself an unlettered foremast hand. He dashed off a distinguished signature on each page.

"You may return to your ship," said Gardiner neutrally, standing. Kydd rose also, satisfied with the catharsis of at last telling his tale. "We will call upon your testimony as the court decides," Gardiner added. Kydd nodded politely and left.

*　*　*

Renzi sat on the sea chest he shared with Kydd. They had lost everything in the shipwreck, nothing to show for their great voyage around the world. Kydd was fashioning a trinket box from shipwright's offcuts and bone inlay to present to his adoring sister when he finally made his way up the London road to the rural peace of Guildford.

"Nicholas, you'll be right welcome at home, m' friend, y' know, but have ye given thought t' your folks?"

Renzi looked up from his book, his eyes opaque. "I rather fancy my presence will not be as altogether a blessed joy as yours will be to your own family, dear fellow." He did not elaborate and Kydd did not pursue it. The sensibilities that had led to Renzi's act of self-exile from his family were not to be discussed, but Kydd was aware that in becoming a common sailor Renzi could only be regarded as a wanton disgrace by his well-placed family.

Renzi added casually, "If it does not disoblige, it would give me particular joy to bide awhile *chez* Kydd." He didn't find it necessary to say that this would renew his acquaintance of Cecilia, Kydd's handsome sister.

Kydd sighed happily. "I told 'em everythin', Nicholas—I say my piece afore the court, an' we're on our way home!" His keen knife shaved a thin sliver from the lid, rounding the edge.

Renzi looked at his friend. Kydd's account of his questioning was disturbing. In his bones he felt unease.

"Yes indeed, and we shall—" He broke off. Above the comfortable patter of shipboard noises a faint thud had sounded, as of a light-caliber cannon in the distance. Activity ceased on the lowerdeck as men strained to hear. Another thud. Eyes met—random gunfire in a naval anchorage was unusual to the point of incredible. Some got to their feet, faces hardening. A move to the hatchway turned into a rush as a third shot was heard.

On deck all attention was on the harbor entrance. Officers on the quarterdeck had telescopes trained and tense chatter spread.

Some men leaped for the foreshrouds to get a better view.

It was a naval cutter under a full press of sail, flying through the narrow entrance of the harbor, an enormous ensign streaming and some sort of signal on both shrouds. A white puff appeared on her fo'c'sle, the thump arriving seconds later.

"Despatches—she's a packet boat," Stirk growled. "An' goin' rapful—she's got some noos fer us, mates!" he said, with unnecessary emphasis.

The cutter raced along, and made a neat tack about opposite the signal tower. Backing her single topsail she subsided to a stop and hove to, her boat launched almost immediately. It passed close to the receiving ship, the single officer ignoring the shouted pleas for news echoing over the water. It made the landing place, and the officer hurried up the stone stairs. He disappeared among the buildings while the boat shoved off again, to lie off.

It was galling to know that something of deep importance was taking place within a stone's throw, and speculation flew about, opinions ranging wildly from the French at sea on their way to invade to the death of the sovereign.

They had not long to wait. A deeper-throated great gun, probably from the fort more inland, sullenly boomed out and a line of soldiers emerged, trotting in a single line along the waterfront. On deck the excited chatter died away. Another gun boomed, but then Renzi cocked his head. "The church bells are ringing. It seems we must celebrate a victory!"

More bells joined in, and more. From the halliards of the signal tower burst hoists of flags, and the water became alive with craft furiously crisscrossing the harbor. In exasperation men hung from the rigging, watching the growing excitement ashore. A receiving ship's main purpose was as a floating barracks for the victims of the press-gang before they were sent out to their ship, and had well-tested means of keeping men aboard; they would have to contain their frustration for now.

Happily, it soon became clear that boats were putting off to spread the news. A pinnace sped toward them, a midshipman standing perilously in the sternsheets waving madly. Indistinct shouting tantalized, but soon it was close enough for the shrill words of the excited youngster to come through: it was a great victory by Admiral Howe, out in the stormy seas of the Atlantic not three days before. In a rush the boat was alongside and the midshipman flew up the side, pelting aft to the quarterdeck to report.

The seamen lost no time in hanging over the side and getting their story from the boat's crew, the tale disjointed and wild but plain in its essentials. Admiral Howe had been at sea for weeks, knowing that a desperately needed convoy of grain was coming from America to relieve revolution-racked France, heavily guarded, of course. The two fleets met at sea and a running battle over three days had culminated in a titanic clash on 1 June and a crushing defeat for the French.

Willing hands hauled on lines of flags as the receiving ship dressed overall, her token four-pounders banging out to add to the bedlam all around, a delirious show from a nation at the news of a great victory in a major fleet action at sea.

Ashore, the dockyard and the town were filling with people, their shouts carrying faintly to the frustrated men who knew full well what was developing in the taverns and pothouses of the town.

But to their unspeakable mortification, the *Artemis* survivors were not allowed to join in the merrymaking—and it was so easy to remember their own wild reception after their victory in a sea duel with a French frigate, the first fight among equals of the war, and they wanted to relive the euphoria. There was nothing to do but stare longingly at the shore and endure, a hard and bitter thing for men who had suffered as they.

The court-martial flag remained at the masthead, but Kydd was not called. Neither was he the next day, and when the flag was hauled down on the third day he shrugged and made ready to leave for home.

It was also the day that Earl Howe and his victorious fleet arrived at Spithead. The town erupted for the second time, and enviously the *Artemis* seamen watched as the liberty boats swarmed ashore at Portsmouth Point. Incredibly, they were still being kept aboard.

Renzi's disquiet turned to unease. This was neither humane nor sensible treatment for shipwrecked souls, and did not make sense. The loss of *Artemis* would be overlooked in the delirium of the victory of the Glorious First of June, so there was no point in keeping the men from their families.

A boatswain's mate appeared at the hatchway and pealed a call. "*Artemis* hands! *Haaaaands* to muster! *Aaaaaall* the *Artemis haaaands*—muster in th' waist with yer dunnage!"

"Well, bugger me days!" said Stirk. "An' the bastards 'ave remembered we're 'ere!" There was a scramble for their pitifully few possessions, Kydd's own fitting into one small bundle. With lifting heart he tugged on his hat and hastened on deck into the evening sun. Hooked on below was a big launch, manned by a subdued set of seamen he did not recognize. An older-looking lieutenant was standing at the tiller, his mouth a thin line.

"Hey-ho, mates—and it's bad luck t' any who ain't chirpin' merry in one hour!" said one *Artemis,* his eyes shining.

"Got th' gormy ruddles sittin' in this hooker!" said another, hefting his bag, "an' the only thing'll cure it 's me comin' alongside some willin' piece who'll show a sailor the way home!"

Kydd grinned, and after their names were marked off in the muster book, he went down with the others into the boat, Renzi close behind. They settled all along the center, between the rowers. But there was no answer to their jocular barbs. The crew of the launch were mute and serious and they kept their eyes in the boat facing aft. Slowly the happy chatter of the *Artemis* hands died away under a sense of apprehension. The boat shoved off, the men at the oars pulling slowly but economically, as if they had a long stretch ahead.

Kydd looked at Renzi in appeal—he only shook his head. Suddenly a cutter shot out from the other side of the ship. With a shock Kydd saw that it carried a party of marines, complete with muskets and accoutrements. It curved toward them and fell in close astern, the officer not glancing at it as the launch shaped course to parallel the shore.

"The poxy shabs!" roared Stirk in disbelief. "We're bein' turned over!" He stood up and grasped the gunwale.

"Try it, 'n' you'll get a ball in the guts!" growled the lieutenant. Stirk stood rigid as a storm of protest broke around him. It was not uncommon for ships returning from a distant commission for docking and refit to transfer their company bodily to another ship, without the chance of liberty ashore. But survivors of a shipwreck?

"Silence!" bellowed the officer. "You're under discipline, you damned rascals, and I'll see the backbone of any who doesn't agree!"

CHAPTER 2

~~~///~~~

The boat, borne away at speed by an ebbing tide through the harbor entrance, passed scenes and sounds of merriment ashore as the seamen of the victorious fleet gave vent to their feelings. In the launch there was a grim silence, just the creak of oars in their rowlocks and a regular, hypnotic splash as they dipped into the sea.

Kydd felt bleakness take hold. A lump grew in his throat as his eyes took in the land. So far! And so much had happened on the voyage! His sorrow left no room for rage.

Altering to starboard after making the open sea, the boat made for the gaunt shapes in the dusky light of men-o'-war at anchor at Spithead, but not before they had passed close to the raucous revelers in the rickety old buildings of Portsmouth Point, close enough to hear individual cheers and oaths.

Kydd's eyes fixed on the shore. Renzi tapped him on the shoulder and he looked around to see down the massive length of a 74-gun ship-of-the-line. They passed around the stern, with its old-fashioned open gallery, and Kydd looked up. In faded gold there was a big heraldic ribbon. The name *Trajan* was elegantly lettered inside.

Bitterness welled up and choked him. Kydd gripped a rope at the edge of the foredeck and stared back at his homeland, unwilling to let the fast-receding land disappear. The seas lengthened as *Trajan* met the first Atlantic rollers coming up the Channel, sending men staggering. The two-decker was soon clawing to windward as close as she would lie, two other vessels astern and one ahead. The land finally turned to a misty anonymity and vanished, and the lump in Kydd's throat deepened.

"I must declare myself truly gulled," Renzi said, appearing at Kydd's elbow shaking out the chinckles in a light line for coiling. Kydd was supposed to be at work on the fo'c'sle, but no one felt inclined to make a point about it. The *Artemis*es were sadly ill-used, was the general opinion, and they were left alone to their misery.

Kydd glanced at him. "Gulled? Not th' word I'd choose f'r it m'self," he muttered.

Renzi paused. "Is the loss of the flying *Artemis* so much on the public mind that we are all to be kept out of the way? Or is the fleet so in need of seamen that they press even the shipwrecked mariner? No! What we have is a political act, a move to shield the reputation of one who should be brought to account. Instead, and with the exercise of interest at the highest level, Rowley has been excused of blame, your evidence is suppressed—it is only a deposition—and we . . . we are an embarrassment. . . ." His voice trailed off, for Kydd's thickening anger was apparent on his face.

"We're shipped out t' the Caribbee to save Rowley's hide!" His face white with anger, Kydd said harshly, "T' the West Indies, fever . . ."

"I fear so. But, dear fellow, it is also the Spanish Main, treasure, the richest islands in the world—and glory, too, as we mercilessly seize the sugar islands from the French!" Renzi winced inwardly at the last, but Kydd had to see some purpose in this twist of fate.

"In this old scow!" Kydd's scornful words were heartfelt. After the trim beauty of *Artemis,* the elderly *Trajan* was all that Renzi knew he despised. A ship-of-the-line, she was lumbering and massive, her timbers old and decaying—and she had big-ship discipline: master-at-arms and corporals, trumpeter, boatswain's mates. And his previous rate as acting petty officer had not been accepted in *Trajan*: she had her full complement and no need of him. He was now no more than an able seaman, even if a topman, and he had to sling his hammock with the rest instead of in the cozy privacy of a screened-off petty officer's berth.

Renzi said nothing. Kydd's words were powerful and true, and could not be denied. He had every reason to feel aggrieved. Howe's great victory had released forces for the ongoing island invasions in the Caribbean, and *Trajan* was on her way to assist in these. And what better way to be rid of an embarrassment? His gaze lost itself in the tumbling waste of seas stretching to infinity ahead. He tried to swallow his bitterness and went below.

The noon meal was a cheerless affair—no grog this close to home, small beer only on offer. Boiled with dandelion and herbs, it had a bitterness that was intended to hide rankness, but at least it was better than water from the cask, which quickly grew stale and flat, then stagnant. After weeks at sea the beer would give out and they would revert to rum, which was much preferred, but for now Kydd's pot contained a thin brew that did nothing for his mood.

Kydd pulled forward his meal—the square wooden plate he remembered only too well from his first ship as a pressed man: no pewter and crockery here. He glowered at the mush of peas and odd-tasting pork. There was soft tommy taken aboard in Spithead, the bread only a couple of days old and useful for wiping up the last of his meal—there would be only hard tack in the weeks ahead.

"Got yer watch 'n' station, then, mate?" Doggo asked, his grog-roughened voice uncharacteristically low. His ugly, monkeylike face was long and grim.

For as far ahead as could be seen, Kydd would have to perform his sea duties as assigned this morning in his part-of-ship and watch, and this could be onerous or a satisfaction depending on the character of those in charge. And his quarters in battle—this might have been manning the helm, and therefore defenseless before the pitiless musketry of an opponent alongside, or with the ship-smashing 32-pounder cannon on the lower gundeck, or any one of a number of other dangerous duties.

"Second o' larboard, maintopman," said Kydd gloomily, fingering his bread. "An' the fore magazine f'r quarters." To his great disappointment he had learned that Renzi was in the opposite watch. This meant that they would only meet for meals and the odd "make and mend" when they could sit together on the foredeck at work on their clothing. In *Artemis* they had been in the same watch, and had spent many hours happily discussing life, philosophy and other conundrums.

Isaac Larcomb's pleasant, open face creased. "Could be worse, cully, topman ain't a bad start," he said.

Renzi nodded, but did not say anything.

"Aye, and that means I'm in yer watch, Tom!"

Kydd looked across at the tow-headed Luke, a ship's boy from *Artemis*. He smiled, but only briefly. Luke was eager and had come to admire Kydd, but he was no substitute for Renzi.

Kydd was slated to do his trick at the helm in the first dogwatch, and felt immediately better after he had seized control at the man-high wheel. The familiar tug and thrum of the tiller-ropes with their subtle transmission of the sea's temper was medicine enough. *Trajan* felt ponderous but obedient to the wheel, just a little weather-helm, not enough to be a griping, calm and sure.

He warmed to the ship. Glancing up often to the weather leech of the comfortable old main topsail, he tested how far he needed to meet each boisterous sea on the bluff bows, and what she needed to correct the yaw induced when a sea passed at an angle down her length. It seemed she had no real vices, which would be verified or otherwise when the old lady was really put to the test.

He could look forward under her sails the whole length of the ship, a sight he never tired of—the lazy heave and fall of the deck, the blue horizon dropping out of sight then emerging at a slightly different angle, a continuous, comforting, satisfying motion. He nodded, and a smile broke through. She couldn't be mistaken for a racehorse, but as a homely old mare she was perfect.

"Watch yer luff!" growled the quartermaster's mate-of-the-watch. There was no need for his caution—Kydd had been completely in control of the situation and there was never any question of losing way by coming too far into the wind.

He glanced at the man. Squat, powerfully built, he wore rumpled clothing and a glower that triggered a warning in Kydd. "Aye," he said, to be on the safe side.

At the interchange the officer-of-the-watch looked back from his pacing. Kydd kept his gaze politely forward, aware that he was under eye. He had nothing to worry about, and continued in his duty. After a minute or two, the officer came over. "You're one of the *Artemis*es, are you not?" he asked. It was not at all the right thing to engage the helmsman in conversation, but this was an officer.

"Aye, sir," he said. It would be understandable to keep his eyes on the weather leech of the mainsail. *Trajan* sailed on; Kydd sensed interest from the officer.

"You've got a frigate's touch at the helm, I see." That did not require an answer, but it must have been apparent from his many light moves at the wheel instead of the more deliberate, slower action of a ship-of-the-line.

"What is your name?"

"Kydd, sir!" broke in the quartermaster's mate firmly. In direct charge of the conn, the petty officer had every right to deflect any interference from his helmsman.

"Thank you, Coltard," the officer said smoothly, but continued to address Kydd. "So you were in *Artemis* around the Horn?"

"Sir," said Kydd briefly. He wished the officer would go away.

"At the helm?"

"Quartermaster's mate, sir."

"Hmmm." Kydd caught the quick glance at Coltard and wondered what it meant. The stumpy petty officer flushed and looked dogged.

The half-hour trick was over all too quickly, and Kydd felt reluctant to hand over to the able seaman waiting. The officer-of-the-watch contemplated him with a ghost of a smile, and he stood down with a light heart.

Kydd went forward along the moving deck to complete his watch, ready to lay aloft as a topman at the mainmast. The Atlantic's influence was becoming more marked, the longer ocean seas sweeping up the Channel and adding stateliness and a wider range to *Trajan*'s movements. He glanced up at the less-than-white canvas, noticing patches in her sails and signs of hairy chafing in her lines running aloft; as with *Duke William* earlier they were cutting corners to keep the most valuable units of the fleet at sea.

Portland was disappearing astern. They would fetch Torbay on this tack, and from there, rumor had it, they would pick up the convoy to Madeira and then the Caribbean. Another surge of resentment swept over Kydd, this time dulled by resignation.

"An' here's ter pieces o' eight an' a right good frolic in Port Royal!" chuckled Larcomb, raising his pot. His sally drew general approval, and expressions lightened along the table.

"Frien' o' mine in *Daemon* frigate was out there wi' Rodney in 'eighty-two—an' paid off in Plymouth carryin' home twelve guineas o' prize money," said the man next to Larcomb, with evident satisfaction at the prospect.

"Yair, but I got three ol' shipmates went out too an' ain't one of 'em come back yet," Doggo responded.

Kydd put down his tankard. "But y' can have fever anywhere," he said. "C'n remember in *Artemis* we had th' fever after roundin' the Horn, 'n' on our way home—even did f'r the captain."

"Aye, but—"

Larcomb broke in earnestly. "Look, if yer gonna make fishmeat, yer number is a-written down already, no use wonderin' about it," he said. "S' why not rest easy 'n' take yer life as it comes t' yer?"

There were troubled looks, but Larcomb ignored them. "Has anyone bin ter the West Indies?" he asked. It seemed none had, and he lifted his pot.

Renzi stirred. "It would seem that we are doing well in the Caribbean—we have taken Martinique," he said, to general incomprehension. "A big island, and wealthy," he explained. "I believe our intent is to detach, one by one, the enemy islands from the French."

"But if our ships are out there, doin' this invadin', then the French will feel free to fall on England!" Kydd said, with spirit.

"Yet if we leave these islands to themselves, the enemy will take them! No, the islands are a wellspring of English wealth, and we must defend them." Renzi's cool assessments were not to the taste of his new shipmates and the conversation faded.

Auberon, the first lieutenant, was on deck the next forenoon for Kydd's next trick at the helm. He took the wheel from a gray-haired able seaman and squared up. The quartermaster of the previous watch hovered, fidgeting with the traverse board and slate as the minutes lengthened and no one came to relieve him.

"For God's sake, what's the matter?" Auberon said peevishly to him.

"Er, 'aven't had m' relief," he said hesitantly.

Auberon stiffened. "You mean he's adrift?" he snapped.

With some hesitation the petty officer nodded awkwardly. Auberon showed him no sympathy. "You shall quit the deck only when properly relieved," he growled, and began to pace back and forth.

Kydd felt the rising tension, and kept a careful alertness. The duty watch on the quarterdeck fell silent as time extended, avoiding each other's eyes, trimming the sails and coiling down the lines from aloft, carefully and quietly.

The watch was set to exercise—loose and furl. Kydd noted the marked stability the ship showed on the helm even when the big foresail was dowsed and furled, unbalancing the forces of propulsion, then let free and sheeted in to take up again in the brisk easterly. This was a sea-kindly ship.

A single bell sounded from forward, sharp and clear. Instantly, Auberon rounded on the mate-of-the-watch. "Pass the word for the master-at-arms!" he ordered.

In a short while the master-at-arms appeared. He touched his hat to the first lieutenant. "Sir?"

"To wait, if you please, Mr. Quinn," said Auberon coldly.

Kydd handed over the helm to his relief, and went across to report to the captain of the maintop for his duties for the rest of the watch. Clearly the man did not want to miss anything and set Kydd to rehanking the falls around the forebrace bitts nearby.

It was unfortunate for the absent man that the first lieutenant was on deck. This was the officer next after the Captain in authority, and who, more importantly, had the responsibility for the watch and station bill detailing every man's place of duty.

A face appeared at the main-hatch, wary and hesitant. Coltard came on deck as though treading on eggshells, darting looks about him. The rest of the deck watch busied themselves, but made sure they were within earshot.

"You, sir!" snapped Auberon. His cocked hat was jammed on at an aggressive angle, his arms thrust down behind him. There was no question of what was to follow.

Coltard touched his forehead. "Aye, sir?" His face was pale and set; his hat passed nervously from hand to hand.

"You are adrift, sir!" As if to lend point to his words, the bell forward sounded a sharp double strike. "An hour!"

Trajan rose playfully to a sea on the bow, sending Coltard staggering a few paces. "Got gripin' in the guts, sir—feel right qualmish, if y' please sir." His voice was weak and thick.

Auberon's expression did not change. "You have attended the doctor," he stated in hard tones. There could be no answer. If he had, Auberon would have had the surgeon's morning report; if he had not, it would be assumed he was fit for duty. "This is the third complaint I have had of you, sir. What have you to say to that, you rascal?"

"Me belly, it—"

"You have been taken in drink, I believe. And at this hour. You shall dance pedro pee, upon my honor!"

Coltard straightened, but his eyes showed fear. "Sir! I'm a petty officer, not—"

"Master-at-arms!"

This was harsh treatment for a petty officer: they had privileges that stood them above the common sailor, yet Coltard could no longer count on them. Discipline was above all. Quinn moved eight paces away, then turned and faced Coltard. His foot tapped a black caulked seam in the decking.

There was no pretense at work now: everyone turned inboard to watch. Coltard stared down at the black line of tar. "Get a move on!" Auberon snapped. As though it were a high wire, Coltard stepped forward, and within three paces had lost his footing. "Again!" said Auberon.

Within seconds it was over, and Coltard stood dull but defiant.

"Mr. Quinn, this man is fuddled with grog. He is to be triced up in the weather foreshrouds to dry. Then he is to explain himself before the Captain at six bells."

"*Haaaaands* to muster! *Haaands* lay aft to witness punishment!"

Reluctantly, seamen ceased work to make their way aft. Emerging up from the gundecks, dropping to the deck from the rigging, they crowded onto the quarterdeck. The officers stood above on the poop deck, looking down with grave expressions on the little party below.

Coltard stood flanked by the master-at-arms and the ship's corporal. His eyes darted among the mass of sailors; if he was looking for sympathy, it was hard to tell. Kydd caught his eyes and he responded with a sneer. Kydd started in surprise.

The awful words of the Articles of War sounded out, clear and final. Judgment was given: Coltard's head fell as he heard his captain disrate him. He was now a common sailor, turned before the mast. There was more, inevitably. Coltard made no protest as he was stripped to the waist and seized to the grating by his thumbs with rope yarns.

Kydd turned away his eyes as the marine drummer opened up on the poop. A sudden stop and sweeping down and the boatswain's mate's cat-o'-nine-tails mercilessly slammed into the paleness of Coltard's back. It brought only a grunt into the appalled quiet. The second and succeeding lash brought no sound either—Coltard was going to take it all without giving his audience the satisfaction of a cry. Kydd stared at the deck and felt the skin on his back creep.

Making his way below afterward, Kydd could not join in the general hum of jollity at the humbling of a petty officer. It was clear that the man was so much in the thrall of drink that he had risked the lash to indulge his need. It did not take much to surmise that his shipmates had tired of covering for him and, that morning, had left him to his fate.

Before he had reached his mess, a small midshipman tugged his arm. "Able Seaman Kydd?" he squeaked, breathless.

"Aye?"

"Lay aft and attend the Captain," the reefer said importantly. Kydd stared at him. "This instant, you dog!" the youngster shrilled.

Kydd padded aft, and made himself known to the sentry. Dare he hope?

Inside the Great Cabin the Captain sat at his desk, the first lieutenant standing near him with papers. "Ah, Kydd?" It was the first time that Captain Bomford had addressed Kydd directly.

"Sir."

"I understand you are one of the volunteers from *Artemis*." Bomford had a pleasant, urbane manner. Kydd's heart leaped.

"Aye, sir."

"You rounded the Horn, I believe."

"Sir."

"And you were quartermaster's mate at the time."

"Acting quartermaster, sir." He would never forget that exhilarating but terrifying time in the great Southern Ocean, the massive seas and sudden squalls slamming in from nowhere. . . .

"And *Duke William* before that?" The first lieutenant exchanged looks with Bomford.

"Yes, sir." The big 98-gun ship-of-the-line and its memories were well behind him now. No need to add that he had been on her books as a lowly landman and then ordinary seaman.

"Then I am sure that you will do well in *Trajan*," Bomford said smoothly. "It is in my mind to rate you petty officer—what do you think of that?"

Yes! He had been right to hope! A cooler voice intervened: Auberon would have primed Bomford about the presence aboard of a suitable replacement well before the events of the morning; Kydd had no illusions about his good fortune. Nevertheless . . .

"I'd like it well, if ye please, sir." There was no suppressing the smile. "In what rate, sir?"

The captain's eyebrows rose as he studied a paper. "Quartermaster's mate." He met Kydd's eyes again. "If you do your duty strictly and diligently I see no reason why you should not rely on further advancement, if the opportunity arises."

"Thank ye, sir." It was a priceless step.

"Then you are so rated. The first lieutenant will arrange your watch and station. Carry on, please."

Kydd strode back down to the fo'c'sle with his news clutched to his heart, and stopped suddenly. He was now a petty officer: he did not belong with the others. His excitement fell away as he realized that all his messmates were now subordinate to him, every one—even Renzi, his particular friend.

He continued down to the gundeck, but kept his announcement until after the noon meal when he quietly made his goodbyes. He left Renzi to the end. His friend had taken the news with annoying equanimity, hanging back with a slight smile while the others slapped his back and showed gratifying envy. It was time. Awkwardly he held out his hand. Renzi took it with a firm handshake, but said nothing. Kydd mumbled something, and left.

Right aft on the larboard side of the gundeck were the petty officers' messes. Each was screened off with canvas, a little world within a world. Kydd scratched on the entrance of his new home; he was answered by Toby Stirk.

"Knoo you'd waste no time a-gettin' yerself a petty officer's berth!" The hard-featured seaman grinned—with his experience he had been quickly entered as a quarter gunner—and pulled him inside. It was snug and well appointed with pewter mess-traps, and the inside of the screens were splendidly decorated with colorful painted nautical scenes.

"This 'ere is Thomas Kydd—shipmates wi' me in *Artemis,* he was. Right taut hand o' the watch is Tom," Stirk said smugly, his dark eyes glittering. There was no one Kydd would have preferred to serve the compliments: Stirk's courage in battle and skill at the long guns was fabled.

He thumped his gear down on the table, looked around at his new messmates and glowed with happiness.

CHAPTER 3

—◅◆▻—

L aaaand hoooo!" The masthead lookout's powerful hail
stopped all work on deck. "Land ahoy—one point t'
loo'ard!"

In the van of the convoy, *Trajan*'s lofty masts gave the best
height of eye and they sighted Barbados first. A string of flags
jerked up her signal halliards and news of her landfall spread fast
around the eighty ships of the convoy. It had been five weeks since
they had left England, with only a brief stop in Madeira. The men
in the maintop, engaged in the endless task of tarring down the
standing rigging, broke into excited chatter. Kydd listened from
his position at the aft rail.

"Where's this'n?" demanded Larcomb, his face animated.

"The Barbadoes, in course!" said Carby, an older hand. "This
'ere is the first port o' call fer the Caribbean—ev'ry other o' the
islands are t' looard. Includin' the Frenchie ones," he added.

Kydd watched the gray blur on the horizon grow in definition
and broaden, eager white horses hurrying toward the land.
"What's ashore, mate?" he asked Carby. He was unsure quite what
to expect. Renzi had elaborated on the strategic importance of the

sugar islands, but that didn't seem to square with the hazy tales he
had heard of pirates, the Spanish Main and the infamous Port
Royal. Especially the pirates—were they still at large?

"Yair, well. Nothin' much, 'ceptin cane-fields and black-
amoors," grunted Carby. "Yez c'n get a good time at the punch
shops, an' the ladies are obligin', I'll grant yer." His lined eyes crin-
kled. "But don' expect ter be steppin' ashore like in Portsmouth
town, cully."

Within the hour Barbados had transformed from an anonymous blue-gray sprawling land to a substantial island, curiously
weathered into small ridges and valleys, all looking rather brown.
As they rounded the southwest tip, Kydd saw many windmills and
tiny huts on the hillsides in a sea of bright green sugarcane.

One after another the convoy tacked around the point, an endless swarm of sail that filled the sea. As Kydd stood by in the maintop for the evolution of mooring ship, he made sure that Carby
was near to give a commentary.

"There, mates, that's the lobsterbacks' barracks, an' up there, big
place near th' open bit, you has th' hospital. Yer goes in there wi'
the yellow jack 'n' it's a shillin' to a guinea yer comes out feet first."

Kydd gazed at the detail of the land resolving in front of him. A
wide bay was opening up past a large fort on the point, and a small
town nestled in the arm of the bay. "Carlisle Bay an' Bridgetown,"
said Carby.

In common with the other vessels, they would not be entering
the harbor; their anchor splashed down noisily into the innocent
blue-green of the wide bay. As cable was veered Kydd worked at
furling the big main course to its yard. This furl would be concluded with a fine harbor stow, and he was in place of honor at the
bunt in the middle, not at the yardarm. It was some satisfaction
for Kydd to be recognized as a good seaman. "A yardarm furler
and bunt reefer" was what a mediocre sailor was called: the best
men always went to the outer ends of the yard for deep-sea reefing
and the complex center of the sail for harbor furling.

Kydd on one side and Carby on the other clapped on the bunt jigger, and brought the clews over each side of the mast in a neat "pig's-ear." Then they passed plaited bunt gaskets to finish the beautifully even stow. The captain of the maintop let them work on without orders—Kydd's fine seamanship was now instinctive.

Finally at rest, *Trajan* slowly turned to her anchor to face the warm, gentle breeze, which was all that remained of the ceaseless trade winds of the open sea they had enjoyed over nearly the whole breadth of the Atlantic. Here, the waves were tiny, only enough to sparkle the sea, but a swell drove in to the beach in huge, indolent waves, a potent memento of a faraway storm.

A lazy heat descended on the motionless vessel. The boats were swayed out from their sea-stowed position on the skid-beams in the waist, and one by one they were placed in the water. An indefinable warm fragrance came on the winds from the shore—dusty earth, unfamiliar vegetation and a tropical sweetness.

The first away was the Captain's barge with Captain Bomford and the first lieutenant looking uncomfortable in their dress uniforms. The next was the longboat, its sturdy bluff bow pushing the water aside as it made its way shoreward. It would be returning with naval stores too valuable to be left to the local lighters even now putting off from the inner harbor.

Moodily, Kydd watched the boats lose themselves among the throng of other watercraft beetling among the many anchored vessels and the shore. He could see enough of the land's details to feel frustrated: he wanted to know what a Caribbean island looked like.

Trajan creaked in sequence as a swell passed down her length, accompanied by a lethargic rhythm of clacks and slatting from aloft as blocks and ropes rattled against the masts with the movement.

"*Haaands* to store ship!" Kydd's duty as quartermaster's mate required his presence. He took one last reluctant look at the shore. Already lighters were putting off from the distant quay with water, big leaguer casks in rows. He watched, astonished, as just two men fended off, then began manipulating mighty polelike oars—all of fifty feet long—to bring out one of the heavy lighters.

To get at the hold, it was necessary to open the main-hatch on each deck, one under the other. At the orlop the decking was taken up, revealing the noisome darkness of the hold, now made light by the strengthening sun coming down through the hatches. Kydd dropped down to the top of the stores. The empty casks had to be cleared away to allow the full ones to lower down into the ground tier, safely nestled "bung-up and bilge free" in shingle ballast. The stench was thick and potent—the shingle had absorbed bilge water and the stink roiled up as it was disturbed. In the heat it was hard to take, and Kydd felt a guilty pang as he scrambled above. Clear of the hold, he wrote his reckoning on his slate.

"*All the haaaands!* Clear lower deck *ahoooy!* Hands lay aft!" The boatswain's mates sounded distantly above.

Kydd cursed—this was not the time to be stopping work. "Secure!" he growled, at the questioning faces of his work party below.

The Captain had unexpectedly returned and waited patiently at the break of the poop, flanked by his officers.

"Still!" roared the master-at-arms. Conversations faded and the sound of shuffling feet quickly died away.

Captain Bomford stepped forward to the rail. "*Trajan*s, I have asked you here to tell you the news." There was silence at his words. "Our duty to the convoy is done." This was met with stony looks—the slow progress of the convoy across the Atlantic had been tedious.

"Now we are released for our true work." He let the words sink into the silence. "We shall now sail for the French island of Guadeloupe. You will be happy to hear that His Majesty's arms have met with great success in the West Indies. We are taking the French islands from them, one by one, Martinique, Saint Lucia, and now Guadeloupe. We sail immediately. On arrival, all hands should be prepared for shore service. However, I do not anticipate much opposition."

Trajan and the 32-gun frigate *Wessex* sailed unopposed into the sheltered arms of Grande Baie, Guadeloupe. The sleepy island was oddly shaped: to larboard a bulking, rounded beast of land, to starboard a low, rumpled coastline stretching away, the two forming an inward curve. Where they met, the land dipped to a flat joining place.

Sun-splashed and deeply green, the land seemed all that Kydd expected of an isle in the Caribbean. There were no wharves and shantytowns that he could see, just verdancy and, here and there, the golden lines of beaches. The heady scent of land on the brisk wind entered his nostrils, immediate and exciting.

The anchor dropped and cable rumbled out. Motion ceased on the *Trajan*, but *Wessex* continued on. Inshore, from a small, squat coral-stone fort, Kydd saw white puffs appear close to the water's edge. The puny guns seemed to have no effect on the ship, which glided on. Kydd wondered how he would feel if positions were reversed. Here was the equivalent of an entire artillery battery of the heaviest guns of the army coming to punish the little fort.

There was no more gunsmoke from the fort. Kydd guessed that the gunners were fleeing the menace closing in. But there was no time to watch. He was in charge of one party of fifteen seamen under Lieutenant Calley and a master's mate he didn't know, and they would shortly board one of the boats for the shore.

The sudden crash of a broadside echoed around the bay— *Wessex* had opened fire. The smoke blew down on them quickly in the lively breeze, hiding the frigate, but the effects of the tempest of shot on the silent fort were clear. Heavy balls had torn up the ground, sending huge clods of earth and rock fragments skyward. Tropical trees had fallen as if slapped down, and a haze of dust had materialized.

A storm of cheering went up, and the men tumbled willingly

into the boats. Kydd and his party were assigned the forward part of the longboat, and he pushed between the rowers to the bow, his cutlass scabbard catching awkwardly. He saw Renzi board at the last minute; he could not catch his eye at this distance, and wondered what he was doing—he was not a member of Kydd's party.

He looked back along the boat to the rest of his men boarding. His heart raced, but whether this was at the thought of meeting the enemy or anxiety at having his powers of leadership tested in such an alien arena he could not be sure. The men seemed in good heart, joking and relaxed; comforting in their sturdy sea ways.

The boat shoved off, Kydd at the tiller. Bows swung obediently shoreward, bringing the seas smacking solidly onto the bluff bow, soaking him. These seas would make landing difficult—and if there were enemy waiting for them . . .

The smash of another broadside drew his attention. *Wessex* was concentrating her guns on the coast where the boats were headed, and it would take a brave man to stand at the focus of such terrifying, rampaging power.

Kydd looked back. Other boats were converging together, bobbing and surging in the boisterous seas. A deep-laden pinnace stopped, and turned head-to-sea. Rainbow sheets of water flew over the side. He searched the seashore immediately ahead but could not see any beach, just endless vegetation coming down to the foreshore and dark reddish-brown coral at the water's edge. The heartening roar of the frigate's guns ceased, and the ship lay offshore under backed topsails. There was nothing more she could do for them.

Trajan's large cutter approached the landing place to lead the others. It carried marines. Close in now, it did not appear to be under fire but seemed to hesitate at the last minute. It dipped and rolled in the energetic seas, then turned to pass along the shoreline to find a better landing place. In a flash, the boat was seized by the riotous waves and thrown over in a tangle of oars and red uniforms. Yells of fear and despair carried across the water.

Other boats came on. Some followed the example of the lighter pinnace, which stretched out manfully to ground noisily on the dead coral in a surfing rush. Its men scrambled out, but before half had made it, the boat slewed broadside to the waves and also overturned.

The more sea-wise cast an anchor when still off the landing place, and with bows firmly held seaward, veered rope until they were in the shallows. The disadvantage was that men dropped into feet of water and stumbled, soaked and bruised, long yards to the shore. Kydd had the sense to deploy his men in a chain to the tide line, passing over their heads muskets and the small kegs of powder.

There was still no sign of opposition ashore. Military shouts sounded in the glades where the sailors were grouping.

"My crew, t' me!" Kydd called brusquely. He mustered them carefully. Two missing. Should he tell someone to find them? The man might get lost; best to count on what he had. Curious glances came from those waiting for him to show indecision or worse. Responsibility was hard. What *was* Renzi doing in his party? He frowned and turned to him. "Why are you—" he began.

"I was bored."

Kydd took a deep breath. This was no time to be enigmatic. "Then . . ."

"I am, for the nonce, a bona fide member of your excellent party," Renzi said.

"An' ready t' take my orders?" Kydd retorted, then regretted his tone, but stubbornness kept him glowering.

"But, of course, my dear fellow."

One of the missing men arrived, grinning foolishly and showing obvious signs of the bottle.

"Tom, L'tenant Calley wants y'r report," said Luke, who had managed to get ashore as messenger. His wide eyes gazed trustfully at Kydd.

"Thanks, younker," Kydd said, and looked around for Calley.

"Kydd, sir, mustered complete," he reported. If Renzi was so eager to be in his party, he could make up the numbers.

"Very good, Kydd. Be ready to advance in one hour—you will take flank." Calley looked distracted. Flank was some sort of tent or blanket for the officers, Kydd assumed. "We will storm Gozier Fort," said Calley quickly. "The one attacked by *Wessex*," he added impatiently, seeing Kydd's expression. He turned to an anxious midshipman, effectively dismissing Kydd.

As far as Kydd could see, they would be assisting the marines in the assault, a useful mass of armed men coming in from behind. They would carry the familiar weapons of the boarding party, pistols and either a cutlass or a tomahawk with its blade and useful spike. It would be just like carrying an enemy vessel by boarding, no marching up and down like the army seemed to do. He brightened at the familiar focus.

"*Trajan*s ahoy!" Calley's voice blared. "We go to meet the enemy—to the fore, advance!"

Three distinct lines of men began to move into the light, wooded land, the red coats of the marines visible ahead. The columns diverged and, wending their way through the undergrowth, the lead men disappeared from view.

Away from the sea breeze, the warmth turned to heat, sending up the smell of steamy vegetation. The path was well beaten now, and they plodded on steadily.

The man behind Kydd suddenly gave a cry and dropped his musket. It went off with a muffled report, suffusing the ground with gunsmoke. He danced about, waving his arms frantically. Kydd stood rooted in astonishment. Then he saw a large hairy black spider with glittering eyes clinging to the man's lower arm. Suddenly it scuttled over his body, the man fell to the ground and the spider leaped off then disappeared. Shame-faced and trembling, the man rose as Calley arrived in a lather of indignation.

The first sign of resistance appeared with a tiny white puff arising from the undergrowth ahead and the tap of a musket sound-

ing faintly. Kydd's mouth dried. This might be the enemy returning after the sea bombardment, angry and resentful—in their
thousands. He gripped his musket nervously and slogged on,
knowing that the eyes of his party behind—including Renzi—
were on him.

"First section will attempt an enfilade." Kydd had not noticed
Calley return. "That's you, Kydd," he snapped, taking off his
cocked hat to wipe his streaming forehead. His cotton stockings
were streaked now with soft green and his blue coat hung loose.

"Sir—" began Kydd.

"In an enfilade," Calley snarled sarcastically, "the object is to
bring the enemy under fire from the flank."

So much for blankets, thought Kydd.

"We rake him, you ninny!"

Kydd burned. Why hadn't Calley used understandable sea
terms from the first? To rake the enemy at sea was to slam a storm
of shot down the unprotected length of the vessel instead of into
her heavy sides, and was generally credited a battle winner.

Calley glared, then collected himself. "The fort lies yonder, a
mile or so off," he said, gesturing at the dense undergrowth to the
north. "You will move around to take him from the east. But mark
my words! You are to take position only. Do not advance until you
hear the redcoat's trumpet that we are also in place." He breathed
heavily. "Else you will be destroyed."

Kydd led the way. A sea-service cutlass was too heavy and cumber-
some to do much about the thickening ground cover, and he
swore—at first under his breath, and later aloud. His musket, over
his shoulder in its sling, slipped and banged him, and he could
hear his men muttering.

Without warning, the trees and vegetation dropped away to
nothing. Kydd fell to the ground, motioning the others to do the
same. They had reached a track crossing their course. It was the
ideal path for enemy coming down on them from the north, but

there was nothing for it: he must obey orders and carry on eastward.

He ran across the track, followed by his party. The other side was a dense wall of harsh greenery reaching skyward eight feet or more, so thickly sown that it was virtually impenetrable. It would be impossible to keep on their course. Kydd crouched and felt a rising tide of panic. He would do his duty or die in the attempt! But this? What if they were going in the wrong direction, were late, betrayed the brave souls making the frontal assault who believed they would be supported to the east by Kydd's section?

"Give over frettin', Tom!" Larcomb said kindly, coming up to squat next to him. Larcomb had his jacket off, knotted around his waist. "What say we takes a spell here, mate?"

"No!" Kydd snarled.

Renzi loped up at the crouch. Kydd braced himself—he neither wanted to justify himself to his friend nor discuss the philosophy of the situation.

"Should you await me here, I do believe I can find an easterly path for us, my friend." Renzi was looking northward with a keen gaze.

"Er, o' course," Kydd said, caught off balance.

Renzi left his musket and cutlass and sprinted off. Almost immediately he disappeared into the thick vegetation. Kydd waited, debating with himself what to do if Renzi did not reappear—then his friend popped into view, beckoning furiously.

"Sugarcane has to be harvested was my logic!" Renzi chuckled, as they hurried down a narrow break in the cane-field to the east.

Logic, thought Kydd dully. It would have to be logic if it were Renzi, but his heart warmed to the way his friend had made it easy for him.

"D'ye think a mile has passed f'r us?" Kydd asked, as casually as he could, as they moved along the endless, unchanging track. The assault could come at any time. . . .

"I would think so," said Renzi.

Kydd felt annoyed again: it was easy for Renzi, he was not in charge. Not only did Kydd have to be in position to the east, but when the trumpet sounded he *had* to know which direction to push forward, or end up in the empty country while the real battle was being fought and won without him.

"Damn you!" he ground out. Renzi glanced at him, no emotion on his face.

Kydd looked away. At least they were in position now—the fort must be away to their left. He hunkered down for the wait. The others lay around, some on their backs, seeming uncaring of the coming clash-at-arms. Renzi sat, hugging his knees and staring into space, while Kydd got up and paced.

The sun grew hotter. They had no water, as it was all expected to end rapidly one way or the other. The minutes dragged on, with not a sound apart from a bird that kept up a deafening racket. It was agonizing—what was delaying the main assault? Kydd checked the priming on his musket again. Perhaps Calley had received secret knowledge of a greater than expected French garrison, and was waiting for reinforcements. If that was so—

A rustling sounded on the other side of the wall of cane. They were discovered—and before the assault! He would sell their lives dearly, though. Kydd seized his musket and pointed it at the sound. He sensed the others grouping behind him.

Luke wheeled around the end of the cane-field. "I bin a-lookin' fer you!" His face was wreathed in smiles as he ran toward Kydd. Then he stopped and attempted a professional look, such as messengers have when delivering their news. "Er, Mr. Kydd, I'm ter tell yer from L'tenant Calley ter report t' the fort."

"What?"

"He's in a rare takin'—Frogs ran off afore we c'd even get in position, they did!" His face clouded. "An' he says as how yer such an infernal looby as y' doesn't know when the guns ain't firin' there ain't a battle."

Kydd gritted his teeth. Of course! That was what had been nig-

gling at the back of his mind—no firing! A quick glance at Renzi's
blank expression told him that he had known all along that their
advance on the fort would be guided by the sound of battle.

"An' he told the Joey major that he'd be a confounded prig afore
he sounds the trumpet t' advance jus' ter oblige a parcel o'—"

"That's enough o' yer insolence, m' lad!" Larcomb said reprov-
ingly. The party hefted their muskets and followed Luke meekly to
the fort.

Flames flickered ruddily from the cooking fire. The seamen had
left the foraging and other arrangements to the marines, who
seemed well able to cope. Kydd nursed his cracked cup of rum as
he sat morosely against the wattle wall of the chattel house, staring
into the flames. It was not his kind of war, this—crashing about in
the undergrowth not knowing what was going on. Real war was
serving a mighty cannon on a surging gundeck.

The evening was pleasant, the constant breeze from the ocean
reliable enough, but the ground all about was hard and dusty. He
scratched at a persistent tickle in his leg hairs in the darkness, then
saw by the firelight that it was a busy column of ants. He leaped to
his feet in disgust.

They'd eaten a kind of spicy chicken that the previous owners of
the house had thought they would be having that night. It sat
uneasily on Kydd's stomach. Reluctantly he pushed his way closer
to the fire and settled down again on the stony ground.

It seemed like minutes later when boatswain's mates and corporals
roared about to rouse the huddled men. Kydd ached in the
predawn darkness after his uncomfortable doze. A thin overcast
hid the half-moon and the night was full of dull shadows.

Kydd knew the plan in a general way. They would push forward
before dawn toward a much bigger fort, Fleur d'Épée, and fall
upon it at first light. It was hoped that the defenders would not
expect such a rapid resuming of the advance.

"Pay attention, you section leaders." Calley was indistinct in the poor light, but his words came strongly. Kydd stood in the semicircle of a dozen men, listening carefully.

"We advance on the fort shortly. There are two roads. Sections one and three will take the easterly, the other sections the westerly. The roads go each side of the fort. Now, mark this, the fort is on a slight hill, and reconnaissance tells us that the brush has been cleared around to give a good field of fire. "Therefore—and I cannot emphasize this too strongly—we will be bloodily repulsed if they are waiting for us. The advance *must* take place in complete silence. Total silence! Do I make myself clear?"

All traces of weariness and aching fell away as Kydd took in the words.

"For that reason, the first numbered sections will be armed with cold steel only—this will ensure that there are no accidental discharges of musketry. And, do you bear in mind always, you are not to leave cover and advance over the open ground until the trumpet sounds. Then move very quickly, if you please," Calley added dryly.

Kydd took his cutlass, the blackened steel and gray oily blade sinister in the last of the firelight. He remembered the first time he had used one with deadly force. Then it had saved his life, but at the cost of the enduring memory of a young man's face sagging under the recognition of his coming death.

He fitted the scabbard to its frog, and slid it onto his wide seaman's belt. Experimentally, he drew the heavy weapon's greased length—it fell to hand easily, and Kydd noted that the blade had been ground to a good point: it could be relied on to sink through clothing and leather to the heart.

"Form up!" he growled at his section. Renzi was present, although Kydd was none the wiser about his action in joining his party. He had been too tired the previous evening to do more than grunt at Renzi's solicitudes; there had been no comfortable conversation.

They moved off. In the lead were other sections. They paced on rapidly, Kydd grateful for the easy going afforded by a road instead of clinging undergrowth. The road forked. Kydd's section took the lead to the right. The road sank lower and its sides reared as they passed into a defile cut into a rise in the coral rock, until even the least military of them realized that, trapped as they were by the vertical sides of the road, they were easy meat for any ambush.

Kydd paced on, his ears pricking, his eyes staring wide. His men followed behind in file. It was no use trying to listen for strange sounds—the tropical night was alive with unknown stridulations, barks, squeaks and grunts. The road emerged from the defile, and began to trend upward. They must be approaching the prominence with the fort astride it, he reasoned. Sure enough, a curve in the road led out of the wooded fringing area and some-where shortly ahead must lie the open ground—and Fort d'Épée.

"Dead silence!" whispered Kydd, "Or—or . . ." It seemed thin and pathetic against the reality of their situation, but the men nodded, and plunged after him off the road and into the woods. It wasn't long before they came to the edge: the crudely felled and leveled area ahead gave no cover, open ground all the way up to the drab cluster of low buildings inside stout palisades. It was still too overcast and murky to make out much.

"Back—we wait f'r the call," Kydd whispered. It were best they were not at the very edge of the clearing in case a pale face in the night was seen from the fort. They moved inward a few yards and settled to wait.

"I c'n hear . . ." began Larcomb. There was a rustle.

Renzi moved up and looked around questioningly. "There!" he hissed.

It *was* a footfall. Kydd held up his hand for silence. His heart thudded. Another footfall, a rustling of foliage. Someone was entering the woods, and heading toward them.

At the edge of action Kydd teetered. The movement stopped

and Kydd took a deep breath—but then came the tinkle of urine
on the ground.

In a dizzying moment of relief, he touched the arms of Larcomb and another seaman then pointed. They nodded and rose
soundlessly. In a swift flurry they brought the man crashing down.
He was a young sentry, who had laid down his musket to relieve
himself out of sight of the fort. He struggled hard, but was pin-
ioned securely, Larcomb's hand clamped over his mouth. The
struggles spent themselves, and the hapless man stared up.

Kydd knew that Renzi spoke French, and whispered harshly,
"Tell him he's our prisoner."

"I rather think not," Renzi replied.

"Damn it! Do as I—"

"We have no men to spare to look after prisoners." To give
point to Renzi's words, the youth struggled again. Three men
were holding him down—three effectives who would be greatly
missed later.

"You can't just . . ."

Renzi said nothing. The young man's eyes bulged; he seemed
to sense what was being discussed, and tried desperately to reach
out to them.

"Bugger wants ter talk," Larcomb muttered hoarsely, and
looked up.

Hesitating, Kydd shook his head—there was too much risk.
Renzi's logic led one way, pity and humanity, another. He gazed at
Renzi in despair.

Renzi leaned across, and extracted the bayonet in a steely slither
from Larcomb's scabbard.

"No!" breathed Kydd, held powerless in horror as the nightmare face returned.

The youth heaved and floundered, his eyes frozen on the blade.
A rank, unmistakable odor arose. "He's shit hisself," Larcomb
croaked, his voice thick with compassion.

"Make room," Renzi said. Kydd realized he meant Larcomb to move aside enough to enable the bayonet to do its work. Larcomb did so, his eyes down. The boy ceased his struggle, lay petrified and rigid. Renzi crawled over to him and raised the bayonet. There was an inhuman squeal of such intensity that it sounded through Larcomb's tight grip—then Renzi thrust the bayonet firmly into the chest to the heart. A dextrous half-twist, and the blade was withdrawn, the gout of bright life-blood hopeless and final.

Renzi wiped the weapon on the ground and handed it back to Larcomb. He looked up at the anguish on Kydd's face. "Duty can often take a harsh disguise, my friend," he said in a low voice.

Kydd tore himself away from the sight of the fresh corpse, his mind a whirl of confusion. Nobody came to where he crouched, and there was no relief to his emotions. Away to the left, far in the distance, a trumpet bayed, its sound taken up by another, nearer. "Tom!" said Renzi softly.

Kydd pulled himself together. "With me!" he croaked. He cleared his throat. "Let's give 'em a quiltin', then." He broke out of the wood and stumbled up the rise toward the fort, hearing his men follow. Others emerged all along the fringe of wood. It seemed incredible that their drama could have taken place in such isolation.

They moved up the hill. The fort's palisades were topped with continuous gunsmoke in the soft dawn light, and attackers began to drop. The fusillade died away—they had succeeded in their surprise: there were not enough men on watch to maintain the reloading cycle for full defense.

Something seized Kydd's mind in a fierce, uncaring rage—a point of concentration for his incoherent feelings. His legs burned as he pounded on toward the focus of his madness. Behind him panted Larcomb—then Kydd realized he had gone. Renzi was away to his right and all the others he assumed were somewhere close. All the time the weakened enemy fire found victims.

The palisades rose up suddenly. Renzi appeared beside him. He carried a rolled Jacob's ladder and coolly hurled it up, hooking it to the jagged top of the barrier. Faces appeared above, then quickly disappeared. Musket smoke came in gusts, the sound of the shots this time from behind him. Kydd seized the ladder and swarmed up. Other seamen had boarding axes and they were using them in the same way as they would to storm the side of an enemy ship. The seamen's agility told: they were quickly into the inner square and throwing wide the gates for the soldiers before the confused enemy could group.

Panting, hot and aching, Kydd stood watching the fluttering French flag jerk down, then rise again, surmounted by a Union Flag. A disconsolate group of French prisoners flanked by marines began their march into exile. The last of the dead were dragged off and the wounded attended to.

The crisp sound of marching heralded the arrival of the light infantry, with a mounted colonel at their head. Lieutenant Calley removed his hat and awaited the Colonel. "Well done, sir!" the Colonel spluttered, as he dismounted. "Damme, but that was a splendid thing. Blast m' eyes if it weren't!"

The marines snapped to attention; their sergeant needed no lessons in military honors. The "present arms" was parade-ground perfect, yet these men, less than an hour before, had been storming the fort.

The Colonel marched across and inspected them, his gruff compliments making the sergeant red-faced with pleasure. Kydd felt awkward with his ragtag sailors, but the Colonel touched his hat genially in response to the individualistic salutes of the seamen, in no way disconcerted by the sight of their direct gaze and sea-fashion rigs.

"A fine body of men!" said the Colonel to Calley. "And 'twould infinitely oblige me, sir, if they were in my column for the final push on the capital."

"By all means, sir. Your orders?" Calley replied.

* * *

Within an hour the column was swinging along at a measured pace astride the road to Pointe à Pitre, the capital, soldiers four abreast in a serpentine column that stretched ahead of the seamen, with fifes and drums squeaking and rattling.

A sergeant of infantry dropped back from the rear of the column, and stared with frank curiosity at the seamen. "Hoay—the sergeant ahoy!" called Kydd. The hard-featured man fell back to Kydd, still keeping step.

"How long to Pwun a-Peter?" Kydd asked.

The man sized him up. There was no clue for a soldier that might reveal his rank. He was dressed as the others in his usual red-and-white shirt with short blue jacket and white free-swinging trousers. Kydd sensed wariness and added, "Tom Kydd, quartermaster's mate—that's petty officer."

"Sar'nt Hotham."

Clearly a "petty officer" meant nothing either to this army veteran, who peered at him suspiciously from under his tall black shako. The voice was deep and projected an effortless authority that Kydd envied.

"An' these are m' men," Kydd continued, gesturing behind him at the cutlass-adorned sailors.

The sergeant's eyebrows rose: Kydd must be some sort of sergeant, then. "Ah, yeah," he said, easing his stock. "Saw yez take the fort fr'm yer front—plucky dos, mate!"

Feet rose and fell, the rhythm of the march was hypnotic. "Aye, well, how far d'we march afore—"

Hotham flashed a quick grin. "Don't be in such a hell-fired pelt ter get there, m' lad," he boomed. "That there's th' capital town o' the island, an' the Frogs ain't about to give it up without a fight."

Kydd said nothing, the whole business of war on land was a mystery to him.

Hotham mistook his silence for apprehension. "Not ter worry, we've drubbed th' French in every other island, can't see why not 'ere as well."

"So . . ."

"We's three, four mile out, less'n an hour—but then we comes up agin the battery commandin' the town." He sucked his teeth as he ruminated. "We gets past that on this road, Mongseers 'd be hard put ter stop us then."

It was still midmorning when the column came to a halt at the sullen rumble of heavy guns ahead. A flurry of trumpet calls echoing up and down the line; bellowed orders and earnest subalterns hurrying on important missions had the column quickly deployed in line.

The seamen mustered together in the center of the line: they would have the road. With a clinking of equipment, a squadron of cavalry mounted on indifferent horses clattered off toward the battery, which dominated the skyline.

"Poor beggars," muttered a sailor.

"How so?" said Kydd.

"O' course, they's bein' sacrificed to see 'ow far the guns c'n reach." A single gout of smoke appeared at the embrasures of the battery and seconds later a thud came, but there was no apparent harm to the widely separated horses. They cantered farther along the road, now even at the suburbs of Pointe à Pitre.

"Stand to!" Lieutenant Calley ordered. "We march."

The re-formed column, having tested their advance, resumed the march. Eyes nervously on the battery above the town, they tramped along the road unopposed. Kydd looked at the deserted houses and neat gardens. No sign of war, just a sullen silence. The squadron cantered back. It seemed the battery had been deserted by the French, and their other forces were in full retreat. The empty town echoed to their progress, only the odd dog or fowl left to dispute possession. By midday, the seamen were slaking their thirst in the fountain of the town square, and the regimental fifes and drums were bringing in the soldiers.

It was an anticlimax—but welcome for all that. Parties of soldiers were sent out to secure strongpoints. The seamen were marched down to the neat harbor, its white stone walls and red-tiled buildings baking in the heat.

CHAPTER 4

—✺—

The rain hammered down in a tropical burst of furious intensity. Kydd opened an eye lazily. It was relatively dry aft under the awning of the trading schooner and he saw no reason to disturb his repose. There was little that he and his two men could do until someone had found enough sea stores to complete the refit, not just of this little craft on the slipway but the larger brig alongside the quay farther along. The French had not dared to sail these merchant vessels out against the waiting English, or had time to destroy them.

A steamy earthiness arose as the rain eased, then stopped. Kydd took in the landlocked harbor, the vividness of the colors after the rain holding him rapt.

The ladder at the side of the craft rattled and the beaming face of Luke appeared. He and Renzi, Kydd's "men," had volunteered for this task rather than return to *Trajan*; other seamen were working on the brig. "Mr. Kydd!" Luke called, and clambered over the gunwale. He had sheltered under the schooner on the slipway with Renzi.

Kydd grunted and sat up.

"Chucks'll be down on us like thunder," Luke said cheerfully, " 'less we show we done somethin'."

"What?" said Kydd grumpily. Admittedly, they could find small things to do—the departing French had slashed at the rigging, but the reason why the craft had been slipped, a strake or two stove in forward, would have to await the shipwright's attention before the schooner took to the water again.

Renzi appeared from under the round of the bilges and paced along the length of the craft on the hardstanding. God only knew what he was thinking about, mused Kydd. The smell of the schooner's hull close to was pleasant, the essence of the tar and preservatives heightened by the sun; the underwater weed and barnacles produced an intense sea aroma.

"Younker, get y'rself down t' Toby 'n' see if he needs ye," Kydd told Luke. He waited until Luke was on his way to the brig, then dropped overside. "Nicholas," he said. "Might we talk?"

Renzi stopped, and struck a dramatic pose:

> *"Slow glides the sail along the illumined shore,*
> *And steals into shade the lazy oar;*
> *Soft bosoms breathe around contagious sighs,*
> *And amorous music on the water dies!"*

Then, gazing at the broad harbor vista, he said, "Do you not find that—"

"You think I am a weak looby, that I did not—settle th' sentry," Kydd said bluntly.

Renzi paused only for a moment before he replied, "No, dear fellow, I do not." Kydd opened his mouth to speak, but Renzi continued, "I observe that you are driven by the highest considerations of humanity, most laudable, but these are not, *entre nous,* always the ones to bear foremost in such a pass. Your humanity bears you on up false paths while the essential principle remains neglected."

"In this instance," Kydd said stubbornly, lifting his chin, "we could—"

"In this instance, the entire assault is put to the hazard," Renzi replied firmly. "There is no other course. Your duty is as clear as at the helm in a storm. The moral courage lies in attending to the matter *and* without repine."

They paced together to the end of the fine-run bow. Kydd stopped. "Why did ye come ashore with me? Was it t' play the nursemaid? Do I need a keeper?"

Renzi smiled. "Do you believe that I would not be interested in the fate of my particular friend?"

A stab of pleasure shot through Kydd. "Y' must be green at m' rate of petty officer," he said gruffly.

"On the contrary, dear fellow, I give you joy of it." His smile was genuine. "My purpose in a ship of war is in the serving of exile, not to top it the tyrant over my shipmates."

At that moment the boatswain and his two mates came around from the other side of the boat. "Sticks in m' craw," he rumbled, "but yez are stood down f'r the day." He took off his hat and mopped his brow. "An' I have a berth for yez—yer'll be livin' wi' a Johnny Crapaud 'n' his family. 'E'll tell y' where," he added, thumbing at one of his boatswain's mates.

"Poxy Frogs!" sneered Luke scornfully.

"Not you, skinker," said the boatswain, "you comes along wi' me."

It wasn't far from the dusty waterfront; in fact, it was a shop in a street leading off the quay. In its neat, small windows Kydd saw tobacco pipes, bone snuffboxes and rows of caddies disappearing into the gloom. Outside stood a small mustachioed Frenchman, his desiccated wife behind clutching spasmodically at him.

"Nah, then, Fronswah, these 'ere are yer guests fer now," the tall boatswain's mate said kindly. "Kydd 'ere, an' Renzi that one. Compree?"

"Ah, oui," the man said doubtfully.

The boatswain's mate looked at Kydd. "So I c'n leave yer with 'em, then?"

Kydd lifted his seabag. "Aye. We've nothing t' fear fr'm these folks."

The sailor grinned and left. The Frenchman looked up and down the street nervously and made shooing gestures to the two sailors. *"Allez—allez!"* he said.

"Mais, mon brave, nous sommes . . ." began Renzi, in mellifluous French, sparking a visible leap in the man's spirits.

"J'ai l'honneur d'être Henri Vernou, et voici ma femme." Careful nods were exchanged after Renzi had translated. His wife began guarded rapid jabber at him, but Renzi turned to her, bowed elegantly and murmured polite words. Her expression relaxed a little.

They threaded through the shop and arrived at the back in a large kitchen-cum-sitting-room. A rotund black woman froze in astonishment at the intruders, but was sharply set about her business. An external flight of steps took them to the upper story; the wife fiddled with a key and stood back to let them enter, her eyes following them unblinking as a crow's.

"Merci, madame," Renzi said. The room was small, but snug—a woman's room. It smelled of fragrances that made Kydd feel his rough-hewn maleness.

"Le dîner est servi à sept heures précises. Voilà votre clé. Ne la perdez pas." She closed the door on them.

"Supper will be at seven, you will be gratified to know," Renzi said.

There were two beds, one an obvious extra. "Turn 'n' turn about," Kydd suggested, for the original bed was the better one. He chuckled. "The throw o' th' dice," he ruminated. "B' rights, we should be in a doss house o' sorts—maybe there ain't any in this town."

"I have my suspicions as to the hospitality," said Renzi, but would not be drawn. The door led to an upper veranda that overlooked the street and, with the jalousie windows, made it acceptably cool. It was infinitely preferable to the careless noise and drunken conviviality of a seamen's boardinghouse.

They went into the kitchen and were ushered to places on either side of that of the head of the house, who entered last. A woman with a frosting of silver hair and an intelligent face was seated at the other end, and at Kydd's glance gave a slight nod and a tiny smile.

The table was spread, the wine was open in the center of the table and the black maid stood by. A warning glare from Renzi was too late to stop Kydd reaching for a stick of interesting bread, which he crunched appreciatively. "Rattlin' good," he said, but was met with a chilly silence.

"I do believe that the French set great store by the preliminaries," Renzi muttered. Kydd felt reproachful stares around the table.

"Seigneur, nous vous rendons grâce pour ce repas que nous apprêtons à partager . . ." The ancient words of the grace droned into the silence. Eyes lifted, and there was an awkward pause.

"Et voici ma soeur, Louise," said Monsieur Vernou reproachfully.

"And his sister, Louise," Renzi murmured to Kydd.

They turned down the table to the woman, who inclined her head graciously and said, "Plissed to mit you."

Kydd gave a broad smile. "Aye, an' we too, er, ma'am!"

"I 'ave been the governess an' ticher of French to ze English before."

"Oh," said Kydd. "Before what?"

At the slight frown this brought, Renzi said firmly, "Pray let us not be accounted boors, my friend." The table sat expressionless. Renzi turned to Louise. *"Madame,"* your English does credit to your calling."

Kydd let the conversation flow around him. It passed belief the situation he was now in. The French were a parcel of mad rascals who had murdered their king and now wanted to set the world at defiance—but here he was, on the face of it one of the conquerors of this island, being politely entertained by them. Perhaps the food would be poisoned? He glanced at Renzi, who seemed to take it all in his stride. He had the attention of the whole table—except Madame Louise, whose quiet gaze strayed from time to time in Kydd's direction.

"Tom, Madame Vernou wishes to know what it is like living in a boat," prompted Renzi, keeping his face a study in restraint. Kydd opened his mouth but recoiled, the task of rendering into polite talk the stern realities of life at sea beyond him. Renzi's smooth flow of French, however, seemed to satisfy the table.

During the meal, a tasty stew, Kydd tried to remember his manners. He grinned inwardly, thinking of what his mother would have to say to him, in this alien place so far from home. The watered wine was excellent medicine for the pork and beans, and he began to relax. "Hear tell th't France is a pretty place," he tried. The comment rippled out under translation, but caused some dismay. Mystified, he turned to Renzi.

"It appears, my friend, that none here has ever been to France."

Kydd gave a weak smile. To his amazement, Monsieur Vernou, who was well into his third glass of wine, suddenly stood up, scattering dishes. He stabbed a finger at Kydd and broke into impassioned speech.

"Monsieur Vernou . . . states that he is not to be mistaken for one of those regicides in Paris . . . who have brought such dishonor on their country . . . who have brought ruin and shame to the land. . . ." Renzi's polite manner was not best suited to the passion of the words.

Monsieur Vernou stopped and, grasping the lapels of his waistcoat, glared down at Kydd.

"In addition, Monsieur Vernou wishes it to be understood that he is proud to be termed a *béké*—which I understand to be of a class in some way superior to others. . . ."

The little Frenchman was still in patriotic flow so Kydd stood up too, and said in a strong voice, "We never killed our king—we yet honor him. An' we say, God save th' King!" He raised his glass and drained it.

From the end of the table, the gentle voice of Louise cut in. "We also, M'sieur Keed—you are in ze company of *royalistes,* you un'erstand."

A rapid volley of French at Monsieur Vernou had the Frenchman staring in consternation. *"Mais bien sûr! Que Dieu bénisse Sa Majesté Britannique!"*

All rose. *"Que Dieu bénisse Sa Majesté!"*

Renzi returned the compliment and the table sat down to a happy babble. "I pray the lunacy on the streets of Paris does not cross the seas to here," Renzi remarked in a low voice to Kydd. "These good people will be its first victims."

The next few days passed in a blur of contentment for Kydd. The boatswain arrived with stores—coils of good hemp rope, six blocks to replace those weakened by tropical rot, and oakum for deck seams. The ship's carpenter put in an appearance to tut-tut over the sprung bow strakes and left with the promise that his mates would come later.

At the billet Kydd settled into a pleasant domestic routine. Louise mended a shirtsleeve he had torn—it was her room that the sailors now inhabited. At family meals she had taken to sitting next to Kydd, her quaint English welcome when Renzi engaged in his long conversations in French. She would gently chide him on his manners, which Kydd found endearing, if disconcerting.

Less than a week later, when the schooner had been brought to readiness but for the stove bowstrakes, they sat down to their meal—and unwelcome news. "The French have made their move," Renzi murmured to Kydd, after the first excited flurry of talk had settled.

Kydd's mouth was full, but he couldn't help saying, "This scran is rousin' good eatin', Nicholas." The ragoût of fish had an elusive flavor of herbs—French cooking was fast persuading Kydd that the English did not have it all their own way in the culinary arts.

"It could prove . . . unfortunate," Renzi pressed.

"What's afoot?" Kydd asked, mouth full.

"They say there are rumors that significant landings have been made to the north of the island," Renzi said in a low voice.

Louise overheard. "So—a few soldier land! We 'ave the protection of ze Engleesh scheeeps and soldiers too."

Monsieur Vernou snapped some words.

"My brothair—he remind that we *béké* are many, and will flock to the color of Bourbon France."

Renzi dabbed his mouth. "These are landed from a frigate. This implies that they are regular troops on a planned invasion—by the revolutionaries," he added, for emphasis.

"But you vill always prevail," Louise said.

"That is not altogether certain," Renzi said carefully.

"Why do ye say that, Nicholas?" Kydd said, with some asperity.

"Consider. *Trajan* and the frigates are away attending to the reduction of San Domingo. They cannot come at our call immediately because they are headed by the winds and current. The garrison here in Guadeloupe is few—we have sent perhaps too many soldiers to San Domingo. The royalists are no trouble and look to seeing out the larger war under our governance, but they may prove unreliable if tested too far. If the Jacobins are energetic and well led, it could be . . ."

Kydd turned to Louise, but her eyes were troubled so he didn't speak.

The following morning there was even worse news. "It seems that the Terror in Paris has come here at last," Renzi told Kydd, after listening to a fear-struck visitor as they prepared to leave for their work. There was no need to lower his voice now: there was a hubbub of frantic speculation. "A guillotine came with the frigate and it is doing its work out there even now." Renzi looked grave.

"One hundred—maybe as many as three hundred have perished in a night of blood. This is serious news indeed."

A torrent of weeping and beseeching from the women greeted the sight of Monsieur Vernou in his ensign of reserves uniform. He made an impassioned speech, then marched out, head held high. The ladies clutched one another. "The royalists go to preserve their very lives now," said Renzi quietly.

Kydd wandered out of the house in a daze. If there was anything in what Renzi had said, the Vernous were in grave danger. He tried to suppress the image of Louise's gentle face. His steps led him to the waterfront, and as he turned the last corner he saw soldiers.

"Hey now!" said the sergeant, coming out from behind a beached boat. "Jack Tar on land still."

"Still are," replied Kydd. "An' you, Sar'nt Hotham, you on y'r way t' stoppin' the Frogs at th' landing?"

Hotham did not reply at first. He looked about, then stepped up to Kydd and spoke quietly. "No, mate, we're not. Nobody is. See, we just ain't got the numbers to face 'em, so many bein' away in Santa Domingy, so we're fallin' back on the town."

"C'n you hold 'em if they attack?"

"Yeah, don't worry."

"An' don't ye worry y'rself," Kydd said stoutly. "Navy'll be sendin' their fleet soon, an' that'll settle their account." *Trajan* and the others would make short work of whatever ships the French had—if they were alerted and could make it back in time.

The new day developed into its usual tropical grandeur. The royalist force marched out with English soldiers to meet the revolutionaries, and that night the Vernou family sat up late, debating events. Kydd lay awake for a long time, haunted by an image of Louise strapped to a guillotine, looking up at the blade.

He was awoken in the dark early hours by sounds from below. There was a scuffle outside followed by a furious hammering on the door. He leaped from bed and hurried below, aware that he and Renzi were the only men in the house. Cautiously he unbarred the door.

"Que Dieu nous aide, nous sommes condamnés!" a middle-aged lady in mob cap cried as she pushed inside. Renzi, close behind Kydd, tried to pacify her. She thrust a paper at him.

Renzi took a candle from Louise, who had just appeared, and read. The flickering light lit up his face from below. "The worst!" he said, his expression as grave as Kydd had seen. "The political leader of these revolutionaries, whose name is Victor Hugues, has made a proclamation, which he has secretly posted throughout the town under cover of night."

Kydd felt his bowels tighten.

"He has stated, in effect, that the glorious revolution promised liberty, equality and fraternity, which applies to the slaves of this island. All slaves are now free and owe no obedience to any *béké* from this moment on."

"C'est la fin de notre société telle que nous la connaissons," the woman moaned. Louise stood stock still, pale and staring.

"What does it mean?" Kydd said, but he knew the answer already. He had no specific feelings about slavery—he hadn't any experience of it—but the effect of uncontrolled freedom on those who had been previously enslaved would have the situation spinning out of control.

Renzi spoke quietly. "It means that with a single move of diabolical genius, this Victor Hugues has turned the tables on us. A large slave population now loose and in disorder is something no military commander can have in his rear. We are finished."

There was a horrified silence.

"As far as we know—"

From the shop came the sudden sound of splintering glass and low animal growls. Kydd pushed open the door, and in the breaking dawn saw figures clambering through the wreckage of the front window.

"Get back! It's not safe!" Kydd called, slammed the door and shot the bolt. The terrified ladies hurried up the stairs while Renzi searched for arms.

There were more sounds of breaking glass, then quiet. Kydd eased open the door and saw that the shopfront was in ruins. He crossed to the door and looked out into the street. It was deserted—but a plume of smoke billowed skyward a street away. Irregular, sinister sounds broke the peace.

"We'd better stay with the ladies, Nicholas," Kydd called.

Renzi joined him. "Hark!" he said sharply, holding up his hand.

Kydd couldn't be sure, but he thought he heard a sharp squeal against the silence. It chilled his blood. "I thought—"

"Shut up!"

Then, from the top of the street, came a boatswain's call.

"Hands to muster!" exclaimed Kydd. He ran into the middle of the street and waved his arms.

The boatswain's mate looked him over with a lopsided smile. "You, Kydd, get yer men 'n' their gear over to th' town square. We needs ev'ry man c'n carry a musket."

At Kydd's reluctance, he snapped, "Sharpish like! Lootenant ain't waitin' fer any wants ter dally." He glared at Kydd and left.

Kydd looked back at the old shop, the front now sad and threatening. How could he abandon the women at this time? He stole a glance at Renzi. His friend was looking steadily at him, his arms folded. He turned away. Perhaps there was time to get Louise and Madame Vernou away—but the schooner was still unfit for sea and . . . What was he thinking? Who was there to man any craft he could find? And how would it be seen by others? That he was running away from a hopeless situation to save himself? There was no alternative: he had his duty. He stiffened. "What are ye waitin' for, Nicholas? Let's get our dunnage."

Their room seemed a fragile relic of gentler times, Louise's fragrance soothing and poignant. Their seabags were stuffed in a trice, but the two women were at the door, the maid nowhere to be seen. At the sight of their set faces, Madame Vernou broke into weeping and Louise simply stared—neither accusing nor forgiving.

"We—that's t' say—we have t' go," Kydd said awkwardly. To his consternation Madame Vernou fell to her knees and clutched at him, sobbing. Her words had no need of translation. Gently he disengaged her. Louise stood like a statue and, on an impulse, he tore off a button from his short blue seaman's jacket and pressed it into her hand. She took it, raised it to her lips and kissed it. Kydd saw her eyes glisten. "We go now, Nicholas," he said.

"Good. Just in time—you go with Mr. Jowett." The lieutenant was harassed and fretful, but his brow cleared at the sight of Kydd and Renzi. The square was crowded with men milling about in anxious groups.

Jowett turned out to be a master's mate of uncertain temper. His men, including Kydd and Renzi, were formed up and the little band moved out. They marched swiftly, Jowett eyeing the streets warily for trouble. Only the four marines had muskets.

"Where 're we headed?" Kydd asked the tattooed sailor next to him.

The man shifted the tobacco quid in his mouth and said, with satisfaction, "Ter th' wharf, ter get the brig t' sea."

Kydd hefted his seabag, a dawning thought lifting his hopes. Yes, they were turning into the last street—and would pass the Vernou shop!

"Mr. Jowett!" called Kydd. "C'n I check on m' billet, as was, when we pass?"

Reluctantly, Jowett halted the band. Kydd knew he would be inclined to trust that a petty officer had good reason to delay the party. Now Jowett would find he had two women passengers on the brig. Kydd called out to the family, but no one emerged. Jowett hailed him peremptorily.

Kydd went in hastily. When his eyes became accustomed to the dark interior, he noticed the charring on the steps to his room, tiny wisps of blue smoke still spiraling—then the blood, trickling over the edge of the floor above. The door darkened and Jowett's angry face swam into his vision. "Well, spread some canvas an' let's be goin'!"

Kydd stumbled out and, seeing his appalled expression, Renzi grabbed his arm. "Too late!" Kydd muttered. He was too shaken to look Renzi in the eye. They trudged on, Kydd in a haze of grief.

The brig had been warped a hundred yards offshore and the wharf was filling rapidly with crowds of frantic humanity, beseeching, imploring and fighting to get passage on the vessel. Jowett established a secure position at the water's edge, the marines making free with their bayonet points. A boat was signaled ashore from the three men aboard. When it arrived it became clear that the brig was in no fit state to sail. Under refit, it had no need for sails: they had all been sent down and kept somewhere ashore.

The strain was beginning to tell: seamen snarled at each other and snapped at the weeping, frenzied mob. Kydd found himself crudely brushing aside an old woman, feeling her withered skin and frail bones, her ancient face distorted with terror.

The sail-loft was found, and sails quickly stowed in the boat. A flat thud sounded above the chaos, then another. Gunsmoke wreathed a ridge above the capital. "They're bombarding the town," yelled Renzi.

Blood appeared in the mass of hysterical bodies as the marines wielded their bayonets more brutally. The guns on the ridge spoke in chorus, but where the shot went was not obvious.

The sailors boarded the boat in a rush, making it pitch alarmingly. The sails were taken out to the brig, some seamen swarming into the tops, others locating the halliards and lifts.

"We go out under staysails an' mizzen," ordered Jowett. There was a ragged hiss and a thump: a plume of water rose in the sea, the cannonball going on to smash a beachside hut to splinters. "They's shyin' at us!" growled Jowett. "Time we wasn't here."

Kydd felt an overwhelming urge to be back at sea where it

would be calm and sane. From the shore came distant screams and cursing—the marines were having difficulty defending themselves. Jowett seized Kydd's arm. "Get ashore, send twenty of 'em out ter me. Twenty is all!" A ball slapped through the fore topmast staysail as it rose up on the stay. "Now!"

Kydd threw a glance at Renzi, who was just descending from the main-shrouds, and boarded the boat. He took the tiller and headed for the chaos ashore, swelled now by royalist deserters who had broken into grog shops.

The marines had fear in their eyes—the mob was near uncontrollable. The boat bumped up against the stone wharf and Kydd fought his way up to the marines. "Watch m' back, you lobsterbacks," he yelled, and took an oar into the crowd, rotating it wildly to clear a space. It gained a minute or two: then what? To whom should he award life, to whom deny it?

One of the men on the oars came up courageously to help him. Together they held the oar as a barrier. There, around two rows back, a mother and daughter, they should go. He pointed them out and beckoned. Under screams of rage from the others, they forced their way under the oar and to safety. Kydd's eyes darted around. The gray-haired man with the proud but fearful expression, a royalist officer, doomed if he remained. As the man came forward, Kydd noticed he was trembling so much he could hardly steady himself. Others—the boat was filling fast. A sharp crack and rending of timber—some spar in the brig taking a ball; there was no time to lose. He made sure the oarsmen were clear—the gunwales were only six inches above the water; he would wedge himself into the stern. Kydd looked around at the crowd for the last time—and, with cold shock, saw Louise on the fringes.

Without stopping to consider the consequences, he pointed and beckoned. The mob howled and tore at her, and she fell—but rose and fought her way through. Kydd tried to think what her presence must imply—whose blood had he seen at the house?

Louise paused in front of him, and he pushed her to the boat. She clambered aboard over the transom into the place Kydd had intended for himself. The boat swayed, nearly dipping the gunwales under. Its passengers screamed in fright. There was no chance for him on this trip.

He watched the boat reach the brig as a cannon shot brought up a vicious plume of spray not five yards from it. The people scrambled for their lives up the side, and Kydd noticed the line of the morning sun lengthening down the brig's hull. Her cables had been cut. The fore and aft sails were shaken out and, with the empty boat drifting free astern, the brig caught the wind and put to sea.

Lieutenant Calley did not look up from his writing. The faint tap of muskets sounded—the French must be close. His shirt stuck to him in the close heat of the small room, and he muttered as he wrote.

Kydd waited patiently. They had made it back to the square and found it empty of friendly soldiery—in fact, empty of most inhabitants. They had only found their way to this "headquarters" after a chance encounter with a hurrying party of infantrymen.

Calley looked up. Kydd was shocked by the dark rings around his eyes and the evidence in his posture of extreme tiredness. "The town is in total disorder: the French are approaching from the east. There is no help for it—we must yield the capital." He spoke generally, not at Kydd but into his immediate front.

"Aye, sir," he said. So much had happened since that predawn awakening. The noon heat was dire in this room and he longed to be out in the steady sea breeze.

"You, er, Kydd." Calley seemed to have difficulty with his words. "We—we must hold until *Trajan* returns, with, er, reinforcements."

The sweat prickled down Kydd's back.

"What I want you to try to do—is take your party to Petit Bourg, our largest remaining stronghold. I shall withdraw into the mountains of Basse Terre and yield up the capital and eastern half of the island to the enemy." His head lowered. "God knows— I have done what I can."

Kydd knew better than to voice his anxieties. "Aye-aye, sir," he said, the age-old response to a naval order, and made his exit.

Outside, the marines waited. No file of men presenting arms, just a group of three in dusty tunics, bowed with fatigue, but with muskets bright and gleaming. Why they should follow his orders he had no idea, but he saw them straighten when he emerged, looking to him. In that moment he understood—they needed from him that nameless quality that drove men on regardless through adversity and battle. They were joined by five seamen.

"We're meetin' our mates," Kydd said decisively. "At Putty Borg—over yonder," he added. It had been pointed out to him earlier, an anonymous huddle of buildings just visible across the bay on the rugged Basse Terre proper.

"That's a fuckin' long way off, cully," said an older seaman, in measured tones.

The group fell quiet. "Y'r right—fifty miles if it's a yard," Kydd snapped. "So, let's be havin' ye."

There would be no rations, no water until they made the safety of the fort, but in fact it could be no more than five miles away. "On y'r feet!" Kydd barked. The men stirred, and got up in ones or twos.

"Marines, get into y'r line an' lead off." They shuffled into file and stood to attention, staring ahead blankly as they always did. "Right—march away!" Kydd shouted, not at all sure of the form of orders to start men marching. The marines, after a moment's confusion, stepped out, and the little band of men tramped off down the dusty road out of town. Kydd felt a swell of pride—his men, obeying his orders, going on a military mission of importance.

Some time later the gates of the small Petit Bourg citadel hove in sight for the footsore and dusty band; security, food, drink and, above all, the warmth of company of their own kind.

"Halt!" This was not a welcome: What had happened? For a moment Kydd thought that the French had reached here and were enticing them into a trap.

"The fort ahoy!" shouted Kydd. "Party o' men fr'm Pwun-a-Peter, come t' join." He could now hand over responsibility for "his" men—he felt a slight pang.

A different voice came from high above, and Kydd saw the shako of an army officer. "Well done, you men." There was a pause, and the head and shoulders of the officer showed. "You should understand that we may have fever . . ." there was a stirring of alarm among Kydd's men ". . . and therefore you may not wish to enter."

"Sod it! Any place 'as vittles, somewhere ter flake out," said the older seaman coarsely.

"Hold y'r jabber," Kydd told him briefly. "Where else c'n we go, sir?" he hailed.

"Wouldn't advise you to remain here," the officer called. "I expect an assault any hour." Kydd's heart lurched. "Yet I do know where there are more of you fellows. You might wish to join them." His tone became apologetic. "It's all of twenty miles or so farther along this road, around the south part of this island—Fort Mathilda." Silence. "I do believe you should make your dispositions soon," the officer said, and indicated across the bay to where they had come from.

Pointe à Pitre was now a bleak scene, ruined gaps in rows of houses, smoke from burning buildings. The smell of devastation lay on the wind. The bombardment had stopped, which meant that the French were in possession of the town. "No choice, is there, mates?" he heard from beside him.

He remembered Renzi's way with logic and forced himself to think. If they entered they would be safe for the time being, but at the risk of yellow fever. If they started on a march of twenty miles or more there was every chance that they would be overtaken by the French. Or they might make it, without exposure to the fever. The elements shuffled themselves in his head at vertiginous speed and came down on a course of cool certainty. They would march on. If there was a chance they could reinforce Fort Mathilda with some able-bodied men, then their duty was plain.

"We march!" he growled. He hailed the fort again. "We go on, sir! Chance o' some rations—an' some water?"

The officer removed his hat. "Very commendable, my man. I will see to it." His figure disappeared downward.

"There is a choice, yer knows." The older seaman confronted him, his eyes fixing Kydd's. "We're not in kilter fer a long piece o' walkin' so we 'as ter do what we must—we gives it all away, we got nothin' ter worry of, not like them royalists, we'll get treated square. . . ."

Kydd's fist slammed into the man's stomach, doubling him over. The next blow took him on the chin, knocking him to the dust, where he lay sullenly, feeling his jaw. Kydd turned back to the fort.

A bucket on the end of a piece of rope appeared. In it, covered by a gray blanket, were army biscuits, two cooked haunches of rabbit and a hand of bananas. Three canteens of water followed. "March!" Kydd ordered. They stepped off, the fallen man left to catch up. As they rounded a curve he saw the officer still looking in their direction. The marines had a rhythm of marching that was relaxed and economic, but the seamen were fast becoming tired and slow.

"Up there," Kydd said suddenly, pointing at the sugarcane field. They stared at him dully. "Are ye thinkin' of *walkin'* all th' way?" It didn't need much smart thinking to realize that cane-fields had carts for the cut cane, and these would be pulled by horses or some other animals.

* * *

It was more difficult than it appeared. "Don' be daft!" One of the marines, an ex-farmhand, chuckled, and took the reins from Kydd's hands. Kydd surrendered them gratefully. The single ox was placid but sure, and the sugarcane cart jerked forward. Sprawled in the back were his men, and he had provided for them. Before he fell asleep under the hot sun, Kydd felt a certain satisfaction.

Fort Mathilda was small, but built securely into the rock of the coast. A surprised lieutenant met them inside the gates and asked immediately about the situation in Pointe à Pitre. Then the little fort stood to, awaiting the inevitable.

It wasn't long in coming: rising dustclouds inland showed the approach of a substantial column—but the satisfying sight of men-o'-war coming around the point with *Trajan* in the van settled their fate in a much more agreeable way.

CHAPTER 5

—✈—

*T*he deck of a ship at dawn was the most beautiful sight he could think of, Kydd decided. Even the swish and slop of the men swabbing the deck did not intrude. The easy, domestic sounds in the cool of the early morning were balm to his troubled soul.

The quality of the dawn light on the anchored ship was of a gossamer hesitancy, a soft emerging of color through gray; the tropical sea began its transition from dark gray-blue anonymity to its usual striking transparent greens and deep-water blue. Within the hour it would bear the hard glitter of the sun, and this magical time would be dismissed into memory. A sigh forced itself on him. The land with all its brutal ways could now be relinquished for the sea—the pure, stern, manly sea. A smile broke through. Renzi had not yet returned to *Trajan* from the brig of refugees, but they would have much to talk about when he did.

The line of men had nearly reached the half-deck. The men on the poop had finished and were stowing wash-deck gear. Stirk sauntered over to Kydd. "D'ye fancy ter step ashore agen, cully?" he said, nodding to the palm-studded coast not a mile away, the sun's light playing stronger on the mass of deep greens and dark ravines of the interior.

"Wish t' hell I could, Toby," Kydd said lightly. "Had m'self a thunderin' good time ashore, the women an' all. . . ."

Stirk kept his smile, but his eyes searched Kydd's face. "Did 'ear 'twas bad cess, them Crapauds, a-killin' their own kind like they did."

Kydd's tone changed. "If they does, only leaves less f'r us." His hands whitened on the rope he held, and his face turned seaward. "Bolderin' weather to the nor'east'd," he said firmly. From the direction of the reliable northeast trade winds the clouds were piling up, more than the usual wet season rain squalls. It would mean soaked shirts for all again that afternoon.

"*Haaaands* to unmoor ship!"

At last! Out to sea, away from the nightmarish memories. From his position in the mizzen top, Kydd could see both accompanying frigates weigh and proceed, a satisfying picture in the trade winds of the open sea. *Trajan* cast to starboard when she had won her anchor and followed in their wake.

When he came on deck after the midday meal for his watch at the conn, the weather was clamping in. On the quarterdeck, Kydd took position next to the helm, and noticed Auberon's set expression. He was gazing at the easterly horizon, at the growing darkness—a peculiar darkness in the clouds, which had an ugly copper tinge. There was also a swell that was out of keeping with the wave patterning, a deepening, driven swell that told of a mighty storm somewhere, raging and lashing. And it was from the northeast.

Auberon rounded on the duty midshipman. "M'duty to the Captain, and I would be happy to see him join me on deck," he snapped.

Bomford did not waste time, appearing in his shirtsleeves and without his hat. Auberon merely indicated. "Sir."

Bomford paused for only seconds. "Pass the word for Mr.

Quist," he said quietly. The sailing master knew these waters well.

The warrant officer deliberated for long minutes. "In my opinion, sir, it looks very like a hurricanoe." He used a telescope to traverse the front of the approaching storm. "I cannot be sure o' more, 'cepting we must shape a more southerly course an' run."

Bomford looked at him sharply. "Why southerly, if you please?"

"Sir, in these parts, if y' faces into the wind then ye'll find the center of the storm nine, ten points on y'r right hand—an' this means we needs t' be athwart it directly."

There was no denying the quiet authority in the man's voice. This was a man who had prevailed in the devastating hurricane that had decimated Rodney's fleet in these very waters less than a dozen years earlier. The master lifted an eyebrow and looked at the Captain. "We can't outrun it—whether we're a-swim on the morrow or no depends squarely on the winds, gentlemen. In the next few hours, if the wind backs, with God's protection we're safe— mauled an' bedundered but we'll live. If th' wind *veers* . . ."

"Very well," Bomford said. A moment's flash of uncertainty shadowed his face. Then he turned to Auberon. "Do you bear away to the south'ard, and pipe the starbowlines on deck. I believe we will clear away and batten down."

There had been other times, in other ships, when Kydd had worked to snug a vessel down for dirty weather but this was different: an apprehensive urgency was building, a knowledge that their very lives could depend on the rightness of a splice, the strength of a preventer. Details now were a matter of life or death.

As quartermaster's mate Kydd held allegiance in the first instance to the sailing master. Quist was calm but firm. There would be nothing left to chance that could conceivably be met by forethought and diligence. For the first time Kydd saw extreme measures being taken at sea, and he absorbed it all.

Quist's first care was to the rudder. If it carried away under stress of weather they could easily broach to, broadside to the deadly combers, and the result would be inevitable—they would be rolled over to their doom. The little party made its way below to the wardroom flat, aft on the gundeck. There, the true origin of control of the rudder lay: the mighty twenty-six foot length of a tiller, high up just under the deckhead, connected by tackle and an endless rope up through the decks to the wheel-drum. As Kydd watched, it creaked and moved with the motions of the unseen helmsman high above, with its powerful leverage ready to sweep from one side of the deck to the other.

Three seamen arrived with a spare tiller to lay along the deck. Kydd's arms ached as he held up one side of the relieving tackles to be reeved. If the tiller-ropes parted in furious seas, these tackles would do no less than save the ship.

"Ask th' boatswain t' kindly step over, lad," Quist told his messenger, a solemn midshipman, when they had regained the deck. The boy darted off. As master, Quist was senior to the boatswain, who arrived without delay. "C'n we have rudder tackles rigged, d'ye think, Nathan?"

There were chains leading up each side of the rudder from its trailing part. They were unshackled and taken to the channel of the mizzen shrouds. A strong luff tackle was applied, its fall led into a gunport, and the chain becketed up under the counter. This was pure seamanship and Kydd looked down thoughtfully while he worked above the noisy foaming around the rudder—he had voyaged around Cape Horn and knew what heavy seas could do.

Back at the wheel, Quist paused as a portable compass was lashed in place near the binnacle. Nodding approval, he said, "And we'll have a quartermaster on th' wheel, and his lee helmsman's going t' be his mate." Kydd would be experiencing his first hurricane from the helm, mate to Capple.

"And we'll have weather cloths in the shrouds." Quist was considerate as well as competent: these old sails stretched along the shrouds to weather would take some of the brutal sting out of the spindrift and blast coming in on the helmsman.

While they labored Kydd kept his eye on the ominous buildup to their larboard. They were crossing the path of the storm rather than trying to outrun it, a rationale that made sense to the master—he would ask about the reasoning afterward. If there was an afterward . . .

Rolling tackles were clapped on to the big lower yards. Vicious rolling could have the heavy yards moving out of synchrony with the hull, tearing sail and rigging; the whipping movement would be damped with the tackles. At the same time, at the ends of the yards where the big braces pulled them around to meet the wind, preventer lines were applied. If the braces parted and the yard swung back it would probably take the mast with it like a felled tree.

It was hard, continuous work, but there would be no complaints. Double tacks and sheets rove, storm canvas roused out; fore, main and mizzen storm staysails were cleared away and baggywrinkle mats seized on everywhere. In the complexity of rigging there was a danger that cordage madly flogging in the bluster of the storm would chafe to destruction.

Kydd took a last look at the vast storm before going below for his meal. It stretched now across half the sky and, laboring at her best speed as she was, *Trajan* was not going to escape. The frigates were nearly out of sight ahead and would probably get away with a battering, but the old ship-of-the-line would be facing the full force of the hurricane.

There was no chatter at the mess table. All the petty officers knew the odds, could bear witness to tempests around the world. There was nothing to be said. Kydd met Stirk's eye: there was an imperceptible lift to his eyebrow but beyond that the hard-featured quarter-gunner seemed unruffled. He had been with Kydd in *Artemis* when the vessel had been racked to pieces on an Atlantic rock and lived through many other dire times that he had never discussed. Kydd felt claustrophobic. The hatches were sealed with tarpaulin over the gratings, which were secured with nailed battens along the sides. Thus battened down there was no air movement and he felt breathless.

With a terrifying creaking along the whole length of the gundeck there was a massive unseen lurch to leeward. "'Ere she comes, mates," Stirk said, and got up. Kydd rose also; he had an urgent need to be out on deck.

The pealing of the silver calls of the boatswain's mates met him on the way up. "All *haaaands!* All the hands ahoy! *All haaaands* on deck! *Haaaands* to shorten sail!"

There was now no point in trying to get away. Like a fleeing animal, *Trajan* could no longer run and had to turn, confront her pursuer, then fight to survive. Reduced to topsails and staysails, the Captain wanted more. First the topgallant and next the topmasts were struck on deck, the lack of high canvas resulting in a different kind of movement, an ugly, whipping roll that felt sullen and resentful. The sight of the truncated masts, only reaching up to the fighting tops, added to Kydd's unease.

The reliable trade winds fell away, then returned, but in gusts. The energetic waves were falling over themselves and the first rain drove in, coming in fretful squalls, chill and spiteful. Capple screwed up his eyes at the onslaught and took up position at the weather side of the wheel, motioning Kydd to the lee side. "Capple at th' helm, Kydd to loo'ard," he called to the knot of officers on the quarterdeck, looking gravely out to the spreading darkness in the northeast. The wheel kicked under Kydd's hands—the vigor in the seas was a reality—and he watched Capple closely as in turn the seaman watched the leech of the reefed topsail aloft. It would be hours before he saw his mess again.

"Dyce—no higher." Quist appeared from behind them, studying the bellying canvas. Far forward, the bows lifted and smashed down in a broad swash of foam as she came around, now going more before the increasingly blustery winds, which Kydd gauged were already at gale strength.

Men moved carefully about the decks, the motion making it more of a controlled stagger. There was still more to be done, and Kydd watched the carpenter at the base of each mast check the wedges for play, the boatswain and his men stropping the anchors with extra painters to hold them securely against the tearing pull of the sea as the vessel's heavy downward roll buried them once again in a roaring mass of foam.

Braced against the wheel, Kydd's muscles bunched and gave with the effort of keeping the rudder straight under the impact of the seas coming in from astern. The shock of the impacts came regularly and massively, and it was difficult to time their movements.

The first seas came over the bulwarks to flood the decks just as the horizon faded in white froth and spume torn from wave crests, but with a thrill Kydd saw from the binnacle that the streaming blast of air was now from the north, tending northwesterly—it was backing! As long as they could keep the seas then, according to the master, they would pass safely through this chaos of sea and air. He looked across the deck to where Quist stood alone, buffeted by the still-increasing gale, his old dark tarpaulins plastered to his body. He felt an upwelling of feeling for the man, who held in his mind so much cool knowledge about this raging of nature, and who—

Under his feet Kydd sensed a sudden rupture, a rending crack— and he fell to the deck, the wheel spinning uselessly above him. Stunned, he heard Capple shout something about the helm before his wits returned and he realized the tiller-ropes must have parted. The ship began to fall away, but Auberon's voice came instantly, bullying over the dull roar of the storm down the main hatchway. "Relieving tackles—get going, y' lubbers!"

A bigger pitch than usual forced the bows at an angle to the sea and a comber crowded aboard in a mad welter of white, crashing, invading. From up the hatchway came an indistinct shouting.

Quist emerged, grabbed Kydd's shoulder and hurled him down the ladder, yelling that the tiller had broken in the rudder head. Capple clattered down behind him.

They raced to the wardroom where a group of men stood staring at a wreckage of broken timber, blocks and a mess of rope. The whites of their eyes showed as the huge rudder thudded sideways, uncontrolled against the counter, and a thump of white spray shot up the rudder casing. The deck canted steeply, then reared up the other way, sending men stumbling and gear sliding. Kydd hesitated—but Capple thrust forward. "Clear that shittle for'ard," he roared, his finger stabbing toward two of the nearest men, who jerked into action. He pushed through the others to look at the rudder. "Get th' fuckin' chocks," he snapped at Kydd.

The carpenter appeared, panting. "Chocks," he agreed quickly, and together, the deck bucking like a horse, he and Kydd eased the first shaped piece of timber into the octagonal opening down which the massive rudder creaked and groaned. "Th' easy bit," grunted the carpenter. "Hold it there, cully, an' I'll scrag ye if y' lets it go."

Kydd held the timber wedge as if his life depended on it. Through the opening he could see the terrifying white-torn confusion of seas hurtling up, tilting, then dropping like a stone. The rudder stock swung over ponderously, thumping and grinding into the rough chock under his hand with an appalling creaking. Capple and the carpenter tried to stuff the remaining chock into the other side, but the rudder spat it out and swung back to thud against the ship's stern. Kydd knew to keep his chock steady in place, but his hands were perilously close to where he knew the rudder stock would return. It narrowly missed crushing his fingers, and this time the other chock slammed in, true.

"Out of it!" gasped the carpenter, and Kydd pulled aside as he swung a big iron-bound mallet in accurate, crashing hits. Miraculously, the rudder had now been jammed into its central position.

On deck they could use a trysail aft to bring the bows back on course. The immediate danger was over.

"Spare tiller, Chips?" Capple asked.

"Aye," said the carpenter, and inspected the immobile rudder head where the tiller had broken off inside. "Second mortice," he said decisively.

With relief, Kydd saw that the spare tiller could be fitted in a lower mortice and, without being told, he had the men hastily ranging the tiller-rope and relieving tackles. When the spare tiller had been shipped, these tackles were clapped on, and they had a fully working rudder once more. It was amazing how quickly a neat, seamanlike scene could turn into a picture of utter despair— bedraggled ropes and anonymous timbers and wreckage—and how quickly it was possible to return to a shipshape condition merely by getting to the heart of the circumstance and doing what was needed. He had seen Capple do just that and acknowledged the lesson.

On deck again, and at the wheel, Kydd saw that the winds had grown marginally less frantic, were definitely more in the west. There was no change in the vista of white-streaked water, horizontal clouds of spume flying over the surface. Huge waves crested, tumbled and were blown downwind to spindrift. The master paced down the deck past Kydd, who flashed him a grin.

Quist stopped, as if surprised in his thoughts. "Good lad," he said, against the wind noise, "An' if it stays as is, we're thrown clear o' the blow betimes." He smiled amiably and paced on.

So, it was only a matter of time. The old ship-of-the-line plunged on before the relentless wind. The hours passed. Kydd remembered Quist's words of earlier. He mentally faced into the westerly wind and worked out that at nine points on his right hand, the center of the storm was passing somewhere out there in the wildness to the north.

He was relieved at noon, and took the lee helm again for the last dog-watch with Capple, wind to the southwest. By now his eyes were red-sore with salt and his body ached for rest; it seemed to Kydd a malicious cruelty of the fates when the dread cry passed aft, "Land *hooo*—I see breakers *aheeeaaad!*"

Lookouts forward had sighted land in their path. Large or small it was an appalling hazard for a vessel barely under control, flying before the wind as she was. Images of the death of his lovely *Artemis* crept remorselessly into Kydd's skull. He shook his head and beat them back. Now *Trajan* needed him.

"Wear ship—we wear this instant!" Auberon bawled.

Kydd and Capple threw up the helm, and the vessel answered begrudgingly. It would be difficult to wear around with only the reefed course and staysails, but it would have to be done. The storm jib was thrown out at just the right moment and, with violent rolling, *Trajan* turned about.

"Lie to, Mr. Quist," Auberon ordered, as the Captain appeared, driven by the sudden change in motion.

"Lying to, sir," Auberon reported, while Bomford studied the ugly dark line extending across the horizon. "We'll never claw off, you know," he said quietly, gazing at the endless barrier of land ahead. *Trajan* lay over crazily as the low sails took the wind from nearly abeam.

Bomford staggered but continued to observe, then snapped his glass shut. "Clear away both bowers. We anchor!"

The veering crew in the cable tiers needed no telling; the cables would go to their fullest extent, and in the stink and dread of the near darkness of the bowels of the vessel they readied the cable. At the cathead in the bow the conditions for the seamen working to free the anchor for casting were frightful too. Kydd's heart wrung at the white fury of the seas coming inboard, receding to reveal the black figures of men resuming their fight.

First one anchor let go, then the other. The dead weight of the hempen cables, even before the great anchors could touch the seabed, heaved *Trajan*'s bows around, head to sea. The effect was immediate. Taking the seas directly on the bow, she pitched like a frightened stallion, at one moment her bare bowsprit stabbing the sky, then a fearful onrush of seas down her sides, before a heart-stopping drop downward, ending in a mighty crunch and explosion of spray at her bows.

Kydd stood ineffective: *Trajan* was now held by her anchor cables, meeting the hurricane head-on, and therefore his duty at the helm held no more purpose. It gave him time to look back at the line of land, which was nearer than he had thought. The constant mist of spume on the sea's surface had obscured the lower half of the band of hard black, and he quailed.

A perceptible yank and quiver: untold fathoms below, the iron claws of an anchor had come to rest in the seabed. The motion changed: the high soaring of the bows was the same, but after the lurch downward, in the hesitation before the swoop up, the ship snubbed to her cable—a disorienting arrest of the wild movement for a big ship.

"Off yer go, then, cock, get somethin' ter eat, an' I'll see yer in an hour," Capple said. Kydd flashed him a grateful smile. He had not had anything since daybreak: with both hands on the wheel there was no way he could bolt the dry rations on offer.

Stretching his aching muscles he followed the lifeline forward and fell as much as stepped down the hatchway. 'Tween-decks was a noisy bedlam of swilling seawater, squealing of guns against their breeching and a pungent gloom. His mess was deserted, the canvas screens not rigged, so he peeled off his wet shirt and helped himself to another from his ditty bag, which hung and bumped against the ship's side. Condensation and leakage had soaked into the canvas bag and it was a sodden garment that he had to drag over his body. He shivered but gave it no more thought.

In the mess racks he fumbled around and came up with some sea biscuits. He pocketed three, then found a hard lump of cheese that he supposed had been left out for him. Munching the hardtack, he glanced forward to where the patchy light of a clutch of violently swinging lanthorns played on dozens of huddled bodies. He assumed they were marines and landmen, hiding in the depths of the ship in the extremity of fear and exhaustion, racked by panic and seasickness.

Kydd felt a warmth of sympathy. They were better off where they were, out of sight of the heart-chilling insanity of the storm. He would go to them and try to say something encouraging, the least he could do. Holding on to anything to hand, Kydd made his way forward in the noisome obscurity.

But then his senses slammed in. The ponderous wrench at the beginning of the scend had disappeared, and a comparatively smooth rise completed the movement. There could only be one interpretation. With a constriction of his stomach Kydd knew that an empty cable was running now from the hawse. As if in confirmation, *Trajan* gave a fishlike wriggle as she careered astern. Kydd spun around. He hurried as fast as he could to make the upper deck, pulling along hand over hand. As he got to the base of the ladderway, a combined twist and jerk told him that *Trajan* had come up to her second anchor. "Clear away th' sheet anchor!" Kydd heard the boatswain howl into the violence, as he breasted the coaming and came out into the turmoil.

Capple stared fiercely ahead to the foredeck where men fought and struggled. At every plunge they disappeared from view under an avalanche of white water. He noticed Kydd. "Coral bottom!" he shouted. Coral was a deadly menace: it snarled and cut thick cables with razor-sharp edges and normally was never chosen for an anchorage.

A few yards forward Kydd saw Quist. He was yelling something indistinct, but ended by stabbing a finger at Kydd, then pointing forward. Kydd grabbed the wet hairiness of the midships lifeline and hauled himself along the bucking deck to the starboard fore-chains, joining the men at the sheet anchor.

There was no immediate need for this last anchor they had, but they could leave nothing to chance. Kydd drew near and was nearly knocked off his feet by the green water sluicing aft. A cable to the sheet anchor had already been bent and seized in storm preparations, but anchoring in coral had not been foreseen.

"Keckling—get goin', Kydd," the boatswain yelled. A coil of three-inch line was thrown at him; it thumped heavily into his chest. The seas roared against the side, burying the channel, the broad base of the shrouds fitted to the outside of the ship. Kydd caught his breath: he knew they were telling him to climb over the bulwarks and down on to that channel, to work at the stowed black mass of the sheet anchor and its cable.

He looked back resentfully at the row of men, who looked gravely back at him. They were older and more experienced but would be able to remain safely inboard. Then he understood: he had been chosen for this job because he was a *better seaman* than they.

The realization warmed him, proofed him against the elements and, with a jaunty wave, he swung over the bulwarks and dropped to the channel. It had crossed his mind to bend on a lifeline around his waist, but if he was swept away then the sudden jerk at the end of the line might cut him in half. In any case the light line would get in the way.

The sea-glistening sides of the ship dipped slowly, and Kydd hung on grimly to the tarry shrouds. The expected seas came, first his feet, thighs, and then above his waist. A rushing torrent bullying and jostling, tearing at his hold on life. It seethed around the lower rigging and fittings with a deep hissing and roaring—then began to recede.

Kydd snatched a glance at the situation. His task was to apply keckling to the last yards of the cable as it came from the sheet anchor, wrapping his lighter line and stout strips of canvas handed down to him tightly about the strands of cable. It was their only chance, the keckling their sole means to protect this last anchor from the deadly sharp coral and keep the ship from driving ashore.

The sheet anchor was lashed outside the shrouds, outside the channel, and Kydd was exposed to the seas. Edging around the aftermost shroud, he stood on the iron curve of the flukes of the big anchor, then swung to the channel and shuffled along. *Trajan* rolled, the seas rose and battered and tugged at him. He held the thick shrouds in a death grip, pressing his face to their rough surfaces, feeling their sturdy strength.

The seas fell away as the ship began a laborious roll upward. It was time to get to work. Kydd moved outboard of the anchor to the big ring beyond the stock. He waited for the surging seas to return and subside, then bent to begin. The rope had a mind of its own, snarling and writhing, but Kydd forced it around. More seas, but his work held, and when the dripping cable appeared, his keckling was still there. He worked feverishly, his arm hooked about the cable, but such was his concentration that when the next sea came it took him unawares—a momentary vision of the water within inches, then he was submerged, buffeted by giant forces while he hugged the cable, a maelstrom of roaring in his ears.

He emerged, bruised and gasping, his eyes stinging, a salty burning in his throat, but he went on grimly. His first sea friend, Bowyer, a deep-sea mariner of the very best kind, came to mind, and memories of lessons in the sea crafts, and he responded. Every working of cordage and cable would be the best he could manage.

Unexpectedly he felt a tug on his shoulder from above. Stirk's hand came out, and Kydd was hoisted bodily over the bulwarks. He sank to all fours with exhaustion, hearing Stirk's murmured words of encouragement—then noticed buckled shoes and silk stockings. He looked up to see the Captain gazing down at him, then his slow nod of approval.

The second bower anchor gave way within the watch. It was terrifying to see the speed with which they were carried downwind toward the hard line of the shore. The sheet anchor, however, was ready and it plunged into the sea almost immediately.

Now down to her last big anchor, *Trajan*'s company were left with the bleak knowledge that if it parted then the ship would drive ashore—not on a sandy beach, but on the fringing reef a quarter of a mile offshore, its presence betrayed by wild breakers slamming high into the air. The vessel would break up fast on the massive coral heads, and when men struck out for their lives they would be slashed to ribbons in the breakers.

The daylight ebbed and the deck filled with silent men staring across the seas to their last sight of the land. Kydd went below to find something to eat, to bring strength to his weary body. It was sheltered below, the manic howl of the wind muted, its wearisome plucking and battering no longer worrying at his body.

The mess was deserted again, except for a small figure, head bowed, sitting alone at their mess table. Puzzled, Kydd approached. It was Luke, a picture of misery. He did not look up as Kydd drew near.

"Hey now, skinker—light along some clacker f'r a starvin' mariner," Kydd said breezily. Luke didn't respond.

"How's this? Messman f'r the petty officers, an' can't find 'em some vittles?" Kydd came to sit next to him. The bass rumble of some loose gear slamming against the hull forward sounded ominous and loud.

Luke said something in a low voice that Kydd was unable to catch. He leaned closer and saw that the boy had been crying. He hesitated, then put his arm around the lad's shoulders. Luke tensed then swayed and rested his head against Kydd.

"How's this? Pipin' the eye?" Kydd said kindly. "Not as would be fittin' f'r a sailor, you'll agree, cuffin.""

Luke's muffled voice was certain. "Mr. Kydd, t'night I will be in hell."

At a loss for words, Kydd could only squeeze his shoulders.

"I ain't been t' church much—an' that was only 'cos m' mother made me," he continued, in stricken tones. "An'—an' I lied t' her! See, I said as I'd go off t' work fer Uncle Jonathan away in Hounslow, an' I didn't. I ran off t' sea."

Kydd saw with guilty clarity an image of a dusty church, a droning sermon and fiery words of sin, sentence and torment. Luke lifted his face, bright with tears, and blurted, "I don't mean t' be wicked. When Mr. Stirk gave me a grog, I didn't drink it, Mr. Kydd, I threw it away—God's honor I did!"

A moment's hesitation, and Kydd withdrew his arm. "You are indeed a wicked dog, and will probably have t' answer for it," he said, thumping his fist on the table. Luke stared piteously at him. "But not this night." He paused dramatically. "How dare ye have doubts about y'r ship? Is she dismasted? Is the mainstay in strands? D'ye see the Captain in despair? What sort o' jabber-knowl is it, says we're on our way t' Davy Jones?"

Luke's face brightened. "But we has one anchor out only, an'—"

Kydd's voice turned to thunder. "So now y' questions m' seaman's skills? Y' say that I can't pass a keckling without it falls off? I should take a strap to ye, younker!"

A hesitant smile appeared and Kydd pressed on: "First light an' the wind 'll have shifted two, three points, an' then we'll up hook 'n' make our offing." He fisted Luke lightly on the arm. "Then it'll go hard on any as were seen afore not havin' trust in their ship."

A sniff, a shamefaced smile, and Luke's cloud passed. "There ain't much t' eat, Mr. Kydd," he said, "but I'll find y' some—fr'm them shonky lubbers who don't want any," he added, waving at the helpless landmen forward.

Kydd grinned. "I thank ye, but I'll take a turn about the uppers first." He felt a guilty stab at the hero worship he saw in Luke's face, stuffed his pockets with anything he could find, and returned to the upper deck.

In the last of the light he saw tossing white breakers, the anonymous gray coast behind. And then a desolate night clamped in. He hunkered down in the lee of the bulwarks, his feet braced against the loudly creaking carriage of a gun, and pulled his jacket around himself. The subliminal jerk of the anchor cable transmitted itself to him, and he thought of the keckling deep in the sea, his work the only thing standing between the ship's company and their end in the loneliness of the night. He worried for a minute whether the canvas parceling under the keckling was sufficient, but then decided that nothing was to be gained by that, and drifted into a fitful doze.

"On yer feet, matey." A boatswain's mate with a dark-lanthorn was shaking him, but not unkindly. "Larbowlines t' muster."

Aching in every part of his body, Kydd staggered to his feet and lurched toward the quarterdeck, almost invisible in the darkness. There was no diminution in the windblast and the fierce motion of the sea was the same.

The officer-of-the-watch had his orders: the hawse rounding would be inspected hourly, the mate-of-the-watch would make his rounds half-hourly and the quartermaster-of-the-watch and his mate would check the hold for stores broken loose. The rest would remain on deck, on immediate call to the pumps.

As they opened up the forward hold in the orlop, Kydd noticed by the light of their lanthorn that Capple's eyes were red, his face lined. He wondered whether he himself looked as bad as he pulled aside the grating and dropped onto the casks immediately below. He reached up for the lanthorn and held it while Capple joined him. The dim gold light reached out into the stinking gloom, the noise of the hull working in the storm a deafening chorus of shattering cracks and deep-throated creaking. As far as could be seen, the stowage was unbroken. Kydd leaned over the side of the mound of casks to the ground tier in their bed of shingle and saw the sheen of water in the shadows, then heard the hiss of water movement, much like a pebble beach.

"Takin' in a lot o' water," Kydd called back. "Hope Chips 's got a weather eye on't." The pumps had been at work for an hour every watch, he knew, but that would be the seawater flooding the decks making its way to the bilges. The red pinprick flash of eyes caught his attention at the periphery of his vision. "Rats 're gettin' restless," he muttered. In a heavy blow at sea, rats usually found somewhere quiet to sit it out; these were on the move. Kydd didn't know why, but felt the beginning of fear.

"I'm gettin' another lanthorn, Tom, mate," Capple said. "We're goin' to take a good look."

It was dangerous work: the massive barrels over which they clambered moved at every violent roll, opening a vicious cleft between them that would certainly mean crushed fingers or worse if they were trapped. They worked their way down the ancient, blackened timbers of the ship's side, noting the weeping of seams, the visible working of frames and planking. There was nothing.

Up the other side. There did not appear to be anything they could report, but Kydd felt that all was not well in the old ship's bowels. They returned to anchor watch on the foredeck, feeling as much as seeing the catenary curve of the thick cable into the white-streaked dark ahead, and were soaked each time the thump of a breaker against the bows signaled another deluge.

At six bells, an hour before the end of Kydd's watch, they heard that the chain-pump, capable of moving tons of water an hour, was now being manned continuously. This was serious. There must be a near disastrous ingress of water somewhere, but the ship's company was numb after hours of hanging by their sole anchor, and the news had little impact. All hopes were centered on the morning.

Kydd could not go below. At the end of his watch he crouched below the bulwarks again, straining against the darkness to catch the first hint of light. The anchor was holding—that was all that counted. At any moment it might silently give way and then, after a few despairing minutes, it would all be over for every soul aboard. At any moment! But the thought gradually lost its reality and therefore the power to terrorize him.

Cold, aching, stupefied by the hammering wind, Kydd slowly realized that he could see as far aft as the hulking shapes of the boats on their skids. He stood stiffly and looked out to sea.

"What is it, mate?" Stirk said. He had shared Kydd's vigil on the foredeck.

Kydd turned to him. "Dawn," he said. A smile transformed his face. They gripped a rope and gazed out, waiting for the wan daylight to spread. Across the wind-torn seascape the land finally emerged—but implausibly it ranged away at an angle.

"We got a chance now, me ol' griff," said Stirk, his eyes dark-shadowed, his face hollow.

"Show some canvas, why, we'll claw off in a brace o' shakes," agreed Kydd. During the night the wind had backed. Now no longer a dead muzzler, there was a fighting chance that they could use the shift in wind to sail themselves out close-hauled. And in this way, they would no longer be reliant on the single anchor—they would be once more in the open sea.

The light of day spread. It was now possible to see a jagged horizon, which had been impossible the previous day, and Kydd knew that the weather was moderating.

"All *haaands* . . . " The rest was impossible to make out. But it was clear what was required. Hands to stations to set sail; Kydd went aft to the helm to await his orders.

Bomford spoke briefly to his first lieutenant. From all parts-of-ship came the officers and petty officers in charge of their stations; from the fighting tops, the fo'c'sle, the mainmast. They were the ones who would hear what must be done—and make it so.

The Captain stood in the center of the deck, his officers straining to hear, the petty officers about them. "You will know of the peril in which we stand—I will not refer to it again," Bomford said. His voice had a hard, resolute edge that cut through the buffeting roar of the wind.

"We will cast to larb'd and proceed under close-reefed main, double-reefed storm jib and driver." He looked keenly at the group. "You will see that this is very like a club-haul, the latter part—and by this you will know that there is no going back, there is but one chance. . . ."

Kydd had never seen a club-haul, a maneuver reserved for the most desperate situations, but he had heard of it. A vessel caught on a lee coast would let go her anchor, then continue to be blown ashore only to pivot around her anchor to face out to sea again. It was a brutal maneuver but the sting was in what Bomford was saying: there was only one chance, because when the vessel found herself headed back out to sea, she had no choice—the anchor cable had to be cut to enable the escape.

"I will crowd on her all sail she will take," Bomford said, "by my sign to each in turn . . ." He specified which signal would apply to which sail, for shouted orders were useless. ". . . and I apprehend the chief peril to be if the main course is taken aback."

The Captain finished, and looked gravely at each man. He then spoke gently but firmly: "I do believe before we go to put our lives at hazard, it will not go amiss if we put our hopes and trust before He who disposes of all things." A scatter of shapeless tarpaulin head coverings disappeared and, bareheaded, the men of HMS *Trajan* came together in prayer. For a long moment, there was silence as every man's thoughts soared to his loved ones, and the chance of ever seeing them again.

Kydd's eyes lifted from the deck. "To your stations, if you please," said Bomford quietly. The light had strengthened: it was possible to see well ahead to the open sea, the yearned-for goal, but the line of coast was growing in clarity.

Capple stood at the wheel, his arms folded, ready. His was without doubt the single most vital task. Kydd snatched a glance. If Capple felt the pressure on him he gave no sign of it, his eyes slitted against the wind, watching the sails bent on, gaskets loosened, men gathering to hoist—or dowse.

It was time. One by one the stations waved an acknowledgment, the men standing by in fearful anticipation. Out of sight on the deck below the boatswain would be standing with his foot on the cable as it left the hawse—he would feel its live thrumming, the tension in a direct line to the seabed. When the ship had sail on, had speed sufficient not only to meet the seas and beat them, but to make real way, then the boatswain would feel the vibration die away, the cable deaden, relaxed at last as the ship came up on the anchor. Then would be the time for the carpenter to step forward with his razor-sharp mast axe and cut the cable.

"Helm!" the Captain warned. Capple gripped the wheel. Kydd would follow every movement at the lee side, his eyes fixed on the quartermaster. The Captain moved to the forward end of the quarterdeck and gave one last glance aloft. Then he acted: the signal went out. It was the storm jib to hoist, and forward a tiny triangle of sail inched up hesitantly, the white faces of the fo'c'sle party clearly visible as they looked back at the Captain, ready for an immediate countermand. The wheel spun as the helm was put hard over. They would use the effect of the seas seething past to help achieve a cast to larboard.

Higher it rose, flapping and beating with the wind dead ahead. Suddenly it took the wind, board taut: the strong sail in an instant had the bows dipping and the ship shying like a nervous horse. This was the time of greatest danger, before any speed through the water was achieved, sheering across the wind and putting intolerable strain on their anchor.

Another signal, this time aft: the driver, a fore and aft sail on the mizzen, makeshift reefing to show the smallest possible area. Kydd held his breath—the sail flapped and banged, then caught.

Braced right around, the main-yard was slung low in its jeers, but the lee clew of the course appeared. It grew, and the first square sail was set, a tiny corner on one side of the yard, but yet a driving force.

Nervously Kydd snatched a glimpse at the white seas raging past. The ship began to rear: there was an uneasy screwing motion. The Captain was as rigid as a statue, gripping a stay and staring fiercely ahead. Bomford gestured—more sail showed at the main. Kydd could not be sure, but felt that the motion was growing less jerky. Could it be that they were advancing on their anchor?

Raising his arm, Bomford looked all about him. Then, the signal to cut the cable, to launch themselves into eternity—or sweet safety.

Kydd tensed, and in the time it took the carpenter to hack through the great cable Bomford strode quickly back to the helm. Suddenly the ship's bow fell away from the wind. No longer tethered she dropped away to leeward. A massive roll sent men skittering across the deck. A cross sea intervened and the ship lurched sickeningly. Kydd snatched a look astern—they were drifting down on the land. His hands gripped the wheel convulsively. A growl from Capple brought his attention to it. They fought the wheel around together, hard over to try to bring the bows back up to the wind.

The Captain stood unmoving and Kydd felt a pressure on the helm, a strengthening, glorious force that told of power and movement through the water. He determined not to look behind at the land, but couldn't help a prickling in his neck as he remembered the fringing reef, which must be close now.

The bowsprit reared and plunged but it sawed a path in the sky that was unmistakable: *Trajan* was answering her helm. Kydd dared to hope. A little more of the goose-winged main and the old ship heeled obediently in response, the seas meeting her bow with energy and purpose. Minute by agonizing minute, yard by yard, *Trajan* clawed her way out to sea until at last there could be no more doubt. They had won through.

All eyes were on the thickset carpenter as he emerged on deck to report. The pumps had been at work for some time, but it seemed that he had not found any specific leakage.

"Sir, the barky is strained in her foreparts, on account o' the anchorin' pulling and tearin' at the riding bitts and clinches. I can't say as I c'n be sure how long afore she opens up aroun' the cant frames, she bein' so moldy deep in an' all."

It would be the cruelest fortune to founder just as they had found life. Kydd felt resentment flare and wondered bitterly what Renzi would make of it, what philosophical edge might make it palatable. There was talk of frapping, putting turns of rope right round the hull and bowsing tight, but this was impossible while the hurricane lasted. The wind had backed farther and as the hours wore on there was a discernible lessening of the violence, a descent into merely a fresh gale, but not enough.

Just before Kydd's watch finished, lookouts on the foreyard sighted sail, far-off and storm-tossed, but it quickly resolved into a frigate, an English one as far as anyone could tell, scudding before the outer edge of the hurricane.

"Show 'em our colors," snapped Auberon. In reply a blue ensign jerked up the mast in the frigate, proving her one of Admiral Jervis's Leeward Islands Squadron.

Bomford wasted no time. "Signal her to lie to, and attend on us when the storm abates," he ordered, and went below.

"All the *haaaands!* All *haaands* on deck—lay aft!"

Shafts of sun glittered on the gray seas, the wind nearly back in the northeast, warmth beginning to spread, the insanity of the past slipping away. The men mustered on the upper deck to hear the Captain again.

"I will be brief," Bomford began. It was clear he had much on his mind, and he spoke curtly. "I am proud of this ship—I am proud of you all, that you have done your duty so nobly. If you stand as valiantly against the enemy as you did against the might of the hurricane then we have no fear of any foe." Bomford seemed to have difficulty in choosing his words. "*Trajan* will proceed now to Antigua for survey and repair at the dockyard, a bare day or two's sail away." He waited for the indistinct murmuring to die away. "But I have to tell you that we as a ship's company will be transported in the frigate back to Barbadoes while this is done." This time there were mutters of appreciation—the small island of Antigua could not bear the effort of keeping hundreds of seamen idle ashore for an extended period, and therefore they would return to the main base with all its lures. "Yet I would ask for volunteers to form a skeleton crew to sail *Trajan* to her well-earned rest. May the first lieutenant see the hands of those volunteering?"

A tiny scatter of hands rose. It was no contest: Antigua had nothing to offer that compared with the punch shops and entertainments of Bridgetown. Anger rose in Kydd: *Trajan* was now to be deserted by those she had borne so uncomplainingly through her time of trial. He glanced about. Stony faces met his: they were not going to give up their chance of a frolic. Kydd threw up his hand—he at least would remember the old lady.

The volunteers were mustered on the quarterdeck. His eyes resentfully on the deserting seamen, Kydd didn't notice Bomford approach.

"Kydd, it did not escape me, the contribution you made to this ship and her preservation." Bomford had piercing eyes and Kydd stiffened. "This was in the very best traditions of the Service, and shows you to be an exceptional seaman. I look forward to when we renew our acquaintance as a ship's company—and while I cannot promise in the particulars, I have it in mind to recognize your worth with an advancement. Good luck, and thank you."

CHAPTER 6

─⁂─

*T*rajan ghosted over a shimmering sea, her sail reduced so that without an anchor she could back topsails and heave to in plenty of time. The low, pretty island of Antigua lay ahead, basking in tropical sunshine, a long sandy beach visible between two rocky points. The dark stone of a fort stood at a height to the right, and another one extended low down along a point to the left, dashes of red along a crenellated wall obviously soldiers. The sea was a deep royal blue, so calm that only a slight swell marred its flat, glittering expanse.

A boat under sail emerged around the point and turned toward them, her bow-wave white and sparkling. On taking in the last of her sails, *Trajan* ceased her live motion and drifted. The boat arrived and a deeply sun-tanned officer clambered up the side. It took little time for the essence of the matter to be conveyed: the ship would be prepared to enter English Harbour.

It was out of the question to sail into the confines of the harbor: the compact space that made it a first-class hurricane haven made it impossible for a large ship to maneuver. *Trajan* would be warped in. Ropes were taken ashore by boat and secured to strong moorings embedded at strategic points, and all hands of the skeleton crew manned the capstan.

The land came in on both sides, but around the point it opened up. At a prominence farther down in the long harbor a cluster of buildings announced the location of a naval dockyard. *Trajan* was not alone. The bulbous hull of a vessel careening dominated the other side, and everywhere there were brigs, schooners, packets and a swarm of small fry. But the 74-gun *Trajan* was easily the biggest vessel, her grim sides towering above them all.

They hauled themselves farther into the harbor. The dockyard was to larboard, and on a flat area to the fore a lofty mast bore a Union Flag that streamed gaily to the breeze. As her commissioning pennant was not in evidence, there were no naval ceremonies and within the hour *Trajan* was alongside a dusky brown coralstone wharf.

Kydd looked ashore. The little dockyard town boasted imposing, veranda-clad two-story edifices along well-made roads. At the root of the tiny peninsula was a long pillared structure with open sides topped with a wide roof—a boat being floated inside revealed it as a shipwright's boathouse.

Springs and breast-ropes applied, *Trajan* had officially arrived. It was hot and dusty, but the northeast trade winds resumed their cool streaming from over the surrounding hills. All the same, Kydd felt grateful to be wearing a thin working shirt rather than the soldiers' heavy clothing. From *Trajan*'s upper deck, he could see into the busy dockyard. Black men considerably outnumbered others, plodding along economically with their burdens. A number of ducks and geese were fluttering and strutting about.

"Ain't much," Stirk said, mopping his brow with his red kerchief. "We goin' rollickin' ashore, 'n' not a sight of a regular-goin' pothouse anywheres." The close-packed dockyard buildings quickly fell away along what could be seen of the road meandering into the interior. The cane-fields over the surrounding hills, apart from the occasional windmill, were innocent of anything man-made.

"Heard tell th't what y' sees is all there is," Kydd said, remembering the derisive talk in *Trajan* when he had volunteered. "Seems the Navy is all in th' north o' the island, an' here just y'r dockyard an' the redcoats." Stirk gave a grunt of dissatisfaction, and Kydd hoped that they would not be long delayed. A week or two to refit, enough to cross the Atlantic for a full docking in England—then, at last, he would be able to go home.

There was a coming and going of officers and dockyard functionaries up the side steps from the quay, but nothing to say what their future would be. The young lieutenant in temporary command was not going to risk his situation by letting his men leave the ship. They stayed aboard, moodily watching the shore.

At four in the afternoon, as the midday heat lessened, a small party approached. It was led by a man in austere black, and as he stepped down on the upper deck Kydd was struck by the nobility in his bearing, the calm certainty in his features. The party disappeared below.

"Who's that?" Kydd asked.

"Why, that's Zachary Caird, yer master shipwright come ter survey," said a local craftsman. "Second only ter the commissioner in the dockyard, is 'e."

One of the party reappeared on deck, his working clothes marking him as a shipwright. He brushed aside questions, slipping over the side and into the dockyard. He returned with a long cylindrical section auger, and vanished below.

Darkness was drawing in by the time the party came on deck again. From their grave expressions Kydd guessed that the repair would be a lengthy one. "Any word, sir?" he asked the young lieutenant, after he had shepherded the survey team over the bulwarks.

"Yes," said the officer offhandedly, "and we are to be condemned, I believe."

Kydd stared. "We . . ."

"We are strained and leaking in the hull, and it is outside the powers of this dockyard to get us seaworthy enough to make passage back to England." He removed his cocked hat and wiped his forehead. "As they have no dry dock here for a great repair, we are finished. It was being at anchor in a hurricane, the strain and working at the bow, too much for the ironsick old vessel." He gazed away.

"But—"

"It's subject to confirmation by others, but, well, you now know as much as I."

Stirk had no doubts about their future. "The *Trajan*s are no more, cully! We'se goin' ter be sent quicksmart t' Barbadoes an' the Loo'ard Island fleet, or it's the Jamaica Squadron. Either way we gets no say a-tall which barky we're goin' ter ship out in."

Kydd's spirits sank. It was hard to take. Renzi would probably not even know which ship he had been assigned to, all his friends would be scattered and he would not see them again. There was one other thing to add to his dejection. He was now a quartermaster's mate, a petty officer: in a strange ship he would have to work his way up all over again. Captain Bomford's promise of advancement meant nothing.

The next day, *Trajan* was warped deeper into the harbor, well clear of other vessels, and prepared for destoring. After the formality of a second opinion her guns would be removed and the process of hulking her would begin.

A large detachment of seamen was soon taken off for immediate passage to Barbados. A brig-sloop took another six, an armed schooner three. A last-minute call from a passing 64-gun vessel took the majority of the remainder to Jamaica, leaving a silent, echoing ship and a handful of men.

"Kydd!" the lieutenant called. "Mr. Caird has asked if I can spare a good hand to work with him ashore. I told him we can.

Get your gear, the dockyard boat will be calling for you at six bells."

The dockyard? Kydd's thoughts jostled and his first instinct was to object—but, then, perhaps it would be interesting, learning the internal secrets of so many different kinds of vessel. He found himself responding positively.

But there was one left aboard to whom he must say farewell. Luke was stricken at the news. "B-but, Mr. Kydd—you . . ."

Touched by his grief Kydd fumbled for words, knowing the dockyard boat would be alongside soon. "Shall miss ye too, skinker," he said, ruffling the lad's hair, "but we does our duty, an' without gripin'." Luke stared at him but didn't move as Kydd turned and left.

The dockyard hoy was taking advantage of the trip by loading mounds of sails, awnings, cordage and other materials from *Trajan* for return to stores. Kydd found himself wedged in with these as he settled down for the short trip.

The boat hoisted sail. As they made their way to the dockyard landing place, Kydd looked back on *Trajan,* his ship: her age-darkened sides, the ugly truncation of topmasts, the secrets of twenty years and the unknown thousands who had sailed in her. He felt a lump build in his throat as she fell astern. She slowly transfigured into yet another feature of the harbor, an anonymous vessel in the distance with all reality of having been his home now faded. He wrenched away his gaze. A different kind of life was starting for him now.

The boat nosed in to the coral-rock quay, ending up neatly under a stout wooden crane where the single sail was dowsed. "Where's Mr. Caird?" Kydd asked the crew. It seemed that he could be found at the boathouse. Kydd heaved out his seabag and started to head in the direction they had indicated.

Then incredulous shouts came from the hoy. He looked back and saw Luke clambering out from under old sails. "Be damned!

You're a wicked rascal, to think on desertin' y'r ship like this," Kydd said hotly. "Y'r goin' straight back aboard."

"Not wi' us, he ain't—we got other work t'do," came a swift rejoinder from one of the hoy's crew.

"Well, how c'n he . . ."

"Not our problem, mate."

Kydd swore, but saw the appeal in Luke's big eyes, his little bundle of belongings over his shoulder, and knew that if he insisted, he would be condemning the lad. He swore again. "Follow me, y' ill-lookin' swab," he growled, and set out for the boathouse. Obediently Luke fell into step behind.

The boathouse consisted of an extensive loft resting on lines of tall stone pillars. Below, boats were floated inside, then hoisted to the workshop floor. The resinous aroma of timber lay strongly on the breeze that played through the pillars, a clean, welcome scent in the overall reek of a harbor. Mr. Caird stepped out from the storeroom at the back. Kydd recognized him at once as the master shipwright who had surveyed *Trajan*.

"Thomas Kydd, who's been sent fr'm *Trajan* for service ashore."

Caird looked at him keenly. "What was your rate aboard?"

Again Kydd was struck by the calm gaze, the certainty in his manner. "Quartermaster's mate, sir."

Caird nodded. "If I may observe, you're young for the rate, are you not?" A series of flat thumps with a mallet sounded to one side.

Kydd returned his look defiantly.

"But, of course, you will have earned it," Caird added quickly. "You may need it. Have you had experience of men of color?"

Taken aback by the question, Kydd paused. There were no slaves in England, and the only black men he had seen at sea were all free, as he was. "Not as y' might say," he said cautiously.

"I have it in mind to employ you as a Master of the King's Negroes—to take my shipwright's sidesmen in charge."

"Aye, sir," Kydd said carefully.

"To see they're mustered at work each morning, that they're not in want of what they need—but ye need to know, I'll not have them abused, sir."

Thoughts racing, Kydd murmured assent. This was utterly beyond his expectations. Caird regarded him thoughtfully, then his gaze slipped to Luke, who smiled up at him uncertainly.

"And this is—your servant?" Caird said. "You are entitled, of course, as a master, but we have our own, you know."

Caught off balance, Kydd stuttered an acknowledgment.

Caird's eyebrows rose. "Well, if you insist—but he will have to share servants' quarters."

"Th-thank you," Kydd said, not daring to look at Luke.

"Hercules will show you to your lodgings. I will see you at my office at four o'clock, if you please."

Kydd followed the black man along the road, past workshops and sawpits, Luke walking silently behind with his bundle. They went through the dockyard gate and stopped at one of a row of small but neat two-story houses. "In this house—you in the top floor, master."

Kydd opened the little wicket gate and stepped inside: there was an external flight of stairs to the top story. The man looked once more at him, then touched his forehead and left.

At the top of the stairs the door held a key: Kydd turned it and entered. The small room smelled stuffy and unused. There was a low bed, a side dresser with a jug, and little else. Kydd crossed the room and opened one of two doors to a tiny sitting room with armchair and table. The other led to a snug veranda overlooking the hills beyond. "Hey, now," Kydd said, with satisfaction. "So I'm t' be a master, an' live in a house."

By late afternoon Kydd had the place in order. On the lower floor, it seemed, was the chief caulker, now absent. He would pay his respects later.

"Where do I go, Mr. Kydd?" said Luke, overawed by events.

"Why, with th' other servants, o' course." Kydd chuckled. Luke's face fell. Kydd couldn't keep it up. "But then again, I c'd have ye close at hand, see t' my wants at any time. Oh, yes! So I decides I want you to doss down here, younker, but mark you, mind y' has proper respect f'r yer master."

"Yes, an' I will, Mr. Kydd," said Luke seriously.

The office of the master shipwright was with the master attendant and commissioner, right at the far end, but the dockyard was compact and well laid out. Kydd was shown into the airy office. Caird sat at his desk, his quill scratching busily. He glanced up as Kydd approached. "A minute, if you please."

The room was extremely clean, furniture well polished, and ornamented only with a series of charts and half-breadth shipyard models. A Christian devotional etching hung in the center of one wall.

Caird swiveled round. "Please be seated, Mr. Kydd," he said, motioning to a cane chair on one side. "I am the master shipwright here, as you know, and my responsibilities are extensive. It would be gratifying if I could rely on those the good Lord sees fit to set under me." He paused, looking intently at Kydd. "This is not always the case, I am grieved to say."

The interview continued with a clear and unequivocal setting out of Kydd's new duties, which were also carefully listed down for him. It concluded with a stern warning on conduct. "Do you mark my words, Mr. Kydd, I will suffer no man in my charge to corrupt himself by yielding up his body to drink and carnality. Should he so dishonor me, I shall cast him out without mercy."

Kydd was by no means a tippler: he disliked the surrender of will involved in drunkenness, and as to carnality, he had not seen a female of any age anywhere. "Aye, sir, ye need have no fears of me," he said positively.

"Ah, that is good. Your predecessor did grievously disappoint in this. I wish you well for the future, and we may expect your presence on the morrow at the boathouse."

Later, in the privacy of his room, Kydd studied the paper containing full details of his duties. The King's Negroes were slaves, but superior slaves, it seemed, for not only did they have considerable skills but, to Kydd's surprise, some even had slaves of their own. He would have a driver, a foreman, who would be responsible to him for the others, and a line of responsibility to the yard boatswain.

"Y'r pardon, Mr. Kydd," said Luke anxiously. He stood at the door respectfully. "I c'n have yer scran alongside, should yer want it now."

Kydd felt abashed: he had not really meant it when he told Luke he was a servant. Now the lad was taking him at his word. On reflection, however, he realized that, given the circumstances, it might be the best thing. "Thank ye, Luke, I will."

Kydd returned to his paper. The King's Negroes' chief employment was as a skilled crew to assist shipwrights and riggers in major operations, such as in heaving down ships for underwater repairs or replacing whole masts. His would be the first party to board men-o'-war entering harbor having been wounded in battle or savaged by a hurricane.

Luke spread a small tablecloth on the sitting room table. Without looking up, he carefully laid a single place with pewter plate and knife, and withdrew.

Kydd finished the paper, smiling to himself at the strictures on keeping his men sober and diligent.

The cool of the morning showed Antigua in its best light: delicate tints, clarity of air, and everywhere the sparkling translucence of the sea.

On the flat grassy area next to the boathouse Kydd surveyed the

King's Negroes. They returned his contemplation with stony indifference, or looked away with disinterest. Big, well-muscled and hard-looking, they were dressed in canvas trousers and buttoned waistcoat over naked skin. Some wore old-fashioned three-cornered cocked hats, others a bandanna. Unusually for slaves, all carried a sheathed seaman's knife.

"An' who's the driver?" Kydd asked, in even tones. The men kept silent, staring back at him. Kydd tried to sense their feelings, but there was a barrier.

"The driver!" he snapped. If it was going to be this way, so be it, but then the hardest-looking of them pulled himself up slowly and confronted Kydd. "I'se driver," he said, his voice deep and strong. He regarded Kydd impassively from under hooded black eyes, his arms folded.

Kydd looked at the others. There was no feeling in their expressions. They existed in stasis, much like beasts of the field, it appeared. "I'm Kydd, and I'm th' new master," he said. There was no response, no interest. "What's y'r name?" he demanded of the driver.

"Juba," he said.

"What are *their* names?" said Kydd. "They are t' tell me themselves," he added.

A flicker of curiosity showed in their faces. "Nero," grunted an older one. Kydd nodded, and prompted the man next to him.

"Quamino."

"An' you?" Kydd went on.

"Ben Bobstay."

One by one, he had a name from each. He hesitated over whether to make a strict speech of introduction, but thought better of it. "If ye does y'r duty, ye'll have nothing t' fear fr'm me," he said firmly, and turned to greet Caird, who had just arrived.

"I see you have mustered your crew already," Caird said. "Fort Shirley has signaled that *Rose* frigate will be here this morning—

she has a sprung foremast, which we shall in course replace." He stopped to take a sheaf of lists from a waiting shipwright and scanned them quickly. "Where are your roves, sir?" he asked impatiently. "Were you thinking to secure with nails?" His forehead creased, and the shipwright cringed. Caird turned to Kydd again. "We shall not need the sheer hulk—the boatswain of the yard will rig sheers on her foredeck."

Kydd had no experience of such skilled work, and if he was expected to take charge . . .

"The boatswain will be overseer," said Caird, as if sensing Kydd's thoughts. "It only requires that you tell your driver the task—he has done this work, and you may feel sure that he knows what to do."

The 28-gun frigate *Rose* sailed in without warping, even with minimal sail at the fore, a fine piece of seamanship in the exuberant late-summer breezes. She had suffered at the hands of the hurricane—sea-whitened timbers and ropes leeched of their tar, stoppers seized at places in her rigging, the patchy wooden paleness of new repairs showing here and there. But she rounded to, and her sails came in smartly, as if her company were conscious of their fortune in being spared by the fates.

The boatswain of the yard, sitting in the sternsheets of the dockyard boat with Kydd, stared idly ahead. The rowers pulled heavily, towing two massive sheer-legs in the water.

To Kydd, it was strangely affecting to step over the bulwarks and be in a sea world belonging to others. While the boatswain talked to the Captain, his eyes strayed to little things that would be embedded in the consciousness of the ship's company—the dog-vane to point the direction of the wind and fashioned into a red-petaled rose, the binnacle finished with a varnished bolt-rope, the smart black japanned speaking trumpet also with a painted rose—all these would be the familiar images of daily life at sea.

Rose's seamen looked at him curiously, his small band of black men at his back. "What cheer, mate?" said one. "Where's to go on th' ran-tan?"

Spared from having to answer by the boatswain's hail from forward, Kydd reported himself and his men. "You, Kydd, get y'r men out o' the way fer now, but I'll want 'em on the cross spar afore we cants the sheers," the boatswain said, and turned to his own crew.

Kydd stared at the scene with some anxiety. The fo'c'sle was a maze of ropes and blocks laid out along the deck each side from when the topmast had been struck. How it was possible to pluck the feet-thick foremast, like a tooth, straight out from where it ended morticed into its step on the keel he had no idea. Juba did not volunteer a word. He stood aside, watching with a patience that seemed limitless and at the same time detached.

The boatswain's men ranged mighty threefold purchases. The sheaved blocks were each nearly double the size of a man's head, the falls coiled in fakes yards long. Lesser tackles were made fast to knightheads and kevels, and all was ready to bring aboard the sheers. But then the boatswain stepped back, his arms folded. Kydd saw why: in a nice division of responsibilities, it was men of the *Rose* who manned the jeer capstan to take the weight, then lower the heavy seventy-five-foot width of the foreyard, indecently shorn of its usual complexity of buntlines and halliards.

The foremast now stood alone, its wound clearly visible as a long bone-colored fracture under the capstan bars, which had been splinted around it. "Kydd, y'r cross spar!" the boatswain called impatiently.

Kydd had been too interested in the proceedings and was caught unawares but he swiftly rounded on Juba. "Cross spar!" he snapped, stepping toward the sheers. He looked fearlessly at the man, who hesitated just a moment, looking into Kydd's eyes, then moved into action. In low tones he called to the other Negroes, in words incomprehensible to Kydd. The men split into two parties and slid the fore topgallant yard athwartships, then up against the splayed end of the sheers. They stopped and Juba looked up slowly. Kydd turned to the men at the crosspiece of the sheers and told them to pass the seizing.

"Like a throat-seizing an' not too taut," the boatswain suggested.

"Aye," said Kydd, happy with a newfound realization: no matter how complex and technical the task, it could be rendered down to a series of known seamanlike evolutions.

The sheers were duly canted, tilted up so the guys could get an angle to sway the sheer-legs aloft. At the same time tackles at their feet held them firmly in place. It was almost an anticlimax, knocking aside the mast wedges, freeing the partners and hearing the massive tackle creak as it strained in a vertical pull up on the mast, which gave in a sudden and alarming jerk upward.

There was suddenly nothing to do as the freed mast was angled and slowly lowered over the ship's side to be floated ashore, a fearsome thing that could spear the heart out of the frigate if it was accidentally let go. Kydd glanced at the motionless Juba, intrigued by the man's self-possession. Unexpectedly Juba allowed a brief smile to appear. Kydd smiled back, and pretended to follow the progress of the mast over the side.

The softness of a Caribbean evening was stealing over the waters when Kydd was finally able to return to the dockyard.

The replacement foremast had needed work. Awkwardly placed along the deck of the frigate it had had to be held securely on trestles while shipwrights went to work with adze and angled mast axe. As the chips flew, the craftsmen held Kydd in awe at their skill with such awkward tools. He now knew a good deal more than he had at break of day, and he felt happier than he had at any time since he had left *Trajan*: this was better than being a spare hand to whatever ship would claim him.

Closer in to the dockyard, he could hear the cries and laughter of the ship's company of *Avenger*, a ship-sloop whose bulbous, naked hull was heaved right over for careening on the other side of the water. These men would be accommodated ashore while their ship was in such a condition, and were making the most of the relaxing of discipline, taking their evening grog around the shore galley near the capstan house with raucous frivolity. Kydd eased into a grin at the familiar antics.

The injured mast could wait in the water off the mast-house for the morning and he could now dismiss his crew and get some supper. "Well done, m' lads," he said, unconsciously regarding them in the same way as a party of seamen after a hard day. Too late the thought came that possibly he should treat slaves in some other way, more at a distance, perhaps. However, they did not respond, and padded off silently together, he couldn't help wondering where.

The shore galley manned, Luke was able to get a hearty platter for him, complete with leaves of some mysterious local vegetable, and he tucked in with a will. It was hard to eat alone, though, with nothing but a candle and circling moths for company.

The conviviality flowing from the capstan house was hard to resist, and Kydd found himself strolling in the warm dark of the evening toward the sounds of merriment. The open frontage of the low building, with its three great capstans, was a favorite place to gather in the growing soft darkness. The lanthorns hung along the beams welcomed him in with splashes of golden light. Men lolled about, taking a clay pipe of tobacco or drinking deep from their pots, in time-honored sailor fashion outdoing each other in sea yarns and remembrances.

Kydd knew none of them, but could recognize the types even though they were of another ship: the hard, confident petty officers in short blue jackets with brass buttons that glittered in the light of the lanthorns; young seamen bred to the sea, with an easy laugh and a tarry queue unclubbed so its plaited length hung a foot or more down their backs; the lined old shellbacks, whose sea wisdom it would be folly to question.

A man hauled himself up to sit on one of the capstan heads and his fiddle was passed up to him. After a few flourishes he nodded to a handsome seaman with side whiskers next to him. The man stepped forward and sang in a resonant tenor:

> *"Oh! Life is the Ocean, and Man is the Boat*
> *That over its surface is destin'd to float;*
> *And joy is a cargo so easily stor'd*
> *That he is a fool who takes sorrow on board!"*

The well-known chorus drowned the singer, who affected vexation, stumping around the capstan in high dudgeon. Kydd laughed heartily with the rest, and raised his wooden tankard in salute.

Sensing the mood, the singer stalked to the front of the capstan, and stood akimbo, arms folded, glaring at his audience. The chatter died away expectantly.

A movement on the opposite side caught Kydd's eye. One of the seamen had a woman under his arm, a black woman. Kydd shifted his gaze back to the singer, who leaned forward as though in confidence, and there launched into the racy, driving strains of "The Saucy *Arethusa*":

> *"Come all ye jolly sailors bold*
> *Whose hearts are cast in honor's mold*
> *While English glory I unfold*
> *On board of the* Arethusa!*"*

The sailors burst into song, and Kydd felt his cheeks glow with pleasure. The singer bowed and accepted a dripping tankard. Kydd looked about him with a grin.

"Clinkin' good singer, is our Dansey!" A seasoned petty officer grinned back at Kydd.

"Rattlin' fine voice!" agreed Kydd. "Are ye *Avenger*s, then?"

"Aye—Ben Kittoe, gunner's mate," the man replied, taking a pull from his blackjack, a dark tarred leather tankard.

"Kydd, Tom Kydd, quartermaster's mate o' *Trajan* as was," he said.

"D'ye mean . . . ?"

"T' be knackered, poor ol' lady," Kydd said, and finished his pot.

"Bad cess. So where are yez now?"

"Got m'self a berth as master."

"What?"

"Master o' the King's Negroes, that is." Kydd laughed. At the other's curiosity he continued, "Seem well enough at th' work, but wouldn't trust 'em on their own."

The numbers at the capstan house had diminished, the galley had closed its hatches, but Kydd felt in no mind to break the mood. Kittoe stood up and waved his blackjack expansively. "Come wi' us fer a quick noggin, mate."

The two walked back along the stone quay and into the copper and lumber house. Kydd remembered that it was here that the crews of ships being careened were quartered. Above the locked and darkened storerooms was the loft where copper plating for the underwater hull was pricked out to shape. "We got a good sort as owner," Kittoe grunted, as they mounted the exterior iron stairs. "Sees us right in the article of grog an' such." They entered: one end of the loft was agreeably illuminated with lanthorns, the light rapidly falling off into darkness at the other end of the broad expanse.

"Here, mate, take a muzzler o' this." He reached for a dark green bottle from his sea chest and upended it in Kydd's pot. The cloying aroma of prime West Indian rum eddied up.

"To *Trajan*—but f'r our hurricanoe, she'd be out crestin' the briny b' now," Kydd said.

Harsh laughter bayed from a group of sailors at their end of the loft. They were seated around an upended tub, playing cards and swigging hard from bottles. Kittoe allowed his face to go grave. "Yeah, to a barky as any haul-bowlings c'n feel proud ter own to!" They drank together. Kydd let the rum just burn his lips: the evening might develop.

"Ye come fr'm England?" Kydd asked.

"Nah—*Avenger* is taken fr'm the Crapauds at Martinico," Kittoe said briefly. It was the way of it—some clash at arms in these seas. . . .

A tall woman appeared, dressed loosely in colorful red. She moved behind Kittoe and slid her arms down his chest. "Come, Kittoe man, you an' me make jig-a-jig," she purred, but her eyes were on Kydd, wide and lambent.

"Away wi' ye, Sukey," said Kittoe, but with a smile. "We're talkin' together, yer silly biddy!"

The woman's hair was drawn back and had a hard sheen in the light. A large polished mahogany-colored jungle seed hung around her neck. She fingered it, regarding Kydd speculatively. Grunts and cries from the darkness beyond left little doubt about what was going on, and Kydd's senses prickled. "Hey, youse kooner-man!" she said, her voice low and throaty.

Kittoe took up the bottle again and went to top up Kydd's tankard, but only a few drops of rum emerged. He snorted. "Potboy! Look sharp, we're a-thirst!" A figure hurried over from the other side to attend them and came to a sudden halt.

"Luke!" Kydd cried. "What're y' doing here?" It was not hard to guess—here he could earn a few coppers. The boy dropped his head as Kydd laid into him. "You little rascal, this's not the place t' find a fine young gennelman, damn me if it is!"

Obstinately, Luke raised his eyes and said, "Then what 're *you* here for, Mr. Kydd?"

There was a chortling from Kittoe, but Kydd stood up, face burning. "None o' y'r business! Now you get y'self back aboard— I mean, return t' our lodgings—this instant, y' swab!"

At the stubborn look on Luke's face Kydd knew there was no other course. "We return *now,* y' blaggard! I'll have no servant o' mine corruptin' himself with drink 'n' carnality!" Kydd pushed him out into the darkness and followed. He cursed and swore under his breath. He had had no intention of being saddled with the moral responsibility for another, but in Luke's case he felt a certain obligation.

"Show more canvas, younker!" Kydd growled. An idea took shape—he shied from it at first, but it would meet the case splendidly. He sighed. He'd thought he'd left all of that behind in another life. . . .

As they opened the little gate he rounded on Luke. "Have y' made up m' accounts yet?"

Luke's face dropped. "Mr. Kydd, y' know I haven't m' letters."

"Damme! I f'got," said Kydd, with heat. "This means I have t' spend my valuable time a-copyin' and figurin'—may have t' get a proper servant, me havin' such responsibility now." Kydd turned his gaze from Luke's pitiable expression, and frowned grimly. "An' that ain't going to be easy hereabouts."

They went up the stairs. Then Kydd stopped, as though struck with a sudden thought. "There maybe *is* a way. . . ."

"Mr. Kydd?" said Luke eagerly.

"Perhaps not. You're a lazy rascal, an' won't—"

"I will so, I swear."

"Right, me hearty! We starts tomorrow. Y' hoists aboard yer letters at last."

"Yes, Mr. Kydd," Luke said meekly.

Just before noon, a rain squall stopped all work. Kydd and his crew hurried into the shelter of the boathouse while the downpour hammered into the ground and set a thousand rivulets starting toward the brown waters of the harbor.

"I have been hearing good reports of you, Thomas," said Caird.

Kydd looked around in surprise. "Mr. Caird?"

"You have been teaching your servant his letters."

Kydd's face eased into a smile. "Aye, keeps him out o' trouble betimes, the scamp."

Caird's voice softened. "That is what I thought. It is the Lord's work you are doing, Thomas, never forget it."

Embarrassed, Kydd mumbled something, but was interrupted. "If you are at leisure, perhaps you may wish to dine this evening at my house—we eat at six promptly." Noting Kydd's hesitation he went on, "I can well comprehend the godless depravity you are sparing the boy, and confess from the start, I had my hopes of your conduct."

"The salt, if you please, my dear," Caird said to the arid lady at the other end of the table, who, Kydd now knew, was his sister Isadore. She nodded graciously, with something suspiciously like a simper.

It was hard on Kydd: bad enough the enervating warmth, but worse the starched tablecloth, precise manners and formidable air of rectitude. He searched for some conversation. "Luke's not a shab, really, it's just that—"

Isadore broke in unctuously, "And as a sapling is trained, so does the tree grow." She helped herself liberally to the cream sauce.

Opposite Kydd sat the delicate, timid Beatrice. Each time he looked at her she averted her eyes quickly, disconcerting him. She was a slight figure in filmy gray, which added to her air of unworldliness. She had been introduced as Caird's daughter, her mother long departed for a better world.

"Another akee, Beatrice," Caird said, his voice tender.

"Thank you, no more, Father," came her small voice. Caird nodded to the hovering servant who gracefully removed her plates.

"I see *Rose* has her foremast a-taunt now," ventured Kydd.

Caird's eyebrows lowered. "In deference to the ladies, Thomas,

I make it a practice never to discuss at table matters they cannot be expected to know."

"Oh—er, I mean—"

"It is Friday, my friend. On the Sabbath, Beatrice and I go about the good Lord's business in this country, ministering to his children. Do you not feel that it would lift your heart to accompany us?"

Struck dumb by the assumption of his godliness, he noticed Beatrice beaming across at him. "Please do, Mr. Kydd," she said, meeting his eyes for the first time.

"Splendid!" said Caird. "We shall call for you—and your servant, of course—at six on Sunday."

When he returned to his little house, the lower part showed the light of candles: the occupant was at home. He started to climb the steps to his room, but a throaty hail stopped him. "Avast there, cock! Come 'n' show yerself!" It was the chief caulker, his beefy frame seeming to fill the room. He was slumped in a chair holding a bottle. A black woman flitted about with a bowl.

"Has th' mullygrubs," he said, burping. "What's yer name, mate?"

"Thomas Kydd, Master o' the King's Negroes."

"Savin' y'r presence, yez a young one fer a master. How'd yer come by it?"

"I had th' rate o' petty officer in *Trajan*, 'n' when she was let go—"

"A cryin' shame," rumbled the man.

"—I was taken up b' Mr. Caird," he finished.

"Are ye a goddamned blue-light sailor, then?" demanded the chief caulker.

"I never take th' Lord's Name in vain, brother," Kydd said, holding his hands in a prayerful attitude and hoping that his humble tone passed muster.

"B' gob, I never said—God rest ye, mate, an' all that!"

Kydd smiled beatifically, and made his exit, pleased at his escape from future bibulous demands. Then he remembered his mother's firm and steely Methodism, the hours of boredom in church—and winced.

Sunday morning saw them both in best attire—Luke with hair slicked back and shirt painfully buttoned up, Kydd in his best step-ashore rig, feeling utterly out of place. They waited outside the master shipwright's house. Broad, square, imposing, built of stone, the house reflected the importance of its chief inhabitant.

The Misses Caird emerged into the early sunlight, closely followed by Caird, forbidding in black—entirely black, from old-fashioned three-corner hat to severe black breeches and stockings, the whole relieved only by a plain white cravat.

Kydd doffed his hat to the ladies, returned by the unsmiling Caird. Luke's hesitant touching of his forelock was ignored. A dray rumbled grittily around the corner, its load of what appeared to be furniture covered with an old sail. The gray-haired old woman at the reins bobbed her head in glee at the sight of Caird. "Hallelujah! Glory be, oh, yest, Lord!"

"Amen to that, Hepzibah," Caird said in a strong voice. "We have today, joining with us in joyful prayer, Master Thomas Kydd and his servant." Hepzibah beamed at Kydd.

"Then shall we proceed. This day we pass by the plantation of Mr. Blackstone, beyond Falmouth town." Caird handed up the ladies to the single front seat and climbed up, himself taking the reins. "I would wish we had more commodious transport, Thomas. You will have to shift for yourself in the back, I fear."

Kydd pulled Luke in after him and the dray moved off. As they clopped serenely through the dockyard Kydd was glad of the early start—there was nobody abroad to see him. He looked at the swaying backs of the Cairds and wondered at the wild contrasts in his life since he had taken to sailoring.

They wound out of the dockyard and were almost immediately

in scrub and rocks over the higher ground behind. The dray
ground along, Hepzibah breaking into joyful hymns that, of
course, it would be unseemly to join. Scattered houses merged
into a township, but the houses were mean—wattle and daub,
small and mud-dusty. "Falmouth," said Caird, "a Negro village."
Past the town, the sea sparkling to their left, they wound up into
cane-field country. The heat was noticeably stronger. As they
topped the rise, the sound of singing floated to them on the hot
breeze. Finally they stopped at a crossroads in the shade of a wild
tamarind tree of considerable size and age, where people of every
variety, free and slave, had gathered.

"Please to assist me, Thomas, in rigging the assembly," Caird
asked Kydd courteously.

Kydd complied, lifting down chairs and an ingenious portable
pulpit, under the shy direction of Beatrice. These were set out
under the tamarind tree. When he had finished, she turned to him
with a timid smile and laid her hand on his arm. "Thank you,
Thomas. Shall we sit?" She guided him to the row of chairs in the
front, which Kydd was uncomfortable to see was the only seating.
Behind them the blacks squatted in the dust.

Caird took his position in the pulpit, looking stern and majestic.
His voice boomed out. "Psalm eighty-four, the eleventh verse:
'The Lord God is a sun and shield; the Lord God will give the
grace and glory; no good thing will he withhold from them that
walk uprightly.' " A warm roar of approbation and shrill cries of
"Hallelujah, Lord!" resounded, and the first hymn was announced:
"And Are We Yet Alive." It was sung with true feeling, in joyous
counter-harmony.

As she sang, Beatrice's pale face under the muslin bonnet was
pink with animation, her gray eyes sparkling as she glanced at
Kydd. The hymn, despite the outlandish setting, brought back
memories of Sundays in Guildford. His mother in her best
clothes, he in his once-a-week coat and breeches next to his father.
Kydd recalled staring dully at dust-motes held unstirring in shafts

of sunlight coming from the freedom of the outside world into the utterly still church.

"That was well, Thomas. It is our pleasure to invite you to our Sunday dinner, should you be at leisure." Caird had preached powerfully: his sermon was strong on duty, obedience, law and sin but sparing in the matter of joy.

The Sunday roast would not have shamed his mother's table, even if the potatoes had a subtly alien bitterness, the beef a certain dark sweetness. Once again opposite Beatrice, he tried to engage her in conversation. "Thumpin' good singing, th' Negroes," he said hesitantly. Beatrice flicked a glance at him, but quickly lowered her eyes.

Caird interjected. "They do so take joy in entering into the House of the Lord," he said. "Should an assembly in England take such a joy it would be gratifying."

Kydd had been impressed with their spirit: his King's Negroes in comparison to those he had seen today were morose. Should he not be perceiving their better parts, appeal to their spirit? "Y'r pardon, but I can't sort of . . . can't get close to 'em, if you know what I say. . . ."

"Your concern does you credit, sir, and therefore I will speak directly." Caird dabbed his lips and put down his napkin. "It is easy for us to feel sorry for the Negro, his condition, his lot in life, but we must not believe that in this way we are helping him."

Kydd nodded, not really understanding.

"You will nevertheless find that I am the sworn enemy of any who ill-abuse their black people, who grind them to the dust and then discard them." He fixed Kydd with a look of such fire that Kydd was forced to look down meekly at the tablecloth.

"But, Thomas, in my heart I cannot pretend that they are of the same blood as you or I—they are not!"

Kydd looked up in puzzlement.

"The Good Book itself tells us that they are an accursed people.

Genesis, chapter the ninth, tells how Noah placed a curse on his son Ham and all his seed. From that day to this the black man is placed into subjection.

"And scientific studies do show this: Edward Long, a vile, ranting fellow, nevertheless forces us to confront the fact that they are really another species of man, lacking vital parts that give us judgment and moral sensibility. Merely look upon them—they are not of our kind."

Kydd sat silent.

"Therefore, my friend, you really should not look to their natures for the finer feelings. They are not possessed of any." Caird looked down, then raised his face with a gentle, noble expression. "For this it is my life's work to minister to them, to help them understand and be content in their duty and place in the world, to bear their burdens in patience and through God's Grace to aspire to His Kingdom."

"Amen!" breathed Beatrice.

It made things much clearer. If they were a debased form of mankind, of course he was wrong to expect much in the way of feelings. But something still niggled. "An' is slavery right?" Kydd asked stubbornly.

Caird looked at him fondly. "It does seem hard, but you must understand that they need direction, discipline, to control the brutality that lies beneath. Slavery is a mercy. It provides a strong framework in which they may learn to curb their natures." He paused and looked at Kydd directly. "It is not the slavery which is evil, it is the manner in which some do enforce it."

There was time to spare the following forenoon. The *Blanche* frigate was due in for repair, following a spectacular action against a heavier French frigate off Guadeloupe. Rumors flew about that her captain had been killed. Kydd was keen to hear the full story, remembering his own desperate battle in *Artemis*.

Blanche was delayed, so Kydd stood down his crew. Over at the boathouse, with Caird away in his office, he had nothing to do but watch the shipwrights at work. The craftsmen in the boathouse filled the space with the sound of their labor: the oddly musical *thonk* of a maul, the regular hiss of the try plane, the clatter of dropped planks. Steam billowed suddenly from a long chest, and a shipwright gingerly extracted a steaming plank, carrying it to a half-clad boat. Another took one end and they eased it around the tight curve of the bow, faying it to the plank below. Kydd could see that they were fitting it to at least three curves simultaneously—by eye alone.

All along the open side of the boathouse a spar rested on trestles, and Kydd marveled at the mystery of mast-making: How was it possible to create a perfectly straight, perfectly round spar from a rough-hewn length of timber? It was all done by eye alone again, he noted. A straight-edged batten was nailed horizontally to one end; a pair of shipwrights worked together, and another batten was fixed to the other end, sighted by eye to exactly the same level. Then mast-axe and adze were plied skillfully to produce a flat surface the whole length. Another pair of battens produced a flat opposite. By the time they progressed to the octagonal they had a true, workable approximation to a round. Kydd shook his head in wonder.

A sudden shout came from outside. Kydd ducked out and saw pointing arms. The *Blanche* had arrived. All work ceased, and men poured out to see the spectacle. "See there, mates!" one man said, pointing out of the harbor to Freeman's Bay, where the broken masts of a substantial ship showed above the low-lying point of land. "She has a thunderin' good prize!"

As *Blanche* came to anchor opposite, Kydd could see that she was sorely battered—a stump of mizzen, not much more of her mainmast. As she slowly swung to her anchor the stern came into view, blasted into gaping holes. The excited shouting died away at the sight, particularly at her huge battle ensign still floating from her foremast, but only halfway up.

Caird strode down from the direction of his office. "Where is your crew, Kydd? And I'll need you two . . ." he pointed to two shipwrights working in the boathouse ". . . and the blue cutter in the water directly."

With a chest of tools and the men, the cutter was crowded, but Kydd relished his luck in being able to see things at firsthand. He squinted under the loose-footed mainsail as *Blanche* grew nearer, and saw the frightful wounds of war: her sails were torn with holes, her sides pocked and battered by shot.

Caird led the way up the side of the frigate to the upper deck where they took in the results of a harrowing, long drawn-out grappling, a trial of fire that had tried her ship's company to the very limit. Subdued murmuring conveyed the essentials: indeed the Captain had been killed; there was a prize lying to seaward, which was in fact their opponent, a French frigate, a third bigger than themselves.

They clattered down the main hatch. Caird needed to get a sight of the damage to the stern and any cannonball strikes between wind and water that might prove an immediate threat. Returning on deck they saw moaning wounded being swayed down into a boat, wrecked equipment dropped into another, and weary-eyed men staring at the shore. "She comes alongside by sunset," Caird said to an officer with a bandaged head. "I shall see the master attendant directly."

"Yer has the right of it, mates, Cap'n Faulknor, an' a right true sort 'e was, Gawd bless 'is memory," said Kennet, a gunner's mate from the *Blanche*. Kydd dragged his upturned tub closer, the better to hear him over the din in the capstan house.

"We wuz openin' Gron' Bay in Gwaddyloop, a-ready ter spy in the harbor in th' mornin' when we sees this thumpin' big French frigate a-comin' round the point." He paused: a sea-professional audience could be relied on to get the picture. "Now I asks yer, this can't be much after midnight, larbowlines 'as watch below 'n' in their 'ammocks, all peaceful like, an' then it's quarters, ship-mates, 'n' as quick as yer like!"

Kydd could visualize the scene all too clearly: drowsy watch on deck swapping yarns, easy in the mind at the prospect of a spree ashore at the end of the cruise, and then in a flash the reality of war and death in the balmy night.

"Cap'n don't lose a minute—we goes at 'em, clearin' fer action as we go, an' it's all goin' t' be in th' dark." Kennet looked about to see if he had their attention before he went on. "We pass the Frenchie—she's called *Pique* we finds later—on the opposite tack, an' we has a broadside at each other." His voice lowered. "An' that's when m' mate lost the number of 'is mess." He stared into his grog. "Sam Jones, second cap'n o' the foretop . . ."

Kydd stood up and gestured with his tankard. "Here's t' Sam Jones, then, mates, an' if we don' remember him, he won't have anyone else will." In the willing roar that this brought, Kydd drank deeply, remembering the emotions battering at him after his own battle experience, the faces that suddenly weren't there any-more, the world's indifference that they had ever existed—but they would continue to live in men's memories just as long as they were brought to remembrance like this. He took another gulp.

Kennet looked up at him, his grim face softening at Kydd's empathy, then continued, "But then, we tacks about, but *Pique,* she's t' weather, an' wears ready to give us a rakin' broadside, but Cap'n Faulknor, he's wise to 'em, an' we continues on t' wear our-selves. So there we was, mates, broadside t' broadside fer two an' a half hours, thumpin' it inter each other." The cruel smashing match in the darkness, dim battle-lanthorns inboard, leaping gun flashes outboard, unseen horrors in the blackness—it held the cir-cle of rough seamen spellbound.

"But then we shoots ahead. *Pique* 'as taken a drubbin' and 's at our mercy! We turn ter rake her an' finish it—when our mizzen an' mainmast both go by th' board. In a trice we runs afoul of her, an' she rakes us, then she goes t' board, but we're ready an' send 'em screamin' inter the sea."

Kydd noticed that Kennet's eyes had gone glassy and his hand had a tremor: these terrible events could only have taken place less than a single day ago. "Pot!" he shouted, against the hubbub, and personally topped up Kennet's can then added to his own. The rum had a potent fragrance.

"So it's a stalemate, lads. We drifts, then runs aboard her agen by the bow—but Cap'n himself rushes for'ard an' puts a lashin' on our bowsprit t' hold on ter the Frenchman. But—an' it grieves me t' tell it—he takes a ball fr'm a musket, an' falls. . . ."

There was murmuring all round. Kennet waited for it to settle, then offered a toast to his captain, which Kydd could see was being repeated in other groups of seamen around him. He raised his tankard in salute, tears pricking at the bravery he had learned about that night.

"Lashin' gives way, we drift off, firin' all the time, o' course. B' now it's comin' on daylight 'n' we're dog tired—bugger m' days but we was knackered!"

Around him Kydd saw bodies topple in the capstan house, but whether from hard drinking or exhaustion he didn't know.

"Wind drops, we fin' ourselves stern to, an' no guns what'll bear, 'cos we got no stern chasers, no gunports, even. So what does we do then?" Kydd couldn't think what—the rum was deepening his emotions but doing nothing for his concentration.

"Well, lads, we heaves some twelve-pounders around in th' Great Cabin t' face astern, then after we puts men wi' firebuckets on ea' side . . ." he paused dramatically, holding their eyes one by one ". . . an' then we blasts our own gunports through the stern timbers!"

There was no comment, only shocked faces.

"We then has 'em! We pounds away wi' them pair o' guns, one hour, two. Not until we brings down their masts an' finishes more'n two thirds o' their crew do they give up, an' then they strikes their flag."

A growl of satisfaction arose, but no cheers: too many sailors—on both sides—would never know another dawn.

Kydd stood still. He couldn't return to his dark, silent lodging. He felt a surging need for the sea, the slam of excitement at the challenge of sudden peril, the close companionship after shared dangers—the kind of thing that had men rollicking ashore together. There was fire in his blood. The pot-boy hurried past, but Kydd stopped him and snatched a bottle, which quickly went gurgling into his tankard.

He swung around and spied a couple of able seamen arguing together. "That scurvy crew ahoy! Come drink with me t' the *Blanche,* mates, as trim a frigate as ever grac'd the seas—barrin' only th' brave *Artemis!*"

CHAPTER 7

—⁓—

"Mr. Kydd, you said y' wanted ter see m' work this morning wi'out fail. An' here 'tis!" Luke held out his copybook in the early light of morning, the pages filled with spidery, childish writing. "I done it while you was . . . away last night," he continued proudly.

He must have sat by the light of that single candle, scratching away at his worthy proverbs, right into the night, thought Kydd. In spite of his fragile condition he was touched by the lad's keenness. "Show me," he croaked. The letters swam and rotated in a nauseating spiral. "Tha's well done, Luke," Kydd gasped, and gave the book back. He had never before had to pay such a price for a night's carousing. He felt ill and helpless—and despised himself for it. It had been easy to be drawn into the wholehearted roistering of a sailor ashore, but he realized there was a real prospect of sliding into a devotion to the bottle that so many seemed to find an answer to hardship and toil.

Kydd levered himself up on one arm. To his shame he found himself still in last night's stained clothes. His resolve strengthened never to succumb again, and he swung into a sitting position. It was a mistake. His face flushed and a headache pounded relentlessly: it would be impossible to deal with the knowing looks of his crew, to think clearly enough to head off trouble, to face Caird. . . . "Luke, m' boy," he began. He looked up to see the lad's eyes on him, concerned, watchful. "Feelin' a mite qualmish this mornin', think I'll scrub round the vittles."

"Yes, Mr. Kydd," Luke replied quietly.

"Damn it! Doesn't mean you can't have any," Kydd flared, then subsided in shame. "Do ye go to Mr. Caird an' present m' compliments 'n' tell him . . . tell him I regrets but I can't attend on him this forenoon, as I . . . 'cos I has a gripin' in the guts, that's all."

He collapsed back onto the bed and closed his eyes.

He woke from a fitful doze in the heat of the day and sat on the edge of the bed. The nausea was still there, and a ferocious dryness in the throat drove him to his feet in search of water. He swayed, and staggered drunkenly to the sideboard for the pitcher, which he drained thirstily. Slowly and painfully he stripped off his clothes, dropping them uncharacteristically on the floor. Then, thankfully, he curled up on the bed again.

In the afternoon no one came to commiserate, and Kydd knew that his story of "sickness" had been received with the contempt it deserved. To be thought a common toss-pot cut deeply.

Luke arrived in the evening. Kydd had previously sent him away, not wanting to be seen, and now Luke crept about the lodging as though in the company of a bear. Kydd swore at him, and at the gruel he had thoughtfully brought. The evening dragged on: still no one inquired of him. Luke took to hiding. As the illness ebbed so Kydd's headache worsened under the lashing of his irritability. The night passed in a kaleidoscope of conflicting thoughts.

At last the light of dawn arrived to dispel the dark and its tedium. He felt hot, dizzy—he needed water. "Luke!" he shouted petulantly. The sleepy boy appeared and, to Kydd's astonishment, his face contorted. A harsh cry pierced the air and Luke fell to his knees, sobbing loudly.

"What—if this is y'r joke . . ." Kydd felt dread steal over him. "What is it, younker?" he asked, fearing a reply.

Luke looked at him with swimming eyes. He ran out and returned with a mirror. "S-see . . ." he stuttered. Kydd looked into it. His face looked back at him. The hideous jaundiced hue of his skin was more frightening than anything he had seen in his life. It was the yellow fever.

They came for him at noon. By this time Kydd had vomited violently several times, as if his body were trying to rid itself of the invading fever. The fear of the dreaded *vomito negro* seized his thoughts and threw him into frozen horror: he had seen soldiers carried to their graves by it in their dozens, but in the way of youth he had always known it would be some other, never him. Luke sat by his bed, defying Kydd's orders to get away, not caring at the likelihood of contagion. Kydd's mind started to detach in and out of reality.

The bearers, expressionless and silent, lifted Kydd onto the stretcher. The naval hospital was full, and instead Kydd found himself at the door of the army hospital on Shirley Heights, its austere gray lines unmistakable even in his feverish state.

The interior of the hospital was dark, but gradually he could see rows of low beds, one or two orderlies moving among them. Some victims lay motionless, others thrashed and writhed. A foul stink lay on the close air, the putrescence of bodies giving up the fight. Moaning and weeping filled the consciousness, numbing Kydd's senses.

He was placed on the ground while a bed was prepared. A corpse was carried away in a blanket, the ragged palliasse flicked over, the top vivid with dried discoloring. He was transferred, the bearers never once betraying a flicker of interest. They left the blanket rolled untidily at the foot of the bed and departed.

An orderly saw Luke and ejected him irritably, so Kydd lay alone, staring up into the void; the pain, sickness and despair creeping in on him. It was here that he would meet his end, not in some glorious battle but in the squalor and degradation of disease, in this pit of terror. His mind wavered and floated. The wasted hours, the unfulfilled hopes—those who loved him, trusted him. Emotion choked him. Kydd waited in the gloom for it all to end.

Black faces. Jolting, moving. Harsh sunlight. Kydd tried to understand. The lift and bob of a boat—he cried at the poignant motion. Luke's face, looking down, anguished. He smiled up at him and was carried on into an airy space. A woman took charge and gently but firmly removed all his clothes. A clean smell of hyssop and soap; he felt himself laid carefully on a sheet and the woman began to wash him. He couldn't resist. Modesty had no more meaning and he drifted into a febrile no-man's-land.

He woke—how much later he had no idea—in a small room, clean and well appointed. Next to his bed a woman kept up a lazy fanning, smiling at him, and on the other side Luke sat, keeled over in slumber.

"Who—er, what d' ye . . ."

"Now, sah, be still, youse in mah hands, Mr. Kydd, sah," the woman said happily. "Sis' Mary."

The talk woke Luke, who sat up, confused.

A shadow darkened the door. It was Beatrice. "Mr. Kydd?" she asked timidly.

"Aye," said Kydd, with as much strength as he could.

"Thank the Lord!" she breathed, and stood hesitantly at the foot of the bed, holding a lace handkerchief to her face. "When we heard you were sick, we never thought—er, that is to say, we were led to believe by false witnesses that your sickness . . . had other causes." Her eyes dropped. "My father thought it best that you are cared for in a private way—it is the usual thing, you know." She spoke more strongly: "Sister Mary has nursed many a soul to recovery."

"Ye need money f'r this," he said feebly.

Beatrice smiled. "Let us hear no more about that, Mr. Kydd. You are in the Lord's hands and He will provide for His faithful servants." Her fingers twisted together. "I do wish you well—it is not over yet."

But Kydd could feel the fever diminishing and elation built at his escape. He was ready to seize life again with both hands.

Sister Mary took gentle care of him, seeming to know what he needed before he could express it. She had an unvarying bright and sunny manner, not bothered by the violence of his vomiting or Kydd's shameful need for a bedpan. After each spasm she bathed his burning face, whispering comforting words he couldn't understand.

The fever faded, the vomiting grew less, and Kydd thankfully slipped into a sweet sleep. On the morrow he would be on the mend.

He woke in the darkness of the early hours, feeling strange and giddy. A sharp bout of vomiting had him leaning over the bed. He pulled back in, and felt a warm wetness exude from his nose. It stank, and he wiped at it uselessly. His hand came away dark-stained in the semidarkness.

"Mary!" he croaked fearfully. She was asleep in a blanket on the floor and didn't hear at first. Kydd called again, in his nighttime panic hoarsely shouting her name. When she came to him sleepily she saw his face, and at once trimmed the light to full illumination. She tore back the single sheet and stared at his lower body. There was no sunny banter.

Kydd looked down and saw oozing from his body orifices a slow, fetid black bleeding. He sank back. Sister Mary set to work, sponging him, insisting he sat up in bed, placing supports around him. His vomiting was shorter, sharper—but now it was discolored, black and foul. Kydd's thoughts became confused. As the morning light strengthened he saw Mary's figure distort and swell. He screamed and whimpered.

At times lucidity came, a strange calm in which he could see and hear but not respond. He heard Luke's broken, desolate weeping and a regular mumbling—it took some minutes for his mind to register that it was Beatrice at a distance, praying. Caird's tall figure in its accustomed black loomed. He spoke to Kydd slowly but the words were gibberish, as if he were saying them backward. His figure towered over Kydd, grim and foreboding, smelling of sin and death.

Deep inside, Kydd knew that he was dying, but no one had prepared him for this terror, this final process of separation from the world. It was so *unfair*—his was a young life that would live! That would fight and win! Obstinately, from deep within, he claimed the last of his strength, and in a final defiant act, he turned on that which was killing him: he struggled up, facing the whirling light patterns that were all that remained of his world, and screamed at it. Dimly aware that he had fallen out of bed, he flailed and fought, and at last stood swaying and victorious, shouting and cursing at the foul disease, challenging it, daring it to do its worst. Fire jetted into his body, and he exulted.

Images came into focus, the horrified faces of Mary, Luke, Beatrice staring at him. He laughed—strength came to him, he moved, staggered, fought. And won. His eyes clamped on the real world he would not yield up, and in a dignified motion he turned and collapsed again on the bed.

"I do declare, we feared we had lost you, Mr. Kydd," said Beatrice, dabbing her eyes.

Kydd grinned, levering himself to a better sitting position. "D'ye get me another o' the lime cordials, I'd be grateful." The fever broken, he was going to live—and with a bonus: having survived the yellow fever at its most virulent, with no lasting ill-effects, he now had lifelong immunity from its terrors.

He looked across at Sister Mary, quietly getting on with her work, and felt a warmth toward her that surprised him with its intensity. Her homely face was inexpressibly dear to him now. "Has Luke been doin' his words?" he asked, in mock-rough tones.

"Indeed he has," Beatrice answered primly. "I have set him some improving verses, which he promises to complete for you this very night." Her eyes softened. "And . . . welcome back, Thomas," she said tenderly.

Weakness forced Kydd back into the pillow, but he was content. In a week or two he would be back in the world he knew.

"*Lignum vitae*—the hardest wood we know," said Caird, stroking the piece of smooth, olive-green timber. "You will see it as the sheave in every block aboard your ship and it grows right here in Antigua. There are some trees of that sort that we will see on our next Sunday mission," he added, matter-of-factly.

The rain slackened its furious assault, but did not stop altogether, the steamy smell of vegetation heavy on the air. They would wait a little longer in the boathouse before going out to the new-captured French cutter. "You might remark this heavy wood—it is from the mastwood tree, the one with the yellow flowers that the honeybee favors so. And there, the large pieces in the corner, the Anteegans term it 'Black Gregory' and we use it much for its endurance; the guns at the fort have their carriages wrought from its strength."

Kydd nodded, his thoughts far from indigenous trees. His recent experience had thrown his perceptions of life and his place in it into a spin, and he longed hopelessly for Renzi to apply his logic to it all.

"Beatrice tells me you are progressing admirably with your servant's learning," Caird said.

"Aye, the younker does try, that I'll grant," said Kydd.

"I'd be obliged if you'd consider another matter," Caird said, looking at him candidly.

"Sir?"

"In the matter of my stores. Peculation in a dockyard is an insidious evil, consuming its vitals, rendering the thief insensible to sin." He paused, eyeing Kydd speculatively. "I would be most grateful if you could do me a service that strikes at the heart of this abomination." He went on, "Take this key. It is to the stores office in the boathouse. Be so good as to enter it discreetly after work ceases and make a true copy of the day's proceedings. This will be compared to the one rendered to me directly."

Kydd understood: this way it would be easy to detect where and how defalcations occurred in the dockyard. "Yes, Mr. Caird," he replied, pocketing the heavy key.

It was a simple matter, just a couple of pages of short-form notes and figures. Kydd laid down the quill. Stretching, he gathered up the papers and stepped into the early evening. Crickets started up, and from somewhere on a nearby tree came the complacent *wheek-wheek* of a tree frog.

As he turned onto the road to his lodging, he glanced up. A fine sunset was building, but as usual it was obscured by the close-in scrubby ridge overlooking the dockyard. Then something seized him. This time, he swore, he would take his fill of the sight. Scrabbling at the crumbling rocks he clambered through the bushes to the top of the ridge. There, the full beauty of the sunset was in view, only distant islands to include in the broad, breathtaking panorama of sea and sky.

A scattering of low clouds hung far away about the setting sun, tinged by the yellow gilding that radiated out. Kydd found a flat rock and sat to watch. The sun sank lower, the clouds progressed slowly from yellow to orange, and began to stretch in delicate tendrils half across the sky, the dying day converging on the central spectacle.

It held Kydd in a trance, the stark beauty entering his soul. An upwelling of emotion took hold, lifting his spirit to soar free above the world. He had made a journey from death to life: he would not waste his existence on vain striving or useless repine. The surge of feeling brought a lump to his throat, but no focus or resolution. It left him ardent but confused. When the smoky violet dusk had settled and the horizon had assumed a hard blue-black line, he got up and stumbled back down the ridge.

The usual evening sights and sounds of Antigua dockyard met him, happy bedlam around the capstan house. It was *Terrier* sloop this time, after a successful cruise to San Domingo. Rather more genteel sounds of revelry came from the brightly lit officers' quarters ahead, from some sort of assembly in honor of the new major of Fort Berkeley. But to Kydd's intensified senses it was the loveliness of the scene that impacted the most. Lantern light was not merely a dim flame, it was a wash of tawny gold; the darkness was not evening, it was a warm electric sensuousness. The dark shapes of vessels at anchor had tiny golden stars of light about them. This faraway land's dark-blue presence hinted at mystery—life and vitality tugged at him mercilessly.

A swell of hilarity came from the capstan house. Its open warmth held a strong appeal to Kydd, the warmheartedness of company, of human interaction, and he felt a sudden, urgent need. Abruptly, he turned on his heel and hurried toward the boisterous gathering. Curious glances came his way at first, but the sailors quickly resumed their companionable roistering.

Kydd stood irresolute, doubts nagging at him, but they were swamped by one overriding thought: if he could not freely taste the delights of life, then what was life for? "What cheer, mateys!" he said loudly. "Do ye have a glass as will allow me t' hob-a-nob with th' *Terrier*s?"

It was punch from a cauldron, a swirling mix of rum, pineapple and coconut. It slipped down easily, and as he had been unable to take strong drink for some time, it went speedily to his head. He looked round, savoring the energy, the vitality around him: this was what it was to seize life! Yet as the rum took hold he felt somehow unfulfilled, aimless, restless.

"How do, Master Keed!" There was no mistaking the low purr. The woman fingered the polished dark bean she wore around her neck. It lay against the twin swell of her dark breasts, and a predatory gleam showed briefly in her eyes.

"Sukey," Kydd said, feeling the impact of the lazy swing of her hips as she moved toward him. She came very close and her feminine odor invaded his senses as she slowly reached out, letting her hand slide down his arm to the tankard, which she silently detached from his grip with a teasing smile.

The color, light and noise around him fell away as the center of his vision was filled with one thing: a focus at last for the burning thoughts that took his reason.

She half turned. "Doan like th' loft." She pouted. "Too many noise—yo have a lodgin' house or somewheres?"

Kydd's blood roared. "Yes!" he said thickly. His drab rooms would now know something other than solitude. But then he remembered: Luke would be there, manfully at work with his quill and ink, loyally transcribing his improving words. Frustration built into a sweet but driving pain. There was no place in Antigua that offered the privacy he knew he needed to cover his deed. Sukey let her eyes drop and teased at his shirt.

Suddenly a thought exploded. "Come on!" Kydd mouthed, pulling her away. She feigned reluctance, but her smile widened and they ran along the coral quay, past the deserted seamen's galley, the silent, two-story canvas and cordage store, the low joiner's loft. The boathouse was still and somnolent. Kydd found the door to the office and fumbled for his key. Sukey snuggled up behind him, her hands sliding over his body, confident and direct in their purpose. The door creaked open into black stillness, and he jerked her inside. Just remembering to lock it he smiled savagely: they could be sure of their privacy now.

In the dusky light Sukey came to him, but when his responses grew fevered, impassioned, she pushed him away, avoiding his hands. He growled and she pouted, then began undoing his shirt, somehow contriving at the same time to lose her own red shift. Suddenly they were both naked. Their bodies slammed together. Giggling, Sukey pulled him to the floor, taunting him, guiding him. His smile turned to a snarl, his hands dug into her shoulders. Suddenly she froze, her eyes wide open staring at the door. Panting, Kydd stopped, baffled.

The lock turned, and into the office stepped an indistinct figure with a lanthorn. The room was filled with pitiless light that fell on their locked bodies. There was a sharp intake of breath, and the light trembled. "Kydd!" came an outraged shout. It was Caird.

Sukey pushed Kydd off her, frightened and quaking, and scrabbled for her clothes, which she held against her nakedness. Kydd didn't know where to turn in the sickening wash of shame and horror.

With a terrible intensity, Caird bit off his words: "May the Good Lord have mercy on your soul, sir—for I shall not!"

Kydd returned to his lodging, dreading the dawn. Luke retreated, shocked at his expression.

The next day was every bit as bad as he had feared. Caird was controlled, but it was with a cold ferocity that tore at Kydd's pride, his manhood, leaving him shaking and in no doubt of his worthlessness. He was told that his employment as a master was over in Antigua and, as of that moment, he was no longer required in the dockyard.

"And for your damnable depravity," Caird concluded, "your indulgence in lust to the hazard of your immortal soul, sir, I will see to it you go from this island. You shall depart on the first

King's ship that chances by!" Pausing only to draw breath he stood and said, "By some wicked means you have ensnared my daughter's affections. She is at this time undone in her sensibilities. You are a desperately wicked rascal, and will very soon come to the sordid end you deserve! Go, sir! Get you out of my sight! *Go!*"

CHAPTER 8

—⁓⁓⁓—

The day Kydd and Renzi were parted had been a bleak one for Renzi.

The brig gathered way, making for the open sea in the bright morning. Renzi looked back from the tiny foretop. He could just make out the red coats of the marines in the panic ashore, and knew that Kydd must be there too, watching the vessel sail away, leaving him to his fate.

On the crowded deck, moans and shrieks arose from the French passengers at the realization that they were on their way to safety but that their friends and relations ashore would probably soon suffer a cruel death. Only Louise Vernou stood quietly, staring at the shore, frozen in pity. She held an object to her lips: Renzi saw that it was the anchor-embossed button Kydd had given her, around her neck on a thin cord.

If Kydd could escape from the clutches of the mindless rabble and keep the marines with him, he had a chance, but the situation was critical. Despite his cool self-possession, Renzi felt his throat tighten. They had seen so much together. It was characteristic of war, the arbitrary nature of its demands of blood and grief, but he realized that he was not as detached from the world as he had thought.

Jowett, the master's mate in command, stumped over and told him brusquely, "Tell th' Frenchie bastards to go below, t' the hold!"

Renzi cajoled and threatened them, and eventually had them crammed into it. The main hatch was left open to give them sight of the sky.

Square sail was set and the brig settled to a workmanlike beat to round the southern end of Guadeloupe. "We c'n make Antigua in a day—wi' this lot we cannot fetch Barbadoes without we find water 'n' vittles," Jowett said. "We sets course f'r Saint John's."

There was a dockyard in Antigua, Renzi recollected, and it was well fortified. St. John's was around the coast to the north, but had the main naval presence, the Admiral commanding the Leeward Islands station and all the facilities for taking their cargo of newly homeless. Later, no doubt, they would go on to the dockyard. All they had to do was cross the short distance to the island without encountering any of the French invasion fleet.

Some hours later they had rounded the southern tip of Basse Terre and, well snugged in on the starboard tack, they began to slip their way north, past the now hostile anonymous green-splotched coast. The distracted babble died away as the brig met the busy waves of the open sea, responding with a lively roll that had the passengers in the hold huddling down. A canvas awning was spread over the hatch against the frequent spray but there was no protest from below.

By the afternoon they had reached the northern coast of Guadeloupe and began to stretch out over the sea to the bulk of Antigua ahead. Jowett's face set to the northeast, toward the buildup of cloud massing there. He sniffed the wind distrustfully. "I mislike bolderin' weather this time o' the year, this bein' the season f'r hurricanoes an' all." They would have no chance if it came to anything like a gale: merchantmen were always looking to shave corners with the cost of gear.

"Sail *hoooo!*" The lookout in this small vessel was only forty feet up, and his sudden bellow made Renzi start. He followed the outstretched arm and saw a fore-and-aft rigged craft emerging from a kink in the northern coastline, not large but dismayingly warlike. A second vessel appeared and the pair set course to intercept.

"Armed schooners!" muttered Jowett.

"Privateers, an' we ain't got a chance!" a seaman added. In the absence of the bulk of the fleet at San Domingo the French privateers were basing themselves back in Guadeloupe, issuing out to fall on any passing prey. Like corsairs, they were savage and murderous.

"Don' vex 'em more'n we need, Mr. Jowett," an older seaman advised, staring at the two schooners leaning to their hard drawing sails. "We ain't got powder fer our guns, nor a full suit o' sails, so we'll never outrun 'em. Why don't we strike our colors now?"

Jowett's jaw set. "No—we got a chance. If they sees us in Antego, we get help. Hold y' course!" The island was drawing nearer and hardening in definition. Renzi scanned the south coast for any indication that they had been seen and a ship was putting to sea in their aid.

Halfway across, it became obvious that the Frenchmen would come up with them well before they could make Antigua. The white swash at their bows sparkled in the sun, their sails hard and boardlike. They were now close enough to show the sight of their crew, clustered around their fore-part.

The flat crack of a gun followed the sudden appearance of a puff of gunsmoke: the leading schooner was making its intentions known. Renzi swept his gaze over the approaching coast. Even if they were sighted now, help could not arrive before the privateers had done their worst. A half-smile appeared on his face. Logic ruled that he would be either dead or captured within two hours. He folded his arms and awaited events.

Then Renzi saw the leading schooner suddenly surge around, head to wind. Her sails shook until the vessel paid off on the other tack—going before the wind away from them! Shaking his head in disbelief, he looked about, searching for a reason for the sudden retreat: perhaps the headsails of a ship-of-the-line appearing around a headland, a vengeful frigate from the south. Nothing. The other schooner followed suit and, under the incredulous gaze of the brig's crew, the privateers were seen making for Guadeloupe and their lair.

Excited, the sailors jabbered away, looking for an explanation for their deliverance.

Jowett seemed not to share their jubilation. "'Cos they seen that," he said. His arm pointed toward the northeast. The cloud banks had extended across the sky and darkened. "It's a reg'lar goin' hurricanoe, that's what yer sees."

"We bears up fer English Harbour," said the helmsman.

"Nah, we bin holdin' course fer Saint John's an' we c'n never beat back to the east'd in time."

"If we makes it ter Antego west about, we'll be in the lee o' the storm."

Jowett growled. "Shut yer jabber—we goes t' Saint John's."

The brig was battened down tight; it was hard on the unfortunates in the airless hold and if they foundered or struck on the rocks their end would not be pleasant. Renzi cringed as he gave Louise his assurances and asked her to calm her compatriots. She did this without question, quietly accepting imprisonment in the claustrophobic darkness.

They kept well clear of the breakers to the southwest of Antigua but by the time the rock-studded danger of Five Isles was abeam, the brig was bucketing and rolling in ugly seas. "Only a league or so," yelled Jowett, to the men on the yard. They had come up with the little islet of Sandy Island off St. John's and were now within a few miles of safety—but that now seemed impossible, for it lay in the teeth of the fresh gale, hourly increasing in strength.

Seamen gathered on deck. The distant sight of the town, no more than five miles ahead, taunted and beckoned. The little brig strained to her uttermost close-hauled, but could not lie close enough to the wind to fetch harbor.

A fizz, then a sudden gout of choking smoke, and a rocket soared up into the gray evening sky to explode high above. Jowett was trying to get a larger vessel to come to their aid, but it was unlikely that any would risk putting to sea under the threat of a hurricane. It was stalemate: on this point of sailing they could only reach the rocky coast to the south where, without charts or local knowledge, they were sure to be wrecked. Or they could run with the gale, but that was no alternative for the hurricane would grow and overwhelm them. It was only a matter of time.

"Wind's backin'!" screamed a seaman, as the wind shifted into the north and with it came a chance. It would need acute judgment, but at the right moment it would be possible to go about then run down to St. John's. It was a desperate matter, for they would be close up against the coast on one side and the battering storm on the other.

Renzi watched Jowett: the thirty lives aboard were in his hands. Jowett stood facing directly into the streaming wind, his nose unconsciously lifting in little sniffs as he judged its mood. "Ready about," he snapped. The brig seemed to stumble as her bow came up into the wind. Renzi willed the plain little vessel to go through stays without complaint, which she did, and they lay over on the larboard tack, every minute gathering speed in the blasting gale.

Explosions of white heaved skyward from the seas pounding the rocks under their lee. The clouds massing took on an ugly cast, but St. John's grew ever nearer. Soon they encountered the breaking seas over the bar at the harbor entrance and, once inside the headland of Hamilton's fort, the waves lost their viciousness. Weary and weatherbeaten they headed directly for St. John's town.

Renzi survived the storm in the company of Louise and the French in a stone warehouse. Worn out and emotionally drained, he snatched what sleep he could with the insane howling of the storm outside. In the morning he looked outside, in the gusting winds and rain of the dying hurricane, and saw their brig miraculously still alongside the wharf, snubbing and rearing like a spirited horse, but safe.

The time of trial had left Renzi strangely depressed: the lunacy of war was *au fond* the outworking of the crass irrationality that lay in the heart of Unenlightened Man, but he knew that what lay on him was more personal. At least Kydd would not meet the hurricane at sea: he was safe ashore, but in what circumstances? His helplessness in the face of the situation was probably the true reason for his dejection, Renzi realized. Moody and hungry, he awaited events.

Rather later a busy little man arrived from the civil administration to relieve him of his charges. He left Louise with no false hopes for Kydd, and when the good-byes were said, French fashion, he saw the sparkle of tears in her eyes.

The brig was uncomfortable to work in, her movement brisk and jerky, but it would not need much to make her ready for the short voyage south again to the naval dockyard at English Harbour.

In the afternoon, Renzi begged leave and went into town, seeking a bookshop, the well of contentment that might restore his balance. Three hours later he returned, spirits restored, his bag stuffed with gold—another Goethe, for "Prometheus" had awakened in him a grudging respect for the man; a secondhand Raynal, the *Histoire des deux Indes,* which had probably been the property of a

French royalist; and an interesting new work by the Plutarchian Robertson on "conjectural history."

And, most important, a glorious find, newspapers from England a bare six weeks old. He exulted as he tramped back to the brig; this was what it was to be alive! At the gangway a cross-looking lieutenant was waiting. Jowett called down from the deck of the brig and the officer rounded on him. "Are you Renzi?" he huffed.

"I am, sir."

"Parley-vous le fronsay vraymont?"

Astonished, Renzi could only stare.

"Answer, then, if indeed you have the French!"

"Mais bien sûr—qu'est-ce que ça vous fait?"

The lieutenant smiled in satisfaction. "That will do. Follow me."

Without thinking, Renzi fell into step beside the man, but was swiftly told, "Fall in astern, if you please." The officer's look of disdain caused Renzi nothing but secret amusement. A short walk took them to an imposing stone building: a blue ensign and marine sentry at the door proclaimed it a naval establishment. The marine slapped his musket to the present as the officer entered, then winked at Renzi.

The lieutenant paused. "Play your cards right, my man, and your days as a foremast hand may well be at an end." Mystified, Renzi followed him down the passageway. They stopped at a door; the lieutenant knocked and leaned inside. "The man Renzi, sir," he said.

"Send 'im in!" roared the unseen personage within.

"Rear Admiral Edgcumbe," said the lieutenant softly, and ushered Renzi in.

The Admiral sat behind a massive dark-polished desk, his expression more curious than fierce. "So you has the French, an' a manner to go with it, I'm told," he mused, looking keenly at Renzi.

He slid across a piece of paper and quill. "Write 'Render to me your return affecting stores that are rotten.'"

Renzi complied, his hand flying across the page, sure and fluent.

"Damme, that's a splendid hand for a sailor," grunted the Admiral, and looked up sharply. "Are ye a forger?"

"Er, no, sir."

"Pity. First class with a pen, y' forger." His head snapped up. "What's the county town o' Wiltshire?"

"Sarum—which is Salisbury," said Renzi immediately. It was a little too close for comfort: his family were prominent in the next county and he had reason to remember the spires of old Salisbury.

Admiral Edgcumbe smiled. "Ah, quick an' sharp with it," he said, with satisfaction, and leaned back in his chair.

"Flags!" he roared.

The lieutenant instantly poked his head inside the room. "This one'll do. Get 'im in a decent rig an' on the staff."

"Aye aye, sir."

"See he doesn't run, an' have him aboard the packet in good time." He bent his head again to his work, thus dismissing both men.

By the evening it had become clear what was going on. The Admiral was newly promoted commander-in-chief designate to the Jamaica station and was due to sail shortly with his staff to take up the appointment. He had been unlucky in the matter of fever— it was damnably difficult to find good replacement staff at short notice—and word about Renzi had reached him just in time. Renzi would be a writer, a form of clerk entrusted only with duplication of orders and unimportant matters, but would prove useful with his good knowledge of the language of the enemy. The lieutenant clearly felt that Renzi had been plucked from an existence as a sea menial to a prestigious position with real prospects, and should be grateful.

For himself, Renzi felt a lurch of premonition at the mention of Jamaica, but perhaps in the naval headquarters there would be no exposure and therefore little risk of confrontation. A new life of petty politics at headquarters was not to his liking, for he had deliberately chosen the sea life as the purest form of exile.

Next day the packet swarmed with the Admiral's retinue. Renzi, as a seaman, knew precisely where to keep out of the way and watched with wry amusement the fluster and confusion as the pretty little topsail cutter put to sea. A small frigate accompanied them as escort, the pair foaming along in the freshness after the hurricane, heading westward deep into the glittering blue of the Caribbean Sea.

The island of Jamaica was raised five days later without incident, an impressive blue-gray monolith appearing out of the morning on the distant horizon. They had passed St. Kitts during the night and Hispaniola was a disappointing low scrubby headland, approaching then receding as, with the favorable northeasterlies, they headed direct for the southern coast of Jamaica.

Off Morant Bay they hove to, a pilot schooner plunging and rolling as she sent across the Kingston pilot, and in turn took aboard the Admiral's flag lieutenant. They would remain there for the night while warning of the arrival of their august passenger reached the capital overland.

It had been a pleasant, if crowded, passage; the tedium of a sea voyage without duties brought Renzi an unexpected pang of sympathy for the passengers he had previously scorned. More immediately useful was the information he had gleaned from casual talking with the Admiral's staff. In the West Indies there was wealth, more millions than he had ever suspected, a river of silver and gold heading back to England from trade and its support, but above all from sugar. The plantation society, the plantocracy, had high political significance in London and lived like lords, if the tales of high living were to be believed, but with the great wealth there was another of corrupt and unscrupulous conspirators who infested every class.

He had met the First Clerk, Mr. Jacobs, a dry but astute man who weighed and measured each word before it was uttered. From Jacobs he learned that they would be going not to the capital, Kingston, but farther inland to Spanish Town, the administrative center of Jamaica, and would be involved primarily in the necessary dealings of the Navy with the civil administration. It was not a prospect that pleased Renzi.

Morning saw the two ships proceeding sedately westward to the entrance of Kingston harbor. On the sheltered inner side of a low encircling spit of land miles long was the Jamaica station of the Royal Navy: a mighty 74-gun ship-of-the-line, four frigates, sloops of war, and countless brigs and schooners.

The Admiral had transferred to the frigate during the night in order to make his arrival with all appropriate ceremony, and in the light airs of the morning, clouds of smoke eddied about the anchored 74 as her salute crashed out at the sight of the frigate's bunting.

The packet followed humbly in the wake of the frigate, but when the bigger ship went to meet her brethren, it passed across the bay to bring up noisily into the wind opposite a wharf at the end of a street in Kingston town. A heaving line sailed across and they were pulled alongside.

The hot, sandy streets were alive: drays filled with the trade goods of two continents, merchants concluding deals in the broad piazzas, processions of traders with their slaves following behind. The cheery green and white of the houses was complemented by the gardens, which differed wildly from the calm neatness of English cultivation: here there were fruit trees, coconuts, tall palms and a riot of color from vines.

There was little time for Renzi to stand and stare. Mr. Jacobs was clearly discontented with the arrangements for transport. The ketureens—the ubiquitous Jamaican gig sporting a gay raised sun-roof on rods—offered insufficient security against possible rain for the two chests of correspondence. When this had been settled with dozens of Negroes walking beside and an overseer riding ahead to clear the way of wagons and carts, they set out on the flat road to Spanish Town. After passing a great lagoon with vast reed beds, they stopped at the Ferry Inn to refresh and change horses before the final run to the old town.

"It is of an age, I believe," Renzi said to Jacobs, as they wound along among the outer streets of Spanish Town.

"It is. Founded by Christopher Columbus, and settled by the Dons. Captured by us in 1655."

Renzi would have to be content with that bare information, but his mind expanded upon it: two centuries of Spanish indolence and fixed ways, eventless years that were in stark contrast to the tumults in Europe. Then the English had flooded in, upsetting the staid times with their thrusting, mercantile rudeness, turning the old, comfortable social certainties on their head.

The procession ground into a large square with imposing build-ings that would not have been out of place in far Castile. One notable exception was a distinguished white marble edifice set between the two largest structures. They disembarked in its shadow and, to his surprise, Renzi saw that it was a splendid colonnaded statue of an undeniable sea flavor—cannons, rope and the sterns of fleeing enemy ships.

"Rodney," explained Jacobs.

Of course. Renzi remembered. Admiral Rodney had fought the French de Grasse to a smashing defeat in a great fleet action some ten years earlier off Guadeloupe; as a result, Jamaica had been saved from French colonization.

He looked around the square: it had a slightly offended air, as of an older gentleman put out by a younger man not fully recogniz-ing his dignity. But the cool, ocher-painted stone of the govern-ment offices was real enough. There he would see out his working life for the immediate future. These were his prospects. He could envisage only a dreary vista of daily sameness in the months ahead.

The work was easy enough: the endless round of returns, reports, minutiae of the fleet, now lying at anchor. It had to be victualed, clothed, repaired, administered. As Renzi dealt with his tiny part of the steady stream, he grew increasingly respectful of the scale of the operation: tens of thousands of men, the fleet as big as a county town, a moving town that might be anywhere, yet needing the same flow of all manner of goods.

In the main Renzi was left to himself. He often caught flashes of suspicion from Jacobs, but realized that these were because of his reserved, indeed secretive, nature. His, however, was a circumstance of endurance, of serving a sentence, and he had no care of what his interim fellows supposed. His thoughts strayed to Kydd. By now he would probably be a lonely corpse in up-country Guadeloupe, or a prisoner-of-war in a French vessel on his way to incarceration, anything. In the absence of any knowledge, logic was useless, and in sadness he forced his mind to other things.

The Admiral did not live in Spanish Town: his mansion was out of town in the cooler hills north of Kingston, and after several weeks Renzi was summoned there.

Admiral Edgcumbe received him at his desk, leaving him standing respectfully. "What do ye think o' that!" he said, thrusting a newspaper at him and jabbing a blunt finger at the top of one column. It was a copy of the *Moniteur* from Paris, not three months old, and the article about the unstable, now executed Robespierre was interesting and significant. Renzi hesitated—what was he being asked to do? Had the Admiral sent for him merely to ask his opinion on a newspaper article?

"By this, sir, I believe we find that the Thermidor coup has established itself. Robespierre overstepped himself, the Committee felt threatened, combined to overthrow him, execute him, and then—"

"Belay all that, what does it mean?"

Renzi resumed carefully, "It means that the Terror in Paris is spent. The revolution is now controlled." He paused, the Admiral's intense eyes on his. "It would be reasonable to suppose that their attention is no longer distracted by the fratricide, that they are now able to turn their attention outward to the larger considerations of the war, perhaps even—"

"Enough." The Admiral sat back with a loud grunt. "And now be so good as to tell me who in Hades you are, sir."

A fleeting smile forced its way on to Renzi's face. "May I sit, sir?"

"You may." The flinty eyes did not spare him.

Deliberately, Renzi relaxed. He crossed his legs and clasped them over the knee, languid and confident, a London beau *manqué*. "You may believe I am a gentleman," he said, in tones he had last used in the company of the Duke of Norfolk. The Admiral said nothing, but his gaze did not alter. "And you may also know that I have done nothing of which I need be ashamed—you have my sacred word on that."

There was a "Humph."

"My beliefs include a devotion to the Rationalist cause, I do not care for the comforts of the old thinking." He straightened and fixed the Admiral with a level gaze. "Sir, if I am to say more, I must ask for your word, as a gentleman, that this will go no further than yourself." He held his breath. This was, on the face of it, a preposterous impertinence from a lowly clerk to a blue-blood admiral.

"You have it."

Renzi gathered his wits. The only course was to tell the truth: any less would be detected instantly. "Sir, my philosophies compel me to satisfy their moral demands in a way that others might consider—eccentric. I find them sufficiently logical and consistent. Therefore, when faced with a matter bearing on my personal moral worth I must answer for myself.

"My father procured an Act of Enclosure—seizing the common lands that had been tilled for centuries; there was grief and suicide occasioned by it. For the sake of my conscience, sir, I am undertaking an act of expiation. I sentenced myself to five years' exile, not to a foreign shore, but to the lower deck of a man-o'-war."

At first it seemed there would be no response. Then the Admiral's quarterdeck expression eased, and a glimmer of a smile appeared. "A glass of Madeira," he growled, and reached for the decanter. Renzi accepted thankfully.

The Admiral looked at him speculatively. He felt for a key and unlocked a drawer, extracting a closely written piece of paper. "Cast y' eyes over this," he said.

Renzi took it and scanned quickly. "This is a letter, from a Monsieur Neuf. It is to his son, I think."

The Admiral nodded. "Just so. We took it fr'm a brig that thought it was going to France." He smiled thinly. "And now it is not. What I am exercised with is just how to spread half a dozen ships o' force over a thousand miles of sea."

Renzi met his ferocious stare equably—but his heart sank. He could see now where it was all leading, and wanted no part of it. "Sir, I am a perfect stranger to dissimulation, deceit and the other necessary qualities to make a spy, and must decline in advance any such service."

The Admiral's eyebrows shot up. "What do you mean, sir? I wish you merely to exercise your intellects in the reading of any chance material bearing on intelligence the fates throw our way— see if you can sight any clue, any unguarded slip o' the pen, you know what I mean. That is, if y' morals will allow of it."

Renzi found himself quickly removed from the vast hall filled with laboring quill-drivers and sharing an upper-floor room with two others. To his satisfaction, they were uncommunicative and self-absorbed, and he found he could work on without interruption.

Each morning, a locked box would be opened in their presence and each would receive a pack of papers of varying size. On most days Renzi received nothing and then he would assist one of the others. Occasionally the Admiral would call for him, and he would find himself reading a letter, pamphlet or set of orders—there was a pleasing sense of discretion in the proceedings that considerably eased his mind at the odious act of violating the privacy of another.

It was a strange, floating and impermanent existence; and above it all hung the knowledge that at any time he could be brought into confrontation with his past, to mutual embarrassment. When it happened, there was not a thing he could do.

"Renzi, blue office, if y' please." This was where petitions from the populace were initially heard. He was generally included where matters touching the Navy were involved, taking notes in the background and making himself available if explication were needed. He sat at his little table to one side, readying his paper and ink, leaving the bigger desk to Jacobs.

"Mr. Laughton," called the usher from the door.

Renzi froze.

The man came striding in, looking past the lowly Renzi to Jacobs, who assumed an oily smile.

"Another loss!" Laughton snapped. "This is insupportable, sir!"

"Sir, you will recollect that the Navy is much committed in the Leeward Islands—"

"Damn your cant! Without trade this island is worthless, and with these losses you will soon have none."

Renzi kept his head well down, and scratched away busily, taking his "notes." The talk ebbed and flowed inconclusively, Jacobs stonewalling skillfully. Laughton snorted in frustration and rose suddenly. "So, that is all you have to say, sir?" He turned and stormed out without a glance at Renzi, who sat back in relief.

A few seconds later the door flew open again, and Laughton's voice sounded behind him. "Be so good as to direct me to the Revenue Office," he said in a hard tone.

"Mr. Renzi," Jacobs asked mildly.

There was now no further chance of evasion. For the space of a heartbeat or two Renzi stared down at his paper, savoring the last moments of an uncomplicated life. "This way, sir," he said softly, holding his head down to the last moment.

Laughton gave way at the door, and then, as Renzi quickly closed it behind him, his eyes widened. "Nicholas!" he gasped.

Renzi looked up. His younger brother had not changed over-much in the years since he had last seen him, a broadening of the shoulders, an unfashionable sun-darkened complexion, the confidence.

"We—we thought you had . . ." Laughton spluttered.

"Richard, be so good as to walk with me a space," Renzi said, hastening along the wide veranda to the steps that led to the gardens at the back of the building.

"Nicholas, are you in distress of money?" Laughton asked, when they were out of possible earshot on the grass.

"Dear brother, no, I am not." It were better the whole story be told rather than allow wild surmise. "If we could talk at length, without interruption—but you perceive, at the moment . . ."

Laughton glanced quickly at Renzi and gripped his arm. "In Spanish Town I have a certain . . . weight. You shall have your talk. Come!"

They returned to Jacobs. Laughton strode forward. "Sir, I find this, er, Renzi has a certain felicity in explaining the naval situation to me. I beg leave to claim his services for a few days to assist me to formulate a position. Is this possible, sir?"

Jacobs seemed taken aback: a new clerk of such accomplishment that both the Admiral and the influential Richard Laughton were laying claim to his services clearly indicated that it might be in his best interests. . . . "By all means, sir," he stuttered.

Laughton gave a polite inclination of his head and gestured to Renzi. "This way, sir, if you please."

*   *   *

The gig ground on over the bright sandy road with Laughton himself at the reins, past endless bright green cane-fields and black people on foot. Windmills and tropical dun-colored buildings were the only disruptions to the monochrome green.

"For the nonce, dear brother, I would ask that you do not claim me as kin—I will explain in due course," Renzi said, a little too lightly.

Richard glanced at him and nodded. "If that is your wish, Nicholas," he said neutrally, bringing the gig dextrously to the side of the road. They sat patiently as an ox train heavily laden with barrels of crude sugar for the coast approached in a dusty cloud, the yells and shrill whistles of the wagoners piercing the thunder of many wheels as they ground past. The overseer raised his whip respectfully in salute to Laughton; the handle was like a fishing rod and the rawhide tail all of seventy feet long.

They resumed their journey, turning up a neat road lined with what looked like gigantic pineapples, blue, red and white con-volvulus blooms entwined among them. "Penguin hedge," Laughton said, and when the road straightened to a line leading to a sprawling stately homestead, he added, "and this is the Great House."

They approached between immaculate lawns, and Renzi saw the scale of the place, grand and dignified. A bare-legged ostler took the reins as they descended from the gig. Stone steps and an iron balustrade led to a broad veranda and the front doors.

"Do ye wait for me a short time, Nicholas, and I shall show you the estate," Laughton said, taking the steps two at a time. He pointed to a cane easy chair as he strode inside, which Renzi politely accepted. Shortly afterward Laughton emerged, now in a blue square-cut coatee and Hessian boots, and wearing a broad-brimmed straw hat. They mounted the gig again and ground off.

"Over nine hundred acres, an' four hundred to work it, quite sizeable—all sugar," Laughton opened, with just a hint of pride. They passed a gang of field-workers trudging out to the cane-pieces: men, women, children. At Renzi's look he added, "Each has his task, even the pickaninny—follows on behind and weeds the fields. Teaches 'em responsibility."

Reaching a cluster of outhouses, Renzi heard a loud rumble and creaking. Around the corner he saw the open, straw-covered busyness of a sugar mill. The rotating rollers were fed with cane stalks in a crashing, splintering chorus; the mill workers did not raise their eyes from feeding the cane into the maw of the rollers. A large axe with a glinting blade was hung on the mill frame. Laughton observed dryly, "Better a limb severed than being dragged into . . ."

It was a complex operation, a sugar estate, and Renzi's concentration wilted under a barrage of details: slaves gained skills ranging from field-worker to muleteer, sawyer, driver, and varied in origin from "saltwater slave" from Africa to infant born on the estate.

The heat of the afternoon suggested they should return to the Great House, and they sank thankfully into the cane chairs on the veranda. Laughton heaved up his boots to rest them on the rail, and clapped his hands. "Sangaree," he ordered of the white-coated houseman.

The breeze of the trade-winds was deliciously cool and Renzi relaxed. "You have done well for yourself, dear Richard," he said, looking at the rolling lands reaching to the horizon.

"Thank you, Nicholas. It was Father gave me my step, as you know," Laughton replied. He accepted his glass of sangaree, and glanced carefully at Renzi before he sipped the rosy liquid in wary silence. "The letter from home was scarce in details, brother," he began softly. "Said you had—disappeared after an argument with Papa."

That was paraphrasing truth indeed: the bull-headed obstinacy of Renzi's father to acknowledge any culpability in the ruination of ten families and the anguished suicide of the young hope of one was a direct contribution to his decision to take upon himself the moral obloquy of his family's act. "Indeed so—but in truth, this is only the outworking of a decision I made. . . ." He found it easier than he had feared: Richard was from the same mold as himself, strong-minded, obedient to logic, and sympathetic to firm resolve based on moral principles.

Renzi finally ended; it had been said.

His brother did not respond at first. Then he stood up, looking away, out over the estate. He turned, fixed Renzi with an intense look, and smiled. "You were always one to show the rest of the world its duty," he held out both hands, "and I honor you for it."

Another glass of sangaree was necessary before conversation could resume.

Laughton's warm smile returned. "Your name, if you will forgive the impertinence?"

"Renzi? Why, nothing but an impenetrably obscure Italian of another age. He was unfashionable enough to value riches of the mind above that of the world, and I . . . have grown used to it." He reached for the jug of sangaree and splashed more into his glass.

"My dear fellow! But you have been a sailor on the bounding main all this time! You must have a tale to tell—or should that be a yarn?"

"It has been a life of some, er, variety," agreed Renzi.

"But the conditions! You were a common sailor and—"

"And still am, Brother."

A slight frown settled on Laughton's brow. "Just so. Then how could you bear the incarceration and daily hazard? Pray tell—I'm interested."

Renzi smiled at Laughton's attempt to relate to his endurance. "I bring to your recollection, brother, that this is the serving of a period of exile, and tolerability is not at question." He paused, then stretched in his chair. "However, I may tell you I have had adventures ashore and afloat around the world that will keep me warm in memories forever. But, you will ask, what of the company, the common seaman, the brute beast of the field?"

Renzi faced his brother. "And I will answer truthfully that those who have not experienced the especial fellowship of the sea, the profound and never articulated feeling of man for his fellow, out there on the yardarm, at the cannon's mouth, deep in the ocean's realm, can not know both mankind in all its imperfection yet heroism." He gazed into the distance. "There is time at sea to ease the mind, to contemplate infinite truths and consider in their intimate detail philosophies and axioms to complete satisfaction."

"You do not weary of the quality of your company?"

"At times I—but I keep myself impervious, there are ways to remain apart," Renzi said slowly, "and I have a particular friend . . ." He trailed off, for with a rush came a vision of Kydd's face— strong and uncomplicated—which held both intelligence and humor. He continued huskily, ". . . but I regret he has met with— he is probably dead," he finished suddenly.

"I do sincerely mourn with you," said Laughton softly. He busied himself with his glass and said, "It would be an honor, brother, if you could sit at table with us tonight. We generally meet on this night, not in the formal way you understand, but to talk together, perhaps a cigar or pipe while we settle the business of the world." His eyes flicked over Renzi's odd clerkly garb. "And there is probably a stitch somewhere I could give you, should you feel the need to appear, er, inconspicuous," he said lightly.

The cool night airs, which breezed freely through the double doors and on through the large airy rooms of the house, were agreeable to the guests as they sat down in the richly polished dining room.

"Gilbert, might I present Mr. Renzi, an *acquaintance* of mine from England? Nicholas, this is Gilbert Marston. He is owner of the estate that borders mine to the west."

Renzi inclined his head civilly at the stout gentleman to his left, noting the shrewd intelligence in his eyes.

"Y'r duty," the man said gruffly. "In coffee, are ye?"

"No, sir, alas, I am here to visit only," Renzi said, leaning back to allow a vast dish to be placed on the table. "I have my interests, er, in the country—England, that is."

"Ah." Marston sniffed at the dish, strips of dried dark meat. "Jerked hog. Y' got to hand it to the blackies, they c'n conjure a riot o' tastes." Another vast tureen arrived. When the silver cover was removed it proved to be a mound of small, delicate fish. Yet another came: this was uncovered to loud acclamation. "See here, Renzi," said Marston, eyes agleam, "this is y'r Jamaica dish royal—black crab pepperpot."

The conversation swelled happily. Renzi noticed his brother gazing at him down the table, thoughtful and concerned. His expression brightened when their eyes met and he called, "You will require a quantity of wine with that pepperpot, m' friend. Allow me to prove we are not without the graces here in the Caribbean."

He nodded to a houseman, who in turn beckoned in a servant who pulled before him a neat cart. To his surprise Renzi saw that it seemed to be some sort of windmill, which the servant rotated carefully to catch the night zephyrs. "A breeze-mill," Marston confided. "Damn useful." Renzi saw that the mill drove a pump that kept up a continual circulation of water over bottles of wine in cotton bags, ranged together in a perforated tin trough. "Saltpetre an' water—uncommon effective." It was indeed: to taste chilled white wine in the tropical heat was nothing short of miraculous.

Renzi caught a speculative look on the face of an officer in red regimentals. "Have I seen you, sir?" the man said slowly. "In Spanish Town, was it not?"

Laughton put down his glass. "That would be unlikely, sir. Renzi is heir to a particularly large estate in England. I rather fancy he would hardly have occasion to call upon the army."

The officer bowed, but continued to look at Renzi, sipping his wine thoughtfully.

"I see Cuthbert has been broke," Marston said to the table at large. "All he had was ridin' in the *Catherine* brig, an' she was taken off Ocho Rios—less'n a day out."

A murmur of indignation went up. "For shame! What is the Navy about that it cannot keep our trade safe, not even a piddling little brig?"

Marston bunched his fists. "There'll be many more ruined afore they stirs 'emselves," he growled. "Too interested in the Frenchie islands in the Antilles, all their force drawn off b' that."

Laughton frowned. "Went to see the Admiral's office in Spanish Town the other day for some sort of satisfaction in the matter—but was fobbed off with some damn lickspittle clerk."

The conversations subsided as the table digested his words. An olive-complexioned man with curiously neat manners spoke into the quiet. "In chambers they are saying that within the month insurance premiums will be out of reach of all but the grand estates. . . ."

A heavy silence descended. To send a cargo of sugar to sea uninsured would mean instant ruination if it were taken. The turtle arrived and Renzi nibbled at the tongue and crab patties, checking his impulse to comment on naval matters. Farther down the table a grumbling voice picked up another thread. "Trelawney maroons are getting fractious again."

Renzi gave a polite interrogatory look toward Marston, who took up the cue. "Maroons, that's y'r runaway slaves up in the cockpit country, where we can't get at 'em. Damn-fool governor—about fifty-odd years ago, gave in t' them, signed a treaty. They lives free in their own towns up there, doin' what they do, but that's not enough—they wants more."

"An infernal impertinence!" another burst out.

"Wine with you, sir," Marston exclaimed to Renzi. "Your visit should not be damned by our moaning." Renzi smiled and lifted his glass. Around the table, talk resumed: gossip, local politics, eccentricities. The barrister politely inquired of him London consol prices; fortunately, Renzi's recent devouring of the latest newspapers had left him able to comment sensibly.

The claret gave way to Madeira, ginger sweetmeats and fruit jellies appeared, and chairs creaked as they accommodated the expansive relaxation of their occupants. The cloth was drawn and decanters placed on the table. "Gentlemen, the King," intoned Laughton.

Chairs scraped as the diners scrambled unsteadily to their feet. "The King, God bless him!" The simple act of the loyal toast unexpectedly brought a constriction to Renzi's throat: it symbolized for him the warmth and good fellowship of the company to be had of his peers. A blue haze arose from several cigars and the talk grew animated; the evening proceeded to its end, and carriages were announced.

"I wish you the sleep of the just, Nicholas!" Laughton joked as he stood with Renzi at the door of his bedroom. He hesitated a moment, then turned quietly and went.

Renzi lay in the dark, the softness of the vast bed suffocating to one who had become accustomed to the neat severity of a sea-service hammock. He stared into the blackness, his thoughts rushing. It had caught him unawares, he had to admit, and even more, it had unbalanced him. The sight of his brother and the memories this brought of home, and above all the easy gaiety and reasoned conversation, all conspired against his high-minded resolution.

He rolled onto his side. It was hard to sleep with the up-country night sounds—the long snore of a tree toad outside the jalousie window, the *chirr-chirr* of some large insect, a nonstop humming compounded with random chirping, whistling and croaking. An insect fluttered in his hair. He swore, then remembered too late that it was usual to search the mosquito net for visitors first. A larger insect blundered around in the confines of the net and he flapped his arms to shoo it out, but felt its chitinous body squirming against his hand and threw aside the net in disgust.

But then he recalled the usual method of dealing with giant scorpions dropping from above—hot wax from a candle: there was none lit, so he reluctantly draped the net again, and sank back into the goose down.

There was no denying that he had enjoyed the evening—too much. And he could feel himself weakening. It would not take much for an active mind to rationalize a course of action that would release him from his self-imposed exile. Such as the fact that, with his dear friend no longer at hand to share his burden, it might be thought excessive durance; he would then be released, free even to join his brother in the plantation. . . .

Morning arrived. Renzi had slept little, but when he awoke he found that his brother was out on the estate. When he was ready he presented himself at the dining room. A tall black servant offered a chair and a small table outside on the veranda, obviously following Laughton's practice.

A breakfast arrived—but nothing Renzi could recognize. "Ah, dis callaloo an' green banana, sah," he was advised by a worried butler. Renzi smiled weakly and set to. The coffee, however, was a revelation: flavorsome and strong without being bitter.

As he was finishing, Laughton came into sight astride a stumpy but well-muscled pony. He slid to the ground and strode over to Renzi with an easy smile. "Do I see you in good health?"

Renzi had never shied from a decision in his life, and the moral strength to stand by its full consequences was deeply ingrained. "Brother, may we talk?" he responded quietly.

It was done. Although he knew he had made the only decision possible, the resumption of his exile was hard, and time slipped by in a gray, dreary parade. The probability was that he would not visit his brother again: the contrast was so daunting.

Day succeeded day in monotonous succession, the work not

onerous or demeaning but stultifying. While on the one hand he would never need to turn out into a wild night, on the other he would not know the exhilaration of sailing on a bowline, the sudden rush of excitement at a strange sail, or touch unknown and compelling foreign shores.

After the morning's work there was already a respectable pile dealt with and ready for signature. He picked up the next paper: another routine report, a list of names and descriptions of new arrivals from somewhere or other available for local deployment. His eyes glazed: he would need to advise the appropriate departments separately for each individual, a lengthy task. Sighing, he put down the paper, then snatched it up again. It was impossible—but the evidence could not be denied. On the fifth row, in neat copperplate, was the name Thomas Paine Kydd.

Feverishly, he scanned the line. Apparently a Thomas Paine Kydd, dockyard worker, was being transferred from the Royal Dockyard at English Harbour as surplus to requirements. The odds against two men with the same name being in the same part of the world must be colossal—but, then, this one was indisputably a dockyard worker. And probably a bad one at that. Renzi knew by now the code for off-loading a useless article.

On a mad impulse he stood up. He gathered together the pile of papers, hurried outside and found Jacobs. "These are for signature, Mr. Jacobs. I have been called away by Admiral Edgcumbe again," he said, and hastened away. If he was quick, he could ride on the noon mail and be at the naval dockyard in an hour or two.

CHAPTER 9

*T*he boat skimmed over the spacious harbor, on its way
from Kingston town to the naval dockyard at the end of a
seven-mile sandy spit of land, the Palisades. This was Port
Royal, the notorious pirate lair that had been destroyed spectacu-
larly by an earthquake a century before. But Renzi had no eyes for
this curiosity. Furious with himself for his impulsive and unrea-
soned act, he was yet in a fever of expectation and hope that had
no foundation in logic—just a single name on a piece of paper.

He waited impatiently while the boat came alongside the
wharf, then swung himself up and strode ashore. Ignoring the
close-packed victualing storehouses, he followed the road through
the sprawling ruins of the Polygon battery, the odd gray-flecked
sand of the spit crunching loudly underfoot.

As he passed the stinking pitch-house and the bedlam of the
smith's shop he had no real idea how to find his quarry—the
employment return had merely said that this man was a dockyard
worker, no indication of what type. It would be useless to ask any
of the dockyard men about a new arrival: no one would know
him. Over there was a rickety row of Negro houses—Renzi had

found that, generally, sailors got on well with slaves so perhaps . . .

He stopped dead. An unmistakable figure was coming around the corner at the dockyard wall with his head down. Kydd. Renzi stood still, noting the droop of the shoulders, the preoccupied air. He called softly, "Avast there, brother! Spare an old friend a glance."

Kydd stopped as though struck in the face. Incredulity, then joy lit his features. He hurried over and shook Renzi's hand until it ached.

"Do ye leave me my hand, Tom. It is the only one I have left on the right side," Renzi said.

Port Royal town was old, a sea town with a gaudy past, and its superfluity of sailor taverns gave pleasing choice for their reunion. The early hour of the afternoon insured they would not be disturbed, and they selected the Shipp Inn on Queen Street: it had a table in a bay window overlooking the calm of the inner harbor.

"You are safe—preserved!" Renzi said, with great feeling.

Kydd looked up, surprised. "Oh, yes. 'Twas nothin', really. L'tenant Calley told us t' march out to Putty Borg on Bass Tair, but there they had th' fever, so we went to t' other side, Fort Mathilda, an' were picked up b' *Trajan*."

Renzi had shared too much with Kydd to believe that this bare account was all there was to tell, but it could wait. "You're in the dockyard line now?" he asked.

"Aye," said Kydd, his brow creased, "but I'd give a bag o' guineas t' get back t' sea."

"How—"

"*Trajan* was surveyed 'n' condemned, I had th' chance f'r a spell in a reg'lar-goin' dockyard."

"And—"

"An' I ran afoul of a blue-light shipwright. Seems m' spirits were too—who should say?—ardent with the ladies," Kydd explained, without rancor.

Renzi contemplated this. He knew that Kydd was not a concupiscent and signaled to the pot-boy. "The punch here is considered of the first class," he offered.

"Thank ye, no. I had th' yellow fever not a month past. Lost m' taste f'r grog lately."

"Then we have your lemonadoes, rap, cacao-drink—"

"A small beer will answer," Kydd said.

It was indeed satisfying to see Kydd again, and once more Renzi realized that here was his only true friend. He dreaded the parting that must come. Rebellion forced itself on his consciousness, but he conquered it. "What are you about at the moment?" he asked, unwilling to confess to *his* impulse in coming.

"Scullin' about—seems I have t' wait for assigning," Kydd said moodily. "What're you doin' for y'rself?"

"Oh, somewhat in the character of a clerk. My small French is of value here, it seems. I labor in Spanish Town." It was depressing, the very thought. "Shall we not view the ruins of the old pirate town?" he went on quickly. "I have a yen to see the very streets of Captain Morgan."

They walked along the narrow streets of Port Royal. It was small and compact, occupying the tip of the Palisades, and it didn't take long to discover that there was no trace at all of the notorious city.

"Ah, dearie, ye have ter unnerstan'—all th't was wicked and godless, one arternoon, jus' ups and slides down inter the sea! All th' people fallin' into great cracks in th' ground an' screamin' an' being carried ter their doom—a judgment on 'em all," the old washerwoman told them with relish. "They're still dahn there!" She cackled.

They passed back along the other side of the spit, seeing its inner prospect of the fleet at anchor in all its puissant presence, the

Admiral's pennant floating proudly atop the 74-gun flagship. Renzi saw Kydd's forlorn attention on the ships as they paced along.

Kydd stopped. He lifted an arm and pointed to a small vessel anchored much closer, in Chocolate Hole. "There!" he said. "Like a yacht, 'n' with saucy lines. If ever I get th' chance t' ship out again, she'd be m' choice."

"Is she not overmuch small?" Renzi teased.

"Be damn'd t' that! She'd be everywhere, all over th' Caribbee, never rottin' at anchor 'n' seein' parts o' the Main where y'r ship-of-the-line would never touch in a hunnerd years!" Kydd went on. "An' th' best chance o' prize money ye'll ever get."

Shielding his eyes, Renzi tried to make out the vessel.

"She's *Seaflower* cutter," Kydd said in a low voice. "With a commander new promoted, an' he can't fin' a crew," he said, finally tearing away his eyes.

An idea came to Renzi in the wagon to Spanish Town. A stupendous, fantastic idea. He elaborated and tested it on the rest of the way and, during the night, planned his move.

Requesting the muster lists of all the ships in the fleet was easy—they were filed together and no one questioned his sudden use of them for undisclosed purposes. He sat down and started work, scanning the names and making the occasional note.

The "pack" on *Seaflower* was not large: a swift riffle through the papers told the story well enough. A tiny unrated vessel, she was beneath notice and would be left far behind the sloops and frigates in the competition for skilled men. He picked up the latest letter from her captain, a young lieutenant in his first command. A third piteous plea for hands—she had been stripped of men while her previous commander was dying of fever and was at the moment unable to sail. The signature was in the same hand as the body of the letter: it seemed her captain had to write his own correspondence.

Renzi smiled. He picked up a fresh sheet, checked his quill nib and started.

Captain, His Majesty's cutter *Seaflower.*

The Secretary of the Cheque views with concern your letter to this office of the 19th inst. concerning your sea readiness.

It has long been the practice on this station to render full returns in the form governed by Commander-in-Chief's Fleet Orders dated 21st Nov. 1782 which provides fully for the correct procedure. Your attention to detail on this matter in the future is most earnestly requested, touching as it does on the effectiveness of this department in the carrying out of its duties.

As a closing paragraph he added, almost as an aside:

Attached a list of seamen to be sent into *Seaflower* to answer your deficit of skilled hands.

Your obed servant, etc., etc.

That should suffice. Now the usual to the dockyard commissioner, answering the availability for employment return and directing the assignment of Thomas Kydd to *Seaflower,* quartermaster.

And the others: they would be all of the same form and it should not take long. He glanced at his notes and began, his pen flying across the paper.

Captain, His Majesty's Ship *Cumberland*

You are directed to detach Tobias Stirk, gun captain, for service in *Seaflower,* with immediate effect.

And the next, concerning Ned Doud, and another for Doggo—or William Shea, as he would appear on the ship's books. He finished the others, then took the sheets across and slipped them randomly into the pile awaiting signature. They would never be noticed by the hard-pressed secretary to the Admiral.

"Nicholas!" Kydd yelled. "You'd never believe—I can't credit it—I'm to be made quartermaster into *Seaflower*!" He laughed.

"Why, my felicitations, to be sure," Renzi said smoothly, joining his friend.

"An' Toby Stirk is t' be her gunner's mate!" Kydd exclaimed in glee. "Come an' sup wi' us at the King's Arms."

Stirk, conspicuous in his usual red kerchief and gleaming earrings, was holding loquacious court at the tavern table, vividly describing the last moments of *Artemis* to an admiring throng. Kydd's heart swelled at the pleasure in his old shipmates' faces.

The riot of noise was broken by a gleeful shout from the door. "Tom—Tom Kydd!"

Kydd stood to get a better view over the crowd. To his delight he recognized Doud, the born seaman and pure-voiced singer from *Artemis*. "Well met, Ned, m' old shipmate! Warp y'rself alongside, cuffin!" he called.

Doud pushed his way through, closely followed by Elias Petit's seamed old face. They nodded in pleased surprise at Stirk and Doggo, then eased themselves onto a seat.

"What ship?" Kydd asked.

"We're Irresistibles mate," Doud said, referring to the big seventy-four out in the bay, "but the damnedest thing—we've jus' bin turned over inter that squiddy little *Seaflower* cutter, an—"

Stirk stared at Kydd in amazement. Suspicious, Kydd turned to Renzi, who suddenly found the view from the tavern window over the harbor remarkably absorbing. "Nicholas, do ye know—"

"The most amazing coincidence this age," Renzi replied quickly. "Especially in view of my own somewhat precipitate wrenching from the felicity of Spanish Town to the uncertain delights of this same vessel."

Kydd reached out and gripped Renzi's hand. "M' dear friend . . ." Whatever had brought about their reunion he would not question it in the slightest particular.

"Could be a mort interestin', mates," said Petit seriously.

"How's that, then?" Doud asked. Petit, the hoary old seaman, could be relied on in the matter of sea sense.

"*Seaflower* ain't a-goin' ter be swingin' around her anchor fer long. Ships like 'er are off doin' all th' jobs that's goin'— despatches, carryin' passengers, escortin' merchant ships, not ter mention takin' a prize or two."

Doud frowned. "But ye'll have ter say she's small, the smallest, an' if we comes up agin even a half-awake brig-o'-war, we'll be in fer a hazin'."

Leaning forward, Stirk gave a hard smile. "As a nipper I were in th' trade outa Folkestone." Knowing looks appeared around the table—there was only one trade of significance so close to the remote fastness of Romney Marsh. And the Navy was always keen to press smugglers for their undoubted skills as seamen.

"An' I learned t' have a care when the Revenooers were out in th' cutters, so much sail on 'em, like ter hide the ship. Fore 'n' aft rig, sails like a witch snug up to the wind—you don't 'ave much ter worry of, 'less yer gets under the lee of some big bastard." His smile twisted. "An' *Seaflower* is right sim'lar t' yer Revenoo cutter."

Petit nodded slowly. "Just so, Toby. But I reckon as we should get aboard, mates, else we chance t' lose our berths if she sails."

In the boat approaching *Seaflower* eager eyes assessed the qualities of the ship that was their future. She was a cutter, single mast with a dashing rake, but an enormously lofty one, and with a splendid bowsprit that was two-thirds as long as the vessel herself. "Should carry a damn fine press o' sail," said Kydd, noting the sweep of deck up to her neat stern, her lines all curves and graces. Closer to, there were loving touches: her clear varnished sides were topped by one wale in black; her attractive decorated stern—a whorled frieze of gold on bluish green—looked stylish and brave; on deck the fittings were smartly picked out in red.

"Not s' many aboard," Doud murmured. Under the awning aft there was one man in shirtsleeves watching them suspiciously with folded arms. Another was fishing over the side forward of the mast.

"Boat ahoy!" hailed the man under the awning. It was obvious they carried no officers to pipe aboard, but naval ritual demanded the hail.

"No, no," Kydd yelled back, the correct response. They swung alongside, and Kydd pulled himself up to the little quarterdeck and an impression of yachtlike neatness. There was nothing to indicate the rank of the man awaiting them, so Kydd played safe. Touching his hat he reported, "Come t' join ship, sir."

After a disbelieving pause, the man turned to the young officer emerging from the companionway on deck. "New men, sir."

The officer returned his salute punctiliously and looked eagerly at the men piling up the side. He withdrew a paper from inside his light cotton coat. "Are you the men sent by the Admiral's Office?"

"Sir." The deck of *Seaflower* was an entirely new experience for Kydd. Only about seventy feet long she was galley-built and a comfortable twenty-five feet broad. There were eight guns a side, but these seemed miniature to Kydd after a ship-of-the-line.

"I'm Lieutenant Farrell, captain of *Seaflower*," said the officer, his voice crisp, pleasant. He surveyed the group, and consulted his paper. "Do we have Stirk?" Stirk stepped forward and touched his forehead. "This advice is to rate you gunner's mate, Stirk," Farrell said. "What is your experience?"

Kydd glanced at Stirk and suppressed a grin.

When Farrell came to Kydd he paused doubtfully. "Ah—quartermaster? Your experience is . . . ?"

"Acting quartermaster, *Artemis* frigate," Kydd told him firmly. "An' that around Cape Horn," he added, in case Farrell had not heard of the crack frigate and her fate.

Farrell's eyes widened. Kydd caught a look of incredulity on his face: *Seaflower* now had a core of prime hands that would not be out of place in a top fighting warship, let alone a humble cutter. Farrell turned to go, a fleeting grin acknowledging his incredible good fortune. "Carry on, please. Mr. Jarman will assign your watch and stations."

The other man straightened. "Jarman, an' I'm the master." He looked guardedly at Kydd: the quartermaster was directly answerable to the sailing master in a man-o'-war.

"We now gets ter see what kinda swabs the *Seaflower*s are," Doud said, as they reached the forward companionway, and went below into a large space extending well over half the length of the vessel. "Well, I stan' flummoxed!"

With the exception of a pair of seamen at a hinged table, the space was deserted. They looked up at the newcomers. " 'Oo are you, then?" one asked, starting in surprise at Doggo's ugliness.

Stirk pushed forward. "Where's yer mates?" His iron voice braced them and they rose warily to their feet.

"We ain't got none—we'se are all there is," the man replied carefully. "Farthing, able seaman . . ."

"Stirk, yer noo gunner's mate. Well, who 'ave we got aboard, then?"

"Ah, we has Merrick, th' boatswain, an' a hard man is he— ashore now. Jarman, the master, a merchant jack, an'—'oo else, Ralf?" Farthing said, turning to the other man.

"Cole, reefer, first trip an' all—"

"Only one midshipman?" Kydd asked. Equating to a petty officer in authority, a raw midshipman could be a tiresome trial up in the tops in a blow.

"Aye. Oh, yeah, Cuddy Snead as carpenter's mate, 'n' that's it."

"Yer fergettin' that scowbunkin' cook. Nothin' but a waste o' space, him—couldn't bring a salt horse alongside wi'out it climbs in the pot itself."

"I see," growled Stirk. All the men left aboard *Seaflower* were her standing officers and these two. They were not likely to get to sea very soon.

"E's goin' ter have t' press men," said Doud gloomily. The press-gang could find men, but they would be resentful, unwilling and poor shipmates.

Doggo shifted his feet restlessly. "Doesn't 'ave ter be," he snapped, his grog-roughened voice an impatient rasp.

"How so, mate?" asked Stirk. It was not often that Doggo put in his oar.

"Yer recollects where we are . . ." he said mysteriously, tapping the side of his nose.

It was well known that, if anything, it was harder to press men in the Caribbean than it was in England—alert to the wiles of the Press they would be sure to find bolt-holes at the briefest hint of a press-gang ashore. They all stared at Doggo.

"Toby, I needs you 'n' Kydd ter step ashore wi' me."

"Er—o' course, mate."

"Then, we sees th' Cap'n an' find out if b' chance he needs a crew o' prime hands."

Farrell, bewildered by an offer coming from the wicked-looking Doggo to have a full ship's company by midnight, nevertheless agreed, and *Seaflower*'s longboat headed for shore.

"Where we off to, cully?" Stirk asked.

"King's Arms, o' course," said Doggo cracking a grin. In just a few salty sentences he told of his plan. Kydd laughed in appreciation.

They entered the warm din of the tavern with a swagger. Stirk's bull roar cut effortlessly above the tumult. "A gage o' bowse fer the *Seaflower*s as needs it, y' scrubs!"

A few faces looked their way, then resumed their talk.

"Get it in yer, cuffin," Stirk told Doggo loudly. "We sails afore dusk termorrow, an' not back fer a while."

A big seaman sitting close by in the packed tavern turned and laughed. "Why, y' lookin' fer some fat scow t' look after, like? An' then orf ter find someone wants ter send a letter somewheres?" He convulsed with drunken mirth.

Another chimed in, "*Seaflower*—she lost all 'er hands, an' can't find any t' ship out in her. She ain't a-goin' anywheres!"

"She is now, cock!" Stirk said.

"Oh, yeah, where, then?" said the seaman, intrigued.

"Ah, can't tell yer that," Stirk said, leaning back. Other faces turned their way. "Cos' fer this v'y'ge—only this one—we has a hand-picked crew." He had attention now. "Tom Kydd here, quartermaster o' the flying *Artemis* as was—Cape Stiff 'n' all, taut hand-o'-the-watch is he! An' Doggo there—best quarter gunner I seen! An' Ned Doud, cap'n o' the top—we got the best there is, mate!"

"Yer didn't say as t' why!"

There were sailors from all parts watching now—merchant seamen, foreigners and privateersmen.

"Why, if yer has—"

"Don't tell 'em, Toby! It's fer us only!" said Doggo.

An older seaman looked thoughtful, and turned to his friends. "Yair—come t' think about it, Elias Petit gets turned out o' *Diadem* an' he's a knowing old sod. Somethin's in the wind, lads!"

Interest was now awakened. A sharp-faced man suddenly became animated. " 'Ere, *Seaflower*, that's the barky th't the Admiral's clerk got hisself transferred inter, all of a pelt!"

"Yeah!" said another. "So what does 'e know that gets him off his arse in Spanish Town 'n' a berth in a squiddy cutter?"

The older man gave a grim smile. "I reckon there's a reason all right—a thunderin' good one!" He waited until he had all their attention, then said in hushed tones, "He's yer tie-mate, ain't he, Kydd? An' you has a soft berth in th' dockyard, right? An' both of ye decides to skin out ter sea in a hurry, not fergettin' t' tell all yer mates? C'n only be one meanin'—yer has word there's summat at sea that's worth the takin', somethin' that yer knows—"

"Yer too smart fer me b' a long chalk, cully!" Stirk said in admiration, then grew anxious. "Now, I didn't say all that, did I? An' ain't that the truth!"

The man sat back, satisfied. "No, mate, yer didn't—we worked it out b' ourselves. Now, what we wants t' know is, y' need any hands fer this v'y'ge o' yours?"

Kydd looked discouraging. "No petty officers, just a few idlers—an' some foremast jacks is all."

Grins broke out all around. "I'll have a piece o' that, then!" the sharp-faced man said, eyes gleaming. "How . . ."

"I'll have a word wi' the Cap'n, can't promise ye a berth—but, mark you, not a word to him that y' knows anything, on y'r life."

The riot that followed was only brought under some sort of order by Stirk setting up in the corner and taking names, for all the world like a farmers' fair. Merchant seamen in hiding from the Press, even privateersmen crowded in, all anxious to take their share of the expected bounty. Well within time *Seaflower*'s long-boat brought out a full and excited ship's company, and a sorely puzzled young captain was making plans for sea.

Storing ship for *Seaflower* was not on the vast scale of a ship-of-the-line with its tens of thousands of pounds' weight of victuals, water and naval stores to last for six months or more at sea. A cutter was not expected to be at sea for more than days at a time.

There was a matter that Kydd felt would make perfect his change of situation. "Cap'n, sir," he asked of Farrell, at an appropriate time, "We now has a prime body o' petty officers, you'll agree?"

Farrell gave a guarded assent.

"An' y'r steward has to make shift f'r the warrant officers too?"

"He does, but what—"

"Then c'd I suggest, sir, we gets a ship's boy t' bear a hand? I have just such a one in mind an', besides, he knows well how t' serve a gun. . . ."

Farrell considered. "We sail before dark," he said.

Kydd knew that, released from temporary service as his servant,

Luke was ashore glumly awaiting an unknown assignment. "He'll be aboard, sir," Kydd said crisply.

Readied for sea, *Seaflower* had still one to join her company. When in the late afternoon the windlass was cast loose and hatches secured Doud made his move.

The boatswain touched his hat to Farrell and reported, "Sir, all aboard save that mumpin' toad of a cook," he said.

"*Still* ashore?" Farrell snapped. The cook had been told to return with last-minute cabin stores for him.

"If yer please, sir," Doud asked humbly, "I got a mate as is a spankin' good cook, lookin' f'r a berth. . . ."

"Get him," Farrell said. Doud's friend had entertained the old cook for hours until he was dead drunk, and was now waiting with his seabag for the signal.

Just as the topmen laid out on the yard to loose sail, the windlass taking up the slack of the cable and Kydd was standing at the tiller, a black face wearing an infectious smile climbed over the bulwarks and the familiar figure of Quashee stepped aboard. He of the *Artemis,* the legendary star-gazy pie and his "conweniences"—herbs and spices. With him aboard they would not starve.

With a fine Caribbean day promising, a fair wind for the south and as happy a ship's company as any, *Seaflower* made for the open sea.

They sailed south, threading through the islets and shoals lying off the harbor, through unruly seas kicked up by a forceful land breeze, and into the wider Caribbean. It was there that they spread full sail, letting the craft show her true breeding. Farrell had made it clear that he would not be reporting *Seaflower* ready for sea until they had shaken down into an effective company, worthy of trust in any mission.

At the helm Kydd found himself working hard. A tiller had the advantage over a wheel in that it was in direct contact with the sea with all that this meant in instant response, but was without the damping and mechanical advantage of a wheel and tackle. *Seaflower,* under her big driving mainsail and eager foresail and jib, swooping and foaming at speed, was as skittish as a thoroughbred horse. Kydd felt the hammering rush of the sea in the tiller and leaned against the pressure of the marked weather helm—the trim of the cutter might need looking to. Going about was a dream. Unlike the minutes that even a frigate took, *Seaflower* shot around in a moment, sheaves squealing, seamen bringing in tacks and sheets hand over hand as if their lives depended on it—an exhilarating ballet of sea skills.

The square sails were then set; by this a topsail cutter had sailing options not open to her bigger brethren, and Kydd felt a stirring of excitement. *Seaflower* leaned happily to her topsail and topgallant, hissing along at a speed that sent a wake streaming like a mill-race past the low deck edge.

Right forward Renzi was having a busy time taking charge of the headsails, the distinctive huge sails spearing out ahead of the vessel. It was a very different situation from the stately pyramids of canvas of a square-rigger, and his cheerful wave to Kydd was just a little harassed.

Farrell stood just forward of Kydd on the weather side of the deck, his hands clasped behind his back, feet braced against the lively movement. His voice as he set the craft about her paces was crisp and authoritative. Jarman stood to leeward; Kydd sensed some reserve between the two men. Farrell gave his orders directly. This left the master with nothing to do but observe, but perhaps this was the Captain trying the mettle of his company.

Merrick, the burly boatswain, stomped about *Seaflower,* his eyes flicking aggressively this way and that. His style was hard and uncompromising. Kydd had been lucky in his previous ships, he knew; no boatswain had really used his position to the sadistic limits possible that he had heard of in other ships.

"Stand down, if you please," said Farrell formally to Merrick.

"Aye-aye, sir," said Merrick, turned to Stiles, his mate, who was fingering his silver call in anticipation, and snapped, "Hands turn to, part-o'-ship f'r cleaning—"

"Belay that," Farrell interrupted. "Secure the watch below and set a sea watch, was my meaning." Significant looks went about: Farrell was going to stand by his men before the boatswain.

The last vestiges of sunset were fading over the Hellshire Hills as they picked their way back to Port Royal, weary but satisfied. This time they anchored close by the fleet—Farrell was clearly going to report his ship ready for sea.

"An' take a turn 'n' clinch at that," Kydd ordered Farthing. He and Stirk were going to make themselves as comfortable as possible below; the senior petty officers berthed right aft within the large space below decks. Farthing finished the knittle line with a seizing, and there they had a taut canvas "wall" screening off their space. In leisure time they would paint the partition with some suitable scene—mermaids, perhaps, or a lurid battle. Kydd surveyed the little space. "Not as who would say oversized," he murmured, head bent under the low deckhead.

Stirk grinned at him. "*Seaflower,* she's two hunnerd tons, makes 'er a big 'un up agin them Revenooers—near three times their size," he said appreciatively. "I say she's snug, is all." At sea a full half of her company would be watch on deck, and at anchor in the balmy weather of the Caribbean many would probably sleep there.

Kydd swarmed up the narrow ladderway to the upper deck, where a sizeable gathering was celebrating *Seaflower*'s prospects. Doggo was leaning on a swivel gun forward of the mast, waving his tankard, with an audience and in full flow. A slightly built man with a leathery face and bright eyes listened. Kydd guessed that this would be Snead, the carpenter's mate, and on the other side was the lean figure of Stiles without his silver call badge of office.

A friendly hail, and Renzi stepped on deck. "Tip us some

words, mate," Petit called. Surprised muttering met this suggestion: few present knew Renzi and his odd predilections.

Renzi stood still and thoughtful, then declaimed into the velvet night:

> *"Majestically slow before the breeze*
> *The tall ship marches on the azure seas;*
> *In silent pomp she cleaves the watery plain*
> *The pride and wonder of the billowy main."*

A respectful silence and scattering of polite appreciation followed, at which Renzi coughed apologetically. "If it were in me to sing a hearty chorus, I would rather—but we have the prince of ballads himself aboard. Ned, dear fellow, entertain us!"

Doud flashed his broad white smile and rose, handing his tankard to Farthing. He struck a noble pose and in a perfect tenor sang,

> *"Come, come, m' jolly lads! The winds abaft*
> *Brisk gales our sails shall crowd;*
> *The ship's unmoor'd, all hands aboard*
> *The barky's well mann'd and stor'd!"*

The Drury Lane ballad, though confected by a landman, was a great favorite, and all joined in the chorus:

> *"Then sling the flowing bowl—fond hopes arise*
> *The can, boys, bring; we'll drink and sing*
> *While foaming billows roll."*

Kydd sang lustily, enjoying the fellowship and good feeling. Luke brought another pot. The lad was growing, and now affected a red bandanna tied around his head like a pirate, with a smile that wouldn't go away. At the edge of the crowd Kydd noticed the wide-eyed young midshipman, Cole, and farther away, the shadowy figure of the Captain, both drawn to the singing.

In the warm darkness something told Kydd that he would be lucky to experience an evening quite so pleasurable again.

CHAPTER 10

Captain Farrell returned from the flagship before ten the next morning, and immediately called the sailing master to his cabin. Overheard, the word swiftly went out.

"The Barbadoes wi' despatches?" snarled Patch, a privateersman. His shipmate, Alvarez, appeared next to him, his olive-dark face hostile.

Doggo glared at him. "Stow yer gab, cully! Yer doesn't think the Ol' Man is a-goin' ter let th' world know, now, do ye?" But Kydd caught his quick look: their tavern story might now be recoiling on them, and gulled privateersmen would be hard to handle. "Cap'n knows what he's doing," he said harshly. "Jus' be sure you does."

"*Haaaands* to unmoor ship!" The boatswain's bellow reached every part of the cutter. Kydd cast off the beckets securing the tiller in harbor and tested the helm through a full sweep. It was his duty to take the vessel to sea, then when sea watches were set, he would take the conn and oversee the duty helmsman for his trick at the helm.

Strong running backstays were needed to take the massive driving force of the enormous gaff mainsail—two linked tackles were rove for this and, unique to Kydd's experience, the forestay had its own deadeye and lanniard secured to the stempost, both together in taut balance.

One by one, Stirk had Doggo and his party moving about the guns—six-pounders, a respectable armament for a mere cutter, eight a side and with swivels forward as chase guns. A cry from forward showed the anchor cable "thick and dry for weighing" and Farrell, in full blues, consulted his watch. The anchor was a-trip. The Captain's arm went up, the saluting swivel forward went off with a spiteful crack and in the smoke both the foresail and mainsail rose swiftly, the steady northeast trades forcing the men at the main-sheets to sweat as they trimmed the sail to the wind at the same time as the waisters brought in the fore-sheets.

Seaflower responded immediately with a graceful heel, falling off to leeward momentarily before surging ahead. Kydd felt the rudder firm and, under Jarman's muttered direction, shaped course westerly to round the end of the Palisades. They slipped past the fortifications and the dockyard, then Port Royal itself, not a soul ashore apparently interested in their departure, and made a competent gybe to place themselves comfortably on track for the open sea. The jib was hoisted and conformable to the fair wind from the larboard quarter, her topsail was set. *Seaflower* quickly left the harbor astern. When they had cleared the hazardous cluster of cays to the south, they went about and headed along the coast for Port Morant.

Sea watches were set, and Kydd yielded the tiller to the helmsman. He took up the slate hanging on the side of the tiny binnacle and checked the course and details that the sailing master had scrawled. In this small ship he would have to maintain the conn himself—nobody to peg the traverse board, no marine to turn the sandglass at the end of a watch.

He stepped back, and saw Patch finish coiling the fall of the topsail sheet. With a careless thump the privateersman cast the coil on the deck against the bulwark and made to leave. Incensed, Kydd shouted and pointed at the untidy twists. Patch saw him, but deliberately turned away. Kydd moved fast, knocking aside another sailor as he confronted Patch. "Take that lubberly shittle and belay it right," he said in a hard voice, referring to the seamanlike practice of taking a single loop of rope to the belaying pin to take the weight of the rest, so all could be cast off instantly when necessary.

Patch stared at him, contempt in his dark eyes. "King's ship ways on a fuckin' cutter? Ye must be—"

"Now!"

Patch paused. Kydd was not getting angry; his voice was iron, his control icy. Drawn by the raised voices, the boatswain approached from behind Patch, who failed to notice him. Merrick watched and waited with a slight smile.

Kydd did not lower his gaze before the case-hardened bigger man. "Do ye take a bight and belay that fall," he repeated.

Patch looked again in Kydd's face. Something passed between them—and Patch moved. He bent and picked up the rope, his eyes never leaving Kydd's as he obeyed grudgingly. Kydd paused, then walked back to his watch position.

In just a few hours they hove to off Port Morant and collected a satchel of despatches, then resumed course. They would reach the eastward tip of Jamaica in only an hour or so, then would keep clear of the offshore banks before shaping course for the Leeward Islands.

With no sign of an eager combing of the sea for an expected prey, there was a definite edge to the mess-deck chatter at dinner. Kydd and Renzi kept the deck to avoid questions. Stirk and Doggo found something to do with the six-pounders, but it was clear there would be an accounting soon.

Gun practice was piped immediately after the noon meal, the hard-bitten seamen making child's play of their weapons. Farrell kept them at it, and just as Morant Point drew abeam he ordered that live firing would take place. *Seaflower*'s decks were cleared, and the pieces manned. Kydd took his place at the helm and silence fell as all eyes turned to Farrell.

At that precise moment the quiet was split by an urgent hail from the lookout on the crosstree. "Sail *hooooo!*" Above the low-lying point could be seen first the topgallants and then the topsails of a square-rigged vessel, and shortly after, the barque slid into view. At least twice their size and a sinister black, she quickly spotted *Seaflower* and her length foreshortened as she turned to intercept.

"Ready about!" Farrell snapped, his telescope up searching her masts for a flag. They slewed around and closed the distance, Farrell seeming to have no hesitation about closing the larger vessel.

There was an apprehensive quiet about *Seaflower*'s decks. "She's a twenty-eight at least, lads," Doud murmured. "Saw her ports." Several faces popped out of the fore-hatch and gazed over the blue seas to the black-hulled vessel. The barque altered her heading to a broader angle. It served to show her gunports opening all along her hull, cannon rumbling into place at each. Still there were no colors aloft. A cold trepidation came over Kydd—the worst situation, with the banks to seaward and the unknown craft closing in to weather.

"Give her a gun, Stirk," Farrell said quietly. A six-pounder crashed out forward, sounding toylike after a frigate's 24s. There was a minute or two's delay, as if the stranger was amused at the small ship's presumption, before a flutter of color at her mizzen peak appeared, shaking out into the stripes and stars of the United States.

"Thank Gawd!" laughed Farthing. "I thought we wuz in fer a hazin'." The barque's sheets eased, and she braced around slowly to diverge, clearly not deigning to dally with an Englisher. Relieved chatter broke out along *Seaflower*'s deck.

"Sir, if y' please . . ." Jarman had not joined in the general relief, and took Farrell's Dollond glass. "Ah! As I thought. There's no Yankee I know of wears a red cap 'n' petticoat breeches. Sir, she's a Frenchie!"

Farrell snatched back the telescope and swept the barque's decks—only Jarman's suspicions and a careless French sailor had given the game away. "Brail topsails!" he snapped. Under fore-and-aft sail only, *Seaflower* sped toward the enemy. She fell off the wind a little and her intention became clear—to pass close astern of the other vessel to send her puny balls smashing through the unprotected stern and down the length of her enemy.

Stirk raced from gun to gun. Fortunate to be at quarters, they were at the ready, but Farrell roared, "Larboard—firing to larboard!"

This was away from the enemy. Kydd was baffled by the order. Then the barque responded. The United States flag whipped down and the French flag rose to replace it in jerky movement. At the same time the vessel came around sharply into the wind, to stay about. Well before *Seaflower* could come up to deliver her blow, the bluff sides of her antagonist were swinging around on the other tack to parallel the little cutter and present her full broadside.

Kydd's throat constricted—a crushing weight of metal would be slamming into them in seconds. He glanced at Farrell who, to his astonishment, wore an expression of ferocious glee.

"We have you now, Mr. Frenchman!" he roared triumphantly. The barque's swing had been a mistake. Farrell snapped, "Ready about! Lee, oh!" and *Seaflower* pirouetted prettily to leave her with her larboard guns laid faithfully on the barque's stern. They passed close enough to see pale faces over the taffrail and sails slatting in confusion as, no doubt, orders were being angrily counter-manded.

There was nothing to miss. The line of windows at the stern gallery dissolved as gun after gun on *Seaflower*'s deck crashed out, the balls' brutal impact causing ruin along the length of the enemy.

Kydd felt a furious exaltation—it was the first smoke of battle he had smelled since the great frigate struggle between *Artemis* and *Citoyenne*.

The last gun banged out and *Seaflower* was past. With her crew cheering madly, the guns were served, but there was a new peril— a square-rigged vessel would back topsails and stay where she was, battering the helpless victim into submission, but with her fore- and-aft rig there was no way *Seaflower* could do the same. She con- tinued on her course, her only hope to get out of range before the enemy could recover, but the black hull was already turning. *Seaflower* lay over under her press of sail, but there was no escape. Kydd's hands sweated at the helm—but he was tied to his place of duty and must stand and take whatever fate had in store for him.

The enemy broadside came. But in ones and twos. Paltry puffs of powder smoke, the thin crack of four-pounders. And a whole gundeck of cannon staring silently at them. "Caught 'em on the hop goin' about!" growled Stirk in disgust.

"They got the yeller fever an' can't man the guns!" someone shouted. Kydd's mind raced: this was no explanation for small- caliber guns.

Jarman smiled. "She's a Mongseer merchant jack, puttin' on a show," he said with satisfaction. It was a pretense: the open gun- ports sported only quakers, wooden imitation guns that could not fire. Her bluff was called. The tiny *Seaflower* had not run for her life as intended, and had dared to attack. Incredulous shouts and cheers broke out while the trim cutter closed in exultantly on her prey.

"Damme f'r a chuckle-headed ninny, but that was rare done!" Patch said, lowering his cutlass to finger the quality of the cordage on the deck of their prize. "Knoo the exac' time she'd weather th' point, and was there a-waitin'," he continued admiringly. "Keeps it to 'imself, he does, an' four hours out we has a fat prize." The

French sailors sat morosely on the main-hatch while Farrell and the sailing master inspected below decks.

It was a matter of small hours to escort the prize back to Port Morant; the talk was all on the astonishing intelligence their sagacious Captain must have had, and happy anticipation of prize money to claim later.

Farrell did not appear affected by his fortune. He appeared punctiliously on deck at appropriate times in the ship's routine, courteous but firm in his dealings with his ship's company, and considerate and businesslike with Jarman and Merrick, who stood watches opposite each other. *Seaflower* seemed to respond with spirit. Square sails set abroad and her prodigious fore-and-aft canvas bowsed well taut, she slashed purposefully through the royal-blue seas at a gallop, her deck alive with eager movement.

By the last dog-watch, deep into the Caribbean, Kydd joined Renzi at his customary pipe of tobacco on the foredeck, ignoring the occasional spatter of spray. They sat against the weather cat-head, the better to see the gathering sunset astern. Renzi drew an appreciative puff at his clay pipe and sighed. "This prime Virginia is as pleasing to the senses as any I have yet tried."

Kydd was knotting a hammock clew. His nimble fingers plied the ivory fid he used for close work, the intricate net of radiating knittles woven into a pattern that ostensibly gave a more comfortable spread of tensions, but in reality were a fine display of sea skills. He had never caught the habit of tobacco, but knew that it gave Renzi satisfaction, and murmured something appropriate. "We're right lucky t' take the barque," he said. Patch had been considerably mollified and was now warily respectful of Kydd.

"Just so," said Renzi, gazing at the spreading red display astern, "yet I believe our Captain must be much relieved."

"Aye, we could not have taken a real pepperin' from such a one." Kydd raised his voice against a sudden burst of laughter from the others enjoying the evening on deck.

Renzi smiled. "A captain of a vessel charged with despatches endangers his vessel at his peril—but his bold actions may be accounted necessary with shoals under his lee and the enemy to weather."

"Doud says as he's a hellfire jack, an' sent into *Seaflower* for the gettin' of prizes f'r the Admiral," Kydd said.

"Possibly—but a humble cutter? Maid-of-all-work? But did not David prevail over the disdainful Goliath!"

Kydd grinned.

"You've done well for yourself, my friend. Who would have thought it? A quartermaster, and so quick!"

"Only a cutter, is all," Kydd said, but his voice was warm. To direct the conn of a ship of war was a real achievement for any seaman.

Letting the fragrance of his tobacco wreathe about him, Renzi mused, "Tom, have you given thought to your future?"

Kydd looked up, surprised. "Future? Why, it's here in *Seaflower*, o' course." He stopped work and stared at the horizon, then turned to Renzi. "If you mean, t' better myself, then y' understand, I'm now a quartermaster an' as high as I c'n go. Any higher needs an Admiralty warrant, an' I don't have the interest t' get me one." He had spoken without bitterness. "Next ship'll be bigger, an' after that, who knows? Quartermaster o' some ship-o'-the-line will do me right well." His broad smile lit up his face as he added, "Y' can't work to wind'ard o' fate, so my feelin' is, be happy with what I have."

Renzi persisted. "Captain Cook was an able seaman to begin with, my friend—and Admiral Benbow."

Kydd's voice softened in respect. "Aye, but they're great men, an' I . . ."

"You sees, Mr. Cole, the boatswain is a mason," Doggo whispered, looking around fearfully.

The midshipman opened his eyes wide and leaned forward the better to hear. It was hard on young Cole, the only midshipman aboard and no high-spirited friends to share his lot, but he was a serious-minded lad who wanted to excel in the King's Service. "I have a great-uncle a freemason, too," he said in a slightly awed voice.

"Do yez good ter get the bo'sun an' you like this," Doggo held two fingers together. "An' he'll put in a powerful good word fer you t' the Captain."

Cole nodded gravely. "I see that, but how . . ."

"Well, the masons have this secret sign, wot they use to signal ter each other." Doggo looked furtively around the sunlit deck. "Like this," he said, and held up his open hand to his face, thumb to nose, and the fingers all spread out.

Awkwardly, Cole imitated him. Doggo pulled his hand down roughly. "Not now! Someone'll see. Now, mark what I say, it's terrible important yez do it the right way, or 'e'll think yer mockin' the masons."

Blinking in concentration, Cole listened.

"Yez waggles yer fingers, like so. An' then yer waits, f'r it's the proper thing fer masons to then pr'tend ter be in a rage—just so's nobody c'n accuse 'em of being partial to their own kind." Doggo paused to allow it to be digested. "An' then—mark me well, if y' please—yer waits fer the show ter blow over, an' that's when y' makes yer salute, both hands, all yer fingers at once."

Later in the watch, Cole had his chance.

"Where's that idle jackanapes?" roared the boatswain, from the group of men aft preparing to send up a fair-weather topgallant sail. "Lay aft this instant, y' lubberly sod."

Cole sauntered aft with a confident smile. Merrick drew breath for a terrible blast—but Cole boldly looked him in the eye and made the first sign.

The boatswain staggered as if struck. "God rot m' bones—you

bloody dog! Damn your impertinence! So help me, I . . ." Merrick paused for control, the enormity of it all robbing him of breath.

In the appalled silence the seamen looked at each other with horror and mirth in equal proportion. Cole saw that this was time for the salute, and bravely brought up both hands and waggled smartly. The boatswain's eyes bulged and his hands clawed the empty air. When the explosion came it was very terrible.

Jarman looked at Kydd speculatively. His cabin was tiny, there was not really room for two people, but there was nowhere else to speak in private.

"Kydd," he said, and paused, as if reluctant to go on. Kydd waited patiently. "Kydd, I'm the sailing master 'n' you're m' quartermaster." This did not need an answer. Jarman leveled his gaze. "What I'm a-sayin' is not f'r other ears. D'ye know what I mean?"

Kydd shifted uncomfortably. If Jarman was sounding him out over some spat with another, he wanted no part of it.

Seeming to sense his unease Jarman hastened to explain: "Jus' a precaution, y' understands, nothin' t' worry of," he said. "No harm keepin' an eye t' weather, like." Kydd maintained a wary silence.

The master picked up a book of navigation tables. "I been to sea since I was a kitling, an' ended up mate in an Indiaman. I know the sea, ye unnerstands—t' get to be master o' *Seaflower* I has to be examined by th' Brothers of Trinity House f'r this rate o' vessel, a tough haul."

Kydd wondered where it was all leading. He had no problem with the master's competence, but then remembered the reserve between him and the Captain. Was he feeling insecure, needing Kydd's approval? Surely not.

Jarman's voice dropped. Kydd strained to hear against the hiss of sea against the outside of the hull. "It's like this—an' please hear me out. Th' Cap'n—an' please t' know I mean no disrespect—is a young man, an' did all his time in a vessel o' size, never in a small 'un. Y' knows that in a big ship ye can make all the blunders y' like an' there's always someone to bring y' up with a round turn, but a small hooker . . ."

Kydd kept his face blank. This might be the first step on the way to a court-martial for mutiny.

"As I said, you're my quartermaster, an' directly responsible t' me."

This looked grave: Was Jarman trying to secure loyalty to himself?

"Consider, if y' please. The Cap'n an' me are the only ones aboard that c'n figure our position, th' bosun never learned. Now, I could say as how I'm a mort disturbed about we bein' carried off b' the fever, but I'd be lying. See, this is m' first ship as master, an' anything goes awry, then it'll be me t' blame—I don't see as how I should give best if it comes t' an argyment over the workings."

Farrell, as captain, had a duty to seek the sailing master's advice only, and could entirely overrule him. Jarman wanted a witness— but what possible use was Kydd?

"So, I'd take it kindly if ye could jus' think about if you'd like to learn how to do the figurin' y'rself."

Kydd sat back in disbelief. But he quickly responded: it was a great opportunity, not the slightest use in his position, but . . . "I'd like it main well, Mr. Jarman," he said, "but how will I learn?"

Jarman eased into a smile. "Don't ye worry—in the merchant service we has no truck wi' pie-arse-squared an' all that, no time!" He tapped the book of tables. "It's all there—ye just takes y'r sights an' looks it up. I learned it all in a short whiles only."

Farrell nodded approval when Jarman brought it up at seven bells. "If you think it proper, Mr. Jarman." Therefore at noon, on the quarterdeck of *Seaflower* could be seen the amazing sight of the Captain, the master, the midshipman and Kydd preparing to take the noon altitude. Midshipman Cole as usual borrowed Farrell's gleaming black and brass sextant, while Kydd gingerly took the worn octant wielded respectfully by Jarman.

Afterward, the master, as was his duty, took Cole aside to examine his reckoning and drill him in the essentials. Kydd hovered to listen. "Now, every point of half th' surface of the earth is projected fr'm the center onto a tangent plane at some point, call'd its point o' contact—but th' plane o' the equator when projected fr'm the center onto a tangent plane itself becomes a straight line. . . ."

While the worried Cole tried to commit the words, Jarman turned to Kydd. "Now, what we have there is a great circle. Nobody sails a great circle—we only steer straight or th' quartermaster-o'-the-watch would be vexed. What we really does is alter course a mort the same way once in a watch or so, an' that way we c'n approximate y'r circle."

There was more, and unavoidably it needed books: Renzi took an immediate interest. "To snatch meaning from the celestial orb—to gather intelligence of our mortal striving from heavenly bodies of unimaginable distance and splendor. Now that is in pursuit of a philosophy so sublime . . ."

With Hispaniola to larboard, they took a southeasterly slant across the width of the Caribbean, the trade winds comfortably abeam and, in accordance with Kydd's shaky workings shadowing the real ones, raised the island of St. Lucia and its passage through to the open Atlantic Ocean. The Windward Island of Barbados lay beyond.

Kydd's shipmates accepted his privileged treatment with respect. He was one of their own, daring to reach for the one thing that set officers apart from seamen. It was a rare but not unknown thing for a foremast hand to take part in the noon reckoning, although in the usual way all officers' results were brought together for consensus while those of lesser beings were ignored.

The rule-of-thumb principles used in the real world, informed by Jarman's utilitarian merchant service experience, Kydd absorbed readily enough—it was really only the looking up of tables. What was more difficult was the bodily technique of using the heavy old octant to shoot the sun against the exuberance of *Seaflower*'s sea motion. A combination of tucking in the left elbow, lowering the body to make the legs a pair of damping springs and leaning into it, and Kydd soon had the sun neatly brought down to the horizon with a sure swing of the arm.

The underpinning of mathematics was beyond him, though. Renzi had the sense to refrain from pressing the issue. There would be time and more in the lazy dog-watches to make intellectual discoveries, and Kydd would benefit by the more relaxed explorations. Besides which, it was only the hapless Cole who was under pressure: he would take his qualifying examination for lieutenant within the year.

Off Cape Moule to the south of the island the boatswain shielded his eyes from the glare of the sun on the calm blue seas— the wind had dropped to a fluky zephyr. "Have ye news of Saint Lucia, sir?" he asked. The island changed hands with the regularity of a clock, and the green and brown slopes could now be hostile territory, around the point an enemy cruiser lurking.

Farrell grunted, swinging his glass in a wide sweep over the hummocky island, across the glittering sea of the passage to the massive dark gray island of St. Vincent just fifteen miles to the south. "I don't think it signifies," he said finally. "We will be past and gone shortly."

In the light airs, *Seaflower* rippled ahead toward an offshore island and then the open sea. Kydd watched the course carefully: the tiny breeze was dropping and their progress slowed. The big foresail shivered and flapped, and the bow began to fall away. "Watch y' head!" he growled to the man at the tiller.

"Can't 'old 'er," the pigtailed seaman grunted, his thigh stolidly pressuring the tiller hard over.

"We lost steerage way, sir," Kydd told Farrell. With the wind so light the heat clamped in, a clammy, all-pervasive breathlessness. *Seaflower*'s sails hung lifeless, idle movements in the odd cat's-paw of breeze. Blocks clacked against the mast aimlessly and running rigging sagged. Kydd looked over the side. Without a wake the sea was glassy clear, and he could see deep down into the blue-green immensity, sunlight shafting down in cathedral-like coruscations.

Jarman broke the dull silence. "We have a contrary current here-abouts, sir," he said heavily. *Seaflower* lay motionless in the calm— but the whole body of water was pressing inexorably into the Caribbean, carrying the vessel slowly but surely back whence she came. "'Twould be one 'n' a half, two knots." That was the speed of a man walking, and even within the short time they had lain becalmed they had slid back significantly against the land. A bare hour later they were back at the point they had begun their passage.

A few welcome puffs shook out the sails, died, then picked up again. A tiny chuckle of water at her forefoot and *Seaflower* resumed her course, heading once more for the offshore islet. Once more the fluky wind betrayed them, and they were carried back again. "T' the south?" asked the boatswain.

"No," said Jarman, moodily watching the coast slip back. "Can't beat to weather in this, an' if we goes south we have t' claw back t' Barbadoes after." Unspoken was the knowledge that a French lookout post might be telegraphing their presence even now to Port Castries and any man-o'-war that lay there; any improvement in the wind later could bring a voracious enemy with it.

A darkling shadow moving on the sea's surface reached *Seaflower,* and the welcome coolness of a breeze touched Kydd's face—and stayed constant. Again, the cutter moved into the passage but this time the land slipped by until they had made the open ocean and were set to pass the little islet. "I believe we may now bear away for Barbadoes," Farrell said with satisfaction, but his words were overlaid by an urgent shout from the crosstrees.

"*Saaail hoooo!*" There was no need for a bearing. By chance occluded by the islet at the same rate as their advance, the sails of a square-rigger slid into view, heading to cross their path.

"Brig-o'-war!" snarled Merrick. There would be little chance against such a vessel and, with the wind gathering, the farther they made the open sea, it favored the larger craft.

Farrell's telescope went up and steadied. "I think not, Mr. Merrick—to quarters this minute."

But the merchant brig was not ready for a fight and struck immediately—to the savage delight of *Seaflower*'s company. They entered Bridgetown with a prize in tow, sweet medicine indeed.

To muted grumbles *Seaflower* was ordered to sea immediately: the niceties of adjudicating shares in prize money between the Admiral whose flag *Seaflower* wore and the Admiral in whose waters the capture took place would have to be resolved before the sailors saw any, and in any case the Vice Admiralty Court would have to sit first.

As they put to sea again after storing, busy calculations were taking place in a hypothetical but blissful review of personal wealth. "Merchantmen—so we don' see head money," Petit grumbled.

Farthing pulled up a cask to sit on. "An' gun money neither."

Kydd arrived down the hatchway and joined in. "Ye're forgettin' that a merchant packet has cargo—that's t' be included, y' loobies." Gun money and head money were inducements to take on an enemy man-o'-war but the value of a merchant-ship cargo would normally far exceed it.

He paused for effect. "D'ye know, we return to Port Royal, but if we fall in wi' the *Corbeau* privateer, we're t' take her?" As a privateer counted as neither a merchant ship nor a man-o'-war, there was no real profit in an action; and even if they did encounter her, a privateer was crammed with men and would make a fierce opponent. "Could never meet up wi' her, y' never knows," Kydd said cheerfully, collecting his rain slick and going back on deck. It was a maddening combination of sun and sheeting rain, and Farrell would be on deck shortly to set the course.

Seaflower now sported a pair of chase guns in her bow—and carriage guns at that instead of the swivels of before. Admittedly they were four-pounders only, but a three-inch ball slamming in across the quarterdeck could cause real discomfiture in a quarry. Stirk was eager to try them, but they were crammed in the triangle of bow forward of the windlass and the bowsprit beside. His gun crews could not rely on the usual recoil to bring the gun inboard for loading; they must reload by leaning outside, exposing themselves to enemy sharpshooters.

"Know anythin' about this *Corbeau*?" Kydd asked Stirk.

He straightened from his gun and wiped his mouth. "Patch says as how she's a schooner—not yer squiddy trader, but a big bastard, eight ports a side. Guess at least six-pounders, hunnerd men—who knows?"

Farrell, appearing on deck, put an end to the speculation. "Mr. Jarman. Be so good as to shape course north-about Saint Lucia."

"North-about, sir?" repeated Jarman in puzzlement.

"Please," said Farrell, with some asperity.

"He's chasin' the privateer 'cos he's worried she won't find us," croaked the helmsman out of the side of his mouth; north-about would place them between St. Lucia and the large island of Martinique, a favorite stalking ground for the more lawless afloat.

They reached the southern end of Martinique in the midst of another rain squall, curtains of white advancing over the sea under low gray skies, the wind suddenly blustery and fitful while it passed.

Afterward there were the usual wet and shining decks as they emerged into bright sunlight—but crossing their path directly ahead was a schooner. A big vessel, one that could well mount sixteen guns and carry a hundred men. She instantly put up her helm and went about, slashing directly toward *Seaflower* as if expecting her presence, her fore-and-aft rig robbing the Navy craft of the best advantage, her superior maneuverability.

"Hard a' larb'd!" Farrell cracked out; they were sheering off not to retreat, but to gain time. The schooner followed downwind in their wake, her two lofty masts allowing nearly twice the sail of *Seaflower.*

There would be no stately prelude to war, no pretense at false colors: the two antagonists would throw themselves at each other without pause or pity. Aboard *Seaflower* there was no fife and drummer sounding "Hearts of Oak," no hammocks in the nettings, no marines drawn up on the poop. Instead there were men running to whip off the lead aprons from gunlocks, and gun equipment was rushed up from below: rammers, handspikes, crows, match tubs. Tompions protecting the bore of the cannon were snatched away and *Seaflower*'s full deck of six-pounders were run out.

Farrell waited, then turned *Seaflower* on her pursuer. Right around she swung—her broadside crashed out into the teeth of her foe, the smoke swiftly carried away downwind, leaving a clear field of fire for her chase guns, which cracked out viciously in a double fire.

First blood to *Seaflower,* thought Kydd exultantly, as he centered the tiller. It was, however, a new and unpleasant experience, standing unmoving at the helm, knowing that he was certainly a target for unknown marksmen on the schooner. He glanced at the vessel: there were now holes in her sails, but no lasting damage that he could see.

Seaflower completed her turn, her other side of guns coming to bear, but the schooner was already surging around to bring her own guns on target—the two ships opened up almost simultaneously. Kydd heard the savage, tearing passage of cannonballs and was momentarily staggered by the displaced wind of a near miss. Through his feet he felt the bodily thud of a shot in the hull, the sound of its strike a crunch as of a giant axe in wood.

The smoke cleared. The schooner, certainly the *Corbeau,* was racing along on the opposite tack to *Seaflower*, her outer jib flapping free where the sheets must have been shot away. Her decks were crowded with men.

Farrell reacted instantly. "Hard a' starb'd!" he ordered. They would stay about and parallel the schooner—but *Corbeau* was there out to windward, she had the weather gauge, she could dictate the terms of the fight. Firing was now general, guns banging up and down the deck, smothering gunsmoke blown down on them, obscuring points of aim. *Seaflower*'s own guns were served with a manic ferocity.

"It's a poundin' match," shouted the boatswain to Farrell.

"Better that than let those murdering knaves board us," Farrell replied coolly, lifting his telescope once more.

Kydd could see little of *Corbeau* a few hundred yards to weather, but could feel the injury she was doing to *Seaflower*. He worried about Renzi, gun-captain of one of the forward six-pounders. If it came to repelling boarders he would be with the first of the defenders, probably going down under the weight of greater numbers. But if—

A sudden shudder and simultaneous twanging from close by made Kydd grip the tiller convulsively. The cause was ahead of him—there, the weather running backstay had taken a ball and was now unstranding in a frenzied whirl. Kydd instantly threw the helm hard over, sending *Seaflower* down before the wind.

Farrell saw what had happened and rapped out orders to ease away sheets to conform to the change in direction. The running backstays were vital sinews in taking the prodigious strain of *Seaflower*'s oversize mainsail, without which the mainmast would certainly carry away with the asymmetric forces playing on it. The stay now had some relief—but for how long? "Mr. Merrick—" But the boatswain was already calling for a rigging stopper, shading his eyes and gazing up to where the final strand was giving way. The lower part of the stay fell, its blocks clattering to the deck, leaving the upper length to stream freely to leeward.

Corbeau had been caught unawares, but now fell in astern in pursuit, the sudden silence of the guns from her bow-on angle allowing the victorious yelling of the enemy seamen to come clearly across the water.

The fighting stopper, a tackle with two tails, would be applied to each side of *Seaflower*'s wound, drawing the stay together again to be tautened by heaving on the tackle, but so high was the wound that someone would have to climb to the ratlines in the face of the storm of shot and musketry. Merrick took the hank of rope and blocks, the lengths of seizing, and without pausing draped them around his neck and swung up into the shrouds.

"Sir." Jarman was pointing to the little islet not a quarter of a mile ahead: he seemed to be suggesting some sort of hide-and-seek around the island.

Farrell stroked his chin. "One hand forward," he said, common prudence with coral about, "and we'll keep in with the island until we are to leeward, then . . ."

Kydd eased the tiller, snatching a glance astern. The schooner thankfully had no chase guns, but she was clapping on every stitch of sail and was gradually closing on *Seaflower.*

Jarman went forward with the lookout, staring intently into the water ahead, and indicated to Kydd with his arm where they should go. Musket balls occasionally hissed past, and one slapped into the transom, but the real danger would be when *Corbeau* reached and overhauled them. With the size of her crew, aroused to an ugly pitch, the privateer would be merciless.

Kydd clamped his eyes on Jarman. They were up to the island, and now began to round its undistinguished tip.

The schooner must have sensed their desperation, for she continued to crowd on sail, her crew clearly visible on her fo'c'sle, the glitter of edged weapons catching the sun as they waved them triumphantly.

"She's slowing!" Farrell's incredulous gasp came. "She's—she's taken the ground! *Corbeau*'s ashore!"

Kydd snatched a look over his shoulder. *Corbeau* was untouched, motionless on the course she had taken. She had misjudged the off-shore reefs and her deeper keel had become firmly wedged among the coral heads.

Seaflower curved around, but *Corbeau* lay unmoving.

"God be praised—we get t' live another day!" muttered a voice.

An angry shout sounded from above. Merrick had passed the seizing on the upper length of the stay, and was demanding the rest to be hauled up to him. They had the luxury of dowsing sail while the operation was completed, *Corbeau* a diminishing image in the distance. The jury stay rigged, they could then beat a digni-fied retreat.

"Ready about," ordered Farrell. "We finish the job," he said firmly. They carefully returned on a track that kept the bow of the schooner toward them. He hailed Stirk. "Grape."

Seaflower shortened sail to glide in within a hundred yards, then put up the helm and let go the stream anchor forward and kedge anchor aft. They came to a standstill, but were now in a position to adjust cables to aim her entire broadside to bear on the unpro-tected length of the big schooner.

With terrible deliberation Stirk went from one gun to the next, sighting carefully and touching off an unstoppable blast of man-killing grape-shot into the hapless vessel. It took until the third gun before activity was seen in the *Corbeau*—they were launching their longboat.

"That will do, Stirk," Farrell called. Kydd was struck with Far-rell's humanity in allowing the enemy to abandon ship without unnecessary killing, and felt ashamed of his own bloodlust.

"Give y' joy on y'r prize, sir!" Jarman said, with considerable respect.

"Renzi!" *Seaflower*'s captain ordered. "The longboat—do ye take possession of our prize."

Grinning, Kydd watched Renzi climb into the longboat with his crew, but they were only halfway across when the first wisps of smoke arose. The boat's crew lay on their oars and watched blue smoke bursting into flame as tarry ropes caught, spreading the consuming blaze to the upper rigging. A crackling, bursting firestorm turned the schooner into an inferno, the shape of her hull only just perceptible in the flames. The climax came when first her foremast and then her main crashed down in a gout of sparks and the rapidly charring ruin forlornly settled to the reef. *Corbeau*'s crew watched silently, lined along the shoreline. They were still there when *Seaflower* brought her longboat aboard and sailed away.

"Barbadoes?" asked Jarman. They had been cut about; it stood to reason they refit.

The beady eyes of Snead, the carpenter's mate, announced his presence on deck. "Sir," he said, touching his shapeless felt hat, "we've taken a ball in midships, an' takin' in water." The clinker build of *Seaflower*'s hull was proving its worth—the strake where the ball had entered would need replacing but the rest were sound.

"How bad?" Farrell asked.

"Can swim a-whiles," said Snead, "but she can't take a blow."

"Dockyard," said Merrick.

Snead looked at him and nodded.

Jarman turned to Farrell. "Antego," he said, without hesitation.

"Antigua—a couple of days only, thank the Lord," said Farrell, but Kydd flinched. Of all places . . .

CHAPTER 11

———

*E*nglish Harbour shimmered under the noonday heat; it was quite the same as Kydd remembered—the beauty, the rank effluvia, the calm solidity of spacious stone buildings. Here it was that he had nearly ended his existence on earth, here it was . . .

Seaflower came to anchor a few hundred yards off. There were hardly any ships in harbor, only a small sloop alongside at the capstan house without her upper masts. Signal flags mounted *Seaflower*'s main topgallant peak. Kydd knew what they were asking and determined to be elsewhere when Caird came aboard for his survey.

Uncaring of the still, clammy heat building below decks in the absence of a clean sea breeze, the boatswain ordered the platforms in the crew space overlaying the hold taken up. Kydd as quartermaster had the task of restowing their stores—firkins of butter, barrels of salt beef, hogsheads of water—over to one side of *Seaflower* in order that the damaged strake could be lifted clear for repair.

When the master shipwright made his survey, unaccountably the cutter's quartermaster was not free to accompany him, but from his busy job shuffling the master's charts, Kydd was able to hear through the skylight. "A strake 'twixt wind and water—a trifling matter," came Caird's voice. "As we have so few to care for at this time, my party will attend on you presently."

Indistinct words came from Farrell, and Caird replied, "No, I do not believe that is necessary. Our riggers will perform the task. We have skilled hands among the King's Negroes, you'll find."

A bumping on the hull told Kydd that the dockyard boat was putting off. He waited a little before coming on deck. The shipwright's punt would be making its way out soon, and there were some he would welcome to see again, but in no circumstances would he venture ashore.

Farrell did not go ashore either. Curiously, Kydd saw him in the shade of the after awning, his attention seeming to be on the nondescript sloop tied up off the capstan house. Farthing said quietly, "Old ships! That's *Patelle,* it's fr'm her that he got his step, Cap'n o' *Seaflower.*"

A distant boom sounded—Kydd looked automatically to Shirley Heights, the army post high up on the point. Smoke eddied away: strange sail had apparently been sighted far out to sea. Signal flags appeared, and were answered in the dockyard. Minutes later a boat under sail left the shore and headed directly for them. Kydd hoped that it wasn't a French squadron out there: English Harbour was particularly helpless now with only one warship—their own—available to meet them.

"Four strange sail sighted!" hailed a seaman in the boat, "An' *Patelle* unable ter shift!"

Farrell stiffened. "Secure the vessel, Mr. Merrick," he rapped. "Do you and Mr. Jarman remain aboard—I am going ashore. Stirk, you and Kydd attend on me in the longboat."

Reappearing in full uniform, Farrell saw Kydd and Stirk in their comfortable loose shirts and snapped, "Jackets, at the least, please!"

They tumbled down the hatchway and Kydd grabbed at his blue jacket with the brass buttons that marked him a petty officer. "What d'ye think, Toby?" Kydd asked, slipping it on.

"Dunno," Stirk said flatly, and they bounded up the ladderway.

Farrell took the tiller and they rapidly pulled ashore, the bowman hooking on at the stone steps while they landed. It was close by, the Admiral's House, but the absence of the appropriate flag showed it had no occupant. Mounting the steps in a hurry, Farrell bumped into a clerk. "Who is the senior officer?"

Eyebrows lifting in astonishment, the clerk replied, "The commissioner is with Captain Mingley in Saint John's at the moment—sir."

"Then, sir, who is in command, may I ask?"

The clerk paused, as if to take his measure. "Sir, in the absence of Captain Mingley that would necessarily be the senior officer afloat."

"Is Captain Fox still with the *Patelle*?"

"He is at Saint John's at the same court-martial."

"Then who is in command?"

"*Patelle* is under the temporary command of one of her lieutenants."

Farrell, followed by the clerk, entered an anteroom on the ground floor, and glanced about. "I shall set up headquarters here. Desire the Shirley Heights garrison to send an officer to attend me here for an immediate council of war."

The clerk looked affronted but, at Stirk's grim look, quickly left. A sergeant of marines shortly appeared and gave a crashing salute. "Sah!" With his local knowledge, Kydd helped to pull things together, and within the hour a captain of the Royal Scots Fusiliers was in respectful attendance.

Meanwhile, Farrell had the marine messenger busy with orders:

"To the officer commanding, Shirley Heights: 'It would be of some service to me should you see fit to begin heating shot as of this moment.'" Guns mounted on the commanding heights above the harbor could send red-hot shot among invading ships.

"My compliments to the commander of *Patelle* and he is to send her longboat, mounted with a swivel, to lie at grapnel in the entrance to the harbor."

There was a small number of marines, less the usual number of sick, but the army was in some strength in forts at Shirley Heights and Blockhouse Hill. Barracks at Monks Hill and The Ridge held an unknown number of soldiers, depending on how many had fallen victim to the yellow fever. Would it be enough?

"Sah!"

"Yes, Sergeant?" Farrell looked up from his desk. The man looked ill at ease. Farrell frowned. "What is it, man?"

"Sah!"

"Yes," said Farrell impatiently. "Get on with it."

"Sah, Lieutenant Powell o' the *Patelle* says—er, L'tenant Powell tol' me that 'e's unable ter comply with y'r orders, sah!"

Farrell rocked back in his chair. "Do I understand you to say that Lieutenant Powell is unable to send his ship's boat out?"

The sergeant hesitated. "Er, it's like this, sah. L'tenant Powell says as 'ow he, er, don't recognize yer orders, like."

Everyone in the room froze. The dockyard clock ticked heavily.

"Where is the officer now?" Farrell asked finally.

The sergeant, still rigidly at attention, said tightly, "Don't rightly know, sah."

Farrell opened his mouth, but Kydd broke in, "You mean t' say he's in the capstan house, do ye not?"

The sergeant's eyes swiveled to Kydd. "Could be."

Kydd went on carefully, "Sir, seems th' l'tenant is enjoyin' an evenin' jug, didn't quite understan' y'r orders."

Farrell gave a wintry smile. "As it happens, I know Mr. Powell."

The smile vanished. "Send word to the master of *Patelle* that Lieutenant Powell is to be confined to his cabin immediately." The sergeant saluted and left hastily.

Stirk looked meaningfully at Kydd but said nothing.

Another languid sunset was on its way, but there was tension in the air. "Have my orders been carried out?" Farrell demanded. The unknown four sail at last sighting were lying becalmed fifteen miles away: the focus of attention was now narrowing to this vexing insubordination.

"Oi!" Outside, the sergeant of marines beckoned furiously to Kydd. "Yer L'tenant Powell—y' knows about 'im an' Farrell?"

"No?" said Kydd guardedly.

The sergeant pursed his lips. "Well, see, they was both lootenants in *Patelle* t'gether, but hated each other's guts somethin' wicked. Now, I got a bad feelin' about this, I has, goin' to end in no good a-tall fer anyone."

Kydd looked at the sergeant intently. "Is Powell confin'd?"

"No. See—it's the sailin' master he's bin drinkin' with," he added, "an' now, well, yer Jack Tars are gettin' upset at their Cap'n being taken in charge like, an—"

One of the dockyard men approached with a strange expression. "Ye'd better give this t' yer officer, lads," he said, holding out a document.

Kydd took it. It was written orders for the disposition of soldiers to the dockyard, and it was signed, "Powell, Lieutenant, Royal Navy, Senior Officer of ships in English Harbour for the time being."

"Sergeant!" shouted Farrell, from inside. "Has Lieutenant Powell been confined in accordance with my orders?"

Kydd entered, and touched his hat to Farrell. "No, sir, an' I think you should see this."

Farrell read it, and stood, his face white. "Sir," he said to the army captain, "you will oblige me by taking a file of six soldiers and placing Lieutenant Powell under arrest." The captain, barely managing a salute, collected his shako and made to leave. "And, Kydd," added Farrell, "please to accompany him, in the event he goes aboard a ship."

Outside in the gathering dusk, Kydd watched while the army officer formed the men into line, had them crashing to an "order arms," then "shoulder arms." The word was getting out, and figures were beginning to emerge from buildings to line the roadway.

"Into file—right *tuuurrn*! By the right—quick *maaarrrch*!"

Kydd fell in behind the officer, but felt a fool, tagging along behind the quick-stepping soldiers. The little party wound along the roadway, Kydd feeling every eye on him. Chattering died away as they approached. They turned the final corner to the flat coral-stone area between the capstan house and the ship alongside. Spectators crowded around the capstan house, but the space was left clear as though it were an arena for some future duel. Along the deckline of *Patelle* her ship's company crowded and there was an ugly buzz of talk shot through with angry shouts.

"*Partyyyy*—halt!" The redcoats clashed to a standstill.

There were two gangways from *Patelle* to the stone landing, one forward for the men, one aft for the officers. Kydd indicated the after brow to the army captain. But before he could proceed, a man who looked very like a boatswain stormed down in hot confrontation. "Damn y'r blood, but I know why ye're here," he said, "and ye can't have him!" Behind him hostile eyes glared in the somber gloom. Lanthorns were brought and hooked into the rigging, their light casting a theatrical glow over events.

"In the name of His Majesty, I order you to yield the person—"

Furious but indistinct shouting sounded from inboard. It brought an immediate answering roar from the seamen on deck, and a sudden burst of activity.

"Fall back on the redcoats," the army officer said breathlessly to Kydd and hurried to stand next to the stolid file of soldiers. From the forward brow the ship's company of *Patelle* poured forth armed with boarding weapons—naked cutlasses, boarding pikes and tomahawks.

Kydd stood firm, but a feral terror of the pack dug into his mind as the angry seamen surged about them. Bystanders scattered, then formed a cautious semicircle around the fray. By a trick of the light, Kydd caught sight of Juba in the crowd of onlookers, motionless, arms folded. He wondered for a moment if he should appeal for help—then thought of what it might mean if he were denied.

The seamen surrounded the party, and began jostling, thumping with the heel of their cutlasses, hoarse cries urging the soldiers to run away. One toppled forward under a blow. The army officer swung around and ordered shrilly, "Load with ball!" At the cry, the crowd began to scatter in disorder. The sailors spread out and hefted their weapons. If the soldiers opened fire they would be instantly set upon. But Kydd knew that the soldiers would do their duty without question. The end was therefore inevitable, and the shouts and cries died away into a breathless silence as all waited for the final spark.

Distantly, the sound of the measured tramp of men-at-arms sounded. It swelled, and a column of marines appeared. At its head was Farrell, in full uniform. The men came to a halt and Farrell strode purposefully to the center. "Where is Lieutenant Powell?" he demanded.

The sailors fell back, unsure.

"If by that you mean your superior officer, I am here," came a strong, resonant voice at the head of the brow. A short but well-built man in loose shirt and breeches came down. His face was robust but lined, the marks of hard drinking on him.

As the two men met, the others fell back.

"You have your orders, sir, why do you not comply?" Farrell snapped.

"Because—because you know well enough, damn you, Charles!"

Farrell's tone hardened. "You are under arrest—"

"Poppycock! You know as well as the whole *world* that you are junior on the lieutenants' list to me, and therefore I am your superior officer." Powell squared away. "And now you do take my orders or . . ."

Kydd was appalled. By the immutable rule of the Navy, the lieutenant whose date of commission was even a day earlier was automatically the senior officer. It even applied to admirals, and Powell's claim appeared to be legitimate.

Farrell's eyes flicked to the mass of silent seamen. Powell caught the look and snarled, "I have only to say the word, and these good men will sweep away your—"

"You'd shed good blood in such a cause?" Farrell exclaimed in astonishment, then stiffened. "I am your superior officer because I hold the King's commission as commander of a King's ship. You are acting commander only. Now, are you prepared to obey orders?"

Powell folded his arms. "No. You are in contempt of naval law, sir."

Kydd tensed. All it needed was for Powell to shout an order and the stones would be drenched in blood. Farrell did not pause. "Your pistol, sir," he asked of the army officer, never taking his eyes from Powell. The captain fumbled at his slung leather pouch and handed over the heavy weapon. Farrell took the pistol and cocked it, aiming at the ground.

"Do you now comply with my orders, sir?" he asked, in an icy monotone.

"If you seek to affright me, sir, you have failed."

The pistol came up, the dark cavity of the muzzle directly on Powell's chest. "For the final time, sir. Lieutenant Powell, do you accept my authority and obey my orders—in peril of your life?"

Both men stood rigid.

"You wouldn't fire, Charles! That would be—"

"Sir?" demanded Farrell in a steely hiss.

"Since you ask. No!"

The pistol blasted out, the ball taking Powell squarely in the chest, a sudden crash of sound in the awful stillness. It filled the air with a hanging cloud of gunsmoke and flung Powell back in a limp huddle. Nobody moved, all held motionless by the horror of the moment.

Farrell lowered the pistol. He turned to the army captain. "Sir, I surrender myself to you as senior officer and consider myself under open arrest."

The soldier's hands were shaking as he tried to make deprecating gestures.

Farrell's face was set, controlled. "I do demand a court-martial on my conduct at the earliest moment."

Seaflower did not rate a coxswain, and Captain Farrell chose Kydd as his personal attendant in his subsequent trial in St. John's. Kydd was thus witness to the solemn spectacle of a court-martial, and was present as his captain returned to the room—to see his sword on the table, hilt toward. The court had unanimously ruled that Farrell's conduct was justifiable in the face of Lieutenant Powell's actions, which amounted to mutiny, and Lieutenant Farrell was most honorably acquitted.

"An' when the president o' the court says the words, his face didn't change one whit," said Kydd to the throng in the crew space. "Jus' bows 'n' thanks 'em all, cool as you please." He had been impressed by Farrell's bearing, his calm replies to barely disguised needling about his earlier relationship with Powell as lieutenants in the same ship—and, equally, his return to *Seaflower.* In his place Kydd thought that he would perhaps have celebrated a trifle, but that was not Farrell's way.

Without delay, they put to sea, newly repaired and bound for Port Royal. As Kydd pulled out the charts to exercise plotting a route, Jarman smiled and said, "Well, how's y'r Danish, then?" Taken aback Kydd didn't know what to say. Jarman tapped at the chart. "First island you comes to after weatherin' Saint Kitts," he said, "Saint Croy, Danish these forty years, very peaceable, but Cap'n wants t' call on 'em f'r some reason."

There was a growing friendliness between them, and Kydd benefited in the learning of his sea craft. Jarman's plain-thinking explanations were the rock on which he was able later to elaborate the whys from the hows and give body to his knowledge. It touched Kydd's imagination, this reduction to human understanding of the inscrutable vast restlessness that was the sea; to be able to bring a world into compass on a single chart, the legendary sights he had seen on foreign shores all rendered tactile and biddable to the will of man.

"When I learned m' figurin' it was always the three Ls, 'lead, latitude 'n' lookout,' an' no more," Jarman told him. "An' that is not t' say they should be cast aside these modern times. But now we just adds a fourth—longitude."

Longitude . . . The deep respect Jarman accorded the two chronometers gave Kydd a feeling for what a fearsome thing sea life must once have been. No sure knowledge of their place in the trackless wastes of ocean, a starless night, a rocky coast—and it might be sudden death in the darkness. The gleaming brass and enamel devices were a true miracle of man's achieving. Now when it became local noon and the sun's altitude was taken, he knew for a certainty that in Guildford, if he could transport there instantly, the big old clock overhanging the High Street would be solemnly showing four o'clock in the afternoon.

They raised the island of St. Croix late in the afternoon, a low grassy seaside so much like parts of Cornwall as to be astonishing. This transformed into the usual lush rainforests farther along, but the helm was put up, and they came to anchor to seaward of an island to the northeast. "We approach Christiansted in the full light o' day," Farrell said. It was prudent: the Danes were a proud nation and touchy of their honor. They were neutral, but could throw in their lot with the Jacobins at any time.

They lay offshore to seaward, out of sight of the main island and snugged down for the night. The sunset's golden tendrils faded to a deep blue and then soft darkness, and without a moon the stars glittered fat and tremulous. After supper, Kydd and his shipmates repaired to the upper deck with their grog, making the most of their unaccustomed inactivity. Kydd settled next to Renzi, who was enjoying a pipe of tobacco, and Stirk sat on the main-hatch.

"Amazin' that," Stirk mused. The black, calm sea stretched into impenetrable darkness on each side, but the slap and chuckle of water around *Seaflower*'s cable was soothing to a sailor. "Puts me in mind o' Mount's Bay," Stirk went on. "Not as I'd want ter be reminded."

"Why so?" someone asked.

Stirk sat back against the mainmast and ruminated. " 'Cos o' what happened while I wuz there," he said finally.

"What was that, cuffin?" the voice persisted.

"Well, mates, if yer wants to know the full story, I warns yer, it's a tough yarn, but I tell yer, it's as true as y'r mainstay is moused!" Stirk teased.

"Cast loose yer tongue, matey," an invisible voice urged.

"Spread more sail!" another said. Luke scuttled up and squatted under Stirk's feet, agog to hear the yarn.

"Right, I'll fill and stand on," Stirk agreed. "When I was a younker, I was in another trade," he began.

Kydd hid a smile.

"Reg'lar run fr'm St. Marlow ter Penzance in brandy. Had a shipmate aboard name o' Cornish Jack, liv'd nearby. Now, he was a right frolicsome cove, always in wi' the ladies. An' he snares a real spruce filly—Kitty Tresnack she wuz called. Trouble is, she's married, see, to old man Tresnack 'oo owns a sizeable tin mine.

Didn't stop 'em—he'd step off soon as he knew 'ow, back aboard last minute, 'n' all the time off in the hills wi' this Kitty."

Stirk gave a snort that some might have interpreted as disapproval.

"He comes back aboard jus' as we're about t' sail, but there's noos. Seems old man Tresnack goes down wi' a fever 'n' dies real quick. So Cornish Jack can't wait t' get back 'n' marry Kitty—but when we does make port agen, he finds 'is intended in clink, arrested fer murder of 'er 'usband!

"They 'as the trial, an' she's found guilty, sentenced ter 'ang. Cornish Jack can't believe it—'e sleeps outside the prison walls till the day she's due ter be choked off. He asks permission to go with 'er to the scaffold. They agrees, an' on th' day he goes up ter the gallows 'oldin' 'er 'and and when it's time 'e clutches 'er tight. The rope goes around 'er neck, an' she asks 'im, solemn like, 'You will?' Jack gets uneasy, but says, 'I will.' She then goes calm and it's all over fer 'er."

Stirk paused for effect, and continued. "After that, Kitty's ghost wuz seen twice, three times or more on the road b'tween Penzance an' Hayle, an' Cornish Jack's a changed man. Goes pale 'n' thin, never laughs—terrible change if y' knew 'im. At th' tavern 'e was 'eard ter say, 'She gives me no peace, follers me everywhere.' We all knows 'oo 'she' is.

"Just a year after this, Cornish Jack was back at sea wi' us, an' in the fo'c'sle. He then finally tells what it was they said on th' gallows. 'She made me swear that on this day, one year more at midnight, I'd marry 'er.' See, not bein' able to get wed in th' flesh, she would in th' spirit.

"An' that's where it gets right scareful, we bein' in our 'ammocks 'n' jawin' together, it all goes quiet, like. That's when we 'ear these sharp small steps on the deckhead, comin' fr'm forrard. He goes white as chalk an' gets th' trembles. They stops right above where Jack 'as his hammock. His face goes mad wi' terror, but he drops ter th' deck and makes 'is way topsides. We rushes t' follow—but jus' in time ter see 'im leg it over th' bulwark ter throw 'imself in th' sea."

Stirk took a deep breath and said, in a low voice, "We catches only a couple o' white faces in them black waves, so 'elp me, an' then 'e's gone!"

The long silence following was Stirk's satisfying reward.

From seaward, Christiansted turned out to be a cozy, settled piece of Denmark in the Caribbean, all cream-colored buildings with red roofs, before lofty hills inland. At the sight of *Seaflower*'s ensign a warning gun thumped from Fort Christiansvaern, marked on the chart as "in want of repair." Obediently, *Seaflower* rounded to, let go her anchor outside the reef and awaited the boat putting off from the town.

The Danish officer boarded quickly, his glance taking in the clean lines, neatness and loving detail that only a sailor's pride in his ship could evoke. "Løjtnant Holbaek," the man said, in crisp military tones. His red-tasseled blue uniform looked odd on the deck of a Royal Navy cutter.

Farrell advanced with outstretched hand. "Welcome aboard His Majesty's Cutter *Seaflower,* er, Loytnant," he said. Holbaek shook hands. Turning meaningfully to Jarman, Farrell said loudly, "Loytnant Holbaek takes back to Christiansted the best wishes of His Britannic Majesty for prosperity and peace, and our hopes that the Jacobin upstarts will soon be swept from the seas."

"*Mange tak, Kommandør*—thenk yo," Holbaek said, with a clicking of heels. He seemed to bristle a little under the curious stares of *Seaflower*'s sailors. "An' my packet?"

"Of course." Farrell handed over the sealed package, which Holbaek quickly slipped inside his uniform. The dour officer did not seem inclined to linger, so Farrell handed him over the side with profuse expressions of regard, and the boat pushed off. "Now we shall proceed. Course for Port Royal, Mr. Jarman."

* * *

"Crusty bugger" was Stiles's judgment. He had been invited in with the petty officers, notwithstanding that as boatswain's mate his was probably the least popular job aboard. So far there had been no call on his services with the cat-o'-nine-tails, a tribute to the sense of harmony that Farrell was achieving.

The noon meal was well under way, rum sweet in the glass. The morning exercise at the after six-pounders had been particularly impressive and the light breeze was sending *Seaflower* along at a relaxed pace, the seas with barely a swell or more than a stipple of waves. Doggo poked his head inside the canvas screen, which by now had its full quota of mermaids and Davy Jones painted on it, and announced, "Might like ter come topsides—could be a bit of a to-do brewin'."

On the horizon to windward a tall pillar of smoke, hazy and pale with distance, rose straight up. "Ship afire," said Doggo bluntly, then nodded significantly aft at the Captain and Merrick in urgent conversation.

Detaching himself, Farrell called to Kydd, "Bear up for that fire."

Kydd ordered the helm over, *Seaflower* obediently turning toward. It was dead to windward, in the teeth of the light breeze, and even with *Seaflower*'s fore-and-aft rig she could lie no closer than four points off the wind before the luff of her sails began shivering and she lost way. The deck fell quiet. It didn't take much imagination to think of what must be happening in the unknown ship: the visceral terror at the flames rampaging, the bravery of those on board—then mortal despair taking hold.

Jarman reached the deck and quickly took in the scene. Kydd opened his mouth to comment, but Jarman held up his hand, keenly sensing the wind direction. Kydd noticed Farrell watching him closely as well. The vessel would know by now that they had been seen and their hearts would be leaping—but all would depend on how speedily they could reach the scene. "A bridle for bowlines on the topsails may answer, sir," Jarman said at last, "an' Kydd will bring her more by th' head by restowing."

Jarman's order meant sending a line to the forward part of the square sails to haul them even more flat to the wind, and shifting provisions and water barrels toward the bow to deepen the stem to give more bite. Kydd hastened below, grabbing hands for the task, which was soon completed. On deck he was joined by Renzi. "A nice problem," Renzi murmured, shielding his eyes to make out the approaching details.

"Aye," said Kydd. The ship afire was dead into the wind—how to get to her? To tack toward, of course, but the problem lay in whether to do short but direct boards and much tacking about, or long fast boards with few delays in tacking, but considerable distance to each side of the goal.

Given the constant of time necessary to go about, Jarman compromised on seven-minute legs. The breeze was frustratingly light, but even so the disastrous tableau came gradually closer. Every glass available was on the harrowing scene.

"Has a sea anchor over th' stern . . ."

"Yair—keeps 'er poop inter the wind, flames don't reach 'em."

"See it blaze at th' main-hatch! Give 'er less'n a dog-watch afore she goes up altogether. . . ."

Kydd took a telescope and trained it on the smoky ruin. The flame-shot vessel leaped into sharp focus. He could almost hear the devilish roar of the fire, the sharp banging and crackling of timbers in hopeless conflagration. There were dark figures against the flames, jerking and moving, but the main body were massed on the as yet untouched after end of the vessel. Kydd swept the telescope along—it was impossible to say which nationality the ship was, or even what species it was.

"Get th' longboat overside," urged some. *Seaflower* was now only a mile off but the wind was so soft and light that the cutter only made a walking pace through the calm waters.

"Longboat, stand by for launching," warned Farrell, "but avast lowering, we have to be closer." *Seaflower* was still just faster than men could row. The towering pillar of smoke darkened the whole area, tongues of flame an angry wild orange against the smoke.

As Kydd stared at the ruin, the stern fell off the wind—the line to the sea anchor had given way. He whipped up the telescope. In sharp detail he saw the after end of the vessel sag away to leeward and the fire leap up triumphantly. Dark figures fell into the sea as the flames advanced on the poop.

The calm seas around the stern became agitated. Flickers of white in dark flurries puzzled him for a moment until he understood—survivors in the water were being taken by sharks. His hands shook as he held the telescope. With a sick horror he saw the remaining figures on the poop hesitating between being burned to death or eaten alive by sharks. One by one they toppled into the water or danced insanely before crumpling into a briefly seen dark mass in the flames.

Seaflower curved smoothly into the wind and her longboat splashed into the water. Kydd watched as it pulled toward the hulk, now no more than a blackened wreck, a dying ember. The hideous twitching around the stern was now irregular and the desolate stink of the fire drifted down on them. The boat reached the still smoking hull and circled around. It returned with a pitiably burned corpse. "Weren't none made it, sir," the bowman said softly. "We c'n give 'em a Christian burial, like."

"No—they stay with their ship. They go together."

"Tom, mate!" whispered the carpenter's mate, plucking Kydd's sleeve. "Come an' 'ave a squiz 'tween-decks." Wondering at Snead's peculiar air of anxiety, Kydd followed him down the forehatch below.

Chasing aside seamen at the galley, Snead lifted the access grating to the forward hold and dropped inside, listening intently in the musty gloom. Satisfied, he hauled himself out. "Tell me what y' hears," he said, his lined gray eyes serious.

Kydd let himself down. As quartermaster he had the stowage of the hold, but that was in port or calm waters. Now, in this increasingly boisterous sea, wasn't the time to be rummaging among the big water barrels or tightly tommed-down stores. He hunkered down in the cramped space and listened carefully, bracing himself against the cutter's roll. Nothing at first, but then he heard over the swish of sea on the outside of the hull an intermittent sibilance as quiet and deadly as a snake. In time with the roll came a sudden rushing hiss which for a seaman had only one meaning. "We've sprung a plank somewhere on th' waterline—takin' in water fast!"

Snead looked at him peculiarly. "Yair, but when I sounds the bilges, ain't any water!"

"What? None?" Kydd asked. It was peculiar to a degree—the rushing hiss returned with every roll, and at this rate the water should be at least a foot deep in the lower hold.

"Don't like it, cully," Snead grumbled. "What say you 'n' I 'as a word wi' the Cap'n?"

"Heard o' this happenin' to a cargo o' rice—swells when it's wet, it does," Merrick said.

Jarman stroked his jaw. "Nothin' stowed below that I knows of like that," he said slowly. "But there's some kind o'—something—that's soaking it up fast. . . ."

"No chances. We heave down and get at it from the outside," Farrell said with finality. "I believe Islas Engaño will answer."

Kydd was relieved. A small cutter like *Seaflower* could easily find an island to beach between tides and get at the hull planking from the outside, and in this case the sooner the better. They raised the island late in the afternoon. Because the leak was getting no worse—in fact, the vessel was still mysteriously dry—they anchored in its lee to wait out the night. A passing rain squall spattered and then deluged the decks. Only the disconsolate lookouts fore and aft remained, the rest were snug below.

In the free discipline of a cutter, there would be no "pipe down hammocks" or other big-ship ways. And now at anchor was a time when a sailor could relax, no fear of an "All the *haaands!*" to send him on deck, no sudden course-change requiring the vessel to tack about—instead the sewing "housewife," the gleefulness of dice play, the scrimshaw, the endless letter . . .

Lanthorns spread a warm golden glow in the crew spaces and the hum of his shipmates' conversation was a reassuring backdrop to Kydd's thoughts. Renzi's musings about his future had awakened possibilities that were unsettling. It seemed that Renzi believed he was destined for something beyond quartermaster— that could only be master's mate, which required an Admiralty warrant. . . .

He watched Stirk throw a double trey at the dice with a roar of satisfaction—did *he* concern himself with times unknown? Unforeseeable circumstances? Himself in twenty years? Of course not! Kydd settled back in his hammock and listened to the drumming of rain on the deck above, grateful to be dry and warm. The rain eased, then stopped. Kydd slipped into drowsiness, unperturbed by the noises of his shipmates' pastimes and merriment, sure of himself and the world he had made his own.

A soft dawn revealed their island to have a long sandy beach, suitable to heave down *Seaflower* and get at the leak. Kydd had tried to localize the sound of inrushing water but, bafflingly, it had died away as they anchored.

The cutter gently grounded on the sand of the beach and was brought broadside to in the gentle waves. Snead waited in the longboat while lines were secured to her mast, taken to a tackle on a sizeable palm ashore and back to the windlass. Snead only needed to see the waterline region and it took little effort to achieve the required cant to one side. "'Tain't this side," he called from the boat, after going the length of the cutter. *Seaflower* was laboriously refloated and rotated for a survey of the other side—with the same result. A perfectly sound hull.

"Only one thing left t' do," Kydd muttered. They would have to rouse out the entire contents of the hold to put paid to the mystery, a long and tedious process. Starting from forward the first of the stores were brought out and laid against the after end of the crew space. Kydd saw that the men were well positioned in chain to pass up the provisions, and turned to go.

He was stopped by an incredulous shout. "God rot me! Come 'ere, Mr. Kydd!" Hurrying over to the fore hold, Kydd looked down. A seaman was standing and pointing to what he had found in the close stowage of the hold. It was a substantial-sized cask with its head knocked in, and in it was the remains of what it had contained—peas, dried for stowing, a sea of seven hundredweight of hard peas. And as the ship rolled, the peas had swished from side to side in the smooth barrel, sounding exactly like the hiss of inrushing water.

They made good sailing in clear conditions and secured a morning landfall on the odd-looking island of Alto Velo, off the southernmost point of Hispaniola. "We will take the inside passage, I believe, Mr. Jarman," said Farrell, inspecting the stretches of low, flat land to the north and the peaked dome of Alto Velo to the south.

The swell increased as they approached, a peculiar, angled swell that felt uneasy. Over to the northwest a serried rank of sharp-peaked mountains appeared out of the bright haze, white-topped and distant. Kydd growled at the helmsman when the *Seaflower*'s topsail fluttered, his eyes flicking astern to check her wake. It was straight—the ever-reliable trade winds were slowly but surely backing: it was not the fault of the helmsman. "Wind's backing," he called to Jarman.

"Just so," said the sailing master. "Those mountains, t'

weather." His mouth clamped tight and he glared generally to windward.

"We have the current in our favor, Mr. Jarman," Farrell said mildly.

"Sir."

The swell angled more and met a south-going counterpart that had *Seaflower* wallowing in confused jerking in the cross seas. Unfriendly green waves slopped and bullied onto her decks, sluicing aft to wet Farrell's shoes. They passed through the passage, the wind backing so far that *Seaflower* had to strike her square sails entirely. Once through, the predominant westerly current and northeasterly winds reasserted themselves and the way was clear for the final run to Jamaica. But for one thing. A brig-of-war. Five miles ahead across their path, her two masts foreshortening as she altered course purposefully toward them.

CHAPTER 12

B e damned," said Merrick, as he came up from below and saw the vessel. The meeting was most unfortunate: having emerged from the island passage *Seaflower* was prevented from going to windward by the lie of the land, and to bear away to leeward would favor the bigger canvas a brig-sloop could show.

"We put about an' return, sir?" Jarman asked immediately. There was no dishonor to fly before a vessel probably carrying half as many guns again as they.

Farrell turned on him angrily. "What do you conceive is our duty, sir? To run at the sight of every strange sail?"

Jarman grunted. "Well, we—"

"Clear for action, Mr. Merrick," Farrell ordered. *Seaflower* kept on her course westward toward the brig and girded for war. All eyes were on their opponent. The brig seemed nonplussed at *Seaflower*'s aggression and fell off the wind somewhat.

Kydd took the tiller, feeling the willing restlessness of the craft, and even through his own anxieties he felt for the lovely cutter and what she must suffer soon. The enemy brig was longer than they and therefore could array a greater broadside; being square-rigged with the ability to back sails she was more maneuverable in a clinch. *Seaflower's* chance lay in her speed and nimble handling— much would depend on Kydd's steadiness at the helm.

A gun thudded on the brig and a large battle flag unfurled at her mizzen peak. There would be no preliminaries, they would grapple and fight and the contest could well be over within the hour. The brig yawed to starboard. This brought her broadside to bear. It thundered out, but at more than a mile it was a ragged display, balls skipping wide on each side.

Merrick grinned. "Too eager b' half—a green-hide cap'n, I shouldn't wonder."

"They's sixes and fours, 'n' we has all sixes!" Stirk said with satisfaction. Kydd did not share his confidence: they had six-pounders, but only eight to a side. The brig resumed an easy close haul, knowing that *Seaflower* must close and endure their wrath before she could swing about and bring her guns on target.

"Stirk, be so good as to set your pretty ones to work," Farrell said with a grim smile.

Clambering over gear to the eyes of the ship, Stirk hunkered down and sighted along the black iron of his four-pounder chase guns. They were an older pattern and were not fitted with gun-locks; over the priming he held clear a glowing piece of match and, when satisfied with his quoin and at the right point in the pitching motion, his hand went down and they spoke with a ringing crack.

Kydd stared intently at the brig, but Stirk scrambled over the heel of the bowsprit to the other chase gun to repeat the exercise while the first was reloaded. Again the sharp report: gunsmoke temporarily obscured her, but when it cleared the brig showed in some confusion.

"Don' know what they wants ter do," Farthing observed. He was behind Kydd standing ready if Kydd fell in battle. The brig's square yards were at odds with each other—it looked like someone had shied away from the balls slamming across her decks, and had tried to bear away, but then a more experienced hand had intervened to send her back. It was hard for *Seaflower* to have to wait to come up before they could reply with their own guns.

"Told yer, it's a right green hand there," Merrick said, and looked at Farrell.

"Ease sheets, no need to rush at things," the Captain said smoothly. *Seaflower* slowed, and Stirk kept up his gunplay. The brig yawed and let go another broadside, but the little cutter's head-on profile was much too narrow a target, and all it achieved was to give Stirk a broader aiming point.

Seaflower tacked about to open the range once more. Her own broadside crashed out as she spun about, a French one not eventuating, as they were in the process of reloading. Stirk resumed his punishment, taking time to lay his weapon. "If'n she had chase guns th' same as we . . ." Merrick reflected.

Abruptly, the brig loosed a broadside, then turned away before the wind and retired. Derisive yells erupted in *Seaflower*—the brig's plain stern presented itself as she turned in retreat, the shouts became an urging to close and finish the vessel with close raking fire.

Kydd glanced at Farrell, who was studying the brig through his Dollond glass. He seemed not to hear the crew's jubilation, but then spoke to Jarman. "She wishes us to close. She is much the bigger—we keep our distance." As if to add point to his words, the brig flew up into the wind and her guns fired, some of the balls coming uncomfortably close. *Seaflower* took immediate opportunity to slew round and return the compliment in kind.

"If y' please, sir," Jarman had the chart. "I believe she means t' round Cabo Falso an' head f'r French waters."

"The nearest port she can find there?"

"Ah—that 'd be, er, Port des Galions. Small, but has a mole f'r the sugar trade."

"Any fortifications, do you think?"

"Always some kind o' unpleasantness at th' end o' the mole," Jarman ventured, looking at Merrick.

"Aye, sir, if she gets inshore o' the mole, we 'ave ter give it away, I fear," Merrick said.

Farrell remained pensive. The brig was too big to take on directly, they were being drawn away from their proper route to Jamaica and there was a possibility that a French man-o'-war was lying in Port des Galions that really did know his business. Straightening, he made up his mind. "We let Stirk have his amusement for a little longer—if he brings down a spar we reconsider, but if the brig makes port we let her go."

The rest of the afternoon was spent with periodic banging from the bow in a wash of powder smoke. Kydd and others spelled the gray-grimed and red-eyed Stirk in his task. The considerable swell angled across and *Seaflower*'s motion became a complex combination of pitch and roll. Behind the breech the sighting picture was jerky and swooping, and having to use a port-fire, instead of the instant response of a gunlock and lanyard, made the job nearly impossible. "Makin' it a mort uncomfortable for 'em," Stirk said hoarsely. He gulped thirstily at a pannikin of vinegar and water.

Beyond Cabo Falso the land trended northwest and within less than thirty miles they entered the French waters of San Domingo. The brig's course then shaped unmistakably for Port des Galions, a far-off thin scatter of buildings amid palm trees and verdure.

There was no result yet from the chase guns, which were now uncomfortably hot and radiated a sullen heat, but Stirk's crews worked on. The mole could be made out, a low arm extending out to enclose a tiny bay with a sandy spit on the opposite side, and no sign of any other vessel within. "Give 'er best, mate," said Farthing as the brig prepared to enter the little harbor and safety and Farrell prepared reluctantly to tack about and retire.

"We'll give 'em a salute as we go," Farrell grunted.

Seaflower stood on for a space, then put her helm up, turning for a farewell broadside. But it was what the vengeful brig had been waiting for—she yawed quickly and at last had the whole length of the cutter in her sights. Her guns crashed out: a storm of shot whistled about *Seaflower,* splintering, crashing, slapping through sails—and ending the life of *Seaflower*'s only midshipman. Cole had cheered with the best of them when the brig had turned tail, and his fist had been upraised when a ball took his arm off at the shoulder, flinging him across the deck. Stupefied, he tried to raise himself on all fours, but failed, rolling to one side in his own blood.

Farrell, himself winded by the passage of the ball, lunged across to the mortally wounded lad and held him gently as the life left him. He remained still as *Seaflower*'s own guns answered. His head fell, and when he looked up there was a murderous expression as his eyes followed the brig past the end of the mole to the inner harbor and safety.

Obedient to his last command, *Seaflower* headed for the open sea, but Farrell slowly got to his feet and breathed heavily. "Do you mark my words, we'll make them pay for this day."

For half a day *Seaflower* sped out to sea, Farrell pacing thoughtfully, at times disappearing below with the sailing master. Toward evening a plan had been hatched that Farrell laid before *Seaflower*'s company that afternoon around the main-hatch. "The port consists of a narrow point of land, with a mole on the other side like an arm enclosing a harbor. The brig will undoubtedly be alongside the inner face of the mole. Now, it were vain to think of carrying her in a direct assault in the open—the longboat can bear but fourteen men, this is not sufficient."

He paused, then smiled. "But we have a chance. I mean to 'borrow' a sugar lighter from farther up the coast. This is how the joggaree—the raw lump sugar—is carried to the port to be shipped out. These are mean and unworthy craft, having but one masterly quality: they may carry concealed as many stout men as we choose. "This lighter will approach the entrance, but it will be a sad parcel of lubberly rogues who try to bring her in. I have no doubt she will run afoul of whatever unfortunate vessel is lying alongside. . . ."

A restless murmuring and then grins broke out, followed by hearty chuckles. Farrell held up his hands for silence. "We still have a use for the longboat. With her fourteen men, it is landed before dawn on the far side of the point. The boat is dragged over the sandy point and therefore launched inside the harbor, where it may fall upon the enemy from a quite unexpected direction."

This time there was silence. It was broken by Farthing, who shouted, "An' it's three cheers fer Cap'n Farrell, mates! One, two, six—an' a *tigerrrr*!"

Farrell's smile of pleasure was unexpectedly boyish. "It is the custom in the Royal Navy on hazardous duty to call for volunteers. . . ." Kydd found himself coxswain of Stirk's longboat and Renzi was detailed for the lighter to assist with the French language. Nearly the whole of *Seaflower*'s crew would be involved in the venture, but five needed to be held back to keep the cutter at sea.

"I must request, Mr. Merrick," said Farrell, "that you remain to take the charge of *Seaflower*, therefore—"

"Sir! This is monstrous unjust!" the boatswain protested. "You do me dishonor—"

"I'm sure, Mr. Merrick, you will always do your duty in the best traditions of the Service."

The longboat was lowered from *Seaflower* when darkness fell. The quarter-moon would last for half the night and then would set, making it easy for the longboat to see its way to creep in to the seaward side of the point. In *Seaflower* hands were raised in farewell as she made off to the north to find the lighter, disappearing silently from view in the subdued moonlight.

The boat hissed to a stop on the sandy beach. Fourteen men

around the sturdy craft quickly had her up the beach and out of sight in the greenery. Stirk motioned to them to conceal themselves while he and Kydd went forward to reconnoiter.

It was absolutely quiet, a light susurration of breeze, gentle and soothing, and no sign of human presence on the dry, sandy landscape. Sharply contrasting black shadows on silver light made it hard to pick a way—the task was to get the boat over the point and in position to launch just before dawn. They chose a low saddle, sand with small rocks and little vegetation. It was harder than it looked to drag the heavy boat across the small, gnarled scrub with feet stubbing on rocks and sand.

Stirk's whispered "Two, six—*heavyyyyy*" became monotonous and hypnotic, but they made good progress, and well before time they were on the other side among the fringing shrubbery near the water's edge—and opposite the mole. The moon had set in the early hours and it was difficult to make out the dark mass of the brig across the darkling waters, but there were the two pinpricks of lanthorn light in the rigging to mark her out.

They rested, waiting for daybreak. It was very quiet; only the odd night noise from the small town around the curve of the bay, the plop and splash of fish, muffled curses at the coolness and restless movement from fourteen men. A blue edge came to the darkness—it would be light soon, arriving with tropical swiftness. Stirk called them together. "Now, mates, we's got a good chance if we goes in fast. An' I means fast—I want ter see yez stretch out on the oars like yer've never seen, an' up 'er side like monkeys wi' their arses on fire."

There was an impatient muttering: the men had been picked for the job, and were more than ready. As the light strengthened, features emerged in the clarity of the morning: the mole, the brig—and movement along the length of the mole. Kydd tried to make out what was happening. A trumpet cut into the morning, a thin baying at this distance but its significance was undeniable. There was a force of soldiers of unknown size on the mole.

Kydd knew that everything had changed. He looked to Stirk. Stirk's tough expression was set and his voice became grave. "This is a-lookin' hickey. Our shipmates is standin' into hazard, they don' know there's sojers a-waitin' for 'em." He stared across at the soldiers forming up, and his jaw hardened.

"We're goin' ter take 'em b' surprise, the Crapauds." He sighted along the line of beach. A couple of small fishing boats were drawn up nearby but otherwise it was clear along to the town, a mile or so away. "We pelts along, through th' town and takes 'em from th' inside. Won't know what hits 'em. An' this'll make 'em take their eyes off of the Cap'n while he cuts out th' brig." He glared around the group of seamen, as if daring comment.

Kydd could see the peril that Farrell would face, coming out of the dawn to find too late the soldiers ready to fall on his band. It couldn't be allowed to happen: Stirk was right to take action. But a frontal assault on soldiers? It was courageous, but against armed troops in their own positions—no, they would have no chance except to sacrifice themselves in the hope that it would not be in vain. The emotional switch from exhilaration, through apprehension to dogged acceptance was cruel.

A quiet voice announced, "There they is." The low bulk of a sugar lighter crept into distant view from the north. They were committed: Farrell had no idea of the soldiers, and when he saw them closer to he would probably press ahead rather than let down his other party.

Kydd forced his mind to go cool. There had to be a diversion to take attention from Farrell to themselves. But did it have to be a full assault? Could it be . . . "Toby," Kydd said. Stirk swung about to face him. "Might be, we c'n do it another way."

From Stirk's compressed lips and glittering eyes, Kydd knew that he was keyed up for what had to be done. "Yeah? I can't see one, cuffin."

Kydd persevered: an alternative was forming in his mind. "Look, we don't have t' go at 'em front on. We c'n just—"

Stirk stepped up to him. "Kydd, we do it the way I said!" he snarled. "In case yer've forgotten, I'm in charge."

"Aye, Toby," Kydd replied carefully. "Youse in command right enough—just sayin' that we don't have t' take—"

Breathing heavily, Stirk grabbed his shirtfront by both hands. Then he spoke slowly and savagely: "Kydd, I didn't reckon on it, but you're a piggin' shy cock."

Kydd was aware of the circle of silent men around him, but felt a rising anger. "An' you're fuckin' blind! Why don't you want t' hear of somethin' else?"

Stirk released Kydd's shirt slowly. "Let's hear it," he said finally. His eyes held Kydd's unblinkingly.

Kydd tried to bring a lucidity, a logical sequence to his ideas as Renzi always did. "We've got to get the Frogs t' pay attention to us, right? Look away fr'm the lighter, get worried about us. We c'n do that. We launches th' longboat an' has a go at the brig."

"That's yer idea?" said Stirk incredulously.

"Not yet. See, the longboat is chasin' one of the little fishin' boats, who o' course are screamin' f'r help. Frogs'll be wantin' t' see if they c'n make it across to them."

Stirk's brow creased.

"Best part is—well, if you were them soldiers, what would ye think?"

An indistinct murmur came from behind, but Kydd pressed on: "You'd think that this fishin' boat is just escaped cos the English were invadin' th' town fr'm the other side! An' you'd want t' get there sharpish."

Doggo's rough voice came from the left. "So th' soldiers get flustered 'n' rushes off ter deal with it, leavin' it clear f'r the *Seaflowers*!"

"Yeah."

Stirk hesitated—but the lighter was in clear view and would begin its final approach shortly. A small smile appeared, and he mock-saluted Kydd. "What's yer orders, then, mate?"

Kydd wasted no time. "We six in th' fishin' boat," he said, indicating the nearest five men. "Wait f'r us t' get afloat, an' get after us. We get aboard t' the for'ard—you lay off until Cap'n comes up, an' we all go at it together."

The light was stronger. Before they broke cover to take the small boat, Kydd thought of something. "Strip off, or they'll see we ain't Frenchies." They whipped off their jackets and shirts, naked to the waist. "Right, mates, we're mortal scared o' the English, we are. Let's away!"

Shouting hoarsely, the sailors raced to the fishing boat, waving arms, desperate to make the safety of the brig. The little boat was rushed into the water and with Farthing and Doggo at the oars it thrashed in a panic-stricken course across the harbor. Kydd kept looking astern nervously, urging the men on. As an afterthought he tied his striped shirt to the single pulley line and hoisted it as if in distress to the top of the stumpy mast.

Stirk performed his part perfectly. Raging like a bull at the edge of the water, he threatened and menaced with a cutlass until the longboat could be launched. It took the water with a splash, and a fierce and bloodthirsty crew tumbled aboard to go in deadly pursuit of the poor "Frenchmen."

A scattering of pops sounded. Soldiers knelt on the mole, taking aim at the longboat, in little danger at that range. Kydd thought of the naked steel lying concealed in the bottom of his boat. A warrior's rising bloodlust made his heart pound.

At the end of the mole, the lighter seemed to hesitate. Kydd ground his teeth. If it didn't arrive soon to do its part, his theatrical performance would fail. The few figures on the lighter seemed to dispute together, then the long sweeps began again—and the ungainly craft careered around the end of the mole, bumping and scraping in a shocking parody of seamanship.

A shouting on the mole drew his attention. With a burst of triumph Kydd saw that the soldiers were turning into file and trotting back along the mole, presumably to defend the town. Events moved quickly. The longboat sheered off under the threat of a swivel gun hastily manned in the brig, leaving the fishing boat to reach "safety." They reached the fore-chains, laughing Frenchmen urging them up. Kydd watched the lighter out of the corner of his eyes, seeing Renzi berating Quashee's hapless bulk at the tiller, while Farrell jumped on his hat in exasperation.

The French leaned over the bulwarks, offering hands to help, but Kydd played for time. Yelling incomprehensibly, he pointed at the "exhausted" oarsmen and gestured for a rope ladder. By this time the lighter was nearly upon them. Shouting angrily, men from the brig jumped to the stonework of the mole with bearing-off poles and fenders as it threatened to drift across the brig's bows.

Kydd knew that the time had come. The lighter thumped violently to lock across the brig's forepart. "Seaflowers! Huzzah for the King!" shouted Farrell, and swung himself up into the bowsprit of the enemy. A storm of cheering rose from all around the Frenchmen—an unstoppable stream of seamen boiling up from concealment in the lighter, Kydd's wildly excited men swarming up the fore-chains, and Stirk's longboat, racing to board by the stern.

They had minutes only before the soldiers found they had been fooled. The French sailors recovered quickly from their surprise, grabbed pikes and weapons from their ready-use positions around the mast and rushed to the sides of the vessel.

Kydd landed on the deck of the brig, and was immediately met by a sailor in a red cap, who jabbed a long boarding pike at his face. Kydd's cutlass blade went up and deflected the lunge, keeping pressure on the haft until he was close enough to grab it with his left hand and yank the man off-balance. The gray steel of Kydd's blade then thrust forward and took the man in the stomach. He dropped to his knees, grabbing at the pitiless steel. Kydd's foot slammed into his face as he wrenched the cutlass free.

A pistol banged somewhere and Kydd felt the violent passage of the bullet past his ear. Seconds later the pistol itself crashed into the side of his face, hurled by its owner. Kydd crouched instinctively at the pain, the swish of a blade sounded above and his head cleared. He thrust up with his cutlass at the man's extended armpit. With a howl of pain the man dropped his weapon and fell to a fetal position. A foot kicked into Kydd. Across him an English sailor was being hard pressed by a bull of a Frenchman. Kydd stabbed upward into the unsuspecting man's bowels, bringing an inhuman screech and the man's blade clumsily and brutally down on his back. A burning line of pain opened, but a second later the man was skewered by his original opponent. Heaving himself to his feet, Kydd snatched a look at the man he had saved: his eyes were wild and unseeing as he turned back to the fight.

From aft a wave of men advanced. Kydd braced himself and turned to face them, his head thumping and his back a cruel red-hot bar of pain—but these were Stirk's men, and in a startlingly short time the deck was cleared.

Farrell's voice sounded loud, commanding. Men dropped to the mole, axes rose and fell on the mooring ropes. A warning shout came—soldiers were racing back along the mole, many soldiers. The ropes fell free, and the axe-men scrambled aboard. The lighter swung away and drifted into the harbor. More shouts from Farrell and men were in the shrouds, racing for the yards. Kydd staggered, pain and nausea swamping his senses. He sank to his knees, retching into the slime of blood.

The brig's foresail dropped and flapped impatiently before taking the wind. The vessel's bow began to open clear water next to the mole. The soldiers, seeing this, came to a stop and knelt to fire at the brig, but their hard running was not conducive to good shooting and their balls whistled past harmlessly. Others made a charge against the brig, but were decimated by the quarterdeck swivel gun cracking out above, plied by English seamen.

The brig parted from the mole, more sail was set and, while

Kydd held his head on his knees, they victoriously put to sea to rejoin *Seaflower.*

"Ye had us a mort worried, m' friend, coming in so strange-like," Kydd told Renzi, remembering the stop–start dispute he had seen on the lighter. He was lying stomach down on the main grating of *Seaflower*, Renzi gently applying goose grease to the angry weal down his back.

Renzi paused. "It was not the best of times to be seeing a pack of soldiers waiting for us—were we betrayed?" He resumed his soothing strokes. "Then the Captain sees our longboat chasing fishermen! His comments on undisciplined rabble disobeying their orders were a curiosity to hear, please believe, but then I recognized your shirt hoisted up the mast and we understood."

"As y' should have," Kydd said crossly. The treatment hurt, and his head throbbed, broken skin and a dark bruise extending out from his hairline were where the pistol had struck. The surgeon's mate had been dismissive of the head wound and, in Kydd's opinion, ham-fisted in his ministrations to his back.

He brooded, but by raising his head just a little he could see the fine sight astern of the French brig-o'-war lifting and bobbing— his prize money must now be growing significant and the prize agent would soon have golden guineas to hand out. This was a happier thought: What would he and Renzi enjoy ashore on the proceeds? *Seaflower* was only hours from Port Morant. She would soon make her number to the small naval station there, and all the world would then know that saucy *Seaflower* had been lucky again.

"Mr. Kydd!" Luke's eager voice broke in on his thoughts. "Cap'n desires yer should attend on him, if ye should be at leisure t' do so," he recited. The odd phraseology set warning bells ringing. Warily Kydd got to his feet. For a moment he wondered whether he should put on a shirt: he had received dispensation while his wound was still sore and decided that this still held.

He went down the after hatchway to the Captain's minuscule cabin. Farrell was seated at the tiny desk. He turned, and held a sheet of paper. "This is my despatch to the Commander-in-Chief, to be landed at Port Morant."

Farrell found the right place and read:

. . . but as we approached, a body of soldiers hitherto concealed from us became evident. I was minded to abandon the venture, were it not for the clever ruse of Thomas Kydd, coxswain of the longboat and quartermaster in *Seaflower.* He caused his party to be split, one part of which went ahead in a fishing boat in the character of a craft under pursuit by English seamen, the other part in the longboat that followed.

The action was most successful, surprise being complete. The soldiers were lured away from their place by the supposition that a landing in force was under way in the town. The brig was carried at slight loss . . .

Farrell could easily have claimed that Kydd was acting under orders. Kydd glowed at the tribute—being mentioned in despatches was an unusual honor.

Renzi looked at him oddly at the news, but said nothing. On the matter of where they would celebrate, he smiled secretly and assured Kydd that he would not be disappointed were he to trust him to find somewhere.

For such an insignificant man-o'-war as *Seaflower* there was no manning of yards in honor from the ships of the fleet when she entered port, but the enemy brig demurely astern, so much bigger than *Seaflower,* was proof enough of their prowess. There was no real need for the elaborate sail-handling when curving so prettily around to anchor under the envious eyes of the fleet, but it was another chance to show the world what kind of man-o'-war the *Seaflower* really was.

Within the hour, Farrell had returned from his call on the Admiral bearing deeply satisfying news. *Seaflower* was due for refit, and her people could rely on two weeks at least of liberty ashore. The Vice Admiralty Court sitting at Kingston had duly condemned their barque as prize, and they had tickets on the prize agent for a gratifying amount.

Kydd considered his ticket. There was the choice of parting with it now, suitably discounted to a moneylender in town, or cash it for the full amount later when the prize agent could be cajoled into drawing on account. He would see what mysterious entertainment Renzi had in mind first: he hoped it would not be a curious pile of stones or the residence of some worthy poet.

"Tom, mate, yez has a letter." Stirk handed over a folded and sealed packet. "An' that's fivepence y' owes me fer the post, cully." Kydd took it gingerly: the writing was small and well formed—a feminine hand. He frowned, then his expression cleared. This was from Cecilia, his sister. The date was only five weeks earlier, and with pleased anticipation he took it forward to open and read in privacy.

He broke the wafer; it was a single sheet, closely written. As usual she wasted no time and went straight to the point. Kydd's eyes widened—he read quickly and stared outward. It seemed impossible.

He found Renzi searching in their sea chest for a suitable kerchief: in his blue jacket with the white whalebone buttons he looked ready for the delights of Port Royal. The mess-deck was rapidly emptying for there was every incentive to get ashore to make this a time to remember: the Seaflowers were going on the ran-tan. Kydd waited until they were alone, and held up his paper. "Ye'd never have guessed it, Nicholas, but here's a letter fr'm Cecilia!"

"I pray she is in good health," Renzi said, perfectly in control.

Kydd grinned. "Aye, she is that, m' friend. An', can you believe it? She is here in Kingston!" Renzi stood quite still. "Ain't it prime?" Kydd laughed. "Here, listen to this, 'My dear brother, I found how I might write a letter to you, and I have news that will make you stare! You may offer your felicitations, Thomas, for you see, I am to be wed.' "

Kydd paused to see the effect on Renzi. His friend had always got along well with Cecilia, and Kydd knew he would be pleased. Oddly, Renzi stared back at him with unblinking eyes.

Shrugging, Kydd went on, " 'Peter is a very amiable man, and he has the most wonderful prospects. I met him at one of Mrs. Daryton's assemblies. Oh, yes, she wishes to be remembered to you, and of course dear Nicholas.

" 'But what I really want to tell you is that Peter is going to Jamaica to be under-manager of a sugar plantation. You've no idea how happy that makes me! It will only be a few years and we will set up our carriage, and a little time after that we will be rich, and I will look after Mama and Papa—but I am going too fast! I have to say that we have an understanding. Peter will return to Jamaica and next month I travel with Jane Rodpole (you remember, the one at school with the long hair and hopeless giggle). She goes to Jamaica for the same reason. We will take lodgings together until—' " Kydd broke off. "So, y' sees, she must even now be in Kingston, Nicholas. We have t' find her, an' celebrate all together."

CHAPTER 13

Kydd and Renzi's appearance—smart man-o'-war's men—attracted some curious looks in Kingston town. Sailors rarely left the more direct pleasures of Port Royal for the commercialism and bustle of Kingston, across the harbor from the Palisades.

It was not hard to find the newcomers: there were streets of hostelries providing rooms for merchants, traveling army wives and the like, and with rising excitement Kydd found himself outside one of these. The door was opened by a mistrustful housekeeper. Kydd shyly inquired about Miss Kydd. The woman agreed to see if she was in to two sailors, but firmly closed the door on them while she did so.

The door opened again: a young lady with laughing eyes, hair whirled in a tight bun in deference to the heat, looked at them both. "Do I fin' m'self addressing Miss Jane?" Kydd inquired, holding his hat awkwardly in his hands.

"You do, sir. Might I ask . . ." She looked puzzled, but there was a barely repressed animation that was most fetching.

"Thomas Kydd, Cecilia's brother."

Her hands flew to her mouth.

"An' my particular friend, Nicholas Renzi."

She bobbed a curtsy in return to Renzi's studied bow, but her eyes were on Kydd, wide and serious. "Cecilia is out at the moment," she said quietly, "but if you are at leisure, you may wish to await her return?"

Kydd grinned widely. "That's kind in you, er, Miss Jane," he said. She flashed a smile, but it disappeared quickly. They eased past the discouraging gaze of the housekeeper, and were ushered into the front parlor.

Kydd sat on the edge of a faded chintz chair. "Ye must be happy f'r Cecilia, I believe," he began.

Jane lowered her head for a moment, and when she spoke, it was controlled, formal. "It were better she will tell you about it herself, Mr. Kydd."

He felt the first stirrings of alarm but suppressed them. "An' I got word that you will be hearin' wedding bells y'rself, Miss Jane."

She bit her lip and replied, "For two months hence." An awkward silence developed, and Kydd glanced at Renzi, who sat opposite. His expression had that frustratingly impenetrable quality, which Kydd knew concealed his understanding of a situation that he himself could not grasp.

Tea arrived, the china rattling on the tray. They sipped decorously, in their sea rig the little graces seeming incongruous. Kydd caught a furtive look from Jane, a look of frank curiosity, and he wondered what the girls had discussed concerning him. There was, however, something about the present situation that was not right.

A rattling at the front door had Jane recovering her poise. "This is your sister, I believe," she said brightly, and rose to her feet. "Oh, Cecilia!" she called. "You have guests, my dear." Footsteps sounded along the passage, and the door opened.

Kydd advanced to meet her—and faltered to a stop. It was

Cecilia, but the pale, drawn face, the black dress and veil? His smile faded. Uncertain how to continue, he hesitated.

"Thomas!" Cecilia seemed to wake, a small smile breaking through as she threw back the veil. "How wonderful!" A little of the old spirit came through. "My, you look so handsome in your sea costume!" Her eyes strayed to the livid bruise on his head, "Oh!" she said faintly.

"Jus' a wound o' battle," he said. She approached and hugged him with controlled passion, the wound on his back making him gasp. "Cec—what is it?" he blurted out.

"Oh, I declare, I'll be late for my dancing lesson," Jane said. "Please excuse me, I must rush."

Cecilia noticed Renzi, standing unmoving in the background. "Oh, Nicholas," she said warmly, "How good to see you!" Renzi inclined his head, but stayed where he was. Impulsively, Cecilia crossed to him and embraced him as well. "Nicholas, your complexion is like a Red Indian's, not the thing at all at home," she said.

When Cecilia turned back to Kydd, her expression was rigid, brittle. "It is only the ten days I have been here in Jamaica, Thomas, but . . ." Kydd pulled her toward him, and held her tight while sobs racked her. Neither noticed Renzi slip from the room.

"It's so—so unfair!" she wept. "He was so happy to see me, and a week later he's in his grave!"

"Er, what . . ."

"On Wednesday he had dreadful pains and sickness, and by Sunday . . ." The tears were all the harder to bear for their brevity and harsh depths. "I was with him until . . ."

"I'm so sorry f'r it, Cec, truly I am." If it were the yellow fever, and she was involved in his nursing, then the end would have been unspeakably hard to bear. "Did ye—were you, er, fond of him? I—I mean . . ."

She dabbed her eyes and looked away. There was now only the emptiness of destroyed hopes.

Kydd released her and said, gently, "Cec, you're here in Jamaica with nothin' anymore. Have ye any means?"

"Of course," she said, but would not look at him directly. Kydd was stabbed with pity: he knew his sister was strong and independent, and would rather die than admit to any weakness. But a single woman without substance far from home . . .

"Have ye any plans? There's nothin' t' keep you here."

She glanced at him. "If you mean, what do I next, then . . . I will attend on Jane for her nuptials, of course."

Kydd's mouth opened in amazement. "But . . ."

She looked at him with fondness. "That is to say, my dear brother, that I crave time to think, to put this nightmare from me—you do understand?"

Kydd let a small smile show. There was time enough for brother and sister to get together later. He felt doubtful, but blurted out, "Nicholas an' I, we were on our way t' kick up a hullabaloo on account of our success in *Seaflower*—I know y'r not feelin' s' spry, but if ye'd like to . . ."

"Thank you both—I hope you'll forgive me, but I need to be alone for just a little while." Her sad smile touched him deeply.

Then he remembered. "Here, Cec, if y' please." He brought out his prize-money ticket. "Do ye see? Y'r Jack Tar is a foolish wight ashore. They say, 'Sailors get money like horses, 'n' spend it like asses.' I'd take it kindly if ye could look after this f'r me—takes th' temptation away."

She looked at him steadily, then kissed him.

"Y' presents it at the prize agent when he's got word fr'm the Admiralty—sign on th' other side an' be sure the mumpin' rogue doesn't chouse ye."

Renzi was waiting outside, and they fell into step as Kydd told him of the conversation. Renzi listened, and nodded gravely. Cecilia was right, she needed time to herself for the moment to settle her feelings. Therefore there was no reason why they shouldn't carry on with his original plan. "Brother, there is some-one that it would give me the greatest of pleasure that you should meet." Kydd looked at him curiously. "And it requires that we go up-country in a ketureen."

On Broad Street they found one, the driver at first disbelieving that two sailors wanted to head away from the delights of the port. "On'y dese sugar pens dere, nuthin' else, kooner-men!"

They made Spanish Town before noon. The ketureen waited on the Grand Parade while Renzi impressed Kydd with the sea splen-dors of the Rodney Memorial, the noble portico of the King's House and the Rio Cobre of Columbus. They dined at a roadside stall on rich yellow akee, salt fish and bammy bread before resum-ing their journey. By late afternoon they had reached May Pen where they took the road north.

Renzi felt that the time had come, could no longer be deferred. "My dear friend . . ." His hand lay on Kydd's arm. "Do you listen to what I say."

Kydd looked at him.

"The personage we will stay with tonight is—my brother, Richard."

Kydd kept his silence.

"He is a gentleman of some consequence in this island, I may say, and is an ornament to the family." Renzi stared into the dis-tance. "He knows of my—resolve in the matter of my moral judg-ment, and respects it. Dare I ask it, it would infinitely oblige, should you feign ignorance of my true position."

Kydd agreed solemnly.

"Then I will touch on another matter, one which is perhaps the more delicate of the two." Renzi glanced at him before speaking. "Do you not take offense, dear friend, if I point out that in the article of polite formalities, you are as yet . . . untutored, natural." He watched Kydd's expression tighten. "But these, of course, are an accomplishment obligatory only on those with pretensions to genteel society," Renzi continued carefully.

"Ye're saying I'm goin' t' shame you to y' brother?" Kydd growled.

"Not as who would say," Renzi muttered.

The ketureen clattered on over the sandy, rutted road and Renzi thought perhaps he had gone too far. In fairness it had to be said that it was really for Kydd's sake that he had felt it proper to bring up the subject, in order that Kydd himself would not feel uncomfortable in polite company rather than for any selfish motive of his own. Cecilia had rapidly acquired a natural affinity with the formalities of gentility, as was the way of women, but her brother, while absorbing the deep-sea mariner's fine qualities of courage, humor and sturdy self-reliance, had also absorbed their direct speech and impatience with soft shore ways. In many ways it would not be a kind thing to do to him. . . .

Kydd glowered, staring obstinately away. But then he recovered. "Y'r in the right of it, Nicholas." He sighed. "F'r you only. But what . . ."

"It will be very agreeable to me if you keep station on myself, mark my motions and do the same and you will not be so very far from success."

"Aye," Kydd said briefly. In the sugar field they were passing there were women with baskets on their heads, gay in red and yellow, some weeding, others scouring the stubbled ground. A snatch of singing came floating over the distance. Kydd looked out, brooding. Then he turned to Renzi and said firmly, "Be s' good as t' give me a steer on y' manners when it's time f'r vittles, Nicholas."

"Why, it's not so perilous, dear fellow," Renzi said with great satisfaction: he would now provide a clear and seamanlike course to follow, perfectly suited to a plain-thinking sailor.

Their ketureen arrived at the Great House, and the two travelers were made cordially welcome.

"A fine surprise, Nicholas!" Laughton declared, his delight

obvious. "And a distinct pleasure to make acquaintance with your friend, back from the dead," he said, looking at Kydd keenly.

"Would it inconvenience," Renzi asked, with the utmost politeness, "were we to beg the loan of attire perhaps more in keeping with the country?"

"But of course, dear fellow."

The days that followed were a haze of impressions for Kydd— the vast fields of sugarcane whose harvest would end at some point as pungent Royal Navy rum; the slow daily round of field-work with the lines of slaves moving across the fields, the younger ones bringing up the rear weeding and clearing with their own "pickney driver." It was utterly at odds with Kydd's world.

Laughton was a fine host, and at sundown always joined his visitors on the broad veranda for easy conversation. "Your visit is most welcome, Nicholas, but I fear not at the best of times," he mentioned one evening. "We've been sadly inconvenienced in our trade by these devilish predators—you'll find the Navy not popular here."

Renzi hastened to change the subject. "And of your maroons, are they as cantankerous, unsatisfied as last you spoke?"

"Worse. They're more or less in open revolt now." He stared out over the fields. "They want more land for 'emselves—which plantation is going to give it to them? They're rambling about at night, causing general trouble. Had two cows taken and another with its throat slit. It's unsettling my fieldworkers, who know they're only over yonder," he said, gesturing toward the tumble of hills and mountains to the northwest, just visible in the dusk. "That's what we call 'cockpit country,' and there the maroon is untouchable. And it's only a short ride away." He took a long pull at his drink. "Don't forget, we're only some thousands with an enslaved population of around a quarter million. Concentrates the mind, don't ye think?"

Fortified by his courteous acceptance by Laughton, Kydd was able to face with equanimity the prospect of a social occasion, an

informal dinner of the usual sort. Seated opposite Renzi, he prepared nervously to do his duty.

"Th' currant sauce, if y' please" was Kydd's first daring foray
into polite society. It was passed to him without comment and,
reassured, he looked around furtively at the members of the table.
The olive-complexioned lawyer farther down caught his look and
nodded pleasantly. Taken aback, Kydd had the presence of mind to
raise his glass in salute. As he placed the glass down again he
became aware of the fierce glint of eyes diagonally opposite.
"Marston," the man growled, and lifted his eyebrows in interroga-
tion.

"Er, Kydd," he said carefully, not knowing if handshakes were
the thing at table, and deciding that it would be safe to do nothing.

"Got th' look o' the sea about ye," said Marston, when it
became obvious Kydd was not going to be more forthcoming.

"Aye, y'r in the right of it, sir."

Marston smiled. "Can always tell. Which ship?"

Renzi broke in smoothly, "Thomas is with me, Gilbert, come to
see where sugar comes from."

"*Damn* fine place to see." He started, then twisted round in his
seat to the lady on his left. "If you'll pardon th' French, m' dear."
She nodded shyly.

Laughton was at the head of the table, his wife at the opposite
end, near Kydd. "Er, Mr. Kydd," she called decorously, "do y' not
feel a trifle anxious out on the sea, what with all those nasty pirates
an' French privateers?" She helped herself to more of the succulent
river shrimps in salt and pepper.

Kydd's own mouth was full with the spicy jerk, but he replied
manfully, "Not wi' the Navy t' look after—"

"Pah!" Marston's face lowered and his eyes slitted. "I've lost
three ships 'tween here 'n' San Domingo, an' it's *disgraceful*
the Navy still ain't come up on 'em! If I was their admiral, I tell
you—"

At the other end of the table Laughton frowned. Outside there was some sort of disturbance. The talking died away. High words sounded and a flustered butler entered, bowed to Laughton and whispered urgently. Laughton put down his glass quietly. "Gentlemen, it seems that the Trelawney maroons are abroad tonight." His chair scraped as he got to his feet. "A mill is afire."

The room broke into a rush of talk.

"Stap me, but they're getting damnation uppity!"

"D'ye think—God preserve us!—it's a general rising?"

"Where's the militia, the blaggards?"

Laughton took off his jacket and carefully laid it on the back of his chair. In his evening shirt he accepted his sword and belt from the butler as calmly as he had accepted his dinner clothes earlier. "I won't be long, gentlemen, but in the meantime pray do not ignore the brandy and cigars." Kydd sensed the assembling of men in the rising tension outside.

Marston stood up. "Richard, dammit, you can't go on y'r own, dear fellow!"

Laughton held up his hand firmly. "No, Gilbert, this is my plantation. I shall deal with it." He turned and left.

"Don' like it—not one bit of it!" Marston rumbled.

"Nor do I," said the lawyer. "You know how they work—set an outbuilding on fire, then when all attention is on that, they fall upon the Great House!"

The ladies stayed close together, chattering nervously, the men pacing around the room puffing cigars. Kydd looked through the open windows into the warm darkness. He glanced at Renzi, who was talking quietly with the butler. Renzi looked across at Kydd and beckoned discreetly. "I do believe we should stand sentry—go around the house. I have asked for weapons."

These turned out to be large, ugly blunderbusses, with their flared muzzles a strong deterrent to any kind of unrest. "I will take the north side, if you would be so good as to patrol the south," Renzi suggested. The rest of the room watched respectfully, and as they left there were low calls of encouragement from the other men.

Outside, away from the bright glitter of candlelight and silver, it was impenetrably black. The darkness was the more menacing for its total anonymity and Kydd felt hairs prickle on the back of his neck. From the windows of the Great House, houseboys looked out fearfully. There was a movement behind him. Kydd wheeled around: it was Marston.

"Come to keep ye company," he said, breathing heavily. Kydd muttered thanks, but at the same time he didn't want to worry about having someone about him on whom he could not rely. Marston, however, fell into step next to him. "Get worked up, they do," Marston said, his cigar laying a thick fragrance on the night air. "Have this obeah man—kind o' witchcraft, calls it voodoo. They does what he says under fear o' death."

"C'n they fight?" asked Kydd. "I mean, in the reg'lar way, against soldiers." He continued to pace slowly, looking out into the night.

Marston nodded vigorously. "Damn right they can, you can depend upon it. But not as you'd say—they disguise 'emselves as trees with leaves an' all, jumps into life in our rear, devil take 'em. Not for nothin' they calls it 'Land o' Look Behind.' "

Kydd thought of Juba, the driver of the King's Negroes on Antigua—if he and his kind were to set their faces against the forces of the Crown he could not be at all certain of the outcome. He remembered the opaqueness of character, the difference in Juba's expression of humanity—was it so hard to understand a resentment, a striving to be as other men?

From the darkness a group of figures emerged, Laughton easily recognizable at their head. He saw Kydd and waved. "Thank you, Thomas. There was no need, but I honor you for it. Shall we rejoin the ladies?"

It seemed the alarm was over. Kydd handed over his blunderbuss and he and Renzi reentered the brightness of the big dining room to murmured words of approbation. Laughton resumed his chair at the head. "Gentlemen!" He raised a glass and drank deep. The ladies could now withdraw gracefully, leaving the men to their blue haze, brandy balloons and conversation.

"Somethin' has to be done!" Marston said forcefully. "They've broken their sworn treaty, the damned rascals. If they take it into their heads to come down from the hills all together, it's up with us. We'd never control a general mutiny. Military is here, an' I hear they're even sending us a general." The announcement did not seem to mollify: snorts of derision were heard around the table, despite the presence farther down the table of an officer in red regimentals. He didn't comment, but a confident smile played across his face as he enjoyed his cigar.

"So what's goin' on, eh, James?"

The officer paused for a moment. "Yes," he drawled, "quite true—General Walpole is expected daily."

"An' with how many damn soldiers?"

The smile widened. "Not so many, I understand."

"What's so funny, damn your whistle?"

"It's—he'll be bringing much more effective reinforcements than soldiers."

"Blast m' eyes, you're speakin' in riddles, man!"

"This is not for public knowledge, gentlemen, so keep it under your hat. No soldiers. Instead, Cuban hunting dogs!" A baffled quiet descended. Enjoying the effect, the officer elegantly lifted his brandy. "Half the size of a man, these brutes are trained up by the Spaniards for man-killing. Can pitilessly run to earth anything on two legs in the worst country, the hardest climate. A runaway slave stands no chance at all, and neither will these maroons."

Kydd felt for them. All their advantages of knowing the country, blending with the landscape, melting into the scrub rendered useless at a stroke.

"We send the dogs in, we can smoke 'em all out from their hidey-holes, finish 'em for good at last." The roar of merriment that followed was heartfelt, but Kydd could not join in.

He turned to the lawyer. "Is it so necessary t' take such hard ways with th' poor beggars?" he asked.

The man frowned. "Are you not aware that these sugar islands are the richest lands in the world? That if we lost their yield for any reason, it would of a certainty mean the collapse of the City, a run on gold, our ruination as a nation just when we are locked in battle with the greatest threat to our civilization ever?"

There could be no answer to that, but Kydd felt a stubborn need to have his misgivings laid to rest. "But slavery, where is y'r rights there?"

The lawyer's eyes turned stony. "If we had no slaves then, may I ask, where do you think that the free men to take their place— thousands, tens of thousands—will come from? No white man will come of his free will to labor in the sun. The black man is eminently suited. They would have no employment, were it not for this."

"But—"

"Do you propose, sir, to abandon the islands? Sail away, leave them to the French, throw away six generations of development?" The contempt in his voice was ill-concealed.

Kydd knew in his heart that Renzi would sadly concur—it was a matter of simple logic; besides which, he was a guest and would not embarrass his friend with an argument. "Of course not, sir, that was never in question," he said.

All too rapidly the remaining days of their stay passed, until the time came, on the last evening, to bring it all to a conclusion. Laughton arrived late for the sundown glass, flopping wearily into his rattan chair. There was little talk as the sangaree splashed into the glasses, each man with his own thoughts. Laughton's wife joined them, but left discreetly at the solemn mood.

Kydd broke the silence, saying civilly, "Y'r sunsets are capital in this part o' the world."

Laughton looked up, a tight smile flashing briefly. "There are many things here which a distracted mind would find pleasing." He sat back and looked directly at Kydd. "It does not take a deal of penetration to see that you are a particular friend to Nicholas—you have shared too much of life together for it to be otherwise. Therefore I conclude that he has confided in you. In short, you know of his—decision, and the noble impulse that generated it.

"I am his brother, as you are no doubt aware, and tonight I ask you very sincerely if you will intercede with him. Ask him to accept my offer of an honored place here—indeed, to include your own good self—and see out these tumultuous times here together."

Kydd was surprised: he had no idea an offer had been made. He glanced across at Renzi, whose expression was as usual inscrutable. "I do thank ye f'r the fine offer for m'self, but must say no," Kydd said firmly. "But as f'r Nicholas . . ."

"No," Renzi said quickly, and stared intensely at his glass. Kydd waited, but there was no further elaboration. Renzi's face was set in stone.

The *chirr* of a cricket sounded in the dusk, immediately joined in a chorus by others. A clatter and laughter sounded far-off in the chattel houses, and the breeze played softly about them. Laughton put down his glass. "Then I think I have my answer, Nicholas," he said softly. "But one moment." He rose quickly and went inside. A short time later, he emerged with a dusty bottle and crystal glasses, which he placed on the marquetry table, then set to carefully opening the bottle. "Let us make this last night as agreeable as we may." He poured the deep gold liquid into crystal. The dark-skinned butler arrived with a candle, and each man held his glass. "Armagnac—the elder Pitt was a boy when this was bottled," Laughton said lightly. "I give you Fortune—may she treat you as a lady."

CHAPTER 14

—※—

It was good to see *Seaflower* at her moorings across the harbor at the Palisades, looking yachtlike at that distance. Kydd and Renzi gave a cheerful wave. Soon they would be aboard in their familiar berths and life would carry on as before.

Kydd caught the strong, clean whiff of linseed oil and freshly tarred rigging as he swung over the side to the deck, the most obvious sign of the work the dockyard had done on his ship. He moved over to the tiller: its arm had been replaced, and in good English ash, he noted with satisfaction. It had a flexibility that absorbed the direct shock of seas coming in on the quarter, which could be a tiring thing for a helmsman.

"Hey-ho, the travelers!" Doud's cry came from forward where he was leading the fore preventer stay to bring its upper wooden heart to the lower, right in the bows.

Kydd wandered up, keen to hear the gossip. "What cheer, cuffin? An' have ye any news, b' chance?"

Doud gave a knowing smile, passed the lanniard loosely through the two hearts and tied off before straightening. "We has a new owner," he announced importantly.

"Does we indeed?" Kydd said, with interest, looking around for Renzi, but he had gone below. "An' what happened t' Cap'n Farrell, may I ask?"

"Been an' got his step. You calls him 'Commander' now, cock." He stepped aside to let his two men finish bowsing in on the lanniard and added, "In course he's too grand fer this little barky, gets a sloop-o'-war or some such, I wouldn't wonder." In the matter of prize money alone, *Seaflower* had become a valuable unit for the Admiral, and her captain had proved he was lucky in this regard. With a larger ship he could do even better.

"Do we know then who's to have *Seaflower*?"

"We don't, but we're gonna find out this afternoon," Doud said. "Due aboard three bells, I heard. We'se t' priddy the decks an' set all a-taunto."

Kydd slapped Doud's arm and hurried below to shift into his loose, sea-going rig. The master was visibly pleased to see him. "Ye know our new cap'n, Mr. Jarman?" asked Kydd.

"I do. L'tenant Swaine, Admiral's staff—comes aboard at three bells."

Kydd was puzzled by his laconic reticence, but put it down to disappointment at the departure of the patrician Farrell. "Are we ready f'r sea?" he inquired. As quartermaster he was responsible for stowage of stores. Jarman told him in full detail: in essence, within a day they could be ready for whatever task *Seaflower* was called upon to perform.

Renzi seemed a little preoccupied when Kydd passed on the news of the name of their new captain. All Kydd could learn from him was that Renzi had seen Lieutenant Swaine on the Admiral's staff in Spanish Town.

At three bells, *Seaflower* was ready for her new captain, with her boatswain's mate, Stiles, in his hat with the ship's name picked out in gold on a red background, and Luke, the sideboy, complete with white gloves, stood at the ship's side. Jarman, as senior, stood waiting on the tiny quarterdeck in his best uniform, with Merrick close at hand.

They waited. It was a gray day, the rain catching them unawares at one point, and the muggy heat afterward was a trial—and still they waited. At five bells Merrick went below and Luke sat on the deck. Kydd was not required but he joined others standing about, curious to see their new commander.

At seven bells, as the late-afternoon sun put in an appearance, there was a stir on the shore. A dockyard wherry put off, a single occupant in the sternsheets. Jarman growled a warning and the side party reassembled. The boat bumped alongside, and an officer in cocked hat and sword stepped aboard. A piercing single blast from Stiles greeted him. Until he read his commission, this officer was not entitled to be piped aboard. Jarman removed his hat and stood attentively.

"Lieutenant Swaine, to be Captain of this vessel," said the officer formally.

"Aye, sir," said Jarman. "William Jarman, master, and might I present Mr. Merrick, bosun." Swaine lifted his hat briefly to each, then stepped quickly to the center of the deck, pulling out a parchment. In a monotone he "read himself in," the sonorous phrases rendered flat and uninspiring by the lack of inflection and speed of their delivery—but it was sufficient: Lieutenant Swaine was now indisputably captain of HMS *Seaflower.*

Carefully folding the parchment, he placed it back inside his coat. For a moment his eyes passed over the neat decks of the cutter, then he turned to Jarman. "Carry on, please." But he made no move to go to his cabin: instead, he stepped over to the side of the deck. The wherry had not shoved off, but lay alongside, and Swaine stood at the deck edge, with a frown deepening on his face. Merrick hastened over to the side with a mumbled apology—it was the last thing to be expected, that the Captain would be off ashore just as soon as he had come aboard.

"I desire that the longboat call for me at the careening wharves at nine—no, make that ten. Have you trusties enough to man?"

Merrick flicked a glance at Jarman before responding stolidly, "We're all volunteers in *Seaflower,* sir."

"Very well," said Swaine after a moment's pause.

Merrick's piercing call of piping the side sounded as *Seaflower's* new lieutenant-in-command, now entitled to special attention, went ashore.

"Means nothin', mate," said Stirk. "He must 'ave engagements ashore, like."

Stiles was unconvinced. "An' did yer see 'is coat? Lace was tatty as a whore's petticoat, 'n' *brass* buckles—must 'ave a light purse. . . ."

Kydd bridled. "Not everyone's flush in the fob as we," he said. "Three prizes wi' our name on 'em, more t' come—what we want is a good square hand who c'n show us the way to a few more."

Stirk lifted his drink and sank it with a grimace. "Somethin' about the cut o' his jib sets me teeth on edge—I just dunno. . . ."

"Yair, somethin' slivey about 'im," Stiles agreed. "Wouldn't like ter trust he's on yer side, kinda thing."

"You would grant, however, that the man should have a chance to show something of himself before judgment is passed?" Renzi's words only produced a restless grumbling.

The two double strikes of ten o'clock sounded from on deck. "Not yet back aboard," Stiles said. "Not allowed ter sleep out of 'is ship, is he?" he added needlessly.

Kydd disliked the way the talk was headed and made his excuses. Jarman had the deck, but responded to Kydd's cordial conversation with monosyllables, staring at the pinpricks of light ashore where Port Royal's taverns continued their raucous trade.

Kydd made to leave, but Jarman said softly, "Do you kindly remain with me, I'd be obliged."

"Is there anythin' amiss, Mr. Jarman?"

"Nothing you can't help b' being here."

Uneasy, Kydd kept the deck with Jarman, seeing the lights douse on other ships, and the shore lights wink out one by one. It was after midnight when the longboat returned. And in it were two passengers.

Jarman lifted his hat to the Captain, who was followed by a figure that tripped as it came over the bulwark and sprawled headlong. "Shit!" came a voice, as the figure picked itself up.

"Midshipman Parkin," Swaine said in a surly tone. Rounding on the lad he snarled, "Damn your eyes, an' you're a useless lubber!" before making his unsteady way to the after hatchway. A muffled roar for a steward had Jarman exchanging looks with Kydd.

Seaflower proceeded to sea the next day after completing stores. Kydd took the helm himself, keeping a wary eye on Swaine. To his relief, Swaine seemed content in the main to leave the direction of the vessel to Jarman, indicating his desires in grunts. The new midshipman was useless. Large and raw-boned, he seemed disinclined to join in with the seamen in their hard work at the running rigging of the huge sails, but on the other hand threw anxious, beseeching looks at the boatswain or others when called upon to take charge.

"Seen it all before, mates," murmured Doggo, at the shroud batten lashings. "Tradesman's son. Reefer's been wished on 'im b' some tailor 'e's got debts with." He yanked at the cordage viciously. It could go either way, depending on how far the Captain shielded the lad.

They tacked about when clear of the cays to the south, and shaped course to round the east of Jamaica for the small naval base of Port Antonio on the north coast. They made the customary stop off Morant Bay to pick up packets and bags; this was easier than carrying them by mule over the almost impassable Blue Mountains inland. Shaking out their sails they rounded the turbulent Morant Point before sunset, and headed northwestward past the red cliffs of Sail Rock.

"This will do, Mr. Jarman," growled Swaine.

"Sir?" said Jarman, puzzled.

"Manchioneal Bay. Good enough holding, I'd have thought."

"We anchor?"

"For the night—no sense in risking a night passage inshore, when we can arrive early tomorrow." Swaine looked narrowly at Jarman.

"Aye-aye, sir," Jarman said, his face blank. The anchor went down off the muddy river between the reefs, the stream flowing fast from the recent rains. *Seaflower* swung to her anchor, facing into this, and the cutter stood down sea watches.

Kydd dropped down the fore hatchway to the hubbub of the mess-deck. On one side Patch was holding court, men clustered around his table. As Kydd approached he looked up, resentment and anger in his face. He spoke to Alvarez but his eyes were on Kydd. "So where's our piggin' prizes comin' from, we lie with our hook down all th' time? This ain't work worth a spit, all hard-lyin' an' no purse at th' end of it—we're nothin' but a parcel o' scranny-pickers."

Farthing muttered, "Some says as how we's a Judas boat now—sittin' like this, we ain't a chance." Others joined in.

Kydd waited patiently for them to make their feelings known. By long-hallowed custom of the sea, seamen in their mess were free to voice their grumbles to each other, short of mutiny or sedition.

It subsided, as Kydd had known it would, but when he resumed his way forward to the petty officer's mess, the privateersman pushed to his feet, locking his gaze on Kydd's. His hand dropped to his knife. Kydd froze. The knife came out. Then, in a vicious one-handed movement, the blade flickered from his palm and thudded into a deck beam between the astonished men of the opposite mess-table, pinioning a hapless cockroach.

The talking died away in an edgy silence. The reality was that they were only a King's cutter, whose duties were mainly despatches and reconnaissance, their prizes before were a lucky chance and not to be relied upon. Patch was not the only privateersman aboard—Kydd realized it could get ugly if their captain . . . "If y' askin' to have y'r blade cropped, I can oblige ye," Kydd said mildly. His hands dropped loosely to his side but he tensed. Any hasty words from Patch now and he'd see him in irons: there was no other way.

At the sudden quiet, the canvas screen of the petty officer's mess at the end of the mess-deck suddenly pulled back. "What's th' gripin', mate?" Stirk called.

"Nothin', Toby. Shipmates talkin' cat-blash is all," Kydd said loudly, but he continued to stand, watching Patch. Slowly, the privateersman unwound and, turning away his gaze, moved to retrieve his knife. Kydd followed him with his eyes, then continued on.

"Gettin' worried they can't see us takin' prizes with this owner," he said briefly, accepting a pot from Renzi inside their mess.

"An' ain't that the truth!" said Stiles, lifting his tankard in disgust. "He'll be a-kissin' his dear ones just this minute, if y' believes young Luke."

"Kissing . . . ?"

"His dear ones—loves 'is bottles so much he's a kissin' of 'em every day," Stiles grated.

Stirk gave a brief smile, then leaned forward. "Other ways yez c'n get a taste o' gold, these parts . . ."

The others leaned forward to hear. "Yair, wasn't it in the Caribbee yer Cap'n Kidd buried 'is treasure? Nearly a million in gold 'n' jools! An' guarded b' ten dead men an' never found till this day?"

Eyes gleamed in the lanthorn light, then he turned to Kydd. "Now then, cully," Stirk said, "yer must know somethin' about it, 'e bein' kin an' all."

Kydd smiled. "Terrible great pirate, I grant ye, but no kin o' mine—he comes fr'm Scotland, 'n' the Kydds are fr'm the south. An' he has an I in 'midships where we have a Y." Embarrassed, he added, "An' I'm the only one—the first one, that is—t' follow th' sea in the Kydd family."

"An' a right shellback you is turnin' into, if'n I says so," Stirk said warmly.

Clearing his throat, Renzi attracted attention. "A great pirate— I have to disagree. He was only a merchant, an investor of Wall Street, which is in New York, no seaman he. But he married a lively lady, and bethought to go a-roving—one voyage only, and his crew is so dissatisfied with his conduct they set him ashore, stranded, in Antigua."

Renzi grinned at Kydd. "But he gets another ship, and continues—and finds an East Indiaman, which in course he captures with a great treasure. A simple-minded creature, he sails straight back to New York, but takes the precaution first of burying the treasure nearby to bargain with in case he meets trouble for his actions. It didn't work, and he pays with his life at Tyburn tree. The treasure is still there, my dear friends, but somewhere close by New York, not here in the Caribbean, I do regret."

Stirk growled, "Aye, but y' had some real pirates hereabouts."

"Take Calico Jack, mates," Stiles began. "Lures an Irish lass ter leave 'er 'usband fer a life a-piratin' together. They takes a Scowegian hooker an' in it there's this other lass. So he has this Anne 'n' Mary too, an' they are the equal ter any in bein' ready ter board, and the cuttin' of throats."

Stirk broke in. "But in th' end, as ye knows, Calico Jack wuz turned off at Tyburn, but 'is women, both on 'em, pleads their bellies. And says he weren't no fighter, lets 'em all be captured."

The thoughtful quiet was broken by Renzi. "Not all came to a bad end," he said. "Take Henry Morgan—"

"You musta 'eard of 'im while you wuz clerkin' in Spanish Town." Stirk chuckled.

"Indeed," said Renzi. "And you can say in truth that we are here today because he was the one who secured Jamaica as our Caribbean center for trade. Top class as a freebooter, as you know, took Campeche just in order to seize fourteen prizes in one go, and there was so much plunder after the sack of Panama that Spanish pieces of eight were legal tender in Jamaica for years afterwards."

Kydd's shipmates became preoccupied: it was not beyond the bounds of possibility that Spain could join in the present war, the old times return.

"Morgan came back to Jamaica?" prompted Kydd.

"Yes—when it was peace with Spain, he retired to England, but it was war again, and the King thought he was best placed of all to know the Caribbean, and appointed him Governor of Jamaica with an eye to its defense, and a fine fist he made of it, too. Sad, really, he missed the buccaneering life, and spent much government time in the Port Royal taverns, lifting a glass with his old shipmates. That's when Port Royal was at its most lively, a rousing good time guaranteed for any seaman. . . . He drank himself to death, and within three, four years a mighty earthquake finally sent most of Port Royal into the sea. Let's raise a pot to Cap'n Henry Morgan!"

Wiping his mouth, Stirk said loudly, "If y' wants a reg'lar-built pirate, then m' grand-daddy can tell ye—he saw Blackbeard 'imself! Back in Queen Anne's day only, scared th' piss outa him. Comes swarmin' aboard, black beard wi' ribbons, an' all this slow-match strung through, alight 'n' smokin' away, roarin' and shouting. Carries four pistols an' a 'eavy cutlass, ain't none can stand against him.

"Colonies see their trade go somewhere else, so they puts a King's ship on to his tail, sloop-o'-war. Lootenant Maynard—that's it. Hides 'is crew below while Blackbeard boards, then takes 'em! Th' l'tenant meets Blackbeard face on, 'n' isn't shy. There's this great fight, the two on 'em, but Maynard wins, and sails back t' port wi' Blackbeard's head a-danglin' from the bowsprit fer all to see."

The anchor was won the next morning in a sullen rain squall, hissing and lashing at the men on the windlass and sending *Seaflower* in a skittish whirl around her moorings. When the anchor finally tripped, the cutter was facing inshore, into the swollen river current emerging to carry her seaward. At the same time the wind strengthened from the sea, prevailing over the current, and *Seaflower* duly drifted toward the shore, not three hundred yards distant.

"Sheet in the main, y' bastards!" It was the first time Kydd had heard Jarman swear as he gave orders to carry sail aft with sheets afly forward. The cutter would rotate to face the sea under the leverage of the big after sail.

"What? Belay that, you dogs!" yelled Swaine. His eyes were red and hair plastered down his face by the rain. "What are you about, sir?" he threw at Jarman, before screaming down the deck, "Let go anchor!"

The men forward were making ready to cat and secure the anchor shank painter and were totally unprepared, the windlass taut and the cable on the pawl. The gawky Parkin had charge of the operation and floundered.

"God rot me bones!" spluttered Merrick, and thrust forward hastily, but the situation was already in hand: Doud's furtive bringing in of the main sheets had given force enough for the bows to swing. Swaine seemed to ignore his previous order with the promise in the bow's swing. "Carry on, then, Mr. Jarman," he said testily, handing the deck to the master.

"Never seen such a dog's breakfast," Doud muttered under his breath—but not quietly enough.

"You, sir!" Swaine rounded on him. "Damn your sly ways—I heard your vile words. Y' think to slander your ship, do you? Bosun! Do you gag this infernal rogue."

Kydd watched with growing anger as Stiles found an iron mar-
line spike, which he forced between Doud's teeth, securing it in place
with spun-yarn. The quarterdeck fell quiet at the manifest injustice.
Doud would wear the "gag" until given leave to remove it.

Seaflower made the open sea and shaped course for Port Antonio, some small hours away. There they landed their packets and
bags and took on two slim packages before resuming their voyage
to St. Kitts and thence Barbados.

Kydd thought it an unworthy spite that Swaine did not have the
gag removed until *after* the noon meal—and the grog issue. In the
way of sailors Doud would later enjoy their sympathy and illegally
saved rum, but that was not the point.

A fine northeasterly had them bowling along the familiar passage south of Hispaniola and by evening they had the precipitous
knife shape of Cape Rojo abeam. "Up spirits" was piped, but there
was not the usual happy hum on the berth-deck as the grog was
measured out. The popular Doud was well plied with good cheer,
but all the talk was on the Captain's character.

Watch-on-deck turned to: there was not a lot for them to do in
the steady sailing weather, and they hunkered down in the warm
breeze. Doud made himself comfortable on the main-hatch gratings and, looking soulfully at the stars began singing softly, his
voice coarsened with rum:

> *"'Tis of a flash frigate, La Pique was her name,*
> *All in the West Indies she bore a great name;*
> *For cruelly bad using of every degree,*
> *Like slaves in the galley we ploughed the salt sea.*
> *So now, brother shipmates, where'er ye may be*
> *From all fancy frigates I'd have ye steer free . . ."*

Too late Doud recognized the dark figure of Swaine looming
and scrambled to his feet. "Do y' wan' the second verse?" he said
truculently, to his Captain.

Swaine didn't answer at first. Then he bawled, "Mr. Merrick!" down the deck to the helm.

"Aye, sir?" said the boatswain, hurrying to the scene.

"What's this, that you have a man on watch beastly drunk?" A thick edge to the words betrayed the Captain's own recent acquaintance with a bottle, but there could be no answer to his question: there was a fine line to be drawn between the effect of the usual quarter-pint of spirits and that of more. Swaine turned back to Doud. "I came to tell this rascal to hold his noise but I see this—seize him in irons, and I shall have him before me tomorrow."

"We have no irons in *Seaflower*," said Merrick, expressionless.

"Then shackle him to the gratings right here, you fool," Swaine hissed.

At seven bells of the forenoon the following day, the ship's company of *Seaflower* mustered on the upper deck. Kydd saw the sanctimonious expression on Swaine's face as he gave a biting condemnation on drinking. The inevitable sentence came. "Twelve lashes—and be very sure I shall visit the same on any blackguard who seeks to shame his ship in this way!" Kydd felt a cold fury building at the man's hypocrisy.

Doud was stripped and tied to the main shrouds facing outboard. Stiles came forward, slipping the ugly length of the cat out of its bag. He took position amidships and experimentally swung the lash, then looked at Swaine.

"Bosun's mate—do your duty." There was none of the panoply of drumbeat and marines, just the sickening lash at regular intervals and the grunts and gasps of the prisoner. *Seaflower*'s company stood and watched the torment, but Kydd knew that a defining moment had been reached. The fine spirit that had been *Seaflower*'s soul was in the process of departing. His messmates cut Doud down, and helped him below. On deck Swaine glanced about once, to meet sullen silence and stony gazes.

The cutter sped on over the sparkling seas, but the magic was ebbing. Kydd felt her imperfections slowly surfacing, much as a falling out of love: the suddenly noticed inability to stand up below, the continual canting of the decks with her fore-and-aft rig, the discomfort of her small size. He pushed these thoughts to the back of his mind.

Parkin was mastheaded at three bells for "rank boneheadedness" but at the beginning of the first dog-watch it was Stirk who ran afoul of the increasingly ill-tempered Swaine; told to flat in the soaring jib he turned and ambled forward, his scorn for the uselessness of the order only too plain. "You bloody dog!" raved Swaine. "Contemptuous swine! But I'll see your backbone at the main-shrouds tomorrow—silent contempt—depend upon it. Mr. Merrick!"

Shackled on deck Stirk was a pitiful sight, not so much in degradation but in the sight of a fine seaman brought to such a pass. Merrick carefully avoided the side of the deck where Stirk lay, but Stiles merely stepped around him—in the morning he would be the one to swing the cat on Stirk's back and there was no room for sentiment in a boatswain's mate.

The evening arrived, and with it a convenient anchorage off an island south of Hispaniola. *Seaflower* immediately swung on her anchor to face into an offshore current of quite some strength, and as soon as the longboat was placed in the water it streamed astern to the full length of its painter, ready with its oars aboard for any lifesaving duty.

"Holding should be good even so," Jarman told Kydd. "Sand an' mud because o' the river yonder." Swaine disappeared and, after securing the vessel at her moorings, supper was piped.

It would be a dispiriting meal. Thinking of Stirk, Kydd winced as he heard rain roaring on the deck overhead. The berth-deck filled as men chose its heat and fug over the deluge above, leaving the luckless lookouts and Stirk the only ones topside.

"What cheer, Luke?" Kydd said, when the lad brought the mess kid of supper. Luke didn't look up, his bowed head sparking concern in Kydd. "How's this?" he tried again, but the boy didn't respond. "Luke, ol' cuffin, are you—"

"He called me names, Mr. Kydd, no call fer that," Luke said in a low voice. His eyes were brimming. He had served the Captain first, so there was no need to know who it was had taken it out on this willing soul.

"F'r shame, o' course," Kydd said softly, "but a good sailorman knows how t' take hard words fr'm his officers."

Luke stared back obstinately. "But he called me . . . it ain't right what 'e called me." He turned and, with great dignity, left.

"I seen bilge rats worth more'n he, the shonky fuckster," Doggo growled.

Renzi said nothing, but stared at the table. Kydd tried to lift the mood: if things got worse, *Seaflower* could easily turn into a hell-ship. "There's no one seen him with a Frenchie in sight—could be he's a right tartar, he gets a smell o' prize money."

"Don't talk such goose-shit, cully," Stiles said wearily.

The table lapsed into a morose quiet, and the wash of talk outside on the larger berth-deck became plain. Patch's voice came through loud, his tone bitter. "I tell yer, we flogs up 'n' down the Caribbee in this ol' scow, yer ain't never goin' ter feel a cobb in yer bung again!"

"Yair, but—" someone began.

Patch's tone rose in contempt. "Drops hook fer the night, never 'eard o' such shy tricks. We choked up inter this squiddy cutter . . ." The never-ceasing background babble rose and fell, and Kydd pictured the pugnacious seaman glaring wildly about. ". . . blast me eyes if it don't stick in m' craw, nothin' but this fer ever. . . ."

There were sounds of scuffling and mess traps falling to the deck, then Alvarez calling, "Where ye goin', *camarada*?"

"Topsides—I've had a gutful."

"Wait—"

Kydd met Renzi's eyes. "It can only get worse," said Renzi slowly. Kydd knew he was right: *Seaflower*'s captain was alienating his own ship's company, treating them as some necessary evil in his own problem.

Kydd agreed. "No chance o' this one gettin' a promotion out o' *Seaflower*," he added. The probability was that he had been given the command of a lowly cutter to satisfy some Byzantine relationship of obligation, knowing that he would not be put to the test so easily. *Seaflower* would gradually decay from within, her heart and spirit wilting and fading under the disinterest and neglect of her captain. It was intolerable that the willing and exuberant soul of their vessel was to be wasted so.

A discordant sound—it might have been a muffled shout, thumping—jarred Kydd's ear against the general noises. It seemed to originate from on deck. If the lookouts had failed to see an approaching attack in time . . . Kydd scrambled to his feet. "Somethin' amiss on deck."

Renzi did not move, but looked up with a dry smile. "I can conceive that Toby Stirk may well be a trifle restless!"

No one else seemed to have noticed as he forced his way aft. Kydd had no idea what he would see on deck, and his mouth went dry as he mounted the ladder. It was dark, and he stopped short of emerging on deck while he blinked furiously, trying to pierce the murk. It had stopped raining, but the deck was wet and slippery. He caught movement around the stern but could not detect any other as he climbed out on to the upper deck.

He hurried aft, to where bumps and thuds sounded, and nearly fell over the lookout, who was on all fours trying to pick himself up. Kydd looked around hastily. In the longboat were Patch, Alvarez and two others. Patch had his knife, was sawing at the painter. Kydd shouted, and the chorus of snarls and laughter from the boat as it fell away left no doubt as to what they intended. The oars came out and it disappeared quickly into the night.

"What is it?" puffed Merrick, appearing next to him.

"Deserters," Kydd replied. "Skelped th' lookout an' took the longboat."

"Who?"

"Patch, Alvarez 'n' a couple of others."

Desertion was a continual worry for the Navy—a good seaman could greatly improve his wages in the merchant service, or do even better by shipping out in a privateer. Theoretically, it could be punished by death or, worse, flogging around the fleet, but practical considerations usually led captains who recovered men to treat the offense lightly rather than lose a good hand. But Swaine . . .

"Get below an' tell the Captain," Merrick muttered. Without another boat there could be no pursuit.

Kydd went down by the after companion and knocked at the door. "Cap'n, sir!" he called.

There was movement inside, and the unmistakable clink of glass. "What is it?" came a hoarse reply through the closed door.

"Sir, the longboat's been taken b' deserters."

At first there was no response, then Swaine's angry face appeared. "Deserters? Did y' say deserters?" He pulled on his coat. The thick odor of drink in the tiny cabin turned Kydd's stomach.

"Vile set o' lubbers, I'll have y'r livers at the gangway t'morrow, try me like this!" The diatribe continued until Swaine had made the upper deck, where he staggered upright. "Poxy crew, this's an aggravated offense an' I'll see you all at th' yardarm, so I will!" he shrieked into the darkness.

To his disgust Kydd saw that Swaine had on his naval officer's coat, but no breeches. Lurching along the deck forward Swaine continued until he came to Stirk, still shackled to the main-hatch grating. "Don' ye dare cross my bows li' that, y' scowbunkin' brute," he snarled, kicking viciously at Stirk, who recoiled against the blow. It threw Swaine off-balance—he flung out an arm to seize a shroud batten, but missed, and fell headlong into the sea.

The current carried him swiftly down the side of *Seaflower*, splashing and choking. A line was thrown but Swaine was in no condition to snatch it, and within seconds he was disappearing into the dark astern. The knot of men stood paralyzed. There was no boat to go to the rescue, and nervous eyes turned to the boatswain. "We has to get under way an' go after him," Merrick said, shaken.

Jarman appeared, drawing on his shirt. "No! We have blashy weather an' coral under our lee, no time t' be standing in t' the land in the dark—"

"Y' misses m' point!" Merrick said, in a stronger voice, and with a peculiar emphasis. "I says we have t' get under way, Mr. Jarman."

Jarman stared at the boatswain. Then his face turned masklike, and he replied, "O' course we must." It was madness—but there was a chilling reason for the dramatic play. Each of the warrant officers was acting a part, knowing that every word and action would replay at the court of investigation that was certain to come.

"*Haands* to unmoor ship!" Stiles's pipe was made in a complete and appalled silence, the deck filling with apprehensive men. No good would come of this night, that much was clear; but they would go through the motions all night if need be.

At noon the next day *Seaflower* somberly reversed her course after spending all night and the following morning searching for her captain. His body was never found. At Port Royal Jarman and Merrick both went to the flagship; they swiftly returned, and with them a lieutenant and file of marines. *Seaflower* was effectively under arrest.

The court of inquiry was over almost as quickly as it was convened—the overwhelming number of witnesses made it so, and it became clear that their evidence concerning Swaine came not as a complete surprise.

Kydd felt a pressing need to be out of *Seaflower*, ashore and somewhere different, and when it was learned that the new captain would not be appointed for some time, he lost no time in suggesting that he and Renzi call on Cecilia.

The housekeeper's disapproving look was just the same, but when Cecilia hurried to the door Kydd was amazed. "Thomas, my dear!" she cried gaily. "How sweet of you to call!" She kissed him soundly, then noticed Renzi with a bob and dropped eyes.

"Cec, you look so, er, in rousin' trim!" Kydd said awkwardly. And, indeed, there was color in her cheeks, her eyes held their usual sparkle and the warm vivacity of her nature shone through.

"Yes, dear, life must go on, must it not?" she said quickly. "And you, Thomas, are you not the picture of good health?"

It was established that the men would stay for an evening meal. Cecilia quickly took charge. "I shall invite Jane, of course, and I want you to meet her betrothed—it's so exciting!" Dinner would be in the front parlor due to the unexpected number of guests, and Kydd helped the frosty housekeeper with the table.

As Cecilia laid places and bustled about, she told Kydd and Renzi her news. "Lady Charlotte—that's the wife of Lord Frederick Stanhope—met me at Mrs. Burchell's rout!" The idea of a Kydd meeting a noble lady socially was astonishing. "It's the very place to meet people, here in the colonies, you know, Thomas. It would never do in Guildford, would it?" Her infectious laugh made Renzi smile.

Then she went on, her manner a fetching mix of youth and sophistication. "And you'd never guess, she wants me to be her companion when they go traveling." Kydd said the expected, and Renzi murmured encouragement, and she concluded, with what looked suspiciously like a pout, "Who knows who I may meet on our travels? Why, there are gentlemen in this part of the world worth millions."

They sat down to table with only the barest discussion as to seating; Jane's intended was a young ensign of Foot in regimentals and quite at a loss when confronted with a requirement to sup with a brace of thoroughbred sailors. "Wine, er, gentlemen?" he said stiffly.

"Thank you," Renzi said. He twirled the glass elegantly before a candle. "I do find the Margaux a martyr to travel—this color has a pallid quality, perhaps not your foremost *cru.*"

Kydd dabbed his lips with his napkin: those weeks up-country had not been wasted. He raised his eyes and said unctuously, "Y'r claret is a sensitive flower, o' course. F'r m'self a hardy Burgundy would be more t' my taste," he added easily. "I'd recommend a Chablis were we t' be granted a breeze-mill in the cooling. But y'r very good health, sir."

It was worth the pain of all Renzi's patient efforts just to see the expressions around the table.

CHAPTER 15

N ame's Kernon," said Doud, "an' I don't think we're goin'
ter have the same kind o' grief fr'm him." He finished his
seaming of the jib and bit the thread. "'Sides, he sets me
up as yeoman of the storeroom," he added with satisfaction. This
made him a man of influence, of some moment in the small ship,
for he was in charge of the boatswain's sea stores.

"Give y' joy, Ned," said Kydd. He'd only been back on board an
hour or two, and there were definite signs of improvement about
Seaflower.

Doggo smiled grudgingly. "O' course, we lost s' many men b'
deserting, Cap'n just has to fin' senior 'ands fr'm somewhere."

Renzi came up on deck. "What cheer, mate," said Doggo, "an'
what's the griff?" Renzi, acting as clerk to the Captain, would
know ship's secrets.

"I'm not so certain that I should allow Captain Kernon's confi-
dences to become public property," he said, frowning. Kydd
caught his quick wink.

"Public? We's yer backbone o' the ship, has t' be in on th' noos

so we c'n plan things out, like. C'mon, tell us what yer knows!"
Doggo's hoarse wheedling brought a grin to Kydd's face.

Renzi leaned forward and said earnestly, "This must not get
out—it's of the first importance to the future of this ship."

"We understands, mate," said Doggo eagerly.

"Ship is under sailing orders!"

"Yeah, we knows that."

"And tonight . . ." Renzi halted, looking dubious.

"Yeah?"

"Well . . . it involves your own good self, you understand."

"Strike me dead—clap on more sail 'n' get on wi' it!"

"Tonight—but we're so shorthanded . . ."

Doggo drew a deep breath, but before he could erupt, Renzi
ended, ". . . that you're to lead a press-gang!"

"Press-gang?" Doggo spluttered.

Kydd grinned broadly.

"And Thomas Kydd is to assist him. . . ."

The grin vanished. It was now years since Kydd had been a victim of the Press; in the frigate *Artemis* there had been no pressed
men in her famous voyage around the world. And since his lucky
rescue from the dockyards to *Seaflower* he had had no contact with
pressed men. Now *Seaflower* had to fall back on impressing hands
from wherever she could.

"Where 're we raidin', do y' think?" Doud asked. It was well-
nigh impossible to attract good seamen to a King's ship in the
Caribbean—there were too many better-paid berths competing:
merchant ships commanded good rates to man ships for the
Atlantic run, and privateers could rely on the lure of fat prizes.

"Kingston town, I'd wager," said Doggo, his face alive at the
prospect of the entertainment. "Port Royal 'll be awake up ter the
press-gang."

"I can't do it, Nicholas," Kydd muttered into his grog, at the noon
meal. "I knows about it, is all," he finished lamely.

Regarding him steadily Renzi appreciated that Kydd was exploring his feelings and needed to talk. "So pressing men is an unmitigated evil?" he said coolly.

"I didn't say that," Kydd retorted.

"Some would say it's nought but slavery."

"So what's t' do if there's not enough t' man th' fleet?" Kydd said heatedly. Then he subsided. "You're turnin' it all around as usual, Nicholas. But you can't argue with me that tearin' a man fr'm his family an' all is a fine thing, dammit!"

Renzi lifted his pot and said, before taking a pull at his grog, "Then may I hear what it is you propose in its place?"

Kydd's slow smile was his answer, and Renzi grinned back. "So, we are overborne by logic. It is a disagreeable necessity while we cannot find any other means. Therefore you shall do your duty tonight, as is your bounden obligation."

At an hour before midnight, *Seaflower*'s press-gang formed up on the waterfront of Kingston town. "Do ye mark what I say," Merrick said. "Ye knows the rules—no violence. If they tries ter run, tip 'em a settler on th' calabash." He seemed unperturbed by the contradiction, but nodded at the nervous civilian next to him. "This 'ere is a sheriff's man come t' see fair play."

Plans were laid. The *Sign of the Mermaid* would be their victim, away from the center of the waterfront, and it was hoped to take hands from a merchant ship carousing after a long, hard voyage across the Atlantic. The boatswain would stand back and allow Doggo, experienced at the press-gang, to lead in when all exits had been covered.

Kydd eased his broad belt with its cutlass. This would only be drawn if things grew ugly, and then there would be an accounting to the shore authorities. The main persuaders the party carried were stretchers from the longboat, the narrow lengths of wood against which the rower braced his feet.

A brief memory of the Horse and Groom three years ago in

Guildford flashed by, when sailors of a press-gang had burst in to change his life forever. But he had secretly to acknowledge that there was no question as to which life he now wanted.

"So let's get under weigh," grunted the boatswain, and they padded off at the trot. A few late night citizens out on the street stared at the sailors, and there were scurries in the shadows.

Without speaking, Merrick indicated their positions outside the well-lit seamen's tavern. From within a riot of noise surged and fell, cackles of laughter and rumbles of conversation showing they were not expected, but the operation would not be easy: this was no gathering of unsuspecting rural lads.

The boatswain winked at Doggo, who threw open the door and thrust inside. "So who's fer a life on the rollin' sea? An' we c'n even save yez the trouble o' payin' yer reckoning!" he grated, into the falling silence. His stretcher tapped slowly in his palm.

A female screech pierced the blue haze: "The fuckin' press!" There was instant pandemonium. Tables and chairs scattered as men leaped to their feet in their race for freedom. Into the chaos poured the Seaflowers. Kydd, right behind Doggo, sprang after one likely fellow and seized his collar, managing to avoid a wildly swinging fist. The man faced him, glaring and panting.

"Now, cully, y'r taken fair 'n' square—" At this, the man charged, head down. None too gently Kydd tapped him on the head with his stretcher and he fell to all fours. Around them the scrimmage died away: there was no contest between a sober, determined press-gang and their fuddled victims.

Merrick strode into the taproom, looking pleased at the sight of the eight they had secured. "Well, boys, it's a life in the Navy fer youse now. But I'm remindin' yer, y' c'n still enter as a volunteer. . . ." One of the eight saw the inevitability of the situation and accepted the offer, but the others threw bitter looks at the Seaflowers and stayed mute.

Kydd's man got to his feet slowly, murder in his eyes. Two

*Seaflower*s began to hand him outside, but at that moment there was a scuffle at the entrance and a disheveled woman appeared, heavily pregnant, looking around wildly. Two ragamuffin children clutched her skirts, wide-eyed with fear. "No!" she shrieked, when she saw the man. "Not m' Billy! You can't—God save us, leave 'im!" She threw herself at the feet of the boatswain, her sobs harsh and piteous.

"Now, then, m'dear, y'r husband's off t' join *Seaflower,* as fine a man-o'-war as ever swam!" Merrick stuttered, clearly put out by the woman's emotion.

One of the captives pushed forward. "God rot it, leave jus' Billy Cundy, yer brute, yer has enough." The two children rushed to Cundy's side and clung to him, crying brokenly.

"Leave us m' Billy—an' look on these innocents! Oh, God, what shall I do?" The woman sobbed into her pinafore and patted her belly meaningfully.

Merrick shifted uncomfortably. "This is all very distressin', I c'n see that. Perhaps we'll stretch a point in th' case of y'r Billy boy. . . ."

"Oh, sir, if yer c'n see yer way clear, the bantlings'll pray fer y'r soul every night. . . ."

She tailed off when Doggo and two others descended the stairs with two more prospectives, still in their night attire. "What cheer, Sally?" Doggo said with a grin, taking in the scene. He crossed over to her and the woman's eyes widened fearfully. With one hand he seized her wrists, the other he forced up her skirt.

She screamed in outrage—but Doggo withdrew a large cushion, which he flourished aloft. "Still up ter yer tricks, then, y' saucy tomrig." Her hands turned to claws as she flew at him, but Doggo held her at arm's length until her struggles subsided.

"Take 'im out," said Merrick, annoyed at being caught out.

But the mood in the taproom had changed rapidly, from laughter at the deception to a very real anger. Billy Cundy whipped round to the others: "They ain't about t' take Billy Boy wi'out they has a fight—an' if we get took one b' one, it's all over wi' us. Our only chance is a fair fight all together!"

He threw himself at Kydd, and they went down together. The tavern exploded into riot. Lanterns were caught and doused, screams and hoarse curses mixing with the splintering of furniture in the gloom. Kydd landed a punch on the side of Cundy's head, but was enveloped in a beery bear hug. This allowed his "wife" to sit astride Kydd's back while she seized his hair and yanked it back agonizingly.

A barreling body abruptly relieved Kydd of her weight. The tears in his eyes clearing, Kydd set about subduing Cundy, but the riotous diversion had attracted others from outside and the press-gang found itself outnumbered. The boatswain's piercing call of "belay" sounded, urging them to retreat while they could.

Cundy, nose bloody but still full of fight, laughed coarsely in Kydd's face. Kydd saw red. He pulled the man to his feet and hooked him by his torn shirt. "Aye, but ye're with us, cully!" Fending off flying bodies he propelled the man to the door, where two Seaflowers secured his thumbs behind his back with spun-yarn.

The boatswain brought a charging man to a sudden stop with an efficient straight-arm blow and, giving one last look around, left, Kydd and his prize following. Outside, a crowd was gathering, menacing the sailors who looked anxiously as the boatswain. "Move," he said harshly. The sheriff's man was nowhere to be seen. Surrounding their victims the Seaflowers bullied them off down the street, screaming women throwing dirt after them while gleeful children ran alongside.

The tumult settled only when they boarded their boat and shoved off. "Small pickin's fer our troubles," grumbled one sailor. For all the sore heads and bloody noses there were only three men to show: Cundy, the volunteer and one other, the remainder of their catch lost in the rough-and-tumble. This would hardly count in the need to replace the deserters who had taken the first opportunity to run after the cutter had made port.

"Mates, it ain't over yet, an' I has me spies out," Doggo said hopefully, but it was a long pull back to *Seaflower*. In anticipation of a haul of pressed men she had anchored with the fleet and its regular pinnace rowguard.

"So, you has information," the boatswain said doubtfully.

"An' reliable," answered Doggo. "You'll unnerstan' I has t' sweeten m' man after, like."

"We will," said the boatswain shortly. "Th' Press musters at three bells this forenoon."

Kydd reserved judgment on the wisdom of a raid in full daylight. They headed off not for Kingston but to Port Royal. Scornful jeers met their landing and taunts followed their progress through the shabby streets. "Here we is," Doggo said. With a frown he consulted his paper: his tip-off turned out to be a cooper's yard near the dockyard wall, with the usual two-story living quarters within.

"This yer information?" said Merrick contemptuously. The Seaflowers were in strength, Doud, Stirk and Stiles ready for anything, but looked ill-at-ease at the risk of being made a laughing-stock.

Doggo looked confused, but rallied. "We'll 'ave prime man-huntin' here, Mr. Merrick—me man says as how there'll be nine top hands restin' quietly after a long v'y'ge, an' all unsuspectin'—be sure on it!"

Seamen took up positions and the press-gang entered the yard. Some coopers, knocking down barrels into their constituent staves for better portability at sea, looked up. Doggo pushed through them to the two-story dwelling and thrust inside, Kydd and the others following close behind. Three women in the front parlor paused in their darning of coarse sea stockings, but there were no men anywhere. The sailors swung out to the stairs on the outside of the house and clattered up, bursting into the first bedroom they found.

"Should ye be wantin' a dose of the yellow fever, ye're welcome," said a doctor, easing a poultice onto the poor wretch writhing in pain. The sailors whitened and left hurriedly. Gingerly they entered another bedroom, but this one held an old woman rocking in her chair and her daughter at a large cradle.

"Stap me, but you've led us a rare dance, mate," snarled Merrick to Doggo. The women looked on, quite as if they were used to having their privacy invaded by hard seamen with cudgels and cutlasses. The daughter smiled demurely at Kydd, who blushed.

Even Stirk seemed abashed, his big hands shifting awkwardly. "Aaah," he said, and crossed to the cradle to pay his respects. The daughter's smile disappeared and the old lady stopped rocking. "Aah! Dear liddle diddums." Stirk stretched to tickle the infant under the chin—then straightened abruptly. "Be buggered! An' that's th' biggest baby I seen in m' life!" He wrenched away the covers, revealing a lithe lad with all the muscular development to be expected of a first-class topman. The youngster leaped up, only to be collared by a laughing Stirk.

The old woman's race to the stairs was astonishing to see, but in vain, and the daughter had no chance with Kydd. "Take her," he told a nearby Seaflower. "Toby, I got a feelin' the yellow jack next door's goin' to recover a mort sharpish!" There would be no danger for Kydd if he were wrong, for he, of course, had lifelong immunity.

The women darning had broken for the street but had easily been rounded up under the dumbfounded gaze of the coopers in the yard. "Don't ye give no mind t' us," Kydd called, as they passed, but Merrick stopped. He turned to face the coopers. They went back reluctantly to work under his gaze, but the boatswain did not move on: his unblinking stare seemed to make the workers nervous. They had finished knocking down the barrels to staves and now should take up tools to shape the raw wood of a cask head, but they shamefacedly tailed off. . . .

"Come along wi' me, then, my little lambs," the boatswain said.

Captain Kernon could not have been more of a contrast to *Seaflower*'s previous commanders. A gray, cautious lieutenant, he smacked of reliability before initiative. His words to the ship's company on reading his commission were careful and considerate, but were notable more for the "do nots" than the "do's."

Seaflower left Port Royal with her pennant streaming, bound for the Spanish Main across the width of the Caribbean. But, to Renzi's disappointment, it seemed they would not be touching on the vast continent to the south, with its lure of amazing wild creatures and history of blood and conquest. Instead, as Kydd explained, having studied their passage plans with Jarman, they were to reconnoiter Aruba, an island off the mouth of the vast Gulf of Venezuela.

"A Dutch island," Renzi said with interest.

"Are they not our friends?" Kydd remembered hazily that the United Provinces had been one of the first to declare an alliance with Britain in the feverish times in the days following the guillotining of the French king.

"I believe not," Renzi said.

"Ah, so chance o' plunder," Stirk growled.

"Not as who would say," Renzi continued. "If you remember, the French invaded last year and we now must call their country the Batavian Republic."

"So it's French."

"Again, we cannot say. I saw recently that William the Fifth, who is your Stadholder of Holland, has crossed the Channel seeking refuge at King George's court. He still rules—or so we must accept. I think it an imprudent commander who makes the assumption that his possessions are for their plundering."

"They are our allies?" asked Kydd, in disbelief.

"It is safe to say that they are neither our friends nor our enemies. I rather fancy that our enterprise is one of prudent inquiry."

"Spying," said Kydd.

"Judicious reconnaissance."

The ship sailed on, knifing through the slight swell southward, and Kydd felt contentment build. *Seaflower* seemed to realize this, and lay more snugly to the quartering wind, the hiss of her passage always at the same eager pitch but rising and falling in volume. Kydd sent the helmsman below for an early supper and took the helm himself, letting the recurved tiller press against his hip with the slight weather-helm.

Out to starboard a fine sunset promised: he and Renzi would probably sit on the main-hatch gratings and see out the dog-watches in companionable conversation. Muffled laughter eddied up from below as supper was served at the mess tables. The watch on deck sat forward, little to do but spin yarns and watch the night steal in.

Reluctantly, Kydd gave up the tiller to the relief helmsman and murmured the hand-over mantra to the quartermaster's mate relieving him, together with the slate of course details. Luke arrived with a plate of supper and he joined Renzi forward. The golden sunset spread gradually and silently to a vast scarlet spectacle, an unfolding heavenly splendor perfectly unobstructed to the far bounds of the darkling seas. It was not a time for idle talk and the two friends took their victuals in appreciative silence.

When Luke came with their grog pots, Renzi took out his clay pipe and prepared it, letting the fragrance of the smoke drift away until it was whisked into nothing by the higher stream of air above the bulwarks. "Little enough chance of a prize," he said idly.

At first Kydd didn't reply. Then he gave a small smile and, still gazing at the copper ball of the sinking sun, said, "But ye have other things in y' sea life, Nicholas."

"A sight better than town or country alike, these troubling times."

"Aye," said Kydd, his eyes still on the majesty of the sunset. "Nicholas, I've been thinkin' over what y' said before," he said slowly, "about betterin' m'self." He eased himself to a more comfortable position. "I own that it would be very agreeable t' see m'self in a gunroom as Master's mate, an' in course o' time to take m' ticket with Trinity House as sailin' master—is that idle dreamin', do ye think?"

A master in the Royal Navy was as high as it was professionally possible for a seaman to go: he had his own cabin and advised the Captain himself. Kydd was a natural seaman, having the skills and rare combination of moral courage in a decision with an instinctual understanding of the sea. Yet he was only a few years into the sea service—but that, by fortunate coincidence, in some of the most testing regions of the globe. It would not be impossible. "Indeed it is not, given the time and opportunity, dear fellow." Renzi smiled. "Who knows? This war is spreading like a canker over Europe and its dominions. Soon England will be wanting every man of skill and enterprise to man its fleets. Your course is set fair for the greatest things."

Kydd's secret smile did not escape Renzi.

"You may find it happens sooner than you expect," he added.

Shifting uncomfortably, Kydd hesitated, then said, "Rattlin' good news from Cecilia, she meetin' this Lady Stanhope an' being rated companion. D'ye think she'll make a good 'un?"

In turn Renzi paused. "Inasmuch as she values politeness above all things, a quality her brother is only now achieving, yes, she has the vivacity, or we might say the liveliness of wit, that the position requires. . . ." he said dryly.

When the smoky blue of Aruba island rose grand and distant in the shimmering sea the next day, *Seaflower* shortened sail and altered away to stand off and on until night stole in. "Mr. Jarman, I will not risk the vessel by closing on Oranjested," Kernon announced.

Jarman looked uncomfortable. This was taking caution to the limit: a cutter like *Seaflower* had reconnaissance as one of its main purposes, and risks had to be taken. The harbor might well have a larger warship ready to put to sea in chase, but this was an acceptable part of their duty.

"I have it in mind to despatch the longboat to oversee the port," Kernon continued. This was hard on the boat's crew but would reduce the risk to *Seaflower.* "I will need a steady hand to command, one with the sea knowledge and the skill to navigate the boat there, and back to the rendezvous."

Kydd stepped forward and touched his hat. "Sir, I have m' figurin' an' can do this."

Kernon said nothing, ignoring Kydd, and continuing to regard Jarman gravely.

"It'll be me who takes th' boat, o' course, sir," Jarman said calmly. "You'll have y'r chance in good time, lad—please be s' good as to assist the Captain. Sir, Kydd is a fine quartermaster and knows his charts. I leave him with ye."

"Thank you, Mr. Jarman, I knew I could rely on you. Kydd, please to wait on me presently with the charts. We approach the island at dusk."

The reality was more perturbing than Kydd had imagined: the sea details to be won from the austere lines of a chart—the bearings, tide sets, implied wind variants inshore—were exercises in imagination compared to the reality on deck: a moonless night, the longboat bobbing alongside being boarded by Jarman and four men, who must push off into the blackness and trust that *Seaflower* would be in exactly the same position for their return. The quiet faith of others in his powers—this was the true end of his sea learning.

A barricoe of water was passed down: they would be holed up for a day in the craggy hills overlooking the port and would rendezvous the next night. There was little chatter, and when Jarman was ready, he climbed into the boat, settled his hat and ordered, "Bear off for'ard—give way together."

The boat slipped into the darkness and out of human ken; Kydd's farewell wave faltered when Jarman did not look back. *Seaflower*'s sheets were taken up and she surged ahead, safely out to sea on a fixed course. At a calculated time, she would reverse her heading and run down the line back to this position—in theory. The wind dying or freshening, and her speed over the ground would be different. An unsuspected current in these heated tropical seas, roiling to the surface at right angles to their course, would displace her bodily from her intended track—even the shape and strength of waves at different aspects of the hull would result in a deflecting.

Kydd watched intently as the watch prepared to launch the logship. This triangular float would be cast astern with a log-line to measure the ship's speed. Kydd himself held the twenty-eight-second sandglass, and when the logship had exactly reached its mark he instantly inverted it and stared at it by the small light of a dark-lanthorn. The log-line whipped away from the roller held above his head by a seaman until Kydd saw the last sand grains slipping away. "Stand by!" he growled. The glass emptied. "Nip!" he bawled, and the point reached by the log-line was noted. The number of knots tied at equal distance that passed out with the line would give the speed directly. While his crew hauled in the wet log-line, Kydd chalked in the speed on the slate, and set about worrying over the wind direction.

Kernon was cautious, but considerate: he treated Kydd like a master, consulting and discussing, allowing Kydd's concerns but meeting them with his greater experience. The next day wore on, and the evening drew in. Now was the testing time, whether the miracle could take place of a conjuncture in the dark out at sea of the two craft.

In the last of the light as they headed in once more, Kydd yet again took bearings of the headland and single islet that he had selected as his seamarks, additionally using Jarman's octant to determine their angle laterally, fixing their position by triangulation. The geometry was not onerous, but still intimidated Kydd, and he was grateful for Renzi's easy way with the formulae. He was only just beginning to see them not as some kind of machine that took in raw ingredients and out the other end came a neat and finished product: now he could, with Renzi's insights, dimly discern the elegance and fine reasoning behind them.

The moonless night was impenetrable, the soughing breeze and shipboard noises reducing awareness to a narrow circle of perceptions. The boat might be either in their path—or passing blindly by. "Mr. Merrick," said Kernon, consulting his fob watch. There was fumbling in the gloom and sparks flew in the wind. A red glow and fizzing, then a blinding blue light issued from a wooden tube held aloft by a seaman. The acrid smoke caused Kydd to choke, but the ghostly blue radiance shone out into the night in a goblin splendor, and threw the vast mainsail into a stark, pale relief. The tube spluttered busily and hissed, pouring towers of cloud downwind, each man on deck motionless and bathed in the unearthly light.

"Deck *hoooo!*" The cry from forward was quickly followed by the challenge, "*Booooat* ahoy!" and a faint cry from out in the blackness. *Seaflower* altered course—and her company was made whole once more.

Their welcome at Port Royal was puzzling: a lowly cutter returning from her servile duties, yet before she had taken up her moorings her number was hung out importantly on the flagship summoning her captain, and a pinnace pulled energetically from the shore.

"Barbadoes—an' not a moment t' be lost!" the dockyard functionary said with relish. "Lord 'n' Lady Stanhope an' one other."

Kydd recognized the name with a start, and before Captain Kernon returned from the flagship, Cecilia was aboard, gazing warily about her, something about her manner repelling Kydd's greeting.

The boatswain called tersely for Kydd as the senior hand responsible for stowage of the hold. "Do you consult Miss, er, Cecilia, concernin' the passage o' the noble gennelman," he ordered.

Cecilia's eyes flashed a warning as she drew herself up. "That is kind in you, Mr., er, Kydd."

"This way, Miss," Kydd mumbled, holding his hat awkwardly, and led the way to the broad midships. "Cecilia—"

"Thomas, please!" Cecilia hissed. "I cannot acknowledge you as kin, you must understand that. It were best that we stay at a distance, if you please." She looked around warily. "It is not often Fortune smiles on such as we, and I will not allow this opportunity to slip through my fingers." Kydd smiled bleakly, while Cecilia continued, "And, besides, you've no need for concern on my behalf. I rather like Lady Stanhope, she's kind and good." She looked at him with a touch of defiance but more a plea for understanding.

Kydd straightened with a grin. "Then, Miss Cecilia, we'd better be about y'r master's business."

His sister was gratifyingly practical. It was urgent that Lord Stanhope reach Barbados as soon as possible to take ship for England on a matter of some high diplomacy, the details of which would be disclosed, no doubt, to Captain Kernon on his return. There was no expectation of special treatment—it was known that *Seaflower* was a small, but fast, vessel, best suited for the purpose, and Cecilia had personally seen that their baggage would not exceed four sea chests in all. They themselves would board only when *Seaflower* was ready.

The wherry with the chests arrived at that instant, and Kydd tasked off three seamen to rig a tackle and sway them aboard. Kernon returned in some degree of distraction, giving immediate orders that his day cabin and bedplace be turned over to his noble passengers, arrangements for others to be put in train in due course.

Seaflower had to be stored for the passage and her extra passengers, and Kydd was hard put to plan the stowage and as well take in private stores required *en voyage*. A polite message came off from the shore inquiring whether four P.M. would be a convenient time to board. Cecilia's approval of the cabins and Kydd's report on stowage allowed Kernon to send a civil reply.

"A great honor, my lord," Kernon said, very politely. Lord Frederick Stanhope was a thin man with oddly black eyebrows against his snow-white hair, and a slight stoop. His eyes were penetrating.

"Thank you, Captain, for accommodating us at such a notice," Stanhope replied. His voice was soft but clear. His wife looked every inch the grand lady, and Kernon visibly shrank at the duty of greeting her.

"Sir, I will show you to your cabins," he said, with a bow, but Lady Stanhope cut him off with a flourish of her gloved hand.

"Nonsense. I'm sure Cecilia knows the boat by now, you have much more important work to do. *Tempus fugit,* Captain?"

Cecilia moved up silently on cue. Kernon took the hint, and without delay the boatswain's mate was pealing his call, "*Haaands* to unmoor ship!" *Seaflower* readied herself for sea. Kydd took position at the conn and heard a last interchange as Cecilia helped Lady Charlotte down the near-vertical ladder below. "Young lady, I was traveling in boats before you were born—do not fret so!"

Seaflower weighed in late afternoon and, breasting the tide, slipped along the colorful Palisades to the untidy clutter of buildings at the tip, Port Royal and Fort Charles, then gybed for the passage south.

"If'n ye pleases," the boatswain rumbled, indicating to the interested party emerging on deck that they were to occupy the more spacious midships area. Kydd had used some forethought: a grinning Doud stood by to warn the noble group should the mainsail boom decide to traverse the deck in an untimely fashion.

They emerged into the open sea past reefs and islets, which Jarman took delight in pointing out—Gun Cay, Salt Pond Reef, Drunken Man's Cay, Turtle Heads; all well known hazards to Kydd, who remained alongside the helmsman with a sharp eye. His gaze strayed occasionally to Cecilia, who stood at ease with Lady Stanhope, clearly enjoying the experience. *Seaflower* lifted gently to the broader swells of the Caribbean when Kydd was free to hand over the conn; but it was passing strange to see his sister in such a context.

Jamaica became an anonymous patchwork of green and brown, and Kernon approached Stanhope. "We strike south first, m' lord. In the central Caribbean we shall not be annoyed by corsairs or privateers. We then alter to th' east, and should make landfall in Barbados in no more than three or four days, for agreeable to your request I shall bend on all sail for a fast passage."

"Thank you, Captain," Stanhope answered courteously. "Now, my wife is wondering would it be convenient if perhaps we supped on deck rather than in the cabin—not that our accommodation is in the least objectionable," he added hastily.

"Of course, sir," said Kernon with a wrinkled forehead. This was not an easy thing to achieve in a lively cutter. "However, might I take this opportunity to present Petty Officer Renzi, whom I have detailed as your personal aide, and Master Luke who will be your servant."

Renzi stepped forward: the elegance of his small bow incongruous in his plain sea-faded seaman's gear. He did not look at Cecilia. "My lord," he said quietly.

Lady Stanhope smiled, then glanced at her husband, who had a preoccupied expression. "What is it, Frederick?" she asked curiously.

Stanhope's face cleared. "Nothing, m' dear," he said lightly.

Under the interested gaze of the watch on deck a table was

brought up from the master's cabin to be lashed into place next to the main gratings and both cabins were deprived of chairs so supper could then be spread.

"Could I suggest the veal and ham pie and cold tongue, m' lady?" Cecilia said, standing by, eyeing Luke's efforts with the cloth and cutlery doubtfully. "And the orange custard will not keep, of course."

"Charlotte?" Lord Stanhope extended an arm to his wife, and politely helped her to her place, which in keeping with other sea-service furniture was compact and neat.

"Oh, Mr. Renzi, would you be so good as to open a hock for Lord Stanhope?" said Cecilia, looking at him through her eyelashes.

Lady Charlotte watched the evening sea hiss past from her chair and sighed. "How wonderful, Frederick, just we two again." She turned to Cecilia and smiled sweetly. "My dear Cecilia, on this small boat we simply cannot stand on ceremony—be so good as to join us at supper."

Blushing, Cecilia took her seat to the side and glared secretly at the grinning Luke.

"A glass with you, my dear," said Stanhope. She accepted graciously, careful not to look at the waiting Renzi, standing silently in the shadows abreast the fore windlass.

Lady Stanhope leaned forward, her face alive. "Don't look now, dear girl, but I do believe that you've made a conquest of that handsome sailor at the back of the boat." Unable to resist, Cecilia snatched a glance—and saw Kydd looking at her along the length of the deck from the helm.

"I—I shall beware, milady," she stammered.

They made good time, and before noon the next day had shaped course eastward to Barbados, the trade winds coming comfortably from the beam.

Jarman came on deck with a serious expression. "Sir, th' glass is dropping—one-eighth inch since Port Royal, an' still going."

Kernon considered, his brow furrowing. "The reading now?"

"Twenty-nine an' three-fourths. I'm not happy, sir."

"But is this not your usual for these waters?" Kernon seemed unwilling to face the implication. "Lord Stanhope will not look kindly on any delay, Mr. Jarman."

"Sir."

But Kernon's face was troubled as he returned to his guests. Lady Charlotte and Cecilia thrilled at their leaping passage. They were standing right in the bows gripping a stay, mesmerized by the rush of glittering sea. Lord Stanhope, near the helm, remained preoccupied.

"Should the weather turn out for the worse, we may have to delay, m' lord," Kernon said, hesitating.

Stanhope turned, but did not speak.

"That is, we face a blow of sorts across our path which could be . . ."

"You will make the right decision, of course, Captain—bearing in mind the urgency of my mission, which I now feel obliged to point out is of the utmost moment for the safety of England." As if to underline the point, he drew out his fine watch and consulted it.

"I understand, my lord." Kernon's gray features set in worry, and he trudged off along the deck.

Within the hour the horizon across their path subtly changed in character. To the low band of silver and dark gray of the familiar rain curtains there was now added a trace of menace—a tinging of the clouds with tiny, subliminal amounts of copper verdigris. Kydd had seen this before, and reacted at a primal level.

"Sir! We must return t' Port Royal!" Jarman's forceful plea beat at Kernon's resolve while *Seaflower* plunged on gaily with her sails flat, the taut rigging harping musically. "We must put about now, sir!"

Anxious looks were now being directed aft by seamen who knew of the animal savagery of sea scourged by giant winds. Kydd stole a look at the helmsman, and was comforted by his stolid performing of duty.

"We put back to Port Royal," Kernon announced. It was a measure of his worry that he omitted first to consult Stanhope. "Ease sheets, and we take in the topsail—bear off t' leeward and set course, um, nor' nor' west." He seemed easier, having made a decision.

Seaflower's speed fell off and the ladies looked aft curiously. "If you please, ladies," Kernon called. He explained to the group what had to be done. Lord Stanhope frowned but said nothing, and Cecilia darted a quick look at her brother.

Kydd spoke quietly to Jarman: "In *Trajan* we could never outrun a revolvin' storm. We worked out its position, an' then it was bear away in the safest direction f'r us."

Jarman nodded. "Aye, but in such a cockleshell we needs to go further. These tropic storms are monsters an' go at such a gallopin' pace—it's not only th' center we needs to worry about, it's where they're headed. We plots the center every hour, an' works out a path where it's going, an' hope t' God to outwit the infernal beast."

The ugly skies loomed frighteningly quickly. The ladies stopped their marveling and stared soberly at the massing hideousness astern. Fear struck at the sight of what nature was bringing out from its sack of terrors.

On deck seamen secured as best they could. The cutter was dead before the wind and slashed ahead at an insane rate, like a hunted animal trying to flee a carnivore. But the bearing shifted, slowly but surely, about the starboard quarter. A rain spot spattered the folded chart that Jarman had brought from below. The tiny dots inside circles were their plot of the path of the storm marching across from the east—and curving north. "This is th' worst f'r us," Jarman murmured. His face had a strange, detached calm that struck a shaft of icy fear through Kydd. "That devil will go between us an' Port Royal. There's no returning there now."

They struck south, every sail drawing, then southwest into the vague direction of the reef-strewn interior of the western Caribbean, anything to keep from the path of the rampaging monster. By the dog-watches the vast dark roiling masses of cloud had reached overhead and the wind had turned edgy and fitful.

A presentiment forced itself on Kydd's mind, born of his sea knowledge, his increasing empathy with the deep. This was going to be the time when it would claim its price for that understanding, a hard price that he knew might be his life—and then he thought of Cecilia, and felt a hot misery.

"Sir, if you could go below, it would ease our worries at this time," Kernon said, distracted. Lord Stanhope looked about to demur, but Lady Stanhope took him by the arm. "We are together, Frederick, never forget that. We will see this through with each other, my love." She kissed him. "Come! You shall read to me. Captain, any news . . ."

"Of course, my lady."

They turned away, arm in arm. Cecilia paused for a moment, looking into Kydd's eyes. He felt helpless in the face of emotions that women seemed to meet with such nobility. Her eyes dropped and she went to him, clinging soundlessly for a long time. "Tell me . . . when . . ." she said in a muffled voice. The lump in his throat prevented Kydd answering, but he squeezed her hard. The cutter lurched under a spiteful gust.

"*Haaands* to shorten sail!" They could not run anymore.

"Cec—" He could think of nothing to say, and she pulled herself away and staggered over the deck to the after hatchway; one last long look, and she disappeared below to face whatever unseen madness was in store.

Lifelines rigged fore and aft, square sails struck, lines prepared for frapping, pumps checked—there was not much they could achieve in their little ship. Kydd remembered the violence of a hurricane from the decks of a ship ten times the size. In this they would not survive, but they could meet their fate with courage and dignity.

They lost dead reckoning when the horizon closed about them in a welter of white: from now on they might be anywhere, flying endlessly from nowhere into nothing in the cruel and uncaring storm.

Kydd remembered a true storm being painted by his first sea friend, so long ago: it was seared on his memory. "Comes a time when yer knows that there's a chance yer might not live—sea jus' tears at the barky like it was an animal, no mercy a-tall." Bowyer's iron-gray deep-sea mariner's appearance had reassured him then, but now . . .

The moaning wind turned to a banshee ululation, driving spray into Kydd's face with a stinging spite that made it almost impossible to see. Merrick levered himself aft, shouting in the ear of every seaman he could find. In turn he came to Kydd. It was the closing act. The last remaining scraps of sail would shortly be torn away and with it any control over their fate. *Seaflower* was going to stream a sea anchor: this was a drag on a line over the bows that would bring them around, bows to the sheeting chaos, the final move. Kydd's part would be to bring them up into the wind at the right moment, after which his role as quartermaster of *Seaflower* would no longer have any meaning.

The tiller had relieving tackles seized to its end: Kydd could dimly perceive, crouched on the deck, the hunched bodies of the seamen who must haul on these. Through salt-sore eyes in the screaming wind, he made out the jerking figures of those working in the bows. Seas smashed in, burying them under white torrents.

A hand waved: Kydd sensed the seas then flung his arm at the larboard men. They hauled and fell, staggering and fighting at the tackle, but the bows came round into the blast. The scrap of canvas met the wind end-on and flogged itself to death in an instant, but *Seaflower*'s bow remained headed faithfully into the tempest.

It could not last. At the point when sky and sea were unrecognizable apart, the sea anchor gave way. *Seaflower*'s bows rose like a frightened horse, then fell away in a sickening wallow, the vessel now free of any constraint.

Kydd was aware that, beside him, Merrick was fumbling: he was casting loose his lashing, his lifeline. The boatswain clawed his way forward, a hopeless, heroic thing, for *Seaflower*, it seemed, was now more under water than above. Nearly to the fo'c'sle he was taken by a wave. Clinging to the side he was mercilessly battered by the waterfall until his grip was broken and he was dragged into the rage of sea. Kydd caught sight of him only once as he sped past, the boatswain's face a frozen rictus of puzzlement as he went to his death.

A numb, unreal feeling crept over Kydd, paradoxically insulating him from the insanity. Intellectually he knew that once the blast caught *Seaflower* broadside on, she would roll over, perhaps once, twice, then all life in her would be extinguished, all the struggling, all the care, the pity—all would be over. Then a dark lump intruded itself into his vision, clawing across the deck to him. In these last moments left to them he pulled Cecilia to him, her lovely dark hair now plastered across her skull, the dress a torn and useless rag. He felt her trembling violently as he passed his lifeline around them both and gulped at the sheer unfairness of it, that such an innocent should suffer a sailor's lonely end.

Seaflower's bow swayed off wind: instantly the blast took her and she staggered, beaten. She began a roll, her high side caught more of the hurricane and the roll increased, faster and faster— Kydd hung from his lifeline as the leeward seas rushed to meet them. He turned to Cecilia's upturned face and pantomimed a huge breath. She seemed to understand but then the seas engulfed them both in a roaring, endless finality that was strangely peaceful: they could no longer hear the murderous hurricane.

He felt Cecilia struggle. In the dreamy underwater peace he

knew that she was drowning. He bent his head and forced his breath into her mouth, and prepared for his own end—but suddenly he was aware of a whipping, hectoring worry at his skin. They had come upright and the wind was clawing at him once more.

Seaflower now had her stern toward the wind: the roll would return when they passed the midpoint. It was the moment between life and death, a surreal halfway existence that allowed for the sight of the bow surging up at an impossible angle, fleeting dark shapes flicking by, poking above the rushing seas. The tidal surge paused, deposited *Seaflower* gently among storm-tossed coconut palms, then retreated.

The cutter was held rock solid in the arms of the land.

CHAPTER 16

—⁓⁓—

In stupefied immobility, Kydd waited the long night through on deck, not daring to slacken his lifeline or loosen his grip on Cecilia. The winds howled unceasing, the fabric of the vessel trembled and shuddered, but *Seaflower* was immovably high and dry among the palm trees, which whipped furiously in the outer darkness.

A wild dawn crept in. With it came a true appreciation of what had happened. The improving visibility showed them a good two or three hundred yards inland, quite upright, held there by the densely growing palms of some unknown island. Their small size had enabled them to surf over the offshore reefs and be carried safely ashore: a deeper hulled vessel would have grounded and been smashed to flinders. *Seaflower* had brought them through safe and sound. Tears pricked at Kydd.

Cecilia stirred. Her eyes opened and he saw to his astonishment that she had been sleeping. He didn't trust himself to speak, but Cecilia said something—he bent to hear against the dismal moan of the wind. "Thomas, please don't think to speak of this to Mama, she does worry so."

They laughed and cried together in the emotion of the moment, and Kydd loosened the cruel bite of the lifeline. The fore hatchway opened, a head popped out to look around, and untidy bundles around the deck began to stir. Kydd moved his limbs and stared out at the ruinous scene. Where was Renzi? A wild fluctuation of feeling was replaced by overwhelming relief when his friend's features came into frame at the after hatchway.

" 'And doomed to death—though fated not to die!' " Renzi said with great feeling.

Cecilia got to her feet, futilely trying to smooth her torn dress in the still blustery winds. "Pray excuse me, gentlemen, I fear I'm not fit to be seen in polite company." She smiled at Renzi and lowered herself awkwardly down the hatch.

Movement was now general about the stranded cutter. Kernon appeared, and Jarman. There was an attempt to reach the sodden ground beneath by rope, and after an exchange of shouts, Kernon was lowered by a tackle, followed by Snead and his bag of tools.

Renzi stretched and groaned. "Immured in those infernal regions, waiting for—anything. This I will not relive ever again— I would rather it were ended by my jumping overboard than endure that once more."

While the gale moderated to strong winds, *Seaflower* came to life. An absurd and out-of-kilter existence, but life. Her company assembled on the ground, among the ragged, tossing palms. They looked up to the naked bulk of their ship and gave heartfelt thanksgiving for their deliverance. Then blessed naval discipline enfolded them. The first act was a muster of all hands—remarkably few souls lost, but a number had tried to drink themselves into oblivion. Then the vessel was stabilized with shores: there was no shortage of palm trunks lying flattened and splintered, ideal for the task.

Lord Stanhope had suffered a fall in the storm and now lay injured, tended by Lady Stanhope. Other unfortunates had broken bones, cracked ribs, but they were young: the noble lord, in his seventies, was facing an uncertain future.

Initial scouting had established that the island was an undistinguished, lumpy specimen of some indeterminate miles around and, as far as it was possible to tell, uninhabited. Springs of water had been found, and goat droppings promised fresh meat.

Immediate dangers over, it was time to take stock. "Your best estimate of where we are, Mr. Jarman?" Kernon asked.

"Sir, both chronometers did not survive th' storm." This was bad news: latitude was easy enough to determine, given a sighting of the sun, but longitude was another matter. "And I do not carry tables o' the kind that I c'n work a lunar."

"I see," said Kernon. It was fundamental to the strategics of their plight that they knew their position, and his frown deepened.

Jarman took a deep breath. "As far as I c'n judge, an' this is before a good observation o' the sun, we are t' the south 'n' west o' Jamaica, distance I cannot know." He paused, then continued, "There are no islands in th' central Caribbean, but many in the west. The path o' the hurricanoe was from th' nor' east, but you will know their path often curves north—or not. Sir, this is my best estimate, south an' west o' Jamaica."

Kernon contemplated it for a moment, then turned to Snead. "The ship?"

"Nothin' that can't let 'er swim, but we ain't a-goin' to see that wi'out help." He pointed at the two hundred yards of dry land down to the sea. "Anythin' the size of a frigate c'n tow us off, but fer now . . ."

In the rude shelter where he lay, Stanhope stifled a cry of pain. "Desire Renzi to attend me, if you would, my dear," he whispered. His wife knew better than to object. When they returned he said firmly, "Charlotte, I wish to speak to Mr. Renzi alone."

Stanhope looked up at Renzi with the ghost of a smile. "We have met, I believe," he said in stronger tones, "in—different circumstances, as I recall."

Renzi did not recall, but there was no point in denying it. It was the merest chance that brought together a foremast hand and a peer of the realm, but it had happened.

"Your father is no friend to the government, as you must agree, but I have always believed his son to be made of straighter grain." His smile faded and he winced at the pain. "You will have your reasons for decamping from your situation, I have no doubt—"

"They seem sufficiently persuasive to me, my lord."

"It would be my honor to be privy to them."

It was an impertinence, but Stanhope's penetrating eyes held his unblinkingly—this was no idle inquiry. Renzi felt that deeper matters hung on his reply. Concisely, and with the least possible detail, he spoke of the moral decision leading to his period of exile.

Stanhope heard him out in respectful silence. "Thank you, Renzi. My supposition was not in error." He paused, clearly recruiting his strength for a higher purpose. "I shall respect your position completely, and with all discretion—and may I express my deepest sense of your action."

"Thank you, my lord."

"It serves to reassure me of what I am about to do." He bit his lip, levered himself up to his elbows and looked directly at Renzi. "It is of the first importance—the very first, I say, for me to reach England. The reason is that I have intelligence of certain actions planned by the Spaniards to do us a great mischief immediately war is declared."

"War!"

"Of course. It is planned to move against us once certain matters are in hand, but you can be assured that war is imminent." Renzi's mind raced—Spanish possessions ringed the Caribbean and a whole continent to the south, and he could think of a hundred mischiefs possible against unsuspecting islands.

"I have no despatches, it is too dangerous." He looked soberly at Renzi. "I am not sanguine as to my personal survival, and it is a heavy concern to me that my intelligence die with me."

Renzi said nothing, but feared what would come.

"I must now make all particulars known to you—under the strictest confidence that you can conceive, Renzi."

"Yes, my lord." A loathing of dissimulation made him unfit for the role of intelligence, Renzi knew, but there was little he could do to avoid this duty.

"It may happen that I am able to reach England—*Deo volente*—but if not, then I do require that you make known your intelligence to Mr. Congalton at the Foreign Office by any means you can contrive."

"I will."

He coughed once and lay back. "Every day lost racks at my soul. What are our chances of an early return to civilization, do you think?"

"Sir, this is something for Captain Kernon to disclose, but I should not be hopeful of a speedy resolution."

Stanhope groaned, whether in frustration or pain it was difficult to know. "Nevertheless, do you please attend. Now, the essence of this Spanish plot is . . ."

Satisfied with his immediate steps in the situation, Kernon strode across the clearing to Lord Stanhope's shelter, to see Renzi emerging. "Is Lord Stanhope at liberty to see me?" he asked.

"I do believe he will be more than happy to do so, sir," said Renzi, "but you will be aware that he is considerably out of countenance owing to his indisposition."

Kernon entered, removing his hat. "Sir, do you wish a report on our situation?"

"Thank you."

"I have good news," Kernon began. "We have found two springs of water and there are goats on the island. We shall neither starve nor suffer want of water. In large, this amounts to an inconvenience only, my lord."

"But our chances of rescue, Captain?"

"Equally good, I'm happy to say. The master believes us to be somewhere in the southwestern Caribbean. This means that we are on the sailing route taken by the logwood traders of Campeche and also the hide droghers of Honduras. It is only a matter of time before we are sighted and Port Royal alerted of our plight. In any event at this moment I have no doubt they are combing the seas for you. Our vessel is unharmed and we have only to wait."

"For how long, sir?"

Kernon considered. "I am confident that within a very few weeks we shall be found—a month or two at the most."

"Damnation!" The vigor of his response brought a flinch at the pain. "Captain, I have every reason to desire an early return, you must believe. Can we not use the boat?"

Kernon looked shocked. "I do not recommend such a course of action at all, my lord. The hazards are many, and here we may comfortably await our rescue without risk."

"What hazards?"

"Why, sir, where would we go without we know where we are? If we sail north in the expectation that Jamaica is there and miss it, we face a hard trip to Cuba. If to the northeast we may fetch up against San Domingo and a French prison—"

"Yes, yes, but it is possible?"

"But most inadvisable."

"Captain Kernon, I want you to understand that I must make the attempt."

"My lord—"

"Prepare the boat, sir. I will not be denied."

"If you insist."

"I do."

"You will need seamen to navigate. I shall myself command—"

"You must remain with your ship. And so must your only other officer. Is there no other who can figure a course?" The effort was draining his strength; he grew pale.

"There may be," Kernon said reluctantly, and passed the word for *Seaflower*'s quartermaster. When Kydd appeared, he said, "I cannot order you to do that, Kydd, but are you able to undertake to navigate in a boat voyage to the nearest inhabited place, as determined by Mr. Jarman?"

"I am, sir," Kydd replied seriously.

The decision taken, it was short work to manhandle the longboat to the sandy foreshore. The seas were still up, but would almost certainly be navigable in the morning. The longboat was eighteen feet in length and could carry fourteen men with its eight oars. On the sand it seemed large and commodious enough, but Kydd knew that launched into the vastness of the sea it would magically shrink.

It would be rigged for sailing, a common practice for wide harbors and brisk winds, sloop-rigged with a single mast and runner backstays, but with an extensible bowsprit that would allow it to hoist the two headsails of a cutter.

As seamen padded down with the equipment and began erecting masts, tightening shrouds and shipping rudders, Kydd looked thoughtfully at his first "command." At the very least he would need navigating gear. Jarman and he had held conclave for a long time, reasoning finally that the safest assurance of a civilized landfall was to the southeast, the coast of the continent of South America, a guaranteed unbroken landmass across their path that had a scattering of Spanish settlements continuously along it. Renzi had been unusually positive that in his opinion the Spaniards had not opened hostilities, and that the high status of their passenger would compel immediate assistance.

A boat compass would suffice to keep a straight track, but Jarman pressed his cherished octant on Kydd. "Ye could be grateful t' run a latitude down," he said. "You'll be able t' return it when y'r done."

Stores for a voyage of up to a week were found. Renzi came down the beach with a small package. "We need food for the spirit as well," he said, packing it up under a convenient thwart.

"You're coming?" Kydd said with pleasure.

"And why not? To leave you to enjoy the wonders of the new continent while I remain idle? This is asking too much."

Kydd grinned, suspecting that Renzi's motives came at least in part from the knowledge that Kydd would need a watch-keeping relief at the tiller. Doud had volunteered to work the sails, and could always sleep between activity, but there would be no rest for the man at the helm. More than that, he knew he would be thankful for real intelligence and cool thought to assist him if it came to decisions that might mean life or death.

"Could we perhaps contrive an awning for Lord Stanhope? We can take our rest sitting athwart," Renzi suggested. The beam of the longboat was nearly six feet, and with sails as padding they could lie quite comfortably braced around the sides of the boat.

At first light Kydd was down at the longboat, checking every line and fitting. The awning sewn during the night was tried and declared a success, as was the sliding stretcher hanging below the thwarts.

It was time. Kernon and Lady Stanhope accompanied Lord Stanhope down to the boat, their faces set and grave. Cecilia followed with last-minute comforts for the men, while Stirk carried the heavy water barricoes himself.

"My darling . . ." Charlotte bent to her husband and whispered to him while others averted their eyes.

Stanhope's reply was sad but resolute. "No, my dearest, grant me this only, that of all things I will have the confidence that you are safe from harm. I must go alone and, with God's grace, we shall prevail."

Her hands squeezed his—then let go.

"We must put you aboard now, my lord," said Kernon, sounding choked.

The boat was drawn up at the water's edge. The tumbling seas looked colder and more inimical, and glances seaward showed that Kydd was not alone in his feelings. Stirk came up, shuffling his feet in uncharacteristic awkwardness. "Ye're a chuckle-headed sawney as ever I saw, Tom, but I honors yez for it," he said in a low voice. "Keep lucky, cock, an' we'll step off on a spree some time. . . ."

It seemed that the whole ship's company of *Seaflower* was gathered as Lord Stanhope was placed tenderly in his stretcher. His wife stood motionless, her stricken eyes fixed on her husband.

Cecilia pushed forward. "I shall go with him," she declared firmly. "He needs care. Kindly wait while I fetch a few necessaries."

"It's—that's impossible, Miss Cecilia," said Kernon, scandalized.

"Nonsense! I will accompany his lordship—you know that I must, if he is to be of use to any on whatever mission this is that requires so much urgency."

Lady Charlotte clasped Cecilia and began softly, "My dear . . ."

Impatient, Cecilia told her quietly, "I know we are in the very best hands, Lady Stanhope, do not concern yourself any further on our behalf. We will be quite safe." She hesitated a moment, then said gently, "You see, Kydd is my brother Thomas, Lady Stanhope. . . ."

Arrangements concluded, stout hands were applied to the gunwales and the boat entered the still white-dashed waters, rearing and bobbing. Cecilia was handed aboard, Doud heaved himself into the bows and Kydd and Renzi took their places aft.

A signal to Doud had the foresail soaring up the stay and while

Kydd settled in the sternsheets with the tiller, Renzi cautiously showed main canvas to the brisk wind. A lurch to leeward and the boat started seaward, a bumpy, swooping scurry until they crossed the outer breakers, then the sea winds took hold and they lay to the blow, heading for the open sea.

Kydd thought only then to look astern, to see the dots of people lining the diminishing shore, the scattered waving, the forlorn bulk of *Seaflower* in the midst of the battered palms. He held up his hand in farewell and saw a flutter of kerchiefs in return, then turned forward, his face hardening in resolution.

Cecilia was doing something for Lord Stanhope, and Renzi was busy tying off on the lines. Doud stepped carefully around them. At his approach Kydd steeled himself for bad news, but Doud grinned down at him from a midship thwart, hanging on to one of the shrouds. He gave an exulting whoop, and began singing,

> *"Farewell and adieu, to you, Spanish ladies!*
> *Farewell and adieu, you ladies of Spain;*
> *For we've orders for England, you bold-eyed and lovely*
> *But we know in a short time we'll see you again!"*

To Cecilia's evident delight all the sailors took up the refrain:

> *"We'll rant and we'll roar like true British sailors;*
> *We'll rant and we'll roar all on the salt seas;*
> *Until we strike soundings in the Channel of England,*
> *From Ushant to Scilly 'tis thirty-five leagues."*

At noon Cecilia, by unspoken concession, took charge of provisions, and each in the boat received a ship's biscuit surmounted by cold tongue and a pickle. The wine was recorked after a splash of Bordeaux flavored the water ration agreeably, and a morsel of seed cake completed their noon meal.

An overcast sky still prevented a noon sighting, but a steady southeasterly course was not hard to sustain, and with the winds coming more abeam they made good speed. Toward evening the sea had moderated, the sun finally emerged and the wearisome jerking motion settled to a regular swelling surge.

Cecilia made Lord Stanhope as comfortable as was possible and the boat sailed on into the night. The seamen aboard, used to regular watches, had no difficulty in falling in with the rhythm, but a pale dawn revealed a hollow-eyed, plank-sore Cecilia.

Without a word, Renzi reached for the awning. He loosened its end, lifted it up and secured each corner to an opposite shroud. "Milady's toilette," he murmured, and clambered aft followed by a suddenly understanding Doud.

"Sir, you are too kind," Cecilia croaked and, without meeting anyone's eye vanished behind the improvised screen; the plash of water showed that she was making good use of her privacy.

Later in the morning a cultured cough from amidships drew Cecilia to Lord Stanhope. "Should you be so good as to tighten these bandages? I am certain I may sit, which would give me the greatest satisfaction since it has always been my practice to look the world in the eye—"

At noon, to Kydd's gratification, the sun was bright and beneficent. He took a sighting carefully and, after due consultation with the tables, he turned to the chart with Renzi. "Here, somewhere along this line o' latitude, that's where we are of a surety, Nicholas."

Cecilia could not contain her curiosity. She crowded into the sternsheets with them, her eyes searching eagerly for meaning in the chart. "Pray where are we, Tom? You are so clever; it looks a perfect conundrum to me."

"Well, sis, we are somewhere here," he said, with a sweep of his hand across the chart along the known line of latitude.

"Oh," she said.

Kydd added, "If only we'd a longitude, we c'd tell exactly where we was."

"Yet we must not be accounted lost," added Renzi. "We have but to extend our southeasterly heading and we shall be quite certain to end our voyage on the coast of South America."

Cecilia looked at him with round eyes. "Are the natives fierce there?" she asked fearfully.

"I rather think they have been tamed by the Spaniards by now, dear lady," Renzi replied.

The low, rambling coastline of the continent emerged out of the haze of noon the next day, sending the seamen feverishly to their chart, but it would be no easy fix, and they closed the coastline with some trepidation.

"My lord, you see that we have made landfall at an unknown point," Renzi explained, "and, should we be too far east, we will encounter the Dutch. . . ."

"Wi'out our longitude, sir, we cannot know—" Kydd added.

Cecilia was in no doubt. "Yes, you can, and very easily!"

The men looked at her incredulously.

"So simple. You go and ask where we are—from one of your natives."

It *was* simple. The boat kissed the sand of the unknown land on a small rock-strewn beach, raw red cliffs leading up to a profusion of greenery alive with the noise of animals and birds. Cecilia and Lord Stanhope were helped out, staggering around at the change of sensation.

"And where, then, will we find an accommodating native of these parts?"

Renzi's answer came from farther up the beach, in the form of a barking dog belonging to a figure standing watching them.

"I shall speak with him," said Lord Stanhope.

Kydd waved and hailed with a foretopsail-yard-ahoy bellow. "Hoay—*ahooooy* there!" The man approached. As he moved a small boy hiding behind him became apparent, dressed almost as a miniature of himself, with a wide straw hat and a gaily colored poncho.

Cecilia was entranced. "I do believe he has never seen the English before." His dark brown weathered features were a mask of uncertainty. The man's black eyes flicked from the boat to the two well-built seamen and then to Cecilia, the little boy clinging fearfully to his cloak.

"*Buenos días, señor.*" The eyes swiveled to Lord Stanhope. "*¿Por favor puede informarnos dónde nos encontramos. . . ?*" The others waited impatiently while the exchange continued, at one point the man pointing along the line of foreshore to the right.

"Ah, that settles it," said Stanhope. "We are within Spanish territory, and Cuerda Grande lies just four milliaria beyond. . . ."

The two sailors dived for the chart. "There!" exclaimed Kydd, his finger jabbing victoriously at the spot. The others came over, agog to hear the news. "Hmm, quite a way farther east than I thought," said Kydd. "See, this is Barranquilla, an' here we have your Hollanders," he added, indicating islands not so very far away.

"Perhaps this man can say if war is declared," Cecilia asked.

"He has no knowledge of any war," Stanhope replied, "but, then, I doubt he knows of much beyond his village—I cannot take the risk. We must confer, gentlemen."

The men clustered around the chart; Cecilia sat down on a rock and luxuriously splashed her feet in the clear sea.

"Kindly show me the essentials of our position, if you please."

"Aye, m' lord. Here we are, near halfway along th' Caribbean coast o' South America. Port Royal is here," he indicated to the northwest of the chart, "an' Barbadoes here to the east."

"And how far to return to Port Royal?"

"In the longboat, m' lord?"

"If necessary."

"Hmmm, this is not less'n five hundred miles, but with the nor'east trades a-beam . . . about three, four days."

Stanhope was thoughtful. Renzi looked up with an apologetic smile. "I will earn Cecilia's eternal loathing, but duty obliges me to point out that we are perhaps six days from Barbadoes if we continue, but if we return to Port Royal the vessel we take there must necessarily retrace our course, meaning a total time of around twelve days, even a fortnight. This—"

"We press on, I believe."

"Yes, my lord. Might I suggest her brother be the one to inform Cecilia . . . ?"

A jabbering from the little boy to his warily curious father brought attention back to the man. "If we have coins, perhaps we can persuade him of some fruits," Renzi suggested.

Cecilia was delighted with what was brought—not only fruits but corn bread, dried strips of meat and four eggs. "We shall dine right royally before we face that odious sea again," she vowed, and set Renzi to building a fire, claiming the boat baler as her cooking pot.

Kydd saw braiding in the sand along the beach and knew at that spot there would be water—the two barricoes would be full when they left, more than enough for a six-day voyage. As Cecilia's soup laid its irresistible fragrance on the air, he bent his mind to the job in hand. "Nicholas, we need t' clear the Dutch islands, an' as well keep away fr'm the coast shipping. Do ye think we should run down the fourteen degree line o' latitude to the Wind'ard Islands?"

"I do, dear fellow, but I worry that we are sadly at risk if we cannot fix our longitude for the Barbadoes after passing through the islands. Should we ignorantly sail past, into the empty Atlantic . . ."

"Aye, you're in the right of it, m' friend, but I have an idea." Kydd assembled his thoughts carefully. "Do we not now have, at this moment, complete and certain knowledge of our position—our longitude, in fine?"

"Yes?"

"And when we sail, this is lost. But what if we conjure our own chronometer? Do y' ask Lord Stanhope if we c'n borrow his fine watch. I take m' noon sighting right here in th' usual way, when the sun tells us it's exactly midday." Kydd paused significantly. "This is then our noon at this longitude, which we do know. An' if I am not mistaken in m' reasoning—I pray humbly I am not— then we know fr'm this the exac' time we are here ahead o' Greenwich noon."

"At the rate of one hour for every fifteen degrees—you are, of course, completely right."

"So we subtract this time an' set th' watch to our Greenwich noon, and by this we have a chronometer—an' fr'm now on, the difference between our local noon and this watch gives out y'r exac' longitude."

Renzi, who had seen it coming, nevertheless joined in the general applause. "You are indeed in the character of a magician, right enough." No matter that the watch was a poor substitute for the precision of a real chronometer, it would nevertheless put them well within sighting distance of their goal—and if it did that, then it was all they could desire.

Apart from some far-distant flecks of white there was no indication that they were crossing a major sea highway. In a world with privateers and pirates no ship would be inclined to indulge their curiosity and they sailed on unmolested into the empty seas of the central Caribbean.

Routine set in—the scrupulously doled-out rations, the morning square-away that Kydd insisted on, Doud's never-failing evening songs. And, most crucial, the noon sight. It seemed a fragile thing indeed to entrust their lives to a ticking watch. A frail artifact of man in the midst of effortless domination by nature, yet in itself a token of the precious intelligence that could make man the master of nature. It was the first thing to be stowed safely beneath the thwarts when the rain came down.

Thick, hammering, tropical rain. Tied to the tiller for hours at a time, unable to go to shelter, Kydd endured. The rain teemed down on his bowed head, his body, his entire being. The incessant heavy drops became a bruising torture after a while, and it took real courage to keep to his post. The others crouched together under the slacked-off awning, just the regular appearance of a hand sending a bright sheet of water from the baler over the side from under the lumpy canvas.

It was trying afterward as well; from being comprehensively soaked to a brazen sun warming rapidly. The result was a clammy stickiness that had clothing tugging at the skin in a maddening clinging heaviness. Cecilia's appearance from under the old sail showed that she had not escaped. Patches of damp had her distracted, plucking at her sun-faded dress and trying to smooth her draggled hair; she was in no mood for conversation with the men.

Mile succeeded mile in a near-invisible wake that was a perfect straight line astern. The dying swell of the storm petered out into a flat royal-blue immensity of water, prettily textured by myriad dark ripples from the warm and pleasant breeze. Then the sun asserted itself—there was real bite in the endless sunshine now, a heat that was impossible to escape.

But on the fourth day a milestone was reached: the meridian of 65 degrees west. It was time to leave their eternal easterly progression and shape their course to pass through the Windward Islands chain and direct to Barbados. The empty sea looked exactly the same, but the filigreed hands of the watch mysteriously said that not only had they passed the Dutch islands safely astern but that the several island passages that were the entrance to the Caribbean Sea were now only a couple of hundred miles ahead, say no more than a day of sailing.

"Huzzah!" cried Cecilia, and Doud stood tall on a thwart and sang of England and sweethearts to the uncaring sea and sky. They had adequate water; the food was now a monotonous hard tack soaked in water tinged with wine, cheese of an heroic hardness and a precious hoard of treats—dried meat strips cut into infinitely small pieces to suck for minutes a time, dainty cubes of seed cake and, for really special occasions, one preserved fig between two, with a whole one for the helmsman of the watch.

The boat lapsed into a silence; rapt expressions betrayed minds leaping ahead to another, more congenial plane of existence. The clean fragrance of fresh linen in a real bed. Surcease for body and spirit. What would be the first thing to do after stepping ashore?

And then the wind fell. From a breeze to a zephyr, from that to a playful soft wafting around the compass, and then nothing. The longboat ceased any kind of motion. The sails hung lifeless with only an occasional dying twitch, and the heat closed in, blasting up from the limitless watery plain, a hard, blinding force that could be felt behind closed eyes. The awning seemed to trap a suffocating humidity beneath it, but the alternative was to suffer both the unremitting glare reflected from the pondlike sea, and the ferocious heat from a near-vertical sun.

Time slowed to an insupportable tedium. Rooted to their places on hard wood for an infinity of time, the slap and trickle of water the only sound, the choking heat their only reality, it was a trial of sanity. Doud lay in the V of the bow, staring fixedly ahead. Stanhope sat under the awning against the mast, with Renzi opposite. Cecilia lay in the curve of the lower part of the boat, and Kydd still sat at the motionless tiller, his mind replaying a quite different nightmare—the shrieking darkness of Cape Horn.

The baler was passed from hand to hand, a scoop of seawater poured over the head gave momentary relief, but the sticky salt remaining only added to the misery. Water, precious water, it was no longer a given thing. Life—or death—was in the two hot wooden casks in the bottom of the boat, and when they were broached, eyes followed every move of the person drinking their tiny ration of tepid, rank fluid.

"I fear we have a contrary current," Kydd croaked, after the painful duty of the noon sight. "Only a half-knot or one, but . . ."

Nobody spoke, the idea of being carried back into the Caribbean a thought too cruel to face.

As the afternoon wore on, water in its every guise crept into the brain, tricked itself into every thought, tantalized and tempted in a way that could only call for wonder at the creativity of a tortured mind. Still the implacable sun glared down on them, sending thoughts fluttering at the prison bars of reality, desperate for any escape from the torment. Time ground on, then astonishingly the sun was on the wane—a languorous sunset began, full of pink-tinted golds and ultramarine sea. And still no wind.

Renzi crawled over to a thwart and drew out of his package a small book. "My friends," he began, but his voice was hoarse and unnatural, and he had to clear his throat. "We are at some hazard, I'll grant, but . . . these words may put you in mind of another place, another time, what we may yet . . .

> 'The curfew tolls the knell of parting day,
> The lowing herd winds slowly o'er the lea,
> The ploughman homeward plods his weary way,
> And leaves the world to darkness and to me.
> Now fades the glimmering landscape on the sight,
> And all the air a solemn stillness holds . . .'

"Oh, Nicholas, Nicholas!" Cecilia wept. She moved to Renzi, and hugged his arm while the measured, burnished phrases went on until Renzi could no longer see the text.

Night fell. They lolled back and gazed at the vast starry heavens as they drifted in perfect calm beneath. But bodies were now a mass of suffering from the aches of unyielding hardness every-where—and the sight for them held no beauty.

The night progressed, the moon traveled half the sky and still no wind. Then in the early hours an inconsequential puff from nowhere had the sails slatting busily. Kydd heaved himself up from the bottom of the boat where he had been lying and looked across the ebony black sea, glittering with moonlight. A roughening of texture in the glassy sea away in the distance had his heart hammering. It approached, flaws and ripples in a darting flurry that came nearer and nearer. Kydd held the tiller in a death grip, fearful with anticipation, and suddenly they were enveloped in a brisk breeze that sent the longboat heeling, then in a joyful chuckling of water they were under way again.

Croaking cheers broke out—but the breeze dropped, their speed fell away . . . and then the wind picked up even stronger than before in a glorious thrusting urge. The winds held into the morning; with a steady breeze from the northeast, the heat was under control. Eagerly, the midday ceremony with octant and watch was anticipated with little patience, for Kydd took the utmost pains to insure his workings were unassailable.

Finally he looked up from the frayed chart. "I'm grieved t' say it, but I was wrong," he said, but the staring eyes that looked back at him made him regret his black humor. "That is, th' current, it wasn't as bad as I thought. In fact . . ." he paused dramatically and pointed " . . . there—there you will find Saint Lucia distant but twenty leagues, and there, that is Saint Vincent. We pass between them and to Barbadoes beyond."

It was incredibly elating to be making plans for landfall within the next day. "Can we stop at an island for water on the way?" Stanhope said. His voice was croaking with dehydration.

"No," said Kydd decisively. "We don't know if the French are still in control—after what we've suffered, I don' want us t' end in a Frog prison."

Cecilia lifted a barricoe and shook it. "We don't have much left," she said. Her voice was husky and low, her skin dry and cracked.

"We don't stop," Kydd said, concentrating ahead. His own voice had a harsh cast.

For a long time there was nothing said, then Lord Stanhope murmured, "I could insist. . . ."

Kydd gripped the tiller. "No. Y'r not th' Captain. If y' needs water then you c'n have my share."

"That won't be necessary," Lord Stanhope croaked, "but thank you, Mr. Kydd, that was nobly said."

"We don't stop."

"No."

The passage between the two islands was more than twenty-five miles; at their height-of-eye they would probably not even see them. Kydd concentrated on the boat compass, the card swimming lazily under the lubber's line. He had to be certain of his course for if he steered true, Barbados lay just eighty-odd miles beyond in the Atlantic, less than a day away.

"When we gets t' Barbadoes, th' thing I'd like best—"

Before Doud's thought could be finished there was a sickening crunch and a crazy rearing. The longboat came to a sudden halt, sending all hands sprawling and the mast splintering in two. Then the boat slid backward crazily and into deep water again. The sea was as innocent as it was possible to be, but inches under water, and therefore invisible, a projection of reef not on the chart had been lying in wait. The boat lay in disorder, and Kydd saw clear water in the bottom. "Clear away th' raffle, Nicholas—we're takin' in water," he said thickly.

Without being told Cecilia added her weight to the heaving and bundling, her face set and worried, her dress riding up unnoticed. Doud was in the foresheets, bending over again and again, and in silent agony nursing an injured arm.

It was as bad as Kydd had feared. The very bottom of the boat had taken the full force of the impact and was stove in. By a miracle the worst-affected plank was still hanging by a thread, but the crystal clear water of the Caribbean was gouting in. Their survival would now be measured in minutes unless something could be done. Kydd's mind raced. If they stuffed the holes with clothing it would reduce the flow—but at the almost certain risk of the plank giving way and bringing on a final unstoppable rush of water.

"Nicholas, unbend the mains'l, we have t' fother." They would try to check the inrush by passing the sail around the outside of the boat. "Rest o' ye, bale f'r your lives!"

His fingers scrabbling at the ropes and flaccid canvas Kydd tried to think. Judging by the merest suggestion of misty gray to the northwest they were no closer than a dozen miles from St. Lucia. The wreckage of the boat might sink under the weight of its fittings or remain a waterlogged hulk; either way there was no salvation for them.

The mainsail was won from its rigging by sheer brute insistence and sailors' knives, and Kydd staggered with it to the bows. Somehow the unwieldy mass had to be passed under with a rope each side—that required two men—but as well it had to be hauled away aft.

"Which rope?" Lord Stanhope said tersely, stumbling toward them.

"M' lord—if y' please," Kydd said, and handed him one. Cecilia insisted on the opposite one, freeing Kydd and Renzi to ease the sail foot by foot down the outside length of the boat. The water was halfway to the knees, unnerving and making the boat wallow frighteningly.

"Bale!" bawled Kydd, and with anything they could find they furiously threw the water overside. There was no telling whether they had a chance and Kydd fell to his work in a frenzy of desperation.

He was unprepared for the inhuman screech that pierced the air. It was Cecilia. She stood in the center of the boat and pointed shakily—to a hulking white shape below the water that glided past lazily, a lethal flash of cruel eyes and a semicircle of teeth around a gaping maw. Kydd went icy. He remembered the frenzy of killing around the burning ship, the living flesh ripped and devoured before their horror-struck gaze. "Bale!" he howled.

Cecilia remained frozen near the stump of the mast, her face sagging with fear, staring at the shark. "I—I hate them—I *h-a-a-a-te* them!" she said in rising hysteria. Kydd had never seen her like this before and saw that her terror was unhinging her.

His voice caught in a sob, for he knew there was nothing he could do for her. It was probable that before evening every one of them would be eaten alive—there were now four of the terrible creatures circling the boat. An impossibly huge shark came close, closer. There was a sudden bump and dismaying displacement. Something of its evil ferocity was transmitted in the shock of the blow, a personal message of hatred that was the more terrifying for being felt rather than seen.

Cecilia sat suddenly, her face contorted with terror. Renzi put down his baler and, with an expression of supreme compassion, held her rigid body close, stroking, soothing.

"Nicholas!" Kydd choked. His duty was baling; they must fight—they would play it to the last.

Renzi went back to his baling, his eyes on Cecilia. She gulped crazily and scrabbled over the thwarts toward Kydd, looking to him with eyes at the very edge of madness. "Thomas! *Thomas!* Ple-e-a-se!" Kydd could not look at her. "P-p-promise me, p-please promise me—before it h-happens—you'll k-kill me, with y-your knife, *ple-e-e-se.* . . ." Kydd's hand strayed to the seaman's knife at his belt and felt his mind unravel.

The shark came in again, its bulk under the bright sunlit water sinister and purposeful. Kydd knew that the shark was closing in for a kill. He took an oar and, like a harpoon, rammed it into its loathsome mouth as hard as he was able. The shark twisted in agony, and thrashed away in a fury of spray—but the others took it to be a crippling injury. They fell on the creature and it disappeared in a snapping frenzy of red mist.

"Bale!" Kydd croaked.

But something had changed—the far horizon ahead was no longer a clean line of sea and sky: it was populated with pyramids of sails, and not one but nearly a dozen. Unseen by them in their peril they had stolen up over the horizon.

"Th' Loo'ard Islands squadron!" Kydd gasped. The stately line of men-o'-war stretched several miles over the sea, clearly on its lawful occasions, possibly exercising on the passage to Barbados; an incredibly moving and beautiful sight—but they were many miles distant.

"Ned!" screamed Kydd. Doud leaped to his feet, tore off his shirt and, with his good arm, waved it furiously, for their lives depended on it.

The grand procession sailed on.

"Holy Christ, see us, see us, why don' ye?"

"Bale!" Kydd shrieked.

Cecilia sat with her head at a strange angle, a haunted smile playing on her lips.

The ships, Vice Admiral of the Blue, Sir Benjamin Caldwell's Leeward Islands squadron of the Royal Navy, proceeded ahead in line—sailing inexorably past.

"Y' bastards, y' fuckin' scrovy . . ." Doud raved. But Kydd knew that past the closest point of approach they had little chance. The lookouts were primed to expect things ahead, and with their mast a mere stump their visibility to the fleet would be nothing. A lump came to his throat, emotion flooded him, overwhelmed him.

Then, one after another the great ships-of-the-line majestically put down their helm, the heavy spars braced around, the sails backed then drawing at exactly the right moment to have the fleet pivoting about the one point in succession—and in a faultless exercise, the ships of the fleet tacked and headed directly toward them.

There was weeping, racking, joyous, heartfelt—and this time Kydd let Renzi go to Cecilia.

In a haze of unreality, they saw the leading ship fall out of line, lowering a boat that sped across to them. The sight of the strong, open faces of the seamen misted Kydd's eyes. They heaved the feeble, sun-ravaged humanity into their boat, and left the wreck to settle forlornly. Their pitiful collection of possessions was tenderly removed and the lieutenant in charge spoke kind words. And discovered whom he had delivered. Sailors tugging strongly at the oars, they went back down the line, passing ship after ship in a delirious progression, to the flagship in the center.

For Kydd there followed only disconnected images: the vast bulk of the flagship alongside, figures looking curiously from the deck-line high above. A chair swaying down from a yardarm whip, Cecilia first, the others and finally Kydd. The blessed tar-smelling clean decks, the crisp banging of backed sails above, himself crumpling helpless, concerned seamen crowding around, a vision of Cecilia staring at him, the gold and blue of high officers gathering around Lord Stanhope—and then his body sought peace in insensibility.

"Good God!" exclaimed the Admiral, visibly shocked. "Frederick, to see you like this. Great heavens, you must be—"

"That is not of consequence. May we talk—in private?" His voice was weak but resolute.

The Admiral's Great Cabin, with its dark paneling, ornate silver and polished furniture, did not deter Lord Stanhope from speaking directly. "I have a matter of compelling urgency that requires my attendance at the Foreign Office—"

Strategic naval dispositions were straightforward enough: Ceres frigate would be sailing for England in any event, it would simply leave immediately. Of course it would be in order for the young lady to be accommodated until Lady Charlotte arrived to join her.

But in other naval matters it was necessary for Lord Stanhope to step carefully, for the customs of the Service could not be ordered from above in quite the same way. "It is my most firm resolve, Benjamin, to recognize the quite extraordinary deeds of these men who carried me through so valiantly."

The Admiral stroked his jaw. "A purse of guineas from you is the usual thing, and possibly an address by myself before the ship's company. . . ."

"I rather feel that, in this case, something more in the way of a professional distinction perhaps, a form of honor. . . ."

"I understand, Frederick. You will tell me more of them and I will make a suggestion."

"The one is the quartermaster of *Seaflower,* a perfectly noble specimen of the sea race and in my untutored eyes destined for some eminence in the sea profession. And we have another who is of a most interesting character and who is the most nearly learned of any I have had the fortune to meet. The last is a bold seaman of courage and humor who would be an ornament to any vessel that has the honor to bear him."

"Quite so. Hmmm, it is within my gift to raise them to the felicity of warrant officer, but I rather fancy the last named may prefer more to carry my personal recommendation to his next captain for a fitting advancement to petty officer."

The Commander-in-Chief of the Leeward Islands Squadron looked directly at Stanhope: "Very well. These two are master's mates from this hour, but the warrant will require that the Admiralty do confirm my motions."

"My dear Benjamin, I think *that* is a matter that can safely be left to me. . . ."

AUTHOR'S NOTE

I am a visile—I have to "see" things in my mind's eye before I can write about them. I try to go to the very places that were so important to history, to caress the old stones, to sight along a great gun that men once served in bloody battle, and most precious and transcendent, to step aboard men-o'-war of Kydd's day—particularly the glorious ship-of-the-line *Victory* and the valiant frigate *Constitution*.

Away from the gaudy tourist haunts in the Caribbean there are many tactile relics of rousing times past, unwittingly bequeathed to us by men whose concerns of the hour did not include a care for posterity. Henry Morgan's Port Royal slid into the sea a century before Kydd arrived, but the bones of the dockyard still exist, albeit in a parlous state. More rewarding is English Harbour in Antigua, where Kydd suffered and loved, and which remains much as he would remember—a uniquely preserved jewel of naval history.

There are many who care deeply about the Caribbean's past, and I think especially of Reg Murphy of Antigua dockyard, who told me the story of the deadly confrontation on the quayside, which I faithfully retell in this book, and Desmond Nicholson, whose encyclopedic knowledge so enriched my visit. In Barbados, the staff of the museum were especially kind, enabling me to find Karl Watson at an archeological dig of the eighteenth century; he then provided me with an embarrassment of material. In Jamaica, John Aarons at the National Library proved a fascinating source of his country's deeply interesting past. In fact, my apologies are due to all of them that, within the scope of one book, I have not been able to do justice to their generosity.

Above all, it is to my wife and creative companion that I owe so much: Kathy's cool judgment on my hot imagination, and sturdy practicality in walking and talking the plot delight my publisher with the result. Thus it is with some confidence that I let the juices flow and now set forth on my next—and very different—story in Thomas Kydd's tale.

ABOUT THE AUTHOR

Julian Stockwin was born in England in 1944 and was sent at the age of fourteen to *Indefatigable,* a tough sea-training school. He joined the Royal Navy at fifteen, before transferring to the Royal Australian Navy when his family emigrated. He served in the Far East, Antarctic waters, the South Seas, and in Vietnam, where he saw active service in a carrier task force. After university, he became a teacher and an educational psychologist and lived for a number of years in Hong Kong, where he was commissioned into the Royal Naval Reserve and received Britain's MBE award. He retired with the rank of lieutenant commander. *Seaflower* is Julian Stockwin's third novel, following the successful launch of the series with *Kydd* and *Artemis.* He lives in Devon, England, with his wife, Kathy, where he is at work on the next Kydd adventure. His website is www.julianstockwin.com.

PROLOGUE

—⁓—

D amme, but that's six o' them—an' they're thumpers, Sir
Edward!" The massive telescope that the first lieutenant
of HMS *Indefatigable* held swayed in the hard gale, but
the gray waste of winter sea made it easy to see the pallid white
sails of line-of-battle ships, even at such a distance.

Captain Pellew growled an indistinct acknowledgment. If it
was the French finally emerging from Brest, it was the worst tim-
ing possible. The main British battle fleet had retired to its winter
retreat at Portsmouth, and there was only a smaller force under
Rear Admiral Colpoys away in the Atlantic, off Ushant to the
north, and the two other frigates of his own inshore squadron
keeping a precarious watch—and those an enemy of such might
could contemptuously sweep aside. Heaven only knew when the
grudging reinforcements from the Caribbean would arrive.

"Sir—" There was no need for words: more and more sails were
straggling into the expanse of the bay. Silently, the officers continued to watch, the blast of the unusual easterly cold and hostile.
The seas, harried by the wind, advanced toward them in combers,

bursting against their bows and sending icy spindrift aft in stinging volleys.

The light was fading: the French admiral had timed his move so
that by the time his fleet reached the open sea it could lose itself in
the darkness of a stormy night. "A round dozen at least. We may in
truth say that the French fleet has sailed," Pellew said dryly.

The lieutenant watched eagerly, for the French were finally
showing after all these months, but Pellew did not share his jubilation. His secret intelligence was chilling: for weeks this concentration of force had stored and prepared—with field guns, horses and
fodder—and if reports were to be believed, eighteen thousand
troops. If the entire fleet put to sea, it could have only one purpose. . . .

"Desire *Phoebe* to find Admiral Colpoys and advise," he
snapped at the signal lieutenant. However, there was little chance
that Colpoys could close on the French before they won the open
sea. In the rapidly dimming daylight, the swelling numbers of
men-o'-war were direful.

"Sir! I now make it sixteen—no seventeen—of the line!"

A savage roll made them all stagger. When they recovered it
seemed the whole bay was filling with ships—at least the same
number again of frigates; with transports and others there were
now forty or more vessels breaking out into the Atlantic.

"*Amazon* is to make all sail for Portsmouth," Pellew barked. It
would reduce his squadron to a pitiable remnant, but it was essential to warn England while there was still time.

Yet the enemy sail advancing on them was not a line of battle, it
was a disordered scatter—some headed south, shying away from
the only frigate that lay across their path. Strings of flags rose from
one of the largest of the French battleships, accompanied by the
hollow thump of a gun. The gloom of dusk was fast turning to a
clamping murk, and the signal was indistinct. A red rocket soared
suddenly, and the ghostly blue radiance of a flare showed on her
foredeck as she turned to night signals.

"So they want illuminations—they shall have them!" Pellew said grimly. *Indefatigable* plunged ahead, directly into the widely scattered fleet. From her own deck colored rockets hissed, tracing across the windy night sky, while vivid flashes from her guns added to the confusion. A large two-decker trying to put about struck rocks; she swung into the wind, and was driven back hard against them. Distress rockets soared from the doomed ship.

"Can't last," muttered Pellew, at the general mayhem. The driving gale from the east would prevent any return to harbor and the enemy had only to make the broad Atlantic to find ample searoom to regain composure.

The mass of enemy ships passed them by quickly, disdaining to engage, and all too soon had disappeared into the wild night—but not before it was clear they were shaping course northward. Toward England.

CHAPTER ONE

—◈—

*B*ear a fist there, y' scowbunkin' lubbers!" The loud bellow
startled the group around the forebitts who were amiably
watching the sailors at the pin-rail swigging off on the topsail lift. The men moved quickly to obey: this was Thomas Kydd, the
hard-horse master's mate, whose hellish open-boat voyage in the
Caribbean eighteen months ago was still talked about in the navy.

Kydd's eyes moved about the deck. It was his way never to go
below at the end of a watch until all was neatly squared away,
ready for those relieving, but there was little to criticize in these
balmy breezes on the foredeck of the 64-gun ship-of-the-line
Achilles as she crossed the broad Atlantic bound for Gibraltar.

Kydd was content—to be a master's mate after just four years
before the mast was a rare achievement. It entitled him to walk the
quarterdeck with the officers, to mess in the gunroom, and to
wear a proper uniform complete with long coat and breeches. No
one could mistake him now for a common sailor.

Royal blue seas, with an occasional tumbling line of white, and
towering fluffy clouds brilliant in southern sunshine: they were to
enter the Mediterranean to join Admiral Jervis. It would be the

first time Kydd had seen this fabled sea and he looked forward to sharing interesting times ashore with his particular friend, Nicholas Renzi, who was now a master's mate in *Glorious*.

His gaze shifted to her, a powerful 74-gun ship-of-the-line off to leeward. She was taking in her three topsails simultaneously, probably an officer-of-the-watch exercise, pitting the skills and audacity of one mast against another.

The last day or so they had been running down the latitude of thirty-six north, and Kydd knew they should raise Gibraltar that morning. He glanced forward in expectation. To the east there was a light dun-colored band of haze lying on the horizon, obscuring the transition of sea into sky.

The small squadron began to assume a form of line. Kydd took his position on the quarterdeck, determined not to miss landfall on such an emblem of history. His glance flicked up to the fore masthead lookout—but this time the man snapped rigid, shading his eyes and looking right ahead. An instant later he leaned down and bawled, "*Laaaand* ho!"

The master puffed his cheeks in pleasure. Kydd knew it was an easy enough approach, but news of the sighting of land was always a matter of great interest to a ship's company many weeks at sea, and the decks buzzed with comment.

Kydd waited impatiently, but soon it became visible from the decks, a delicate light blue-gray peak, just discernible over the haze. It firmed quickly to a hard blue and, as he watched, it spread. The ships sailed on in the fluky southeasterly, and as they approached, the aspect of the land changed subtly, the length of it beginning to foreshorten. The haze thinned and the land took on individuality.

"Gibraltar!" Kydd breathed. As they neared, the bulking shape grew, reared up far above their masthead with an effortless immensity. Like a crouching lion, it dominated by its mere presence, a majestic, never-to-be-forgotten symbol: the uttermost end of Europe, the finality of a continent.

He looked around; to the south lay Africa, an irregular blue-gray mass across a glittering sea—there, so close, was an endless desert and the Barbary pirates, then farther south, jungle, elephants and pygmies.

Only two ships. Shielding her eyes against the glare of the sea, Emily Mulvany searched the horizon but could see no more. Admiral Jervis, with his fleet, was in Lisbon, giving heart to the Portuguese, and there were no men-o'-war of significance in Gibraltar. All were hoping for a substantial naval presence in these dreadful times . . . but she was a daughter of the army and knew nothing of sea strategy. Still, they looked lovely, all sails set like wings on a swan, a long pennant at the masthead of each swirling lazily, a picture of sea grace and beauty.

Flags rose to *Glorious*'s signal halyards. They both altered course in a broad curve toward the far-off anonymous cluster of buildings halfway along at the water's edge. As they did so, the gentle breeze fluttered and died, picked up again, then dropped away to a whisper. Frustrated, Kydd saw why. Even this far out they were in the lee of the great rock in the easterly; high on its summit a ragged scarf of cloud streamed out, darkening the bay beneath for a mile or more. He glanced at the master, who did not appear overly concerned, his arms folded in limitless patience. The captain disappeared below, leaving the deck to the watch. Sails flapped and rustled, slackened gear rattled and knocked, and the ship ghosted in at the pace of a crawling child.

Kydd took the measure of the gigantic rock. It lay almost exactly north and south some two or three miles long, but was observably much narrower. There was a main town low along the flanks to seaward, but few other buildings on the precipitous sides. On its landward end the rock ended abruptly, and Kydd could see the long flat terrain connecting the Rock of Gibraltar to the nondescript mainland.

It wasn't until evening that the frustrating easterly died and a local southerly enabled the two ships to come in with the land. Kydd knew from the charts that this would be Rosia Bay, the home of the navy in Gibraltar. It was a pretty little inlet, well away from the main cluster of buildings farther along. There was the usual elegant, spare stone architecture of a dockyard and, higher, an imposing two-story building that, by its position, could only be the naval hospital.

Rosia Bay opened up, a small mole to the south, the ramparts of a past fortification clear to the north. There, the two ships dropped anchor.

"Do you see . . ."

Kydd had not noticed Cockburn appear beside him.

"Er, no—what is it y' sees, Tam?" The neat, almost academic-looking man next to him was *Achilles*'s other master's mate, a long-promoted midshipman who had yet to make the vital step of commission as a lieutenant, but had accepted his situation with philosophic resignation. He and Kydd had become friends.

"We're the only ones," Cockburn said quietly. "The fleet must be in the Med somewhere." Apart from the sturdy sails of dock-yard craft and a brig-sloop alongside the mole in a state of disre-pair, there were only the exotic lateen sails of Levant traders dotting the sea around the calm of Gibraltar.

"Side!" The burly boatswain raised his silver call. The captain emerged from the cabin spaces, striding purposefully, all aglitter with gold lace, medals and best sword. Respectfully, Kydd and Cockburn joined the line of sideboys at the ship's side. The boatswain raised his call again and as the captain went over the bulwark every man touched his hat and the shriek of the whistle pierced the evening.

The captain safely over the side, the first lieutenant remained at the salute for a moment, then turned to the boatswain. 'Stand down the watches. We're out of sea routine now, I believe.'

The boatswain's eyebrows raised in surprise. No strict orders to ready the ship for sea again, to store ship, to set right the ravages of their ocean voyage? They would evidently be here for a long time. "An' liberty, sir?" he asked.

"Larbowlines until evening gun." The first lieutenant's words were overheard by a dozen ears, sudden unseen scurries indicating the news was being joyfully spread below.

At the boatswain's uneasy frown, the lieutenant added, "We're due a parcel of men from England, apparently. They can turn to and let our brave tars step off on a well-earned frolic, don't you think?"

Kydd caught an edge of irony in the words, but didn't waste time on reflection. "Been here before?" he asked Cockburn, who was taking in the long sprawl of buildings farther along, the Moorish-looking castle at the other end—the sheer fascination of the mighty rock.

"Never, I fear," said Cockburn, in his usual quiet way, as he gazed at the spectacle. "But we'll make its acquaintance soon enough."

Kydd noticed with surprise that *Glorious,* anchored no more than a hundred yards away, was in a state of intense activity. There were victualing hoys and low barges beetling out to the bigger ship-of-the-line, every sign of an outward-bound vessel.

The old-fashioned longboat carrying the senior hands ashore was good-natured about diverting, and soon they lay under oars off the side of the powerful man-o'-war, one of a multitude of busy craft.

"*Glorious,* ahoy!" bawled Kydd. At the deck edge a distracted petty officer appeared and looked down into the boat. "If ye c'n pass th' word f'r Mr. Renzi, I'd be obliged," Kydd hailed. The face disappeared and they waited.

The heat of the day had lessened, but it still drew forth the aromas of a ship long at sea—sun on tarry timbers, canvas and well-worn decks, an effluvia carrying from the open gunports that was as individual to that ship as the volute carvings at her bow, a compound of bilge, old stores, concentrated humanity and more subtle, unknown odors.

There was movement and a wooden squealing of sheaves, and the gunport lid next to them was triced up. "Dear fellow!" Renzi leaned out, and the longboat eased closer.

Kydd's face broke into an unrestrained grin at the sight of the man with whom he had shared more of life's challenges and rewards than any other. "Nicholas! Should y' wish t' step ashore—"

"Sadly, brother, I cannot."

It was the same Renzi, the cool, sensitive gaze, the strength of character in the deep lines at each side of his mouth, but Kydd sensed something else, something unsettling.

"We are under sailing orders," Renzi said quietly. The ship was preparing for sea; there could be no risk of men straggling and therefore no liberty. "An alarum of sorts. We go to join Jervis, I believe."

There was a stir of interest in the longboat. "An' where's he at, then?" asked Coxall, gunner's mate and generally declared leader of their jaunt ashore—he was an old hand and had been to Gibraltar before.

Renzi stared levelly at the horizon, his remote expression causing Kydd further unease. "It seems that there is some—confusion. I have not heard reliably just where the fleet might be." He turned back to Kydd with a half-smile. "But, then, these are troubling times, my friend, it can mean anything."

A muffled roar inside the dark gundeck took Renzi's attention and he waved apologetically at Kydd before he shouted, "We will meet on our return, dear fellow," then withdrew inboard.

"Rum dos," muttered Coxall, and glared at the duty boat's crew, lazily leaning into their strokes as the boat made its way round the larger mole to the end of the long wall of fortifications. He perked up as they headed toward the shore and a small jetty. "Ragged Staff," he said, his seamed face relaxing into a smile, "where we gets our water afore we goes ter sea."

They clambered out. Like the others Kydd reveled in the solidity of the ground after weeks at sea. The earth was curiously submissive under his feet without the exuberant liveliness of a ship in concord with the sea. Coxall struck out for the large arched gate in the wall and the group followed.

The town quickly engulfed them, and with it the color and sensory richness of the huge sunbaked rock. The passing citizenry were as variegated in appearance as any that Kydd had seen: here was a true crossing place of the world, a nexus for the waves of races, European, Arab, Spanish and others from deeper into this inland sea.

And the smells—in the narrow streets innumerable mules and donkeys passed by laden with their burdens, the pungency of their droppings competing with the offerings of the shops: smoked herring and dried cod, the cool bacon aroma of salted pigs' trotters and the heady fragrance of cinnamon, cloves, roasting coffee, each adding in the hot dustiness to the interweaving reek.

In only a few minutes they had crossed two streets and were up against the steep rise of the flank of the Rock. Coxall didn't spare them, leading them through the massive Southport gate and on a narrow track up and around the scrubby slopes to a building set on an angled rise. A sudden cool downward draft sent Kydd's jacket aflare and his hat skittering in the dust.

"Scud Hill. We gets ter sink a muzzler 'ere first, wi'out we has t' smell the town," Coxall said. It was a pothouse, but not of a kind that Kydd had seen before. Loosely modeled on an English tavern, it was more open balcony than interior darkness, and rather than high-backed benches there were individual tables with cane chairs.

"A shant o' gatter is jus' what'll set me up prime, like," sighed the lean and careful Tippett, carpenter's mate and Coxall's inseparable companion. They eased into chairs, orienting them to look out over the water, then carefully placed their hats beneath. They were just above Rosia Bay, their two ships neatly at anchor within its arms, while farther down there was a fine vista of the length of the town, all cozy within long lines of fortifications.

The ale was not long in coming—this establishment was geared for a fleet in port, and in its absence they were virtually on their own, with only one other table occupied.

"Here's ter us, lads!" Coxall declared, and upended his pewter. It was grateful to the senses on the wide balcony, the wind at this height strong and cool, yet the soft warmth of the winter sun gave a welcome laziness to the late afternoon.

Coins were produced for the next round, but Cockburn held up his hand. "I'll round in m' tackle for now." The old 64-gun *Achilles* had not had one prize to her name in her two years in the Caribbean, while *Seaflower* cutter had been lucky.

Kydd considered how he could see his friend clear to another without it appearing charity, but before he could say anything, Coxall grunted, "Well, damme, only a Spanish cobb ter me name. Seems yer in luck, yer Scotch shicer, can't let 'em keep m' change."

Cockburn's set face held, then loosened to a smile. "Why, thankee, Eli."

Kydd looked comfortably across his tankard over the steep, sun-lit slopes toward the landward end of Gibraltar. The town nestled in a narrow line below, stretching about a mile to where it ceased abruptly at the end of the Rock. The rest of the terrain was bare scrub on precipitous sides. "So this is y'r Gibraltar," he said. "Seems t' me just a mile long an' a half straight up."

"Aye, but it's rare val'ble to us—Spanish tried ter take it orf us a dozen years or so back, kept at it fer four years, pounded th' place ter pieces they did," Coxall replied, "but we held on b' makin' this one thunderin' great fortress."

"So while we have the place, no one else can," Cockburn mused. "And we come and go as we please, but denying passage to the enemy. Here's to the flag of old England on the Rock for ever."

A murmur of appreciation as they drank was interrupted by the scraping of a chair and a pleasant-faced but tough-looking seaman came across to join them. "Samuel Jones, yeoman outa *Loyalty* brig."

Tippett motioned at their table, "We're *Achilles* sixty-four, only this day inward-bound fr'm the Caribbee."

"Saw yez. So ye hasn't the word what's been 'n' happened this side o' the ocean all of a sudden, like." At the expectant silence he went on, "As ye knows—yer do?—the Spanish came in wi' the Frogs in October, an' since then . . ."

Kydd nodded. But his eyes strayed to the point where Gibraltar ended so abruptly: there was Spain, the enemy, just a mile or so beyond—and always there.

Relishing his moment, Jones asked, "So where's yer Admiral Jervis an' his fleet, then?"

Coxall started to say something, but Jones cut in, "No, mate, he's at Lisbon, is he—out there." He gestured to the west and the open Atlantic. Leaning forward he pointed in the other direction, into the Mediterranean. "Since December, last month, we had to skin out—can't hold on. So, mates, there ain't a single English man-o'-war as swims in the whole Mediterranee."

Into the grave silence came Coxall's troubled voice. "Yer means Port Mahon, Leghorn, Naples—"

"We left 'em all t' the French, cully. I tell yer, there's no English guns any further in than us."

Kydd stared at the table. Evacuation of the Mediterranean? It was inconceivable! The great trade route opened up to the Orient following the loss of the American colonies—the journeys to the Levant, Egypt and the fabled camel trains to the Red Sea and India, all finished?

"But don't let that worry yez," Jones continued.

"And pray why not?" said Cockburn carefully.

"'Cos there's worse," Jones said softly. The others held still. "Not more'n a coupla weeks ago, we gets word fr'm the north, the inshore frigates off Brest." He paused. "The French—they're out!" There was a stirring around the table.

"Not yer usual, not a-tall—this is big, forty sail an' more, seventeen o' the line an' transports, as would be carryin' soldiers an' horses an' all."

He sought out their faces, one by one. 'It's a right filthy easterly gale, Colpoys out of it somewhere t' sea, nothin' ter stop 'em. Last seen, they hauls their wind fer the north—England, lads . . ."

"They're leaving!" The upstairs maid's excited squeal brought an automatic reproof from Emily, but she hurried nevertheless to the window. White sail blossomed from the largest, which was the *Glorious,* she had found out. The smaller *Achilles,* however, showed no signs of moving and lay quietly to her anchor. Emily frowned at this development. With no children to occupy her days, and a husband who worked long hours, she had thrown herself into the social round of Gibraltar. There was to be an assembly soon, and she had had her hopes of the younger ship's officers—if she could snare a brace, they would serve handsomely to squire the tiresome Elliott sisters.

Then she remembered. It was Letitia who had discovered that in *Achilles* was the man who had famously rescued Lord Stanhope in a thrilling open-boat voyage after a dreadful hurricane. She racked her brain. Yes, Captain Kydd. She would make sure somehow that he was on the guest list.

The next forenoon the new men came aboard, a dismal shuffle in the Mediterranean sun. They had been landed from the stores transport from England, and their trip across wartime Biscay would not have been pleasant.

Kydd, as mate-of-the-watch, took a grubby paper from the well-seasoned warrant officer and signed for them. He told the wide-eyed duty midshipman to take them below on the first stage of their absorption into the ship's company of *Achilles* and watched them stumble down the main-hatch. Despite the stout clothing they had been given in the receiving ship in England, they were a dejected and repellent-looking crew.

The warrant officer showed no inclination to leave, and came to stand beside Kydd. "No row guard, then?"

"Is this Spithead?" Kydd retorted. Any half-awake sailor would see that it was futile to get ashore—the only way out of Gibraltar was in a merchant ship, and they were all under eye not two hundred yards off at the New Mole.

The warrant officer looked at him with a cynical smile. "How long you been outa England?"

"West Indies f'r the last coupla years," Kydd said guardedly.

The man's grunt was dismissive. "Then chalk this in yer log. Times 'r changin', cully, the navy ain't what it was. These 'ere are the best youse are goin' to get, but not a seaman among 'em . . ." He let the words hang. By law the press-gang could only seize men who "used the sea."

He went on: "Ever hear o' yer Lord Mayor's men? No?" He chuckled harshly. "By Act o' Parlyment, every borough has to send in men, what's their quota, like, no choice—so who they goin' to send? Good 'uns or what?" He went to the side and spat into the harbor. "No, o' course. They gets rid o' their low shabs, skulkers 'n' dandy prats. Even bales out th' jail. An' then the navy gets 'em."

There seemed no sense in it. The press-gang, however iniquitous, had provided good hands in the past, even in the Caribbean. Why not now? As if in answer, the man went on, "Press is not bringin' 'em in anymore, we got too many ships wantin' crew." He looked sideways at Kydd, and his face darkened. "But this'n! You'll find—"

Muffled, angry shouts came up from below. The young lieutenant-of-the-watch came forward, frowning at the untoward commotion. "Mr Kydd, see what the fuss is about, if you please."

Fisticuffs on the gundeck. It was shortly after the noon grog issue, and it was not unknown for men who had somehow got hold of extra drink to run riotous, but unusually this time one of them was Boddy, an able seaman known for his steady reliability out on a yardarm. Kydd did not recognize the other man. Surrounded by sullen sailors, the two were locked in a vicious clinch in the low confines below decks. This was not a simple case of tempers flaring.

"Still!" Kydd roared. The shouts and murmuring died, but the pair continued to grapple, panting in ragged grunts. Kydd himself could not separate them. If a wild blow landed on him, the culprit would face a noose for striking a superior.

A quarter-gunner reached them from aft and, without breaking stride, sliced his fist down between the two. They fell apart, glaring and bloody. The petty officer looked inquiringly at Kydd.

His duty was plain, the pair should be haled to the quarterdeck for punishment, but Kydd felt that his higher duty was to find the cause. "Will, you old haul-bowlings," he said loudly to Boddy, his words carrying to the others, "slinging y' mauley in 'tween decks, it's not like you."

Kydd considered the other man. He had a disquieting habit of inclining his head one way, but sliding his eyes in a different direction; a careful, appraising look so different from the open honesty of a sailor.

"Caught th' prigger firkling me ditty bag," Boddy said thickly. "I'll knock his fuckin' toplights out, the—"

"Clap a stopper on it," Kydd snapped. It was provocation enough. The ditty bag was where seamen hung their ready-use articles on the ship's side, a small bag with a hole halfway up for convenience. There would be nothing of real value in it, so why—

"I didn't know what it was, in truth." The man's careful words were cool, out of place in a man-o'-war.

Boddy recoiled. "Don't try 'n' flam me, yer shoreside shyster," he snarled.

It might be possible—these quota men would know nothing of sea life from their short time in the receiving ship in harbor and the stores transport, and be curious about their new quarters. Either way, Kydd realized, there was going to be a hard beat to windward to absorb the likes of these into the seamanlike ship's company that the *Achilles* had become after her Atlantic passage.

"Stow it," he growled at Boddy. "These grass-combin' buggers have a lot t' learn. Now, ye either lives wi' it or y' bears up f'r the quarterdeck. Yeah?"

Boddy glared for a moment then folded his arms. "Yair, well, he shifts his berth fr'm this mess on any account."

Kydd agreed. It was a seaman's ancient privilege to choose his messmates; he would square it later. There was no need to invoke the formality of ship's discipline for this. He looked meaningfully at the petty officer and returned on deck.

The warrant officer had not left, and after Kydd had reassured the lieutenant-of-the-watch he came across with a knowing swagger. "Jus' makin' the acquaintance of yer Lord Mayor's men, mate?" Kydd glanced at him coldly. "On yer books as volunteers—and that means each one of 'em gets seventy-pound bounty, spend how they likes. . . ."

"Seventy pounds!" The pay for a good able seaman was less than a shilling a day—this was four years' pay for a good man. A pressed man got nothing, yet these riffraff. . . . Kydd's face tightened. "I'll see y' over the side," he told the warrant officer gruffly.

At noon Kydd was relieved by Cockburn. The bungling political solution to the manning problem was lowering on the spirit. And Gibraltar was apparently just a garrison town, one big fortified rock and that was all. England was in great peril, and he was doing little more than keeping house in an old, well-worn ship at her long-term moorings.

Kydd didn't feel like going ashore in this mood, but to stay on board was not an attractive proposition, given the discontents simmering below. Perhaps he would take another walk round town. It was an interesting enough place, all things considered.

Satisfied with his appearance, the blue coat of a master's mate with its big buttons, white breeches and waistcoat with cockaded plain black hat, he joined the group at the gangway waiting for their boat ashore. The first lieutenant came up the main-hatch ladder, but he held his hat at his side, the sign that he was off-duty.

"Are you passing through the town?" he asked Kydd pleasantly.

Kydd touched his hat politely. "Aye, sir."

"Then I'd be much obliged if you could leave these two books at the garrison library," he said, and handed over a small parcel.

Kydd established that the library was situated in Main Street, apparently opposite a convent. It didn't take long to find—Main Street was the central way through the town, and the convent was pointed out to him halfway along its length. To his surprise, it apparently rated a full complement of sentries in ceremonials. There was a giant Union Flag floating haughtily above the building and a sergeant glared at him from the portico. Across the road, as directed, was the garrison library, an unpretentious single building.

It was a quiet morning, and Emily looked around for things to do. On her mind was her planned social event, as always a problem with a never-changing pool of guests. Her brow furrowed at the question of what she would wear. Despite the tropical climate of Gibraltar, she had retained her soft, milky complexion, and at thirty-two, Emily was in the prime of her beauty.

There was a diffident tap on the door. She crossed to her desk to take position and signaled to the diminutive Maltese helper.

It was a navy man; an officer of some kind with an engagingly shy manner that in no way detracted from his good looks. He carried a small parcel.

"Er, can ye tell me, is this th' garrison library, miss?" She didn't recognize him: he must be from the remaining big ship.

"It is," she said primly. A librarian, however amateur, had standards to uphold.

His hat was neatly under his arm, and he proffered the parcel as though it was precious. "The first l'tenant of *Achilles* asked me t' return these books," he said, with a curious mix of sturdy simplicity and a certain nobility of purpose.

"Thank you, it was kind in you to bring them." She paused, taking in the fine figure he made in his sea uniform; probably in his mid-twenties and, from the strength in his features, she guessed he had seen much of the world.

"*Achilles*—from the Caribbean? Then you would know Mr. Kydd—the famous one who rescued Lord Stanhope and sailed so far in a tiny open boat, with his maid in with them as well."

The young man frowned and hesitated, but his dark eyes held a glint of humor. "Aye, I do—but it was never th' maid, it was Lady Stanhope's travelin' companion." His glossy dark hair was gathered and pulled back in a clubbed pigtail, and couldn't have been more different from the short, powdered wigs of an army officer.

"You may think me awfully forward, but it would greatly oblige if you could introduce me to him," she dared.

With a shy smile, he said, "Yes, miss. Then might I present m'self? Thomas Kydd, master's mate o' the *Achilles*."

"In Stockwin's hands... the sea story will continue to entrance readers across the world."
—The Guardian (UK)

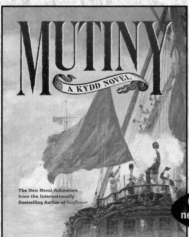

The New Naval Adventure from the Internationally Bestselling Author of *Seaflower*

JULIAN STOCKWIN

"Stockwin bravely goes where Patrick O'Brian has gone before...period dialect and seagoing argot aplenty add credibility to the adventure."

—Publishers Weekly

Coming in June 2004, the next book in the Kydd series

Mutiny
0-7432-5800-2 · $24.00

Previous titles in the
Kydd series:
Kydd
0-7432-1459-5 · $13.00
Artemis
0-7432-1461-7 · $13.00

THE THOMAS KYDD SHIPMATES NETWORK

If you've enjoyed *Seaflower*, why not join the Shipmates Network? One of the comments that readers frequently make is that they wish it weren't a whole year before publication of the next book!

By becoming a Shipmate, you can keep in touch with the author and his hero Thomas Kydd on a regular basis.

Each month you'll receive the free email newsletter the *Bosun's Chronicle*, packed with information about the Great Age of Sail, details on author events, advance notice of new publications, news about Shipmates around the world, and contests for signed editions of the books and other great prizes.

There's also an opportunity to have your own questions about the sea and ships answered in the section "Ask Julian."

Sign up now at the website
www.JulianStockwin.com.